Winter Wishes

eBook Exclusives

Desperate Measures
Seasons of Her Life
To Have and to Hold
Serendipity
Captive Innocence
Captive Embraces
Captive Passions
Captive Secrets
Captive Splendors
Cinders to Satin
For All Their Lives
Texas Heat
Texas Rich
Texas Fury
Texas Sunrise

Anthologies

Mistletoe Magic
Winter Wishes
The Most Wonderful Time
When the Snow Falls
Secret Santa
A Winter Wonderland
I'll Be Home for Christmas
Making Spirits Bright
Holiday Magic
Snow Angels
Silver Bells
Comfort and Joy
Sugar and Spice
Let It Snow
A Gift of Joy
Five Golden Rings
Deck the Halls
Jingle All the Way

Books by Susan Fox

Blue Moon Harbor Series
Fly Away with Me

Caribou Crossing Romances

"Caribou Crossing"
Home on the Range
Gentle on My Mind
"Stand by Your Man"
Love Me Tender
Love Somebody Like You
Ring of Fire
Holiday in Your Heart

Wild Ride to Love Series

His, Unexpectedly
Love, Unexpectedly
Yours, Unexpectedly

Books by Jules Bennett

The Monroes Series

Wrapped in You
Caught in You
Lost in You

Books by Leah Marie Brown

It Girls Series

Owning It
Working It
Finding It
Faking It

Published by Kensington Publishing Corporation

Winter
Wishes

FERN MICHAELS
SUSAN FOX
JULES BENNETT
LEAH MARIE BROWN

ZEBRA BOOKS
KENSINGTON PUBLISHING CORP.

http://www.kensingtonbooks.com

ZEBRA BOOKS are published by

Kensington Publishing Corp.
119 West 40th Street
New York, NY 10018

All Kensington titles, imprints, and distributed lines are available at special
quantity discounts for bulk purchases for sales promotion, premiums, fund-
raising, educational, or institutional use.

Special book excerpts or customized printings can also be created to fit
specific needs. For details, write or phone the office of the Kensington
Sales Manager: Attn.: Sales Department. Kensington Publishing Corp.,
119 West 40th Street, New York, NY 10018. Phone: 1-800-221-2647.

Zebra and the Z logo Reg. U.S. Pat. & TM Off.

First Printing: November 2017
ISBN-13: 978-1-4201-3572-5
ISBN-10: 1-4201-3572-4

eISBN-13: 978-1-4201-3573-2
eISBN-10: 1-4201-3573-2

10 9 8 7 6 5 4 3 2 1

Printed in the United States of America

Contents

Christmas Kisses

FERN MICHAELS

Chapter One

Meredith Clark yawned and squirmed in the driver's seat when she saw the sign for Nashville. Not Nashville, Tennessee. Nashville, Kansas. Not for the first time did she second-guess her method of deciding where she'd go once she left Las Vegas. Taping a map of the United States to her bedroom wall, closing her eyes, spinning around a couple of times, then walking toward the map with her index finger pointing was, perhaps, not one of the best ideas she had ever had.

But, she reminded herself, it didn't matter where she went. Nashville, Kansas, was as good as anywhere. If she didn't like it, she could leave. But she'd promised herself she would give it a try.

She had spent more than ten years literally dancing to everyone else's tune. She had saved her money because dancing, especially in the glitzy, theatrical productions Vegas was known for, was a precarious business at best. And job security was laughable. One injury—and she'd had a few over the years—meant she couldn't work, and there was always another dancer eager to take her place in the line.

But this past year had made up her mind. After yet another ligament tear, followed soon after by the collision with a drunk driver, which had messed up her knee even further, she had had it. Not to mention there'd been hints that, at barely past thirty, she was getting a little too old to be a producer's top casting pick.

The signs were all there. It was time to move on. So she'd collected the substantial monetary settlement from the other driver's insurance company, waited until she'd healed as much as the orthopedist decided she was going to, packed up her recent college diploma with a major in English, pointed at the map, and said, "Bye-bye, Vegas. Nashville, here I come."

She didn't have much to show for the years she'd spent in Vegas, and nothing to hold her there. She wouldn't miss the condo she shared with two other dancers. Or the kind of guys who seemed destined to do nothing but profess to love her, then leave. The glitz, the glamour, the sequins, the elaborate costumes? The celebrities, the casinos, the bright lights? None of it held the appeal it had once had for her.

Meredith signaled for the exit ramp to Nashville and thought, *Small-town middle America, here I come.*

Chapter Two

Meredith's car's GPS guided her to the house she'd found for sale by owner on Craigslist. She pulled into the driveway and parked behind a navy blue SUV. The house was exactly as pictured in the ad. The SUV must belong to the owner, she figured, who had agreed to meet her here. She'd texted him at her last stop for gas.

The SUV was unoccupied, so she opened her car door, phone in hand, ready to text him again and let him know she was here. But she didn't have to because just then she spied him loping around the corner of the single-car garage.

She'd never spoken to him, but somehow she'd created a mental image of him from their brief e-mails and texts. She had pictured a checked flannel shirt and overalls. Perhaps a pair of baggy jeans that showed a little too much skin when he bent over. He'd told her he had renovated the house himself, so she'd thought he'd look a little more like the construction worker of her imagination.

You read too much, she admonished herself. She had

a bad habit of conjuring up ideas about people with
very little information to go on. She did it with cus-
tomer service representatives she dealt with only on
the phone. Or pitchmen in radio ads. She would
create a whole scenario about them just from listening to their voice. She'd done the same thing with this
guy based on his e-mails and texts. And her imagination couldn't have been more wrong.

The jeans, though, she got right. But they fit him.
He looked comfortable in them. Maybe they were his
favorite pair. The flannel shirt she got right, too, but
it was a solid gray, and underneath, he wore a black
thermal shirt against the chill in the November air.

"Meredith?" he said as he approached, his hand
outstretched. "Meredith Clark? Hi. I'm Noah."

She took his hand, and hers got lost in the warmth
of his. She smiled automatically because that's what
she normally did at an introduction. "It's nice to meet
you," she said, because, once again, her internal auto-
pilot saved her.

He released her hand. "Ready for the tour?"

She liked his smile. She liked everything about him
so far, she decided as she followed him to the front
steps. The fact that she liked him probably meant that
he was married. Or at least spoken for. She had a bit
of a history of being attracted to men who were, for
one reason or another, unavailable.

Noah pushed the interior door open and held the
storm door so she could walk in ahead of him. He
stopped behind her because she hadn't given him
much room. She thought she could feel his body
sending heat in her direction. But that was surely only
because of the temperature of the empty room.

She tugged her jacket more tightly around her and

rubbed her upper arms as she moved farther into the living room. "There's a fireplace!" she exclaimed. She crossed the wood floor to examine it.

"It's not very big," Noah said. "And it's gas. But it will put out a bit of heat when it's on."

"Nice proportions," she said as she crossed the room and turned to face him. Already, she was envisioning a sectional sofa, a coffee table, end tables, and lamps.

"Kitchen's through there," Noah said, indicating an arched doorway.

"Oh, this is gorgeous." Meredith ran her hand along the countertops, noting the new gas range and the stainless-steel farmhouse sink.

"Concrete countertop," Noah said. "The cabinets are oak."

"Room for a table and chairs," she noted.

A big window looked out over the backyard. There was an ancient swing set that looked sturdy despite its age. The lot backed up onto a wooded area.

"I have to see this back porch." She fiddled with the door, figured out how to unlock it, and stepped outside. Noah followed, taking a seat on the low wall that surrounded the porch.

Again she envisioned how she could make this place her own. Resin furniture, comfy cushions, maybe a swing or a glider. Hanging plants, trailing vines, and flowers in the summer. That is, if she could find some that would survive her brown thumb.

"The land behind the yard is part of the county's conservation plan. Nothing will be built there."

"I do like my privacy," she joked. His eyes were dark blue, she noted, and she got the feeling they didn't miss a trick. She liked his quiet presence. He wasn't trying to hurry her along. In fact, he acted like he had nothing better to do than be here with her.

They went back inside. "This used to be the dining room," Noah informed her. "But you can use it however you want."

Design ideas began clicking through Meredith's mind again.

Down the hall were two bedrooms with a decent-sized bathroom between them. Next to the bathroom was space for a stackable washer and dryer. That would certainly be convenient. One of the rooms, meant to be the master, she supposed, had a big, custom-designed closet with lots of storage. The window looked out over the front lawn.

"That's an oak tree," Noah said, looking over her shoulder at the bare tree with giant, naked branches. "It'll give you a lot of shade in the summer."

"And a lot of leaves on the ground in the fall."

"But raking them is good exercise."

She looked at him, wondering if she ought to be offended. "What are you implying?"

"I'm not implying anything," Noah said evenly, refusing to take the bait she had offered. "You look like you're in pretty good shape, so you probably work out regularly. I was merely pointing out that raking leaves is good exercise, a benefit, if you will, of having that oak tree in your front yard."

"It's not *my* front yard."

"Well, not yet." Noah grinned at her. "Come on, admit it. This house is perfect for you."

"What I'll admit is that you seem desperate to sell it."

They meandered back to the living room, where he turned to her and said, "You caught me. I would like to sell it because I'd like to buy another fixer-upper. This was my grandmother's house, so it's kind of special to me."

"Your grandmother's? And you're selling it? Why don't you live here?"

"I spent many good times here, trust me, but it's not home to me anymore."

Meredith frowned, wondering at the meaning behind his words. "Can I let you know?"

"You're not going to commit?" Noah's tone sounded teasing, but she sensed that he was disappointed.

"I'd like to sleep on it. Could we meet tomorrow?"

"There's a coffee shop on the north side of the square called the Grind. Ten o'clock?"

"Perfect." And it really was. Actually, this trip was becoming a bit more than perfect.

Chapter Three

Noah Kennedy cranked up his SUV and backed out of the driveway right after Meredith did. He felt cautiously optimistic that he'd found a buyer for his grandmother's house. As a high-school guidance counselor these past few years, he'd become pretty good at reading people. He could see it on her face, hear it in her voice: Meredith Clark loved that house.

Now all he had to do was not blow a sale by insulting her. The way she'd taken his comment about raking leaves led him to believe she was the sensitive sort. And maybe prone to jumping to the wrong conclusions.

As good as he'd become at reading people, he still hadn't figured out women. Correction: just when he thought he had, they proved him wrong. And he hadn't gotten much of a read on Meredith Clark prior to meeting her. She'd told him in an e-mail that she was relocating from Las Vegas, but since she hadn't said why, he was left to wonder how she'd ended up in Kansas. Not that Nashville wasn't a great place to live. He was just curious, that's all.

Curious.

And interested.

He'd been drawn to Meredith the second she stepped out of her car. He'd liked the feel of her hand in his. Liked her smile and the sparkle in her brown eyes. Liked the brunette locks that cascaded over her shoulders and the sprinkle of freckles across her nose. Liked the grace with which she moved.

He could easily picture Meredith living in his grandmother's house. The unsettling part of that was he could also picture living there with her.

Meredith spent her first night in Nashville, Kansas, at a local bed-and-breakfast. According to the Internet, it seemed to be the only place available locally. It was a big, old, well-kept Victorian run by a couple named Walt and Beverly Collins. Beverly, Meredith surmised, was a fount of local knowledge. She kept up a running patter of conversation about the house and a few of its former guests.

"Walt's grandmother left it to us," she said, as she led Meredith up the creaky stairs that were covered with a red runner. "It probably would have been kinder if she hadn't. This old place eats money for breakfast, lunch, and dinner, what with the maintenance and repairs. But Walt didn't want to give it up. He loves this place. That's why we turned it into a B and B. Only way we could keep it.

"Congressman Hicks stayed here one night when he was on his way to Topeka. And the mayor's daughter got married here last year. Never considered having a wedding here before, but it turned out perfect."

Beverly opened the door to a pretty bedroom with walls painted slate blue with crisp white trim. "I always give visitors this room if it's available. It's got a view of the backyard and the nicest bathroom."

"It's lovely," Meredith said. She ran her hand along the handmade quilt covering the bed and tested the cushions on the love seat placed beneath the window. A perfect place to curl up and read, she decided.

"Yard don't look like much now, of course, but in June, it was pretty, with the flowers blooming." Beverly stepped up next to Meredith and pointed. "They did the ceremony there in the gazebo. Rented a bunch of white folding chairs and a tent for the reception. Never had so many people in the house at once. But that wedding paid for the new furnace."

"I think it's a beautiful spot for a wedding."

"Sure was," Beverly agreed. "Gave me ideas, too. Opened up the place for private parties and baby showers and such. The mayor and his wife had their twenty-fifth wedding anniversary party here in September. Put the band in the gazebo and brought in a temporary dance floor."

Meredith covered her mouth and yawned. Her days of being on the road were catching up with her.

"You look done in, honey," Beverly said. "And here I am, talking your ear off."

"It's all right," Meredith said. "But I've been driving for two days. I'm looking forward to a good night's sleep."

"Well, you go right ahead. The other reason I give guests this room is it's the quietest."

"It's just what I need, then."

"I'll skedaddle. We don't serve dinner, but there are menus there in the nightstand drawer. The Pizza

Palace delivers until nine. We serve breakfast from eight to ten. It's included in the price of the room, of course. Dining room's just past the stairs on the right."

"I'll be there," Meredith assured her. She got the feeling that breakfast was not to be missed. Beverly was the kind of woman who inspired confidence. She was probably a fantastic cook.

"Towels are in the bathroom, and there's an extra blanket in the closet. If you need anything, you just dial one on the phone there. Me or Walt will answer."

"Thank you," Meredith said again.

The Twelve Oaks Inn was a far cry from the Venetian or Mandalay Bay, but it had a quaint charm all its own. And an owner who clearly cared about the quality of the business.

Although darkness had fallen, it wasn't that late. If she were still working in Vegas, Meredith realized, she'd be preparing for the first show right about now.

But those days, that life, was over. And she felt free, she realized as she unzipped her overnight bag and found her nightshirt and toiletry case. She'd chosen this new life. A very different life. Tired as she was, she felt a tingle of excitement at the thought of what the future might hold.

She took a long shower, luxuriating in the knowledge that she could sleep in, that she had no schedule, no demands. No classes. No performances. Except that ten o'clock appointment with Noah. Maybe that was causing the tingle of excitement. Partly, she allowed. But not entirely.

The bed held more appeal than a pizza. She told herself she wasn't that hungry anyway. She fell asleep minutes after her head hit the pillow. . . .

She saw herself as if watching from a distance, wearing

a flowing white dress, walking through a garden filled with flowers. In fact, she held a bouquet of flowers. There were flowers in her hair. Flowers everywhere, it seemed. And ribbons. And rows of white chairs. A gazebo where people waited for her, their faces indistinct. She kept walking but seemed to grow no closer to them. She knew a moment of frustration, of indecision. She wanted to move toward that gazebo, to whoever waited for her there. But it was as if she were walking into a strong wind. Something held her back from getting there.

She dreamed of the house she'd seen earlier. But in the dream, the house was furnished. Her subconscious led her through the rooms like one of the computer programs on those design shows on HGTV. There was the sectional sofa of her imagination that fit perfectly in the living room. It was a slate blue just like the walls of the bedroom where she slept. Flames lit up the little fireplace. There were pictures on the walls and knickknacks on the mantel. Lamps on the end tables. A teapot on the coffee table along with two mugs. Why would there be two? the dreaming Meredith wondered before she continued her 3-D tour.

In the kitchen eating area, a small table sat next to the window. Three chairs were placed around the table. Why three? she wondered in her dream.

The dining room held a bigger table, a modern design of dark wood with six cushioned chairs to match. Meredith smiled in her sleep. Noah's grandmother's house was perfect for her.

Down the hallway, the back bedroom held a twin bed. The walls were painted lavender. There was a little white table and two tiny chairs in the corner. A toy tea set was set up. A fuzzy, brown, stuffed bear occupied one of the chairs, and a doll with curly blond hair wearing an old-fashioned pinafore leaned back in the other one. Meredith had the thought that

*the doll was looking down her nose at the bear as if he'd
committed some unforgivable faux pas at her tea party.*

*The master bedroom across the hall held a sleigh bed with
a pillow-top queen mattress covered with the same quilt
Meredith currently slept under. The leaves of the oak tree in
the front yard were green, and dapples of sunlight spilled
through onto the grassy lawn and the wood swing beneath it.*

*Suddenly, Meredith found herself seated on the back porch
with a cup of coffee in front of her and the pages of the newspaper scattered around her. But her focus wasn't on the news
of the day or her coffee cup. She was gazing at the swing set,
where a man pushed a little girl on one of the two swings.
Meredith imagined she could hear the child's squeals of
delight as her dark hair flew out behind her. The man looked
as happy as the child, and when he looked Meredith's way,
he waved. Somehow, Meredith could see him clearly across the
expanse of yard. His eyes were a dark blue. So were those of
the girl in the swing.*

Meredith woke with a start. Sunlight filtered
through the lacy curtains covering the window of her
room at the Twelve Oaks Inn. She stared at the clock
on the nightstand, which told her it was just after
eight.

The faint scent of bacon and something else equally
tantalizing drifted into the room. Her stomach
growled in response. She was hungry but not quite
ready to get up and get dressed. She closed her eyes,
trying to recapture the tendrils of her dreams. They
dwindled rapidly like a barely there whiff of perfume
in the air. Confusing, crazy dreams, but parts of them
had been surprisingly realistic. Especially the tour of
the house she'd already decided would be hers. That
vision, no matter what else her subconscious had made
up, would soon be part of her reality.

She pushed back the covers and dressed in the outfit she'd brought in with her last night. She brushed her hair and used a bare minimum of cosmetics. No more extrathick false eyelashes and overly dramatic makeup created by layers of tan pancake foundation, or cheeks as red as a clown's.

She brushed mascara across her lashes and checked her look in the mirror. She looked normal. Natural. The pinkish red color of the turtleneck she wore was a good color on her. She had lipstick in the same color. She smiled at her reflection. Her stomach growled again. It was definitely time for breakfast.

"There you are," Beverly greeted Meredith as she entered the dining room. "I've got bacon ready. Waffles out in a minute. There's coffee there on the sideboard. Or tea if you want it. Hot water in the carafe. I'll be right back."

Everything smelled so good. Meredith's mouth watered as she helped herself to coffee. She took a plate and snatched two pieces of crisp bacon from the covered tray Beverly had indicated. They were gone before Beverly returned with another tray piled high with Belgian waffles.

"That's what I smelled!" Meredith exclaimed. "Oh my, these look so good."

"Best in town." Beverly blushed with pride. "I've got homemade strawberry jam there or maple syrup, of course."

The jam was in a pretty, glass-covered container. Meredith spooned some onto one of the waffles and took a bite. Her manners seemed to have deserted her. "Delicious," she proclaimed. "You should start serving breakfast all the time."

Beverly poured herself a cup of coffee and took a

seat at the table. "You think so? I've thought about it. Maybe just on the weekends."

"Or you could do a Sunday brunch buffet. Reservations only."

Beverly looked doubtful. "What about church?"

"Church?" Meredith had never been a churchgoer. She decided to tread carefully. "What time is that?"

"The early service is at nine. Or there's one at ten-thirty."

Meredith was used to Vegas, where it seemed most of the Sunday brunch crowd was just waking up after a late night out. But, she supposed, some of them might have been coming from religious services. It wasn't as if they wore identification. She had never really thought about it.

"Obviously, I'm new in town, so I don't know the routines here. In Vegas, what they'd call brunch didn't start before ten-thirty or eleven, and it ran until two or three. Because, of course, brunch is kind of a hybrid, a mixture of breakfast and lunch. Plus, people like to take it easy on Sundays, sleep in, maybe."

Beverly nodded. "That's true. That's not just in Las Vegas. I think it's everywhere."

"If you wanted to do Sundays, maybe you could do some of the prep the night before. Scramble the eggs, mix up waffle batter. Whatever you plan to make."

Beverly thought about that. "Certainly I could do a lot of it ahead of time."

"Maybe you could hire an assistant."

"Oh, I don't know about that."

"I bet there's a high-school kid who wouldn't mind making a few dollars for a few hours of work."

"You know, my friend Charlene mentioned her niece is trying to save money for the senior class trip."

"Teenagers always need money, from what I hear."
Meredith thought for a moment. "You could always
do a Saturday brunch, couldn't you, if you don't want
to do Sundays?"

"I suppose I could. You've given me a lot to think
about."

Meredith reached for another waffle and another
slice of bacon. "You know something else you could
do? Write a cookbook."

"A cookbook? Me?" Beverly looked absolutely
shocked by the idea.

"Why not? Call it *Secrets of Twelve Oaks Inn* or something like that. Because I'm betting you've got more
tricks up your sleeve than just these marvelous waffles
and this to-die-for jam."

Beverly blushed. "Well, I do get compliments on my
cooking."

"And if you decide not to do the weekend or the
Sunday brunch thing, you could still do it for special
occasions."

"Like what?"

"I don't know." Meredith was making everything up
as she went along. "Valentine's Day? New Year's Day?
The Fourth of July? You know—have a theme for
each one. Like maybe for the Fourth of July you do
pancakes with colored syrups or jams. Strawberry and
blueberry and . . . white chocolate, maybe? For the
red, white, and blue theme. You could make fruit
smoothies, too, with the same colors and flavors. And
yogurt parfaits. Those are super popular."

"You sure have a lot of good ideas," Beverly said as
she refilled their coffee cups.

"That's because your food is inspiring."

A timer dinged beyond the swinging door into the

kitchen. Beverly snapped her fingers. "Those are my cinnamon rolls. I'll be right back."

Meredith groaned. She loved cinnamon rolls. She hoped they were the kind with the cream cheese frosting melting down into them. Those were her favorite. She polished off the last bite of bacon, fully intending to make room for at least one of Beverly's rolls. If Meredith kept eating like this, she knew she'd have to do more than just rake leaves to stay in shape.

Chapter Four

When Noah arrived at the Grind, Meredith was already seated at one of the small tables. She had a cup of what looked like hot chocolate and was studying the want ads in the *Nashville News*.

Noah got a cup of dark roast and joined her. "That better not be the real estate section," he joked.

"It's not."

She grinned at him, and he once again felt that tug toward her. She looked more put together than she had last night, like she'd slept well after her exhausting days of driving. She wore a cranberry turtleneck sweater, a tweed jacket, and jeans. Her lips were the same color as the sweater. He wanted to kiss her but managed to quell such an inappropriate impulse. First, he'd sell her the house. *Then* he'd kiss her.

He leaned over and tried to read the newspaper upside down. "Job hunting?"

"I'll need to find something if I'm going to buy the house."

Noah was afraid to ask, but he had to. "And are you?"

"I am."

He wanted to breathe a sigh of relief, but it wasn't a done deal yet. "What about the price?"

Meredith studied him for a moment. "It seems reasonable. Much less than anything in Vegas, certainly."

"You'll want to have it appraised. You'll have to anyway, to get financing."

"I don't need financing," Meredith informed him.

That surprised him. Meredith Clark, he decided, was just full of surprises. "Great. Should I have my attorney draw up the papers?"

"It will take me a few days. I'll have to transfer some funds."

"So, full asking price?" Noah held his breath.

Meredith's eyes twinkled. "Unless you want to give me a welcome-to-the-neighborhood discount."

"How about if I help you find a job instead? There's an opening for an aide at the high school."

"I know. I saw that."

"I could put in a good word for you."

She sat back and studied him. "You hardly know me."

But I'm already half in love with you. Now where had that thought come from? Noah mentally shook himself. "Look before you leap," his grandmother had been fond of saying. It was about time he took her advice. "I work there. I'm on good terms with the principal. He'd be the one interviewing you."

The rest of the week passed quickly, in a whirlwind of activity. Noah gave her a set of house keys as a good-faith gesture. Meredith drove to Greenburg, the nearest large town, to make arrangements for her funds to be transferred to a local bank. Then she

stopped at the mall and bought a sleeping bag. There
was no reason she couldn't camp out on the floor
until she closed on the house and bought some furniture. She certainly wasn't going to buy a sofa and a
bed until the house was hers. *Look before you leap.* She
was learning.

While at the mall, she decided to get a haircut.
Something shorter and sassier to go with all the other
changes in her life.

Nick Collins, the high-school principal, contacted
her the day after she submitted her application. That
made her wonder if Noah had indeed put in a good
word for her. Although there was no reason why he
should; he really didn't know her or anything about
her. But maybe that's the way it was in a small town.
One neighbor doing a good turn for another for no
reason. She'd have to get used to that after the survival-
of-the-fittest attitude she was used to in Vegas.

She shouldn't have been surprised to see Noah in
the school office when she arrived for her interview.
He had told her he worked there, after all, although
she didn't know in what capacity.

Nick didn't look much older than Noah, and that
surprised her. She'd expected someone more . . .
mature. But he appeared to be completely competent
as he reviewed her application and asked her a series
of questions designed to draw her out.

She felt comfortable in this environment, she realized as she sat across from him and told him about
getting her English degree over a period of years, taking
classes when she could, working around performance
schedules. He told her she was overqualified for
the position, but it was temporary anyway, just until

the end of the school year. That was perfect as far as Meredith was concerned. She'd have the summer to look for something else, possibly a teaching position. Even though she had a degree, Nick explained she'd have to get a teaching certificate as well.

Nick walked her to the outer office, where he introduced her to the two secretaries. Everyone seemed so friendly. Noah was at the copy machine. He nudged Nick. "I was right, wasn't I?"

Nick tried to ignore him.

"Right about what?" Meredith asked, her gaze moving between the two men.

"I told him you'd be perfect for the job."

Was Noah psychic? Or had he done his own background check on her? She didn't want to owe him anything, and she wasn't sure how she felt about his "help" with getting this job. If she got it.

"He's right," Nick said, surprising her yet again. "Even though I very much hate to give him the satisfaction of admitting it. You'll have to pass the background check, of course. That usually takes a week or so. But there's no reason for me not to tell you now that the job is yours if you want it."

"She wants it."

Meredith frowned at Noah.

"Well, you do, don't you?"

She decided to ignore Noah and give her attention to Nick. "Thank you. You'll let me know once the background check is complete?"

"Of course."

"I'll walk you out," Noah said.

She didn't want to be rude to him in front of the others, so she allowed it.

"We could celebrate," he said. "School's out at three-thirty. I'll buy you coffee."

She turned to him. "Don't you think you're being just a tad overbearing?"

He seemed genuinely confused. "In what way?"

"First you sell me a house. Then you find me a job. What's next? A marriage proposal?"

"Who told you?"

His delighted grin defused her annoyance. She couldn't decide if that was a good thing or a bad thing. Why did he have to be so cute? And helpful? "I'll take a rain check on the coffee. See you around." She pulled the door open and walked away.

"I like the haircut, by the way," he called after her.

She stopped and turned around. "Thanks." She was virtually certain that he stayed there and watched her walk all the way to her car. With that same grin on his face.

Chapter Five

Noah was filled with anticipation the following week. Just the thought that Meredith would soon be part of the office staff, that he'd get to see her every day, made him smile. She'd seemed so outraged by the thought that his next move might be a marriage proposal. Of course, it was premature, but amazingly, it seemed like it might be a done deal to him.

The heck with "look before you leap." He knew, deep inside, that Meredith Clark was the woman for him. It might take a bit of convincing to get her to see it his way, though. That was okay. He liked a challenge. And working near her every day would give him multiple opportunities to wear her down.

In his attorney's office, they signed papers, and Meredith handed over a bank check. He gave her the second set of keys and knew a tiny moment of sadness. His grandmother's house was gone. It belonged to Meredith now.

Their business concluded, he walked her out. "Now we've got two things to celebrate. You never did let me buy you that cup of coffee." He pointed to the corner. "The Grind is right there."

"Maybe another time. I've got furniture to shop for and a few calls to make. But thanks." She held her hand out to him, and he took it. He was always going to like the way her hand felt in his, he decided.

"Congratulations."

She tugged her hand away.

"Call me if you have any problems," he called, as she walked to her car.

"Oh, I will," she assured him. She ducked inside, then she was gone.

Meredith couldn't believe it. She was a home owner. Excitement bubbled inside her. No more roommates. No more fussy landlords who flipped out if you so much as put a nail in the wall to hang a picture. She didn't have to ask for permission to paint a bedroom or change the window blinds.

She'd already browsed the couple of furniture stores in Greenburg, and she'd also done some preliminary shopping online. She'd bookmarked a number of sites and pages with items she liked and thought would be perfect in her new space.

Meredith drove directly to the house after the closing at the attorney's office. She walked the rooms one more time, consulted the notes she'd jotted down and double-checked the measurements she'd made using an old yardstick she found in the garage. Then she went shopping.

She wasn't really sure what she was going to do with the second bedroom. She didn't really need a guest room. She didn't have any family, and the few friends she had in Vegas weren't really the type who'd come visit her in Nashville, Kansas. Had she moved to the Nashville in Tennessee, the chances for guests might have been higher, but realistically, Meredith knew even that was probably unlikely. They just weren't those kinds of friends.

She'd always been a bit of a loner, she supposed. But here, in the small-town environment, maybe it would be easier to connect with people. The pace of life was certainly a bit slower. And much less competitive. She promised herself she'd be open to new opportunities to meet people and make new friends.

Like Noah? She smiled at the thought. *We'll see*, she told herself. She wanted to get to know her new home better, settle in to her job, maybe meet some of her neighbors. She wasn't going to rush into anything. Not with Noah, if that's what he had in mind. Not with anybody else, either. For a little while, she was just going to *be*.

In Hudson's Furniture in Greenburg, she tracked down the salesman who'd given her his card when she'd been browsing at the store earlier. She'd decided the sectional sofa she liked would be perfect for the living room.

Next she stopped at Gayle's Home Furnishings and Interior Design. She had her eye on a table and chairs for the dining room and also a pair of end tables. She lucked out. They were having a sale.

After that, she stopped at Mattress Outlet and chose a queen set. She'd decided to order a sleigh bed she'd seen online. But until it arrived, she'd have the mattress. No more sleeping bag.

Pleased with the results of her shopping spree, she stopped to stock up on groceries and headed home.

Home.

It had a ring to it that it never had before. Because it seemed like, in some way, she was really going home.

Meredith couldn't believe how quickly she'd settled in to her new life in Nashville. The job in the office at the high school was the perfect beginning. She discovered she liked getting up early, preparing for the workday and having a set schedule. Everyone was friendly and helpful to her, especially the two office secretaries. They were happy to have the position filled as they'd had to do the extra work when the previous aide had to relocate after her husband changed jobs.

Meredith had never worked in an office before, but she quickly got the hang of it after only a week or so. She made copies and entered grades into the computer system for the teachers, covered the phones and the front desk when needed, kept track of the supplies and ordered them when they ran low. She also had a set of keys to let the maintenance people in and out of the areas where they needed to work. Basically, she did whatever needed to be done for whoever needed it to keep the school operating as efficiently as possible.

"Your turn to pick a name for the gift exchange." Janet, one of the two secretaries in the office, stood next to Meredith's desk and held a Christmas gift bag aloft.

"I can't reach it if you're going to hold it way up there."

Janet lowered it a few inches. "Okay. But there can be no peeking. I think we all know what you'd like for

Christmas. Or should I say whom." She winked at Jessica, the other secretary.

Meredith reached over her head and plunged her hand into the bag. There weren't very many names left. "What'd you do? Leave me for last?" She pulled out a tiny piece of paper. "And what do you mean you know whom or what I want for Christmas?"

It was just the three of them in the office at the moment. Meredith liked both of the ladies she worked with a lot. They were warm, good-natured, and easy-going. Janet had worked in the office for almost twenty years. Not much got by her, and nothing seemed to faze her.

"I'm not taking one of those kittens you keep showing me pictures of," Meredith warned Jessica for the umpteenth time. "If that's what you're talking about." Jessica fostered kittens for the local animal shelter until they could be adopted. Every day it seemed she had her cell phone out to share photos of her newest wards.

"Oh, we're not talking about a kitten," Janet assured her. Again, there came that knowing look between her and Jessica. "But since you mentioned it . . ." Janet tapped her phone and held it out in front of her so Meredith could see the screen. "Just in case you know anyone who's looking for a Christmas kitten."

Meredith peered at the screen shot of a fluffy gray kitten with big blue eyes. Perched on top of its head was a tiny red and white Santa hat. The little creature was adorable, and she hoped it found a good home. Just not with her. "Darling," she told Jessica. "I'll keep it in mind if I meet anyone who's looking to adopt."

Meredith glanced down at the piece of paper she'd just drawn, shielding it so that she could read it but

Janet couldn't. She hoped her blush didn't give her away when she saw whose name was written on it. "Good," she said, hastily refolding the slip of paper and rejoining the ongoing conversation. "I'm a dog person. At least I think I am. I've never had a pet, actually. Although I always wanted a puppy."

She'd been thinking about it more and more. She'd learned she could fence in the backyard, which was certainly big enough to accommodate a dog. She could see herself walking some gangly mutt on a leash when the weather was nice. It would be good exercise, and she'd have him for companionship.

"Ah, yes. Puppy love. Ain't it grand?"

Meredith eyed her coworker. "Janet, what is up with you? Have you been drinking or something?"

Jessica giggled. "Come on, Meredith. We're talking about Noah."

"Noah?" Meredith felt her cheeks grow hot again.

Janet swatted her with the gift bag she still held. "He's been following you around like a puppy since you got here. Don't pretend you haven't noticed."

Meredith stared at her desk. She hadn't realized anyone else had picked up on Noah's interest in her. She wondered if he'd recruited these two ladies to further his agenda. "Did he say something to you? About me?"

"Noah?" Janet asked, slightly outraged. "He would never. Not a word. We just can't figure out why you keep shutting him down."

"I . . . don't want to rush into anything." Even to her own ears, that sounded like a lame excuse.

"What? Like having a cup of coffee with him? That's not exactly rushing into anything."

"It's not like you have to marry the guy next week," Jessica put in gently.

"I know. I guess I came here on sort of a whim. I bought a house. I got a job. It all happened so fast, and even though it all feels right, like everything's falling into place just the way I hoped, at the same time, I want to slow down a bit."

"I guess it has been a lot of change for you to absorb all at once," Janet agreed. "New town. New job. Maybe a new guy isn't what you need right now."

"A new *hot* guy," Jessica said. "No woman needs that."

The outer door opened, and Nick walked in with two of the teachers. Janet scooted back to her seat behind the counter, and Jessica picked up the phone. Meredith turned back to her desk and unfolded the piece of paper again. *Noah.* She was pretty sure she knew what he wanted. But she had absolutely no idea what to get him for Christmas.

Chapter Six

Ever since her conversation with Janet and Jessica, Meredith had been second-guessing herself. Certainly, she wanted to look before she leapt any further and created even more change for herself, but every time she looked at Noah, her instincts told her he would be good for her.

She'd decided she had the perfect gift for him. The next time he asked her out for coffee, she'd say yes. She knew for certain that was something he wanted. He'd made it crystal clear. And it would be her treat.

There was only one problem with her plan. Noah had stopped asking.

A thick, cream-colored envelope dropped onto her desk. As if she'd conjured him just by thinking about him, Noah stood next to her chair.

She picked up the envelope. "What's this?"

"Open it."

She did. It was an invitation. "Please join us at our Holiday Gathering . . ." She skipped down to see who had issued the invite. Of course, she didn't recognize the names. The only people she knew were the office staff and the few teachers she'd met.

"I have no idea who this is."

"George Macabee's the head of the Latham County School Board. He and Mrs. Macabee throw what used to be called a Christmas Party but is now the much more PC Holiday Gathering. They invite everyone connected with the county school system. Janitors, the maintenance guys, all the teachers and staff."

"But I don't know them. I've never met them."

"Doesn't matter. They don't know they invited you and won't remember you were there."

"That's . . . hospitable of them." Meredith couldn't suppress a giggle.

"The Macabees are loaded," Noah explained. "It's their way of giving back. They open up their house. Hire a band and caterers. It's a good time. I promise. You don't want to miss it."

Meredith looked at the card again. "There's no way to RSVP."

"No need. They just factor in a certain percentage as no-shows. Makes things easier on the caterer."

"Well . . . great. I guess I'll see you there."

Noah grinned. "I guess you will."

The Friday before the Christmas break began, everyone on staff at the high school brought in a dish for potluck. Meredith and Jessica assembled them as neatly as possible on a long table in the teacher's lounge. There was a festive air as everyone looked forward to the holidays and an escape from school. Meredith secretly wasn't sure who was more excited about the break—the kids or the staff.

There was a round table in the corner covered with a red tablecloth. Those participating in the gift exchange, which seemed to be everyone, had placed their gifts either on the table or underneath a miniature artificial Christmas tree.

All of the gifts were required to have "to" and "from" tags on them. Since not everyone had the same lunch period, if you missed the recipient, he or she could still pick up the gift. But many were on hand to exchange gifts in person.

Meredith didn't have a set lunch period. Usually, she coordinated her breaks with Janet and Jessica so that at least one of them was in the office to answer the phone at all times. Likewise, Noah and Nick, since they weren't classroom teachers, chose their own lunch schedules, often heading to the cafeteria or the staff lounge at the same time.

Meredith had spent what she considered an excessive amount of time trying to figure out what to give Noah. She knew what he *wanted*, of course. His numerous invitations to join him for coffee had made that perfectly clear. It had almost become like a game between them. He asked, always, it seemed, with a good reason behind it. A celebration. Noah, it seemed, found cause for celebration in everyday life. He'd wanted to celebrate her buying the house. And getting a job. When it snowed for the first time, he offered to buy her a hot chocolate if she didn't want coffee. "It's officially winter," he'd said. "We should celebrate."

The cold weather and not actual snow, in Meredith's opinion, officially made it winter, but she had refrained from telling Noah that. She'd looked out at the few swirling flakes of snow that would leave no more than a dusting, which likely would be gone by the next day if the weather report was even close to being accurate, and said, "Tell you what. When it snows for real, I'll let you buy me a hot chocolate." *And maybe I'll pay him back with a kiss*, she thought, but no way would she verbalize this. Yet.

"That's real snow out there." Noah had jabbed a finger in the direction of the window. "It's just not very much."

"Exactly." At that moment, Meredith wasn't even sure she'd ever agree to coffee or hot chocolate with Noah. She'd begun to enjoy the push and pull of these encounters so much she didn't want to give them up. Even though, on some level, she knew deep in her heart that she would. She'd give in. They'd go for coffee. And then, the next time, maybe for a drink. Then dinner. A movie. They'd start dating. Be in a relationship. Something else she knew: it would be a serious relationship. Because Noah was not the kind of guy a girl dallied with. He was relationship material. Long-term relationship material.

But for now, he didn't seem to mind the chase. And she had to admit, she liked being chased.

Noah's eyes had narrowed. "So what's real snow? Does it even snow in Las Vegas? Have you ever seen snow?"

Meredith had pretended outrage. "Of course I've seen snow, Noah Kennedy! It snows in Las Vegas." She giggled at Noah's look of suspicion. "But usually it melts before it hits the ground."

"You deserve a noogie for that."

"A noogie? What's that?"

"You don't know what a noogie is?" Noah had pretended incredulity.

"No. But that's because I think you just made it up."

"I certainly did not. A noogie is a time-honored punishment for minor offenses such as your earlier comments about snow."

"I don't know how my comments about snow could be found offensive."

"That's not a judgment you get to make," Noah had informed her. "Do you want your noogie now?"

She'd backed up a step. "First, I want to know what it is."

"It involves a fist," Noah had said, taking a half step in her direction. He held up his right hand and folded his fingers into a fist. "Then you raise the middle knuckle like this." He demonstrated.

Meredith had watched him with equal parts nervousness and anticipation. "Okay."

"Now usually, I'd get the noogie recipient in a headlock, but in your case . . ." He'd studied her as if trying to make a difficult decision. "But in your case, you get a noogie right here." Making a sudden move, he dug his knuckle into the ribs of her lower back. She grabbed his wrist. "Ah! That tickles!"

He had stopped immediately, but he was so close she got caught up just looking into his eyes, feeling the warmth of his breath and his body. "I didn't hurt you, did I?"

"No." She felt breathless.

"I never would."

"I know." She was still locked in place, lost in his eyes.

His gaze flickered from her eyes to her lips and back. He asked the question silently, but Meredith knew he wanted to kiss her then. She wanted him to. But instead she stepped back. "So that was a noogie, huh?"

Noah snapped out of his trance. "That was such a far cry from a noogie that I'd be embarrassed even to call it a noogie." He looked around the deserted hallway. "Don't tell anyone."

"Afraid you'll lose your champion noogie title?"

"All-county three years running," he said without missing a beat.

"You're a nut."

"That may be true, but let's get back to the snow discussion. Now, I'll need more details. What exactly constitutes 'real snow'?"

Meredith pretended to think while she looked at the few swirling flakes still coming down. "It has to be more than this." She gestured at the weather outside.

"Define more."

"Six inches."

"Six inches? All at once?"

"That sounds reasonable."

"How about three?"

"Are you bargaining with me?"

"I'm negotiating. It could be years before we get six inches of snow all at once." He glanced out at the leaden, gray sky. "On the other hand, it could happen next week."

Meredith knew one thing. She didn't want to wait years before she and Noah had their coffee date. "Okay, three."

He looked at her. "Suddenly, you're awfully agreeable."

"I thought men liked agreeable women."

"Actually, they're suspicious of agreeable women."

"Okay. Six inches it is." She turned to go. "Nice chatting with you."

"Except for me," Noah said. "I like agreeable women. So have it your way. I'll agree to three inches."

She walked backward away from him toward the door. "Three inches. On the ground. For at least twenty-four hours."

"Hey!"

"Bye, Noah."

She swung through the doors, grinning like a crazy woman. Now that had been fun. She tried to remember when she'd enjoyed a conversation with a man as much. The answer was never.

Maybe that was what had been missing in her previous relationships. A sense of fun. A sense of anticipation. Maybe she'd moved too fast and hadn't really allowed herself the time she needed to get to know someone. That's what everyone seemed to do. So there must be something to taking it slow. Even when she wanted to leap right into something with Noah.

She'd finally decided to simply buy him a card. A simple holiday-themed card. Of course, it had to include a wintry snow scene. Inside, she wrote, "There are at least three inches of snow on this card. Would you like to have coffee with me? My treat." Then she'd signed it and sealed it. To make it look like a gift, she found a small flat box and put the card inside. She wrapped it in bright red paper, tied it with a green bow, and put a gift tag on it. She placed it under the tree. At the back. Where it was hidden beneath all the other gaily wrapped packages.

But sometime today, Noah would open it. And soon, she hoped, they'd have that coffee date. She found herself looking forward to it. Because she knew one thing. It would be fun.

She was starting to wish that it would snow.

For real. And she secretly wished it would stick to the ground, leaving her snowbound. With Noah. For days. Just the thought made her feel all warm and tingly inside.

Chapter Seven

When Meredith stepped into the teacher's lounge, there appeared to be plenty of food left. The bell had rung for the start of fourth period minutes before. A couple of teachers were just leaving the lounge with their gifts in one hand and small plates of cookies in the other.

The pile of gifts had dwindled and the few that were left looked a bit neglected and forlorn. The trash can was stuffed with used gift wrapping, curls of ribbon, and crushed bows. All of the discarded gift wrapping was mixed with used paper plates and cups and sticky plastic forks. Bits of paper and glitter as well as a squashed sugar cookie littered the floor. The room looked, Meredith thought, like a horde of picky scavengers had swept through, taken the tastiest bits of food and the best gifts, and left what they didn't want behind.

Meredith found the broom and dustpan in the closet and did a cursory sweep of the floor. She pushed everything in the trash can down to compact it and emptied the contents of the dustpan on top of it. She changed the liner, leaving the full one nearby for the janitorial staff, who would do a much more thorough cleanup later.

Finally, she picked up a paper plate and checked out the potluck buffet. Everything looked good and no calories had been spared. She was pleased to note that the bowl of salad she had brought was nearly empty. She'd cut up chunks of vegetables: broccoli, cauliflower, celery, mushrooms, onions, yellow and green zucchini, and carrots. To that she'd added some shredded kale, spinach, and lettuce. She'd tossed it all in a light coating of homemade red wine vinaigrette. She'd correctly assumed that many of the staff would bring traditionally rich goodies and so would enjoy some lighter fare to balance it out.

The turkey carcass looked like something a pack of hyenas had already attacked, but someone had brought in a deli tray on which a few slices of turkey were still available. She scraped up the crispy edges from a macaroni and cheese casserole, happy that someone had left them for her. As far as she was concerned, that was the best part. There was also a spoonful of a cheesy potato casserole left and a good portion of spaghetti pie.

Carbs. Carbs. And more carbs, Meredith thought. But she no longer worried about a temporary tummy bulge or a costume that was too tight because she'd had a hot fudge sundae or a pepperoni pizza the night before. No more show directors getting on her case if she gained a pound or two.

She'd been walking to and from school because it wasn't far, and she enjoyed the exercise. Nashville was made for walkers. Almost every street had sidewalks that were in pretty good condition considering the age of the town. She liked studying the architecture of the older homes. And it was always fun to watch the young children playing in the yards. Sometimes they stopped what they were doing and stared at her with eagle eyes as she went by. Other times they waved shyly. The bolder ones would yell "Hi!" to her. That made her laugh and return the greeting.

If she had a dog—no, she decided, *when* she had a dog—that would give her a reason to walk even more. Plus she'd be raking leaves in the fall, shoveling snow from her driveway in winter, and mowing the lawn in the summer. She'd also plant a garden. Gardening was supposed to be great exercise. Staying in shape was not going to be a problem at all.

She'd like to take a walk in newly fallen snow. Be the first to leave footprints. It seemed romantic somehow. Maybe Noah would walk with her.

"There you are."

As if she'd once again conjured his appearance just by thinking about him, Noah came through the door. He checked out her plate. "Not much left to choose from after the vultures came through, is there?"

Meredith laughed. "Was it vultures? I was sure it was hyenas when I saw what was left of the turkey."

Noah lifted the turkey's foil covering. "I think you might be right. We should pronounce it dead and give it a proper burial." He picked up a plate and did his own scavenging through the leftovers before joining her. Pleasure and anticipation shot through her. Was that because they were together and alone?

"I thought you ate earlier."

He eyed her plate. "You took the best part of the mac and cheese casserole. All of it."

"What? This?" She held up a bite of the crispy brown stuff that had bits of the softer macaroni underneath.

"Yes. Thief. First you steal my heart, then the almost burnt macaroni."

Meredith couldn't tell if the comment about stealing his heart was a joke or not. She realized she didn't want it to be. Was this what falling in love felt like?

"What's it worth to you?" She held the fork closer to his lips to tease him. "Maybe we could make a deal."

He captured her wrist and held the fork still and ate the macaroni.

"Hey! That was my macaroni."

"Let's call it *our* macaroni." He smiled, something that was clearly intended to distract her, because he snatched another bite of macaroni off her plate and popped it in his mouth.

"Hmpff." She pushed her plate in his direction. "Might as well take all of it now." She crossed her arms and purposely pushed out her bottom lip.

"Is this you pretending to be annoyed?" he asked at the same time he stabbed another crispy bite of casserole.

"What makes you think I'm pretending?"

Noah chewed and swallowed. "Either way it's adorable."

"It is?" She smiled, not caring that her delight was so transparent.

"What's that phrase I've heard the kids use? Totes something."

"Totes adorbs?"

"Yeah," he said. "That's it. When did we start speaking

in partial words, by the way? Are we too busy these days to complete our adverbs and adjectives?"

"Appare."

Noah eyed her before concentrating on how best to approach the spaghetti pie. "Appare? That's not even a word." He took a bite. "Is it?"

"Neither is adorbs. Or totes. Well, it is, but not the way it's used with that phrase."

She drummed her fingertips on her elbows and watched him eat while waiting for him to figure it out.

"Hah." It wasn't a laugh, but it was close. "Good one. You're pretty smart."

"Thank you."

"For a girl."

She narrowed her eyes. He disarmed her with a grin that told her he was kidding. "For a minute there, I thought I'd have to give you a noogie," she said.

"You thought about *trying* to give me a noogie."

"You think I can't do it?"

"I think I'd enjoy letting you try."

"We'll see about that." She glanced at his plate, which somehow was nearly empty. "So you didn't eat earlier?"

"Nah. There was an altercation in Mr. Hartman's classroom. I had to take a couple of the boys outside and have a conversation with them."

"I hope no one was hurt."

"No. But it took them a while to listen to reason and apologize to each other."

"I bet taking them outside instead of to your office sped the process along."

"Maybe."

"Exposure to cold air makes people see reason much more quickly—is that it?"

"That's always been my theory."

"So you said you were looking for me. What for?"

Noah got up from the table, dumped his plate in the trash, and rummaged through the remaining gifts under the tree. He came back with a box messily wrapped in paper that featured puppies and kittens peeking out of stockings hung from a mantel. Meredith decided an entire roll of tape had been used to seal the ends. The ribbon looked like it had been strangled by a madman, and the bow was slightly crushed.

He handed the box to her. "I'm not very good at wrapping presents." She bit her lip. That was an understatement if ever there was one. It would have been more accurate to say Noah sucked big-time at wrapping presents. But since he already knew it wasn't one of his strengths, she saw no reason to rub it in.

"You got my name?"

"Thus the present. Don't let the wrapping fool you. I'm pretty sure I nailed it."

He looked a bit smug, and it made Meredith smile. She'd struggled so much about what to give him and how to present it. Had choosing a gift for her been easy for him?

She set the box on the table and pushed her chair back.

"Where are you going? Aren't you even going to open it?"

She walked over to the gift table and found his gift easily and brought it to him. "Here you go. Please note the precision wrapping and the perfect bow."

"Show-off." He held the box in his hands and shook it once. "It's awfully light."

"Don't let the weight fool you. I'm pretty sure I nailed it."

He looked at her. "Do you think it means something? That we got each other's names?"

"Like out of all the houses for sale and all the high schools in all the small towns in America, I just happened to walk into yours?"

"Something like that."

She didn't know what to say. Had fate or some larger force in the universe brought them together? They'd never know. "Maybe," she allowed.

"Or it could just be we got caught in the randomness of the universe."

"Entirely possible," she agreed.

He lifted her present from the table and handed it to her. "You go first."

"Let's open them at the same time," she suggested.

"Okay."

"But you have to give me a head start. Or better yet, a sharp knife. There's a lot of tape on here."

"I wanted you to enjoy the anticipation."

"Oh, I am," she assured him. "One. Two. Three. Go."

They started unwrapping. Meredith decided to bypass the taped ends of the box and simply rip through the paper, hoping she didn't break a nail. By the time she got the wrapping off, Noah was already reading his card.

His gaze came up to hers. "You were right. You nailed it."

She couldn't help her smile of delight. All her thinking about what to give him and how to give it to him had paid off.

She lifted the lid on her box and pushed aside red and green tissue paper to find two exquisite Christmas mugs, a small package of gourmet coffee, and one of gourmet hot chocolate mix. The mugs were midnight blue covered with snowflakes and the words, "Let it snow, let it snow, let it snow."

Their eyes met. "I guess you know what I like."

Noah smiled. "I guess I do."

Chapter Eight

Saturday morning, Meredith bounced out of bed and skipped into the kitchen. She got a burst of joy as she always did each time she entered the room. It was warm and cozy and just the right size. She could sit at the breakfast table with her coffee and gaze out the window at the backyard and the trees beyond and daydream. Sometimes she wrote in the journal she'd begun keeping the day she left Las Vegas. She hadn't done much journaling in the past, but she'd felt like this new adventure she'd set out on needed to be documented. Maybe someday she'd look back and want to remember the journey. So often she'd heard people say it's not the journey, it's the destination, but Meredith had begun to believe that perhaps it was both. Her destination had been Nashville, Kansas, certainly, but arriving here was only part of the journey. Life was a journey, she supposed, and it had less to do with where you were in the physical world than the experiences you had every day along the way. The people you met. The people who became important to you.

Like Noah.

Meredith started coffee and watched it drip into the carafe. It seemed like Noah was destined to be a significant part of her journey. She hadn't been looking for someone special. Someone like him. She hadn't been looking for anything when she'd left Las Vegas because she didn't know what she really wanted. She still wasn't a hundred percent sure what she wanted, but she knew she wanted Noah to be a part of her journey toward finding it.

She was looking forward to their coffee date this afternoon. He'd wasted no time scheduling it, that was for sure. Last night, she'd washed the mugs he'd given her so she could use one this morning. She took one from the shelf and added some sweetener and a shake of cinnamon. When the coffee was ready, she poured a cup and sat at the table to make a list.

She was planning to do a bit of shopping early this morning. She wanted to get some Christmas lights and maybe a few decorations for outside. And a wreath for the front door. There wasn't really anyplace to hang lights, but she'd thought wrapping strands of white lights around the trunk of that big oak tree would be pretty. She didn't want to have the only house on the block that wasn't decorated. Everyone in her neighborhood would think she was a Scrooge.

In the spring, she'd plant some bushes on either side of the front stoop and hope they got big enough by next Christmas so she could drape lights over them. Plus, by then she'd have acquired a ladder and could hang lights from the eaves of the house. But for now, she was starting small, trying to be thoughtful about what she wanted. Looking before she leapt.

After a light breakfast, she got dressed. She'd quickly realized that layering was the best option for the Kansas winter weather. She wasn't sure how she felt about bundling up to go outside, then unbundling bit by bit depending on the indoor temperatures of stores and restaurants. Then putting everything back on to go out again. On the other hand, she liked the opportunity to wear sweaters and turtlenecks, jackets and scarves. And boots. She dearly loved boots. She already had three pairs courtesy of her initial outing to the mall in Greenburg. A black ankle-high pair that went well with slacks. A knee-high pair that she could wear with just about anything, including skirts. And she hadn't been able to resist an impractical over-the-knee style as well. They were black and shiny and sexy. She'd bought an adorable plaid skirt and a soft angora-like sweater in a shade of creamy white. Paired with the over-the-knee boots, she'd look like a schoolgirl ready to paint the town red. The thought delighted her. Must be her years of wearing costumes in Vegas coming back to haunt her.

It was cold, but the sun was bright, almost glaring in its intensity. Meredith made sure she had her list and donned her sunglasses for the drive to Greenburg. Nashville had the basic necessities for shopping, but there wasn't much variety. The supermarket was adequate but small, and the prices were higher than at the bigger chain store where the selection was more what she was used to. A once-a-week trip to the bigger town to stock up on groceries was probably all she'd need. And it would be a fun Saturday outing. If she needed to shop, she could stop at the mall first. It wasn't a super mall by any means, but it had several of the major department stores.

There wasn't much in the way of scenery on the drive. The roads were straight, and the land was flat. No mountains in the distance, no skyscraper hotels. Farmland stretched as far as she could see on either side of the two-lane road. But, of course, there were no crops planted this time of year. She imagined in the spring, there would be shoots of corn and wheat and whatever else Kansas was known for. Soybeans, maybe. Alfalfa. She should do her homework if this was her new home.

Probably hay was grown here to feed the cattle she saw gathered in muddy lots near the barns she passed. The cows looked cold and unhappy, resigned to their lot in life, she supposed. They, unlike her, didn't have a choice about where they went. Probably they couldn't make a decision anyway. But she supposed they'd prefer a nice green pasture somewhere in a warmer climate, where they'd be allowed to live out their days chewing grass and napping in clover.

Wow. She was making up stories about cows now. Maybe she'd write a children's book about happy farm animals. Pigs and cows and goats. Chickens and ducks and geese who all got along with each other. A picture book with green fields and sunny skies. But all the animals would do fun, humanlike things. And the ducks and geese could race on bicycles. And the cows and pigs would wear roller skates and compete in a roller derby. The chickens would stage a dance contest. The goats were the judges for all the events. Except they ate the scorecards. So everyone was a winner.

The more Meredith thought about it, the more she

liked the idea. There was room for some silliness in the world. And what better place to start than with children.

By the time she reached the big home improvement store, she had the whole book mapped out in her head, complete with illustrations. She'd have to find an illustrator, though, because even believable stick figures were a challenge for her.

The parking lot was already crowded, but she found space near the end of a long row of pickups and SUVs. Her hybrid compact seemed out of place among the bigger vehicles. But it was easy to park, which was one of the things she loved about it. That and the economical gas mileage. Maybe someday she'd need a bigger vehicle. But for now, her car was perfect for her.

Inside, the store was bustling, the aisles crowded with shopping carts and families. It was a popular place, not only for Christmas decor but for gift buying as well. Especially if you were buying for someone who liked power tools.

She was glad she wasn't in a hurry. The only thing on her agenda was her date later this afternoon for coffee with Noah. So she took her time navigating through the aisles. The Christmas lights had been picked over, but the clerks were restocking them almost as fast as they sold. She found the kind of clear white lights she wanted and estimated how many she'd need to wrap the trunk of the tree. She should have measured it before she left. Which made her think she should probably buy a tape measure while she was here because she didn't have one and couldn't have measured it anyway.

She placed several boxes of lights in her cart and edged past a harried-looking woman who had two small children wedged in her cart and two older ones tagging behind her. The cart itself was stacked with merchandise, and the kids were pointing out every single item they passed. "Look, Mom." "We should get these, Mom." "Can we have candy-cane lights?" "I like the red ones." Meredith didn't know how the woman did it. She was having a hard enough time figuring out what to buy without anyone along to offer more suggestions.

But the woman was patiently answering the children's questions and suggestions. Meredith guessed she was used to it and had unlimited patience.

There was an entire section devoted to wreaths and outside Christmas decor. She chose a pretty green wreath with a big red bow and little silver bells placed throughout.

Some of the lawn ornaments were outrageous. Big blow-up Santas and reindeer and snowmen. She couldn't imagine dealing with one of those on her own. Not this year anyway.

She found a jaunty snowman made of wood that would fit perfectly in the corner of the front stoop right next to the door. And then she saw there was a snow maiden meant to match him. Perfect, she thought. For the other side of the door.

She pushed her cart to the back of the store to look at the ladders. They weren't cheap, that was for sure. And she couldn't buy one anyway because she had no way to get it home. It certainly wouldn't fit in the back of her car. She'd have to make friends with someone who had a pickup or an SUV who wouldn't mind helping her get one home. Someone like Noah? Just the thought of him made her smile. Yes. And she'd buy him a cup of coffee in return for his help.

There would be a lot of coffee in her future, she hoped. And someone to share it with.

On the way home, Meredith thought about her future. Although she'd got her degree in English, mostly because she loved to read and write, and she'd thought about teaching English, she'd begun to reconsider that idea. Maybe she'd be happier teaching elementary school. Even kindergarten. She liked the thought of reaching children at a younger age, igniting their interest in stories and school and how to get along with their peers.

She'd researched what it took to get a teaching certificate. There were some classes she'd have to take and an exam to pass. But if she started the classes in the winter semester and continued through the summer sessions, she could complete all the requirements by the beginning of the next school year. Even if she couldn't find a permanent position in the county school system right away, she could substitute teach until one became available. Plus, that would give her time to work on her children's book. On the drive home, she embellished her ideas. There would be one bossy cow, she decided, who'd have to become part of the team. And an older mother-hen type who didn't let age get in her way. It would be such fun creating the story and the characters even if it never got published.

For that matter, she could publish it herself. It seemed like everyone was writing books these days, and it didn't matter whether they had a publisher. She could ask Mrs. Williams, the art teacher at the high school, about illustrations. Maybe she knew someone who would be interested in doing the designs and a cover.

When Meredith arrived home, the sun hadn't done much to raise the temperature. She changed her clothes and got started on putting up the lights. But first she situated her snow people on either side of the front door. She thought they were adorable and imagined them sneaking flirtatious glances at each other when no one was looking.

She hung the wreath on the outer door. *There*, she thought. *Proof I'm not a Scrooge.*

She'd stowed her purchases in the trunk of her car, so she just left it open. There was no sense taking everything inside when she could open all the packages of lights right in the driveway. She started with the extension cord, glad that she'd bought the hundred-foot one because there were only a few feet left after she plugged it in and uncoiled it on the way to the tree. She left it there and went back for the lights.

She pulled the big trash can out and discarded the wrappings as she went. She started at the base of the tree with two strands. It would be better, she decided, if she plugged each strand into one of the three outlet prongs. That way, she could plug additional strands into each one as she went up the length of the tree. She'd read the warning label and knew there was a limit to how many strands could be connected. The last thing she wanted to do was create a fire hazard in her new neighborhood.

She went to work circling the tree, trying to keep the distance between the lights as uniform as possible. She wished she had a ladder and more lights because it would have been pretty to wrap the bare lower branches with lights as well. It would give the impression that the lights were floating in the air at night. Next year, she reminded herself, she'd go all out. But for now, she determined she had purchased just enough lights to cover the trunk up to where the lowest branches began. Luckily, she had a stepladder in the garage to help her reach them.

When she finished, she stood back to admire her efforts. The lights all worked. She couldn't really tell how it would look until it got dark out. It would be easy enough to plug in the extension cord each evening and unplug it before she went to bed.

The front door of the house next to her opened as she was folding up the step stool. An older woman wrapped in a thick cardigan sweater came out. "I never saw anyone put lights around a tree trunk like that before," she called to Meredith.

Meredith looked back at her tree. "It's the only place I could think of to put some lights up this year."

"Bet it'll look pretty at night," the woman said. "I'm Julia," she said. "Julia Johnston."

"Meredith Clark. It's nice to meet you." Meredith leaned the stepladder carefully against the tree so as not to crush any of the lights. She made her way closer to Julia's tiny front porch. "I moved here from Las Vegas a few weeks ago."

"I saw someone had moved in. Been meaning to stop over to say hello. You all done with your decorating?"

"Yes, I think so. Next year I'll do more."

"I've got a pot of turkey soup on. Would you like to come over for lunch?"

Meredith's stomach growled an answer she hoped

Julia couldn't hear. She had enough time to eat before she had to meet Noah at the Grind. "I'd love to," she said. "Let me put everything away, and I'll be right over."

"All right." Julia disappeared inside, closing the door against the cold. Meredith put the stepladder away and brought the trash can back into the garage. She closed the car's trunk and dashed inside. She put on the outfit she'd worn earlier. If need be, she could leave from Julia's and head straight to her date.

Julia's house was about the size of her own, but it was laid out differently and was filled with antiques. Glass-fronted cabinets held knickknacks and a variety of pretty dishes. There was an old rolltop desk in one corner framed by a pair of ladder-back chairs. Lacy curtains crisscrossed the front window, allowing in shafts of afternoon sunlight.

"Your house is so pretty," Meredith said, as Julia led her back to the kitchen.

"Thank you," Julia said. "But mostly it's just old. Just like me." She said this in a matter-of-fact tone without a trace of self-pity.

"You're not exactly old. You're more of a classic."

Julia smiled, and Meredith could see the soft beauty of her features. "Like a Model T?"

"Vintage is all the rage now, you know."

"I like that. I'm not old. I'm just vintage."

"There you go. See? It is what it is."

"We'll see what you think when you get to be my age," Julia said as she removed the lid from a big pot on the stove. "Had a bunch of leftovers from Thanksgiving. Threw most of it in the freezer. I can only eat so many leftovers before I'm ready for something else.

But after a couple of weeks, I take the leftovers out and throw them all in a pot." She stirred the contents of the pot with a great big ladle. "Turkey, mashed potatoes, gravy, stuffing. Chop up some onion and celery. Add some seasoning. We call it stewp. Not quite a stew. Not quite a soup."

"It smells delicious," Meredith said. "Can I help?"

"Nope," Julia replied. "Got it all set up at the table there. Baked some bread this morning." She ladled some of the stewp into a bowl and handed it to Meredith. "Go ahead and sit. It doesn't matter which place."

The table was an old, round, pedestal type that probably weighed five hundred pounds. But it, like Julia, appeared to have aged gracefully and had been lovingly cared for over the years. The wood gleamed dully with the sheen of a recent polishing.

Julia took the adjacent seat and offered the bread to Meredith. She'd already sliced a portion of it onto an old cutting board. Meredith helped herself to a slice and slathered it with soft butter from a little ceramic pot. She took a bite and groaned in appreciation. "Oh, my goodness. I could eat that entire loaf, I think. This is so good."

Julia smiled and spooned up some stewp. "I'm glad you like it." She blew on her spoonful before she took a bite.

Meredith didn't want to abandon her slice of bread just yet, but the aroma from the soup bowl was too much to resist. She also blew on it before she took a spoonful. It was thick, with chunks of turkey and carrots, celery and onion. Bits of other seasonings blended into the broth. It was hearty and definitely tasty.

"It tastes as good as it smells," Meredith told Julia.

She alternated bites of bread with spoonsful from her bowl.

"When it's cold out, I like to bake. And today just seemed like a good day for this."

They ate in silence for a little while before Julia said, "I take it you've met Noah."

"Yes. My first day here, actually. We met at the house, so he could show it to me."

"His grandmother and I were great friends for many years."

"He did mention it was her house but that he had done all the renovations."

"He was always such a good boy. A bit of a prankster though, when he was younger. And he was a bit wild in high school. It always worried Martha, his grandmother."

"He seems to have settled down," Meredith said.

"Well, maybe not the prankster side," she admitted, recalling how he liked to tease. "But he's a high-school guidance counselor now, so he can't be too wild."

"Oh, I imagine when his mother got sick, that took a lot of the piss and vinegar out of him. Poor Martha. Pamela was her only daughter. I don't think she ever got over losing her."

Meredith put her spoon down so she could give Julia her full attention. "I didn't know about his mother."

"No. I suppose you wouldn't. But I knew her from when she was young. She and my Marcus were the same age. That girl had a zest for life like no one else. Always a smile on her face. She'd turn the simplest of gatherings into a party. The tiniest event into a celebration. That's what I remember best about her."

Maybe that's why Noah wanted to celebrate her buying the house and getting the job at the high school, Meredith thought. Why he wanted to celebrate the first snow flurries of the winter.

"When Pamela was a little thing—oh, maybe eight or nine years old—Martha helped her plant a garden from seeds. When those first sprouts came up? You'd have thought it was the Fourth of July. Pamela was so excited. She invited all the neighbor kids over for a picnic so they could see her success. She was a darling, just like her mother."

"You must miss them."

"I do. When you get to be my age, you expect a certain amount of loss. But you have to go on living."

Meredith thought of the parents she barely remembered, who'd died in a car accident when she was four. Of her grandmother who'd raised her in their stead and who had passed away going on three years. She'd had no choice, as Julia said, but to go on living. And now, maybe, she'd take that one step further and start celebrating all the little moments that made life special. Like meeting Noah for coffee.

"What's that smile for?" Julia wanted to know.

Meredith hadn't even realized she was smiling. It seemed especially inappropriate when Julia had been talking about loss. "I'm sorry. I just, well, I have a date later, and I'm really looking forward to it."

"A date?" Julia's eyes lit up. "How delightful. It wouldn't be with anyone I know, would it?"

There didn't seem to be any reason not to tell her that Meredith could think of. "It's with Noah."

"That doesn't surprise me," Julia said. She buttered a slice of bread for herself.

"It doesn't?"

"Not a bit." Julia took a bite of bread and chewed. When she was done, she said, "I've just been sitting here thinking you'd be perfect for him. Even though I just met you."

"You have?"

"You remind me a little bit of Pamela. I can't really say why. Maybe because if an old lady invited her to lunch, she'd have come and complimented her cooking just like you have. She might even have told me I'm a classic instead of just plain old."

"I'll come visit you anytime you want. With or without lunch as part of the bargain," Meredith told her. "I don't know very many people here yet, so it's nice to make a new friend."

"Even if she is a vintage model," Julia said, smiling happily.

"*Especially* if she's a vintage model," Meredith sing-songed, her voice filled with an exuberant amount of cheer. Julia couldn't have chosen a more likable neighbor had she been given the opportunity to handpick one herself.

Chapter Nine

The only place Meredith could find to park in the square was a block away from the Grind.

She'd lost track of time while she visited with Julia, then Julia had insisted on giving her a container of the stewp and a third of the loaf of bread. Meredith was thinking about having the leftovers for dinner later.

She hurried to the coffee shop, knowing she was already a few minutes late. The place was crowded, but she spied Noah at a corner table in the back. He stood and watched her wend her way through the café. "Sorry I'm late. I didn't realize it would be so crowded downtown. I couldn't find a parking place." Her words came out in a jumbled rush. As much as she'd been looking forward to this date, she was nervous.

"It's okay. I just got here. This was the only empty table, so I thought I'd snag it for us."

He helped her with her coat. She draped it over the back of the chair and unwound the scarf from around her neck before she sat.

Noah looked divine. But then, in Meredith's opinion,

he always did. He wore jeans and a gray V-necked sweater over a white shirt. Preppy casual, she decided. And Noah could pull it off. If he were in New York instead of Kansas, he might be gracing the cover of *GQ* or doing ads for Armani. Although she'd never seen a photo of him. Maybe he wasn't photogenic. Maybe he only looked this good in person, and pictures wouldn't do him justice. She was glad, however, that he wasn't in New York. That he was right here in Nashville, Kansas, on his first official date with her.

"Do I have broccoli in my teeth or a zit on my nose?" he asked.

"No. Of course not."

"Well, you're staring at me as if there's definitely something of interest above my neck."

Meredith blushed. "Sorry. I didn't mean to stare. That was rude of me. I was thinking—"

"What?" he asked, intrigued.

"No. It's too embarrassing."

"Well, now you have to tell me."

"Okay. I was thinking that you're good-looking enough to be a model."

Noah looked delighted at her confession. "Really? And you weren't going to tell me?" He leaned toward her. "You know women aren't the only people who like to get compliments."

"No. I suppose that's true. But you already know you're good-looking."

"Beauty is in the eye of the beholder. I'd say I'm average-looking."

"Wow. You're humble, too."

"You're funny."

"I don't mean to be."

"I like it." He stared at her for a minute. "I like *you*."

That information made her positively giddy. "Is *that* why you kept asking me out for coffee?"

"Why did you think I was asking you out for coffee?"

"I don't know. Maybe you'd already dated every single woman in this town before I showed up, so I was just the next in a long line of females whose hearts you've broken."

"Not even close," Noah assured her. "I haven't dated anyone in . . . months, now that I think about it."

"Is that because there are no available single women in Nashville?"

"Oh, there are. Quite a few actually."

"But you're picky?"

"I prefer the term 'selective.'"

"Well then, I guess I'm flattered to be here with you now."

"You should be."

Meredith laughed. "I take back my humble remark."

They smiled into each other's eyes. Meredith knew she'd never felt this sense of delight ever before. Certainly not on a first date. Mostly what she felt on first dates was trepidation. She always expected it to go badly. It was always awkward. Maybe that was because of the nerves. And even though she'd been nervous mere minutes ago, now she was enjoying herself. She liked talking to Noah even if their conversations were a little silly sometimes. She sensed that if she wanted to have a serious conversation with him, he'd go there, too. Maybe she wasn't falling in love with him. But she was definitely falling in like with him.

"So," Noah said. "About that coffee . . ."

"Oh, my goodness! This is your Christmas present, and I completely forgot to ask what you'd like." Meredith was acting like a ditz, which wasn't her usual style. Apparently, being with Noah made every thought go out of her head. *Focus*, she told herself. "What can I get you?"

"I want one of those fancy coffees. With the whipped cream and the chocolate flavoring in it. A big one."

"Big coffee, with chocolate and some whipped cream. Got it. Anything else?"

"Well, since you're offering. They've got these chocolate-filled croissants here. I wouldn't mind one of those."

Meredith looked at him suspiciously. "Okay, wait. Are you"—she leaned in close to him and glanced both ways before she spoke in a near whisper—"a chocoholic?"

Noah laughed. "Not yet. But I'm working on it."

"I knew there was a reason I liked you."

She picked up her purse and smiled all the way to the counter. The crowd had thinned out a little, and she didn't have to wait in the order line very long. She had plenty of time, however, to check out the pastries in the case. She decided she'd try a cinnamon-almond apple blossom. She had no idea what it tasted like, but it looked and sounded yummy. *Carbs, carbs, carbs*, she thought again. She'd need to go for a very long walk or do some extreme power yoga to burn off the calories she was consuming on just this one date. Because she already knew she was getting a hot chocolate.

She made it back to the table with the drinks and the pastries on a small tray. Noah helped her unload it, and she took the tray back to the counter.

"You're very graceful," Noah said. He, of course,

had been watching her the whole time she'd been away from the table.

"Well, as a dancer, that is part of the training."

"You were a dancer? Out there in Las Vegas?"

"Uh-huh. For ten years." She took a sip of her hot chocolate and dabbed her top lip with a napkin just in case there were telltale signs of whipped cream.

"Did you like it?" Noah asked.

Meredith cut into her apple blossom. "I guess I did. You know, I never really thought about whether I liked it. I mean, I loved dancing. I took lessons for years, and I thought it would be fun to be in the shows. But after a while, I guess it's like every other job. It becomes a way to make money so you can live and pay your bills. And there's a downside to every job, isn't there?"

She took a bite of her pastry, and it melted in her mouth. She didn't care how many calories it contained. She took another bite.

"What was the downside for you?" Noah asked.

Meredith sipped some more of her hot chocolate. "The career of a professional dancer can be pretty short. It's very hard on the body, for one thing. If you're injured, you can't dance. Or I should say, you shouldn't dance. Because it only aggravates the injury. But a lot of dancers work injured. I tried not to because you can do real permanent damage to yourself.

"But the wear and tear on your joints and ligaments and muscles adds up. I was in a car accident last year, and that kind of ended my professional dance career."

"You were injured?"

"I was already having problems with my knee. The accident made it worse, and that kind of sealed the deal. On the upside, I got a substantial settlement out of it because the other driver was at fault. I got a new car. I'd finished college, and there was nothing to keep me in Vegas."

"So like all retiring dancers, you decided to move to Nashville." Noah was halfway through his chocolate croissant, but he'd been listening intently.

"I decided to move *somewhere*," Meredith said. "Nashville was just a name on a map. But it seemed like it was as good a place as any other."

"No family in Vegas? No boyfriend?"

"No and no. My parents died when I was a child, and my grandmother raised me. But then she passed away a few years ago. I have some friends there, but no one I'm particularly close to."

"My mom died when I was in college," Noah said.

"Were you close?"

"Yes. My brother had more in common with my dad, I guess. My mom and I were similar in some ways. We got each other, you know? Laughed at the same kind of dumb jokes. She had this way of making a big deal out of everything. But in a good way. Like if I got an A on a spelling test, or if my brother hit a home run in Little League, there'd be some special dessert or our favorite dinner. She was a very positive person."

"She celebrated life," Meredith said, remembering what Julia had shared with her earlier.

"Exactly," Noah agreed.

"She sounds like a wonderful woman."

"She was." He pushed his empty plate away. "You kind of remind me of her," he said shyly. "I can't really say why, but you do."

"I consider that a great compliment." Meredith was truly touched. She fell even further in like with Noah.

By the time they left the Grind, it was getting dark.

Noah walked her to her car. "I wanted to ask you something," he said, as she unlocked her door.

"What's that?"

"Would you want to go to the mall in Greenburg with me tomorrow? It will probably be a madhouse, but I have to do some Christmas shopping and . . . I'm not very good at it."

"Yes."

"Yes, I'm not very good at Christmas shopping?"

Laughter bubbled out of Meredith. "There's no way I could know that. I meant yes, I'd go to the mall with you."

"You will?"

"Sure. Why not? What time?"

"Around noon? I can pick you up. I know where you live."

"I'll look forward to it."

She'd opened the car door, and now it was between them.

"Okay," Noah said wistfully. "Thanks for the Christmas gift."

"You're welcome. See you tomorrow."

Noah headed toward his car, parked even farther down the street. He'd wanted to kiss Meredith. Even a little peck on the cheek would have been acceptable. But he couldn't figure out how to do it. He'd waited too long to ask her about going to the mall. She was practically already in her car before he'd said anything.

As first dates went though, he guessed it had gone pretty well. He knew a few things about Meredith he hadn't known before. She thought he was good-looking. That was an ego boost right there.

The fact that she was a professional dancer explained why she was in such good shape. She moved like a dancer, he realized. Her posture was perfect, and she was very graceful.

She was also alone in the world, it seemed. So it hadn't mattered where she lived. It could have been Nashville. Or it could have been anywhere else.

Again he had that sense of their fates colliding. Whether by divine purpose or some random accident. He didn't really care which it was. He was just glad she'd landed where she had. Literally in his own backyard. Because something else this first date had confirmed—he really, really liked her.

Noah knocked on Meredith's door the next day just before noon. He'd noticed the extension cord and followed its length to the tree. He had to admit the yard looked a little bare. The shrubbery that had been planted years ago beneath the windows had not been in great shape, so when he'd renovated the house, he'd pulled it all out. It had made it easier to paint the outside, that was for sure. And he figured whoever bought the place would want to make his or her own landscaping choices anyway.

Meredith opened the door, and he got that little thrill of excitement he always got when he saw her.

"Come in for a minute, okay? I'm having a bit of a wardrobe malfunction."

He stepped inside and immediately felt like he didn't want to leave. In the short time she'd been there, Meredith had transformed the space into something that was welcoming and looked comfortable.

The sectional sofa seemed made for the living room. A flat-screen TV was mounted over the fireplace. An area rug with shades of dark blue and cream pulled the space together.

"Anything I can help with?" he asked.

"Would you mind?" She turned her back to him, gathered her hair in one hand, then lifted it away from her shoulders. "This sweater buttons in the back, and I seem to be all thumbs today. I keep getting the buttons in the wrong holes."

He saw that she was correct. There were only a few buttons, but they were sadly misaligned from her efforts. He undid them, his fingers itching to touch the creamy skin at the back of her neck. He noticed her hair and wondered if it was as soft and silky as it looked. He hoped he'd have the chance to find out soon.

He bent his head and patiently slid the delicate pearl buttons into the appropriate holes. She smelled good. Like something edible. Apples or cherries or peaches. Maybe a perfumery somewhere had combined the scents of all three into something enticingly light and fresh that temporarily addled his senses. "There you go," he said eventually. "You're all set."

She dropped the handful of hair and turned around. "Thanks. I loved this sweater when I bought it, but those buttons were a challenge."

"It looks great on you." It was the color of a tangerine and complemented her beautifully. She also wore dark denim slacks and black boots.

She picked up her coat. "Ready?"

"Ready."

"So what are we shopping for?" Meredith asked once they were on the road.

"That's just it," Noah said. "I have no idea."

"Okay, then. *Who* are we shopping for?"

"My dad and my brother. I guess I should get something for Tiffany the Snob, too."

"Tiffany the Snob?" Meredith said, and gave him a curious look. "And who, exactly, is Tiffany the Snob?"

"My brother's girlfriend. That's not her name. Well, Tiffany is actually her name. 'The Snob' part is just a title I gave her the first time I met her."

"Lovely. What did Tiffany do to earn that title?"

Noah gave her an uneasy glance. "If I tell you, you're not going to hate me, are you?"

"Doubtful. But we'll see how it goes."

"The first time I met her was at my dad's. He'd invited us for a backyard barbecue. Nothing fancy. Hamburgers, hot dogs. Chips. Baked beans. Potato salad. He tries to make a picnic in the backyard like my mom used to. He puts the red-checkered tablecloth on the table. He's got paper plates and napkins and plastic utensils and cups. A cooler with beer and soda.

"Tiffany shows up with my brother looking like, I don't know, a runway model or something close. She's wearing all white. I guess to her, it was casual clothes, but who wears all white to a barbecue?"

Noah asked the question as if he truly wanted an answer. He seemed to be so baffled by Tiffany's wardrobe choice that Meredith felt compelled to say, "Clearly, she was just asking for trouble."

"Right? So the very first thing she does is grab a handful of napkins and wipe off the picnic bench where she plans to sit. Like she thinks my dad wouldn't have thought to wipe everything down when he was setting it up.

"So nobody says anything. We act like all our guests feel they have to clean the furniture before they take a seat. Dad offers her a cold drink. A beer or a soda, and she says, 'Oh, I'll just have a sparkling water if you have it.'"

"Let me guess," Meredith said, thoroughly enjoying Noah's story. "No sparkling water in the cooler?"

"You guessed it. Dad says he can get her ice water from the kitchen. She says, 'Oh, I never drink tap water.' My brother jumps up and offers to run to the corner market for her. She says, 'Thank you, Hunter,' and off he goes!" Noah shook his head as if still in shock over his brother's behavior.

"He must really like her," Meredith said.

"I guess. He's been seeing her for almost a year."

"Well, everyone has their idiosyncrasies," Meredith observed. "I'm sure Tiffany the Snob has some redeeming qualities."

"I suppose. We found out after we sat down that she doesn't eat red meat. Or legumes. Or processed food—"

"Or, let me guess—potato salad?"

"I don't even know why Hunter brought her to the barbecue, to tell you the truth. She sat there with her bottle of water while we all pigged out, because let me tell you, one thing my dad knows is his way around a barbecue grill. He makes the best hamburgers ever."

"It sounds like fun," Meredith said wistfully, suddenly envious of Noah because he had a family. A sibling. She'd always wondered what it would have been like if she'd had a brother or a sister. "So is this something you do with every woman you meet? Give them a title? Did you give me one, for example?"

Noah gave her a shy smile. "No, I don't do it with everyone. But I do kind of have one for you."

"Oh no," Meredith said. "I'm not sure I want to hear what it is."

"I think of you as Meredith the Entertainer."

"Well, that's certainly better than Meredith the Snob."

Noah laughed. "You make me laugh. Plus, you're a professional dancer. Which falls into the entertainment category, I do believe."

"Former professional dancer," she reminded him.

"But still entertaining," Noah assured her.

Meredith felt a warm glow inside as they approached the mall entrance. People always said a sense of humor was one of the top ten important things they looked for when they were dating. The fact that she apparently had the ability to make Noah laugh without even trying seemed like a good thing.

The mall parking lot was already crowded with holiday shoppers, but Noah found a space at the end of a row. Recorded Christmas music poured from the speakers at the entrance. Inside were all the usual holiday trappings. Every store window sported lots of red and green and holiday sale signs. Families with children and strollers clogged the aisles, but Meredith didn't care. Usually she avoided the stores around the holidays. She bought very few gifts since she had no family. Sometimes she'd find small things to give her roommates and a few friends. But everyone she knew was on a fairly tight budget. She counted herself extremely fortunate not to have to worry about the state of her finances any longer.

"I have no idea what I'm looking for," Noah grumbled. "No idea what to get them."

Meredith steered him into the nearest department store. "Let's start here. Tell me about your dad," she said, as she and Noah navigated the men's section.

"He's the postmaster in a small town just outside Topeka," Noah said.

"And you told me he likes to barbecue. What else does he like to do?"

"He likes sports. Mostly, he watches them on TV, but every once in a while he'll get tickets to a game. The Royals or the Chiefs."

"Go on."

"That's about it."

"There's more to him than his job and sports. What do you talk to him about?"

"Um, my job and sports usually. Cars."

Meredith gave him a look. "Do you want a noogie?"

"You know? I kind of do."

"Well, keep it up, and I'll give you one."

"Is that a promise?"

"We'll see."

Noah grinned.

"What I'm trying to get at is sometimes it's easier to choose a gift if you think about who the person you're buying for is. What's his favorite thing to do? What's the best time you ever had with him? What's important to him? What kinds of things does he like?"

Noah stared at a display of wallets and key chains, spinning the turntable around and around while he thought. "I don't know."

"What's your dad's most treasured possession?"

Noah continued to spin the display. "His wedding ring, probably."

"Does he still wear it?"

Noah shook his head. Meredith sensed she was broaching a sensitive subject. "Does he wear other rings? Jewelry?"

"He always wears a watch. It's ancient. It's pretty beat up, but I think he wears it because my mom gave it to him for Christmas one year."

"Your dad sounds like the sentimental sort. If he had a new watch, do you think he'd wear it?"

Noah paused the turning display. "He might. I don't know."

"Even a good watch doesn't last forever," Meredith pointed out. "Okay, what about your brother?"

"What about him?"

"Same questions. What does he like? What do you talk to him about?"

"Am I going to be in trouble if I say jobs and sports and cars?"

Meredith chuckled. "Of course not. But there must be more to him. For example, we know he likes high-maintenance women. What does he do for a living?"

"He's a stockbroker."

Meredith's eyebrows raised. "Really?"

"Why? Does that impress you?"

"No. I mean, I'm not unimpressed. I just always think of stockbrokers as gamblers, you know, with the market being so volatile. I guess I lived in Vegas too long."

"He loves it," Noah said. "And he's good at it. He's highly analytical."

"Does he like puzzles?"

"Yes, as a matter of fact. When we were kids, it seemed like there was always a jigsaw puzzle going somewhere. But really, any kind of puzzle. The one where you have to pull out the blocks of wood and stack them on the top, but if you make it fall, you lose? He loved that one."

They left the department store and chose a direction at random. "I feel like we're making progress," Meredith said.

"You do?" Noah slanted a look down at her. "I feel like an ant going against a herd of elephants."

Noah was referring to the crowds. Meredith was referring to gift ideas for his family. She patted his arm gently. "We'll get there. Don't you worry."

She saw a big-name designer handbag store and pointed in its direction. "Let's go in there."

"Why?" he said as he followed her.

The store was crowded but not as badly as some of the others. There were several salespeople milling about keeping an eye on the customers as well as the high-end merchandise.

"Because," Meredith informed him, "if you want to get something for Tiffany, it has to be small but worthy of notice. I'm betting, from what you told me about her, that she's into designer labels. Did you happen to notice what kind of purse she carries?"

"Uh, no."

"Did you see any letters or special designs on it?"

"Never looked. Didn't care."

"It doesn't matter," Meredith said confidently. She began circling the counter where small items were displayed in glass cases. "See? Look. There are coin purses and key rings. Cell phone cases and wristlets."

"What in the world is a wristlet?"

"That little purse there? With a strap that circles your wrist. You can carry the bare essentials along without hanging on to a big purse all day. Like if you went to an amusement park or a concert or something."

"Okay," Noah said.

"How much do you want to spend?" Meredith asked.

"I don't know. On Tiffany? As little as possible. I'm not even related to her."

"Yet," Meredith reminded him. "I say you get her a key ring or the coin purse. Probably the key ring is best. Even if she doesn't use it, she'll think you get her, which, apparently, you do. And she'll appreciate that you didn't buy her some piece of junk from a discount store."

"If you say so." Noah looked a little lost. No, a lot lost. He was the only man in the store.

"Which one do you like?"

"Which one do *you* like?" he returned.

"That one." She pointed to a silver one with the designer's logo on it but in a subtle pattern.

"Perfect," Noah said, as a salesclerk approached.

"We'll take that one," they said in unison.

"I think we're making progress," Meredith said again, as they left the store. "And you won't even have to wrap it." The key ring was in a little box with the designer's logo on top, tied with a pretty ribbon in the designer's signature colors. The package was inside a fancy little shopping bag that dangled from Noah's fingers.

"Actually, I was going to ask you to wrap it before I realized they'd do it for free," Noah said.

"I'd have done it for free," Meredith assured him.

"Good. I'll keep that in mind since we have two more gifts to buy."

"Let's wander a bit, or as much as anyone can wander in this crowd," Meredith said as she was jostled by a couple who were apparently on a power-shopping trip. "See if we see anything or get some more ideas."

"Okay." Noah took her hand. He didn't ask. It seemed like the most natural thing in the world. She liked holding his hand. Liked being close to him. Liked the idea that anyone who saw them would assume they were a couple. *This is the start of us as a couple,* Meredith thought. Yesterday. Today. Who knew what the future would bring? There was a new year starting soon. *Maybe it will be the year of us,* she thought.

A lot could happen in a year. Why, a year ago, she'd never even heard of Nashville, Kansas, much less thought of moving here, buying a house, getting a job. But she'd spun her life on its ear, and the past few weeks, she'd felt like she was embarking on an adventure she couldn't have dreamed up on her own, ever.

It was like leaving Las Vegas had inspired her, in a way. It had changed her perspective. She'd certainly never thought of writing a children's book. Or teaching kindergarten.

Meredith slowed as they approached a brightly lit jewelry store. "Do you mind?" she asked Noah. "I can never resist looking at jewelry."

"I've got all afternoon. Look all you want." He let go of her hand but stayed nearby.

Engagement rings were displayed prominently in the first case, which was fine with Meredith because that was her favorite thing to look at. To look at and dream that maybe someone would love her enough to want to marry her. That someday, she'd be one of those patient moms in the grocery store with children of her own. She loved the sparkle of the diamonds and the different designs of the settings and bands. She liked how the styles changed from year to year.

She strolled slowly along, taking them in before a salesclerk approached. "Hello. Looking for anything in particular today?" His gaze flickered from Meredith to Noah. "An engagement ring perhaps?"

Meredith could not help but laugh when she saw the look on Noah's face. Was that panic she saw in his eyes? "No, we're just friends." At this point, that was the truth. "I just enjoy looking at jewelry. It's my reward for helping him Christmas shop."

The clerk's gaze went back to Noah, noting the single, small shopping bag he was carrying. "We're having a holiday sale today on men's and ladies' watches. Buy one, get the second half price. Also, we have a lovely selection of sterling silver jewelry on sale at fifty percent off."

Meredith caught Noah's eye. "Did you hear that? Watches. Let's have a look."

They followed the clerk to the display case with the watches inside.

"I don't know," Noah said. "He's so attached to the watch my mom gave him."

"Well, maybe that's because he thinks it would be disloyal to her memory if he bought himself a new watch. But if his son gave him one, that's entirely different. It's a gift from someone else he loves very much, right?"

Meredith glanced quickly at the clerk, hoping for some support. He picked up the ball. "We can also do same-day engraving at no extra charge."

"Let's just look," Meredith urged. "It doesn't mean you have to buy one."

"Okay."

An hour later, they left the store. "I can't believe it," Noah said, looking at his own watch. "I thought we'd be here all afternoon, and we're done already."

"Well, almost done," Meredith agreed. In the end, Noah couldn't resist the deal on the watches. He'd purchased one for his dad and one for his brother. They were both being engraved and would be ready in an hour.

"Are you hungry? We could check out the food court or get ice cream or something."

"Or hot chocolate?"

He wrapped his arm around her shoulders and squeezed. "Or hot chocolate. Anything you want."

Meredith wondered if that "anything" included him. Because she definitely wanted a future that included Noah. She felt more and more comfortable with him, and she felt she had gotten to see a little more of what made him tick. How he felt about his family. How the loss of his mother had affected them all.

There was a long line at the coffee shop, but it was Noah's turn to stand in it. Luckily, they snagged a recently vacated table before anyone else could. It was at the outer edge of the café's enclosure, so Meredith was able to watch the shoppers. Across the way, a Santa held court, and a long line of children and parents waited to visit with him and get their pictures taken.

She couldn't help but smile at some of the toddlers dressed in their Christmas outfits and the mothers trying to keep them happy until it was their turn to sit in Santa's lap. Meredith was perfectly content to watch all of the action and absorb the holiday bustle while she waited for her hot chocolate.

"I'm not sure how I feel about that," Noah said as he set a tray down on the table. He unloaded it and set the tray near the condiment bar before he took a seat across from her.

"Not sure about what?" Meredith asked. She took the lid off her hot chocolate, delighted to see a sprinkle of cocoa powder on top of the whipped cream. Noah had ordered a warm chocolate brownie for her, too. And one for himself as well, of course. *My little chocoholic*, she thought.

"Santa Claus."

"You have issues with Santa Claus?" Meredith asked. She took a sip of her hot chocolate. It was divine.

"Not the concept itself. The idea of telling kids to believe it's true. That he's real or whatever."

"Well, according to ancient lore, there was someone Santa Claus–like at some point."

"No, I know that. It just sort of feels like you're lying to your kids if you make them think that he comes down a chimney and puts presents under the tree on Christmas Eve."

"Considering an awful lot of kids live in places that don't have chimneys."

"Exactly." Noah took a bite of his brownie and watched the procession to Santa's lap.

"Maybe it would be better just to tell kids that Santa Claus represents the spirit of giving during the holidays. That it's okay to tell him what you want for Christmas or get a photo with him, but he's not who's bringing you presents. He's just a fun guy who hangs out at the mall during December."

Noah laughed, then started to cough. His eyes started to water.

"Oh, my goodness," Meredith said, alarmed. "Are you all right?"

He waved a hand at her and coughed into his napkin. "I'm fine. You kill me sometimes, you know that? Santa's just a fun guy who hangs out at the mall in December. I can just see our kids walking into kindergarten telling their classmates that."

Our kids, Meredith thought. Did he even realize

he'd said that? "Well, we all have to find out sometime that Santa's not real."

"Yeah, but the kid who tries to talk twenty other five-year-olds out of believing is going to get punched."

"Not to mention the fallout for the parents."

"Exactly."

"Maybe that's why everyone lets their kids believe until they figure it out on their own. Nobody wants to be the bad guy."

"Maybe."

"It's still fun to watch them, though," Meredith said. So that's what they did until it was time to go pick up the watches and head for home.

Chapter Ten

They were both quiet on the drive back to Nashville. Meredith didn't know what Noah was thinking about, but she was thinking how much she liked being with him. They didn't have to be doing anything. Although she supposed Christmas shopping was doing something. He didn't try to impress her with dinner in expensive restaurants, although that wasn't possible anyway. Not in Nashville, at least. Probably not in Greenburg, either.

No concert tickets or weekend getaways. *Probably too early for those kinds of things*, she reminded herself. Not like he'd shown up at her door with a dozen roses, either. Which made sense since they weren't even dating. Not really. He hadn't asked her out for anything but coffee, and every time he had, she'd turned him down. But even the coffee-"date" Christmas present she'd given him wasn't really *dating*. Was it?

And his request for help with his Christmas shopping, well, that wasn't a date either. She'd told the clerk in the jewelry store they were friends, and Noah hadn't corrected her. There was nothing wrong with being friends, either, she reminded herself. Because it could always turn into something else, couldn't it?

There was an attraction there. He'd held her hand in the mall. That was datelike at least. She was done looking, she decided. She was more than ready to leap. She wondered if Noah was, too. Maybe he was taking things extra slow now to pay her back for all the times she'd said no to his coffee-date invitations. Maybe he was still enjoying the game they'd started. There was nothing wrong with continuing that, either, because even that was fun.

"I know I've thanked you at least five times, but I have to thank you again for today."

"You more than made up for it with the hot chocolate and that brownie," Meredith assured him. "Besides, it was fun hanging out with you." As your *friend*, she thought.

Noah pulled into her driveway and put the car in park. "So are you going to the Macabees' party? It's tomorrow, you know."

"I don't have anything else planned, so yes, I am going. Janet says their house is gorgeous, and they go all out for the holidays."

"The party is always fun, that's for sure. They're really generous people. Usually everybody from the school system is there unless they've gone out of town for the holidays."

Meredith opened her door. "All right then. I guess I'll see you there." She slid out and waved as Noah backed out.

The Macabees' party was the perfect opportunity to move this relationship out of the friend category and into dating mode. All she needed was an outfit to knock

Noah's socks off. A little dancing, a glass of wine maybe. Who knew what could happen?

Meredith's cell phone rang at a ridiculously early hour in the morning. She squinted at the screen but didn't recognize the number. She was awake but luxuriating in the fact that she didn't have to get up right away, but she answered it anyway.

"Meredith? It's Jessica."

"Hi, Jessica. What's up?"

"I have a huge favor to ask you," Jessica said in a rush. "I run the nursery at my church. There are usually three other ladies, and we rotate weekly. Two of them are out of town, and the third one just called me. She has the flu. Are you busy? Is there any way you could help me out for a couple of hours this morning?"

"In a nursery?"

"Usually there aren't that many kids, but with the holidays, I don't know. I need someone who has already passed a background check. You're the only person I could think of on such short notice."

"I'd like to help you," Meredith said uncertainly. "But I've never been around children much. I don't know how much help I'd actually be."

"Then you'll do it?"

"I guess so."

"You're a life saver! It's the Liberty Community Church on the corner of Oak and Third Street. If you can get there by nine-thirty, you can help me set up."

"Oh. Okay. Did you hear me say I've never been around little kids before?"

"You'll be fine. Thanks a million. I'll see you there, then." Jessica disconnected.

The church was small, with simple lines, painted white and decorated for the season with a nativity scene set up on a small patch of lawn at the front and wreaths on the front doors. Meredith followed the sign that pointed to the nursery in the basement of the structure and found Jessica in what looked like a miniature classroom. There were bright plastic tubs of toys and small round tables and chairs. A changing table sat in one corner, and a couple of infant carriers were on a nearby counter.

"Thank you thank you thank you!" Jessica squealed, enveloping Meredith in a big, enthusiastic hug.

"You're welcome," Meredith said, laughing. "But I'm still not so sure about this."

"They're kids. Most of them are used to coming here, and they're fine once Mommy and Daddy leave. But there are a couple of children who aren't too happy to be separated from their parents." Jessica looked up. "Speaking of the devil, here's one now," she said out of the side of her mouth before turning to greet the mother and her little boy.

"Good morning, Mrs. Keene. How are you? And how's Matthew today?" Jessica gave them a big smile, which Mrs. Keene returned but Matthew did not. He had one thumb stuck in his mouth and clutched a thermal blanket close to his chest. He gazed at Meredith and Jessica with wary eyes.

"We're just fine," Mrs. Keene said. "Aren't we, Matthew?" She jostled the little boy, but his expression didn't change. "I know I'm a little early," she said to

Jessica, "but I need to go over the readings. I'm the lector this morning."

"It's fine," Jessica replied. "Mrs. Keene, this is Meredith Clark. She works with me at the high school."

"Nice to meet you, Meredith."

"Likewise," Meredith said.

"Okay, well, I've got to get going." Jessica slid a diaper bag off her shoulder. "Everything you'll need is in here," she said. Matthew began to whimper. His mother hugged him close. "You'll be fine," she told him. "You remember Jessica, don't you? Mommy will be back in a little while."

Matthew let go of his thumb, and a high-pitched shriek rent the air. Meredith was certain she'd temporarily lost her hearing. Mrs. Keene attempted to hand the child to Jessica, but he put up a fight, clinging to his mother's hair and sweater, nearly yanking her necklace off. He kicked his legs and resisted Jessica once she had him in her arms. He put his head back and howled, while fat tears rolled down his cheeks.

Mrs. Keene beat a hasty retreat to the door and waved good-bye. "Bye-bye, sweetheart. Mommy will be back in a little while. Be a good boy."

Matthew didn't hear her. He was too busy fighting Jessica's hold and kicking her. She finally lowered him to the floor. "Can you?" she said to Meredith, and gestured to Matthew. "Just keep an eye on him. He'll calm down in a minute."

A set of parents arrived with twin girls in tow, and Jessica went to greet them. Meredith hunkered down next to Matthew at a total loss as to what to do to comfort him. His face was red, and he hugged his blanket in a ball close to his chest. He tried to suck his thumb, but it was impossible to do as he continued to sob.

Meredith tried to think what she would like if she were Matthew's age and upset about something. She'd want a hug and a shoulder to cry on, she thought. But Jessica had tried, and that hadn't worked. She saw a stuffed animal peeking out of the side pocket of the diaper bag Mrs. Keene had set on the counter, and it gave her an idea.

She brought it back and sat on the floor in front of Matthew. His little shoulders were heaving, and he looked absolutely miserable. Meredith held the lamb in front of her face and, manufacturing a silly voice, said, "What's the matter, Mr. Matthew? Do you miss your mommy?"

Matthew hiccuped and stared at Meredith and the lamb. "I miss my mommy, too," she said, staying in character. "I got stuffed in a box when I was littler than you, and I sat on a store shelf all by myself until I came to live at your house. But I still miss my mommy."

Matthew stuck his thumb back in his mouth and concentrated on his lamb. "Your mommy always comes back to pick you up, doesn't she?"

Matthew spoke a garbled reply around his thumb. He had dark hair and blue eyes. For some reason, the little boy reminded Meredith of Noah. She wondered what he'd looked like as a child. She'd be willing to bet he was just as cute as Matthew Keene.

"Do you want to come and tell me about how much you miss your mommy?" Meredith made the lamb ask. "You can sit right here by me." Meredith patted her knee. "And tell me all about it. And I bet by then, your mommy will be here to pick you up."

The idea of writing a children's book with talking farm animals was becoming more and more appealing. Seeing Matthew's reaction to her speaking in her "lamb voice" made the idea even more exciting.

Matthew stared suspiciously at the knee Meredith patted. She made the lamb sit on her other knee. Meredith started to talk to the lamb, using her own voice. "I think he's a little shy," she said to the lamb.

"I know," she said in the lamb's voice, making the lamb look like it was shaking its head. "I'm shy, too. But you're so nice. I like you."

Matthew took the couple of steps necessary, reached for the lamb, and plopped down on Meredith's other knee. He wrapped one arm around the lamb and his blanket and stuck his thumb back in his mouth.

Jessica looked over from the table where she had the twin girls coloring pictures along with another little boy who had just arrived. "Don't tell me you don't have experience with children. That's the fastest he's ever calmed down."

"He just needed someone to talk to," Meredith told Jessica. "Isn't that right, Matthew?" She hugged him gently, liking the way it felt when he relaxed against her body. Maybe, she thought, someday she'd have a little boy of her own with dark hair and blue eyes.

Then she remembered the dream she'd had her first night in Nashville. Maybe, she mused, she'd have a little *girl* with dark hair and blue eyes. As long as she was dreaming, why not one of each? And a certain man with the same coloring who'd push them on the swings.

* * *

Meredith popped over to visit Julia later in the day. They chatted over Christmas sugar cookies Julia had baked the day before and a pot of tea that tasted like orange and cinnamon. Meredith told Julia about the party later.

"Oh yes, George and Mary Beth Macabee. Two of the nicest people you'll ever meet. They go to my church. Both their families have been in this town since before it was a town, I think. Those two have done a lot for the community over the years."

"Noah says they throw this big party for everyone who works in the school system every year around Christmastime."

Julia nodded. "Education is important to them. Mary Beth was a schoolteacher for a time. They also fund a scholarship. Any of the graduating seniors in the county can apply for it. I imagine it's helped quite a few of them get through college."

"I'm looking forward to meeting them."

"I imagine Noah will be at the party. You're probably looking forward to that as well," Julia said slyly but without malice. She was obviously fishing.

Meredith saw no reason not to be completely honest with her new friend. "I am. I really like him."

"Of course you do."

Meredith didn't realize it, but the Macabee house was only a few blocks from her own. It was in the opposite direction from the one she usually traveled and on a side street she'd never been down. Even though it was cold out, it seemed silly to drive such a short distance. And not that she planned to drink very much, but she never liked to drive after even one cocktail. So there was no reason not to walk.

She looked through her wardrobe and decided on

a creamy sweater dress she rarely got a chance to wear even though she loved it. It was easy to accent with a red belt and shoes and a pair of silver snowflake earrings she'd bought on a whim just because she liked them.

Snow was predicted for later in the evening. After much debate with herself in front of the mirror, Meredith decided to wear her black over-the-knee boots instead of her red high heels. The heels were simply impractical for the weather, especially if she had to walk home in snow. Of course, she could drive her car, but that seemed even more impractical. Besides, the boots looked very good with the dress. She switched to a narrow black belt and decided she looked quite stylish from head to toe.

The party was more of an open house, so Meredith decided to arrive an hour after it began. She hated being an early arrival in an unfamiliar situation and with people she didn't know well or possibly at all. She should have touched base with Janet or Jessica to see when they planned to arrive, but she hadn't. Surely, someone she knew would be there by now, she thought, as she approached the Macabee place. Maybe Noah. She could have asked him when he planned to be there, too, but she hadn't thought of it yesterday. And he could have offered to pick her up, but he hadn't. Why hadn't he?

The Macabee home lit up the night, and Meredith had to pause when she caught sight of it, because it was simply stunning. White lights outlined every window and ran along the eaves. The bare tree limbs of four trees in the front yard were lit up as well, with a different color on each tree. Red, blue, green, and violet. And on one side of the front walk was a sweet nativity scene; on the other, those pretty, carved, white deer. Spotlights highlighted both.

There were huge wreaths suspended beneath the carriage lights on the pillars of the front porch, and two more adorned each of the double front doors. Meredith couldn't wait to take the tour of the inside.

She knocked, and the door opened immediately. "Come in, come in," boomed an older gentleman with white hair and a neatly trimmed mustache. "I'm George Macabee. This is my wife, Mary Beth."

"Hello, I'm Meredith Clark. I'm an aide at the high school."

"Glad to meet you, Meredith," George said, shaking her hand. He signaled for someone to take her coat.

"We're keeping the coats right here near the door," Mary Beth said, as the assistant handed her a ticket. He hung her coat on one of two long, portable racks that had been set up in what looked like a parlor off the wide entry hall.

"The main buffet is set up in the dining room on the left." Mary Beth pointed in that direction. "Drinks are available on the back veranda. Thank you for coming. We're delighted you're here," she said before more guests arrived, and she turned to greet them.

Meredith decided to check everything out before getting anything to eat or drink. The music she'd heard at a distance before became louder as she approached the rear of the house. There were a few people milling around the buffet table but no one she recognized.

She opened the door to the back and stepped out onto a wide porch. Drink stations were set up on either side of the door, manned by professionals in tuxedo uniforms. Portable heaters fought the chill in the air. Meredith was glad she'd chosen a sweater dress but surprised to find the outdoors not as uncomfortable as she had expected.

A giant tent was set up just beyond the porch steps and was obviously the biggest draw for the crowd. A live band played from an elevated stage at the far end. A portable dance floor covered the space in front of it, and it was currently crowded with guests rocking out to a lively rendition of "Jingle Bell Rock." Portable heaters rimmed the perimeter of the tent. Tables and chairs were available at the back, and mini buffets were set up along each side.

Meredith looked for anyone she knew but there was so much to take in, it was hard to differentiate all the faces in the crowd. The tent was lit from inside, with lots of low-wattage bulbs crisscrossed from pole to pole, and more tiny white lights had been wound around each of the support poles as well. There was light, but it wasn't enough to completely dispel the gloom of darkness. She wondered if she'd be able to find anyone she knew.

She circled around behind the tables and chairs, many of which were occupied. People were eating and drinking and chatting loudly to make themselves heard over the music. The buffet dishes sent out tantalizing smells. Meredith knew she'd have to sample the offerings later. She reached the edge of the dance floor and spied Noah. He looked divine, but when didn't he? He wore a gray sports jacket over a dress shirt and a V-necked navy blue sweater vest and dark-washed jeans. He had that preppie casual thing down cold.

She smiled watching him dance because he looked like he was having such a good time making the steps up as he went along. His dancing had no finesse or style, but his enthusiasm made up for it. Or maybe his enthusiasm was because of whom he was dancing with. Meredith's smile faded as she studied the pretty blonde who held Noah's hand while he twirled her in a circle. She looked like she was having the time of her life, and Meredith's heart sank.

Why had she thought Noah was interested in *her* all this time? She'd been planning on making a move on him tonight, but had he really given her any indication that he was interested in her as anything other than a friend? Maybe she'd allowed herself to get entirely the wrong impression from all those invitations he'd issued for coffee. Maybe Noah was just being friendly to the newcomer in town. Because, clearly, she wasn't the only female he spent time with.

The song ended while Meredith was lost in thought, and she didn't register that he'd seen her and was heading her way with the blonde in tow. She forced a smile onto her face and warned herself to be cool. So what if she'd been wrong about Noah? It certainly wasn't the first time a man had given off mixed signals. And it wasn't the first time she'd jumped to the wrong conclusion about his intentions, either. In fact, it was a recurring theme in her life. She was glad now that she'd put him off, that she'd looked before she'd leapt. She'd saved herself a lot of disappointment this time. She was learning.

"Hi," Noah said. "Did you just get here?"

"A little while ago, yes," Meredith said.

The blonde eyed her curiously. "Oh, sorry," Noah said, as if he suddenly remembered she was there. "Charlotte Taylor, meet Meredith Clark. Meredith's an aide at the high school."

Charlotte nodded and smiled. "Nice to meet you."

"Nice to meet you, too," Meredith replied.

"Charlotte teaches third grade," Noah said. "She won Teacher of the Year last year."

"Oh, Noah, stop." She patted his shoulder. "You're embarrassing me, and I'm sure Meredith doesn't want to hear about it."

Meredith barely heard what Charlotte said. She was too busy staring at the sparkling solitaire diamond ring on Charlotte's left hand. There was a roaring in her ears that seemed to drown out all of the party noise, including the band, which was announcing its next song. "Excuse me," she said. "Are you engaged?" Her gaze moved between Noah and Charlotte before it held on Charlotte.

"Yes, as a matter of fact." Charlotte gazed down at her ring. "I still can't believe it."

"Neither can I," Meredith quickly said, stunned beyond belief. Why hadn't Noah asked Charlotte to Christmas shop with him yesterday? Did she know about their coffee date? If she didn't, she soon would. Meredith strongly suspected there were no secrets in a town this size. But if that was true, how come no one had said anything about Noah's girlfriend/fiancée before now? "Have you set a date?" Meredith asked, feigning polite interest.

Charlotte patted Noah's shoulder again. "We were just talking about that. I'm kind of thinking I'd like to have a Christmas wedding, so maybe around this time next year. It will give me plenty of time to plan."

Meredith's gaze flickered to Noah. He was looking at her, and darn it all, he was still smiling. "Oh. How. Lovely." Meredith had to get away from the happy couple. Right now. "Would you excuse me? I think

I need a glass of wine." Or two or three. Maybe the entire bottle.

Meredith pivoted and made her way through the crowd to the bar, where one of the tuxedoed waiters was more than happy to supply her with a glass of merlot. Meredith stepped away to the railing and sipped, trying to wrap her head around the fact that Noah was engaged. She'd spent all this time wondering how things might be between them next year, but she'd never considered that by the end of the year, he would be married *to someone else*!

Great imagination you've got, she chided herself. Making up stories and believing in dreams. Apparently, she needed a great big dose of reality, and the universe had been more than willing to supply it tonight.

She shrank back behind the pillar when she saw Noah come bounding out of the tent and up the stairs to the porch, but apparently he'd already seen her.

"There you are," he said as he approached. "Why'd you take off like that? I was going to ask you to dance."

"Were you?" She sipped her wine, not looking at him.

"I was hoping you could give me a couple of pointers," he said. He nudged her shoulder. "You being a professional and all. I love to dance, but I've been told I'm not very good at it."

"Seems like there are a lot of things you're not very good at," she murmured.

He frowned at her. "Is something the matter?"

"Apparently not," she said, sipping more of the wine. Sadness seeped into her. She wished she didn't like Noah so much. She wished she hadn't let her imagination run wild, hadn't assumed they were moving beyond friendship. She felt rather foolish now, and it wasn't a good feeling. It also wasn't a good feeling learning that he planned to marry someone else.

"You're not in a very good mood, are you? Would it help at all if I told you you look beautiful?"

Meredith's eyes flashed. "I don't believe you."

"Well, that's my opinion whether you believe me or not."

She straightened away from the pillar, her fingers so tight on her wineglass she was afraid she might crush it. "No. I don't believe you're standing here telling me you think I'm beautiful when your fiancée is . . ." She gestured wildly in the direction of the tent, forcing Noah to step back quickly to avoid being splashed by what was left in her glass. "Right there somewhere," she finished.

"My fiancée? What are you talking about?"

"What do you mean, what am I talking about? You just introduced me to her!" Meredith was beside herself. It was all she could do not to throw her glass at him.

"You mean Charlotte?"

Meredith glared at him. "You're impossible." She made to move past him, planning her escape. She had to set her glass back on the bar instead of throwing it at him. She would make her way back through the house with her head held high. She'd thank her hosts, retrieve her coat, and head home. Alone. And once there, she'd allow herself to cry over her ridiculous behavior. But one thing she wouldn't do was let Noah see how she felt.

"Whoa, whoa, whoa, wait a minute," Noah said. He

grasped her upper arms, and he wouldn't let go. "I'm not engaged to Charlotte. I'm not engaged to anybody. I'm not even dating anyone. Not for months."

"But—but—" Meredith looked up at him. He'd told her before he hadn't dated anyone in months. Now he was telling her again. She so wanted to believe in the sincerity she saw in his eyes, but . . .

"Charlotte's engaged to a buddy of mine. He's a firefighter, and he had to work tonight. I was just keeping her company until you got here."

"But . . . but . . . really?"

He eased his hold on her, his grip turning into soothing strokes that sent ripples of heat through her. "Yes, really. If I was going to start dating anyone, I was kind of hoping it would be you."

"Really?"

"Yes, really. Is that the only word you know?"

The fight went out of Meredith as the adrenaline rush of anger and frustration left her. She sagged against him, dropping her head against his chest. His fingers buried themselves in her hair, and he kissed the top of her head. She pulled back and looked up at him. "I wanted to throw my wine at you," she admitted.

He laughed and smoothed her hair. "And you will probably want to do so again at some point in the future. But are we okay for now? For tonight? Because I was really looking forward to being with you at this party."

"Really?"

He laughed again. "Let's get you another glass of wine." He put his arm around her shoulders and walked her over to the bar. "And a vocabulary lesson. And then maybe you'll dance with me."

And dance they did. All of Meredith's hopes for the evening were surpassed by the reality that Noah turned from some other woman's fiancé into *her* dream date. He took dance instruction well and seemed eager to learn. She gave him extra points for not worrying about appearing foolish in front of such a large crowd of his peers. He held her close during every slow song, and Meredith didn't care at all about what their dance steps looked like. She was too thrilled to be in his arms.

They took a break to check out the buffet and sat at one of the large tables with Jessica, Janet, and Nick and their significant others. The crowd began to thin out after a few hours, and the band announced its last set. Meredith and Noah had decided to dance the last slow song before they left. After that, the Macabees were making their way through the tent, thanking everyone for coming and wishing them happy holidays.

As soon as they stepped outside the front door, the cold hit Meredith and Noah. Meredith still couldn't believe how the portable heaters had kept the tent warm all evening. Of course, all the dancing had kept her warm as well. She shivered, just remembering Noah's arms around her.

"Cold?" he asked, misreading the reason for her reaction. He took her hand.

"Yes. I mean no. I mean . . ."

"Maybe you had too much wine?"

"No, that's not it." Noah had decided to walk to the party, too. It was like they were the only two people in the world, walking in the crisp night air, their breath puffing out in front of them. Meredith hugged his arm. "I had such a good time tonight, I can hardly believe it. I want to pinch myself."

"Really?"

She pinched his arm through his coat, and he laughed. "I seriously can't believe you thought I was engaged. And here I thought I was making it pretty obvious that I was interested in you."

"I thought you were being pretty obviously interested in me, too. That's why I was so mad when I thought you were with someone else."

"Mad? Or jealous?"

"Both, I suppose. I built up this whole scenario in my head about us, and I felt like it had just blown up in my face, and I didn't see it coming. I thought by now I knew better."

"I'm sorry. I never thought you'd jump to conclusions when I introduced you to Charlotte, but I can see now how you could have."

"Look before you leap," Meredith murmured, as they approached her house. The lights she'd wrapped around the oak tree glowed softly and spread light across the front yard.

Suddenly, it started to snow, the flakes falling from the sky to land gently on the ground. She took off her gloves to catch a few of the snowflakes and tilted her head back to watch them fall. "I can't believe it's snowing. And it certainly doesn't look like it's just a few flurries, either." The snowfall thickened while she watched in wonder.

"If there's at least three inches by morning, I'm entitled to another date for coffee, right?" Noah asked.

"Absolutely!"

They climbed the steps and stood for a moment facing each other before Noah framed her face in his

hands and looked into her eyes. "I'm done looking."
He kissed her.

She kissed him back, winding her arms around his
neck as he drew her closer. Through their coats and
layers of clothes, she could feel the chemistry and the
heat between them warming the air around them.

She had no idea how long they kissed. It could have
been minutes. It could have been an hour, but when
Noah finally raised his head and looked at her again,
the look of joy on his face mirrored what she felt in
her heart. "Well," he said, "that's one more Christmas
wish that came true."

"Ditto," Meredith whispered in his ear. "Ditto."

Blue Moon Harbor Christmas

SUSAN FOX

Chapter One

Then I guess we should get married. That was almost the last thing he'd said to Jilly, eight and a half years ago.

Rain slashed the windows of Michael Dhillon's rental Kia Rio, and there were no streetlights to ease the late afternoon darkness of this shortest day of the year. He could barely make out the house he'd pulled up in front of. The house on Blue Moon Harbor Drive where Jilly had made a home for their seven-year-old child.

From the shoulder of the narrow country road, Michael squinted at blurry dots of color. The Christmas lights outlining the door, windows, and eaves revealed the general size and shape of the house. A split level with a single-story wing on one side, it was larger than he'd expected. A family home.

Had Jilly married? Did the baby they hadn't meant to create have a real father? When Michael had Googled her, he'd found no indication she was married, but then she didn't have much of an Internet presence. On Instagram, she posted excellent photos of the Pacific Northwest, some of them aerial, which seemed appropriate since she was a pilot. He'd also found her on the Web site of Blue Moon Air, the local seaplane business here on Destiny Island.

In the Web site photo, she stood on a wharf, slender in jeans and a Blue Moon Air T-shirt, beside a small seaplane painted in white and blue. Her smile was engaging, her blue eyes sparkled, and she wore little or no makeup. Her honey-blond hair tumbled in loose curls around her face and glinted in the sun. The natural look—clothes, hair, lack of makeup—was different from when he'd known her and different from the Toronto women he dated, but it suited her.

She was a stranger now, but then they never had known each other well. Their relationship had been purely casual: maybe a dozen nights together during the spring of their last year of university. He'd never have guessed she'd choose such a challenging career, but nor had he figured she'd want to raise a kid.

He hadn't found her on Twitter, LinkedIn, or any other place except Facebook, where her page was private. He hadn't sent a Friend request.

The only thing he'd sent Jilly since they said good-bye was the monthly payments for child support.

In return, she sent him nothing. Which was the way they'd agreed it would be, back when she decided against having an abortion and then rejected his marriage proposal. A clean and total break, but for the financial support, had sounded right to both of them. Honoring that pact had meant that Michael didn't even know the gender of the child he'd come to see. Aside from an occasional vague curiosity, he hadn't even cared, not until recently.

He stepped out of the car and rain slapped his face. When he'd left snowy Toronto that morning, he hadn't thought to bring an umbrella. He hunched his shoulders in his heavy overcoat, it and his wool scarf at least keeping him warm. An older model minivan was parked in the driveway in front of a closed garage door. The porch light of the house wasn't lit, but the Christmas lights revealed a paved path winding in an S curve to the door, through what looked to be a native plant garden. He could see the house more clearly now and, architect that he was, he thought of a dozen things that would improve on its conventional rancher design.

No light came from the front windows. Ignoring the branch of the walkway that led around the one-story side of the house, presumably to the backyard, he stepped onto the porch. Sheltered from the rain, he stared at the holly wreath decorating the front door. Faint strains of "Jingle Bells" reached his ears.

Yes, the "up for anything" girl he'd hooked up with that spring at the University of Toronto had changed. Probably she had married, had found someone she liked and loved.

He remembered her exact words: "You're proposing because you think it's the decent thing to do. That's sweet, but think about it. You and me, we've never been about decency and sweetness. For us, it's been lust and fun. Party, party, party." So much partying, it seemed, that even though they'd used protection, something had somehow gone wrong.

"That's no foundation for building a family," she'd gone on. "We don't love each other and I'm not sure we even like each other. Take out the booze, the partying, the lust, and what have we got? Nothing. So, thank you for the thought, but no."

He got what she was saying about foundations and,

at twenty-two, he'd never felt the slightest bit drawn to the kind of relationship that would create one. So, to be honest, her answer came as a relief.

They had both graduated with bachelor's degrees and Jilly was returning home to Blue Moon Harbor. "We'll be living totally different lives," she'd said. "So let's make a clean break."

Eight and a half years later, would she be furious when he turned up at her door? He'd thought of contacting her first, but guessed she'd have told him not to come.

And he needed to do this. Jilly wasn't the only one who'd changed. Michael was proving himself as an architect and he loved the job, from the challenges and creativity to the flexibility offered by being his own boss. Though he still dated actively and had never felt a desire to settle down, he was no longer an irresponsible kid. He was, in fact, a man. And that man had a child he'd never seen. Michael didn't feel guilty, because he still believed the decision he and Jilly'd made was the sensible one. But that was then and this was now, and now he needed to know if he could be part of his child's life.

Could—by which he meant so many things. For one, would he still want to after meeting the child? What if he felt nothing, no sense of connection much less a paternal bond? Or, if he did, what if Jilly said no? If she had married, how would her husband feel about it? And would it be a good or a bad thing for the child? Because, after all, the kid's interests counted more than those of any adult.

Under the holly wreath was a wrought iron knocker. Michael took a deep breath.

He'd always been an easygoing guy, reacting against his lawyer and surgeon parents' type A personalities. He'd never felt his heart race so fast that he could hardly breathe. Not until now, as he reached for the door knocker.

He thumped it a couple of times, loudly enough to carry over the music.

What would he say if a man answered the door?

What would he say if it was Jilly who opened the door? Or a boy or girl?

Chapter Two

Jillian Summers's son Cole and her mother sat at her parents' kitchen table. Her dad had just started to slice the maple-glazed baked ham, and Jillian set down the baking dish full of her mom's bubbly, cheesy scalloped potatoes. This family dinner was an early one because tonight—the winter solstice—was special. Each year on that night they trimmed the big Christmas tree that took pride of place in her parents' living room.

Jillian pulled out the chair across from Cole. And of course, wouldn't that be the exact moment the door knocker sounded?

Freckles barked and made a mad dash for the door, tail wagging. Her and Cole's Dalmatian-Labrador cross was definitely not a guard dog.

"Back in a sec," she said. "You get started." They wouldn't, though, because her mother insisted on saying grace before dinner.

Jillian's sheepskin slippers slapped the hardwood floor as she hurried after the dog. Who would come to call at this time on such a nasty, cold day? Some generous soul soliciting donations for a charity? She flung open the door and was hit with a draft of chilly air and a shock that sucked the breath from her lungs. "Michael?"

Oh God, he looked like Cole. She'd pretty much banished Michael from her thoughts before Cole was born, grateful for the money he sent but not dwelling on where it came from. And so, as her little boy grew up month by month, all she saw was her son. She hadn't realized how he was coming to resemble his biological father.

Michael himself had changed. His face was more mature and—*damn it*—even more attractive than that of the student she'd hooked up with. He looked . . . *warm* was the word that came to mind. So warm, standing under the porch light against a backdrop of sleety rain. So warm, with his lovely brown skin and the red scarf wound around his neck, trailing its fringed ends down the front of a black overcoat. His hair was longer, more casual; tonight, the glint on its raven black came from raindrops, not hair product. A five o'clock shadow framed lips that were still utterly sensual—but, unlike in the past, not smiling.

"Hey, Jilly," he said solemnly.

From down the hall, her mom's voice called, "Who is it?"

"Uh . . ." Jillian's brain froze, then she managed to reply, "An old friend from university." Freckles, who hadn't ventured outside, butted against her legs and then, probably remembering the ham, dashed back to the kitchen.

"Well, for heaven's sakes ask her in." Her mother's voice was getting closer. "Dinner's getting cold." Her mom joined her at the door and side by side they gaped at Michael.

For what seemed like ages, no one spoke. Incongruously, the strains of "Rudolph the Red-Nosed Reindeer" came from the front room.

Then her mother said, "Old school friend? You're Cole's father, aren't you?" Amanda Summers was no doubt comparing Michael's beautiful Indo-Canadian coloring to Cole's black hair, dark eyes, and always tanned skin.

"Cole?" he said. "I didn't—"

Her mom cut him off. "Why are you here?"

Jillian snapped out of her trance. "Mom, that's my question to ask." Battling the butterflies that swarmed in her tummy, heart, and throat, she lifted her chin. "Michael, why are you here?"

"I wanted to see you. To see, uh, Cole."

Now? After eight years of sending monthly payments and not showing the slightest interest? Whatever this visit was about, it couldn't be good.

"It's freezing with the door open," her mom said briskly. "And dinner's getting colder by the moment. Get in here, take off your coat, and sit down with us." She scowled at him. "But if you hurt my daughter or my grandson, you'll answer to me."

When Michael gazed questioningly at Jillian, she shrugged. Her brain was too stunned to function effectively. This was her parents' house and her mother was a force to be reckoned with. Besides, her own curiosity clamored for answers.

"Come in," Jillian agreed. "But be careful what you say, both of you. I don't want Cole knowing who you are, Michael." Her son wouldn't connect the dots the way her mom had. His social circle was full of adults and kids of various skin colors.

Her mother started down the hall and Jillian followed, hearing behind her a clack-clack as Michael's hard-soled shoes joined the pile of boots and shoes by the door, and then the soft thud of his heavy coat as he tossed it on a chair in the front room.

As the three of them filed into the kitchen, her father looked up. His eyes widened, he glanced from Michael to Cole, and then, with raised eyebrows, to Jillian. She nodded once and said pointedly, "This is Michael, someone I knew at U of T." She narrowed her eyes in warning.

Her dad's eyebrows remained up for a long moment, but then he said, "Fine. Better get another place setting, Jillian."

Before doing so, she turned to Michael, wishing she'd been able to witness his first reaction on seeing Cole. But maybe she was in time anyhow, because he stood frozen in place, staring at her beautiful boy.

Cole gazed back, looking mildly interested. "Hi," he said.

"Uh, hi," Michael got out.

Michael was still lean, but had filled out through the shoulders and chest. Not with chub but with muscle that gently stressed the seams of the black Henley he wore over dark blue jeans. To her dismay, the heat of desire pulsed through her and her fingers twitched with the urge to explore that new musculature. Just as people said you never forgot how to ride a bike, it seemed her body very much remembered how to lust after Michael. *Damn it.*

Her dad had risen and was walking over to Michael, extending his hand. She regained her senses and made the formal introduction. "Dad, this is Michael Dhillon. Michael, meet my father, John Summers."

The two men shook, taking longer than necessary and no doubt exchanging male messages that Jillian failed to interpret.

"My mom," she went on, "whom you just met, is Amanda."

Her mother moved past her to slap a placemat, a dinner plate, cutlery, and a glass of water down on the table beside where Cole sat. "Jillian, you sit beside your son. Michael, you're across from them."

"I want him to sit beside me," Cole said, getting up to bring the spare chair that sat in a corner of the kitchen. He shoved the chair up to the table and smiled at Michael. "You sit here."

Jillian's mom huffed. "For heaven's sakes, everyone, *sit.* Dinner will be ruined."

Freckles promptly plunked his butt on the floor near Dad's chair. After a questioning glance at Jillian, Michael took the seat beside Cole, and then the rest of them sat down.

"Michael, this is my son, Cole," she said, forcing herself not to glance from one face to the other and catalogue the similarities and differences. "Cole, as I told Gramps, Michael and I went to university together."

"That was a long time ago," the boy said. "Before I was born."

"That's true," she said. "Now hush, Granny wants to say grace." When she and her son ate by themselves in their in-law suite adjoining her parents' house, they didn't follow this ritual. But this was her mom's kitchen and her mom's rules. Jillian extended a hand on either side to clasp her mom's and her dad's. A mix of poignancy and anxiety stabbed her heart when, across the table, Cole blithely extended his small hand and Michael hesitantly met it with his.

As her mom spoke, Jillian tuned out the familiar words. She wasn't feeling the least bit thankful. Her stomach churned so badly she wasn't sure she'd be able to eat a bite of even those yummy scalloped potatoes.

What the hell was Michael doing here? She and Cole were happy. Was he going to mess things up?

Chapter Three

What if Michael had come to ask for access rights, or even shared custody? Jillian's breath caught and she almost dropped the platter of sliced ham her dad handed her. Recovering, she served herself a slice and passed the platter to her mom. No, surely not. He'd never before shown the slightest interest in Cole.

Maybe he intended to stop the support payments. He'd been the one to offer in the first place, and he'd been generous. Of course he could afford to be, spoiled rich kid that he was. She was grateful, though. Those monthly payments had enabled her to pursue her dream of being a pilot, and then to fly part time with Blue Moon Air. The small local seaplane business wasn't busy enough all year round to keep both her and the owner, Aaron Gabriel, working full time.

She squared her shoulders and dished out a dollop of potatoes. Across the table, Michael's head was down as he accepted platters from her mom, served himself, and then held the platters so Cole could help himself.

Not only was it a shock to see Michael again, more

mature looking and still so strikingly handsome, but it was odd seeing him in a domestic setting. Their short-lived relationship had been about partying and sex. Neither of them had ever cooked a meal for the other. He'd never even been to the small apartment she shared with two other students.

Maybe this was a bad dream, Michael here with her son and her parents. Surreptitiously, she pinched her arm through her red sweater.

"I don't like broccoli." Cole's protest drew her attention.

Michael, who had extended the bowl of green florets toward him, gazed uncertainly across at Jillian. Feeling no urge to help him out, she said nothing.

He frowned, refocused on Cole, and ventured, "It's good for you?" It sounded more like a question than an assertion, suggesting that he realized this wasn't a selling argument. And then, for the first time, Michael's face softened and she saw the old charm that she'd never even tried to resist. Leaning close to Cole, he whispered something in the boy's ear.

Cole cocked his dark head, reflected, said, "Okay," and took a small serving of broccoli.

Points to Michael. Later, she'd ask Cole what he'd whispered.

For the first time, it occurred to Jillian to wonder if Michael had married. Did he have another child or two? She glanced at his left hand. No ring.

Oh, how she wished he hadn't shown up on the doorstep. He should have given her a chance to talk privately with him. But of course when he rang the doorbell, he likely hadn't expected to be thrust into a family dinner. Across the table, he was tasting the broccoli. "Hey, this is good." His *oops* expression told her the words had escaped him.

"Let me guess," she said. "You're not a fan either."

"He isn't," Cole said. "But he said it's the grown-up thing to do. When someone cooks for you, you should be polite and eat it. He said he'd eat his if I ate mine."

"True," Michael admitted with a rueful shrug. "But this broccoli's actually good. Normally, I only like it in curry."

"Thanks," Jillian said. "I baked it around the ham. With orange-flavored olive oil." A Destiny Island business made several delicious flavored oils.

"You can cook?"

Did he think she and Cole had survived on takeout and microwaved dinners for going on eight years? "Who knew, eh?" But, in the interest of fairness, she said, "I made the ham and broccoli. The fabulous scalloped potatoes are Mom's." When the whole family ate together, they shared cooking duties as best fit everyone's schedules.

"So, Michael," her father said, "what brings you to Blue Moon Harbor?"

Jillian jumped in. "He and I will talk about that later, Dad." Of course her parents were concerned. When she'd come home from university pregnant, she'd told her family that she and a boyfriend had messed up with birth control, that he'd proposed, and that she'd turned him down because their relationship was casual. She'd never mentioned that Michael had initially assumed she'd want an abortion, much less that she'd considered it even if only overnight. She'd also never told them his name, or her mom and older brother Samuel—the fierce ones in the family— might have flown out to Toronto and hurt him.

"Can I ask him where he lives and what he does for a living?" her father asked dryly.

She nodded. "Yes, why don't you fill us in, Michael?" She'd never checked him out on the Internet. Once they broke up, he was out of her life. Except for the annoying way that, every time she met an interesting, good-looking, single guy and didn't feel attracted, she remembered the crazy chemistry with Michael.

He put down his fork and looked at her. It was the first time their gazes had met and held since that moment of shock at the front door. An unwelcome jolt hit her—of pure lust. Damn him for still being the sexiest man she'd ever seen. She caught herself reaching up to tidy her hair, and redirected her hand to her water glass. It wasn't a bad thing to be glad she'd worn a pretty, curve-hugging sweater, but she wasn't going to primp.

"I live in Toronto," he said. "Still."

"The same apartment?" When he'd started university, his parents had bought him a one-bedroom apartment despite the fact that they lived in Toronto, too. They could well afford it. His mother was a cardiologist, and his father a lawyer who worked for a huge multinational corporation. Michael's apartment had turned into party central.

"No. I'm in a larger, more modern one now."

"Of course you are." A true golden boy: gorgeous, charming, rich, spoiled; a man used to getting whatever he wanted. Likely he still hosted parties, ritzier ones with fancier alcohol. And classier women.

"I'm an architect," he said.

"Really?" Jillian said. They'd never talked much about school. He'd seemed more interested in having fun. And when she'd stolen time away from studies and her part-time job to be with him, she'd been all about fun, too. But she did remember him occasionally complaining about the ugly or unimaginative design of a building. Yes, architecture could be a good fit, though his physique suggested he didn't spend all his time drafting plans on a computer.

"What can I say?" he said. "I loved playing with Legos."

"I like Legos, too," Cole said. "An architect builds houses, right? I build houses and mansions and gas stations and stuff like that."

Michael studied him intently. "An architect doesn't actually build things. He designs them and then other people do the hard work."

Cole considered and then pronounced judgment. "That doesn't sound like as much fun."

Michael grinned. "Yeah, there's a lot to be said for Legos."

Oh God, that smile. It was as devastating as ever. He'd been an utter charmer and she saw that he still could be, when he relaxed.

"We could build things together sometime," Cole offered.

"I'd like that." The words came out quickly, sounding genuine, but then he shot Jillian an apologetic look. "If that's okay with your mom."

Great. Now it was all on her, and if she said no, Cole wouldn't understand. "We'll talk later." She kept her voice even. "Talk about how long Michael will be visiting the island, for one thing. Now, Cole, why don't you, um"—she cast about for a safe topic of conversation—"tell Michael about how Freckles came to join the family?"

Her son launched into a story about how they'd

chosen the Dalmador at the shelter. Then he started to talk about the holiday spectacular his school would put on in a couple of nights.

Michael asked questions and her parents contributed comments, all of them obviously working at keeping the conversation casual. Jillian could barely participate. Or eat. Anxiety cramped her stomach and she couldn't wait for the meal to be over, so she could find out why Michael had come.

Chapter Four

"You live in your parents' house," Michael said. Jilly had brought him over to the one-story wing of the house, which he realized had been made into an apartment for her and Cole.

"It works for all of us, being close like this. Wait a minute. I'm going to take pajamas over for Cole to change into."

Waiting for her to return, Michael remained standing where she'd left him, gazing around the L-shaped living room and dining alcove. She'd done a nice, if not terribly creative, job with the space: simple wooden furniture with brightly colored cushions, framed photographs of scenery and of Cole on the bluish white walls, a basket of wood beside the fireplace, and an IKEA shelving unit holding a medium-sized TV as well as a collection of books, Legos, and other toys. Holly wreaths, twinkly lights lining the shelving and the window frames, and a nativity scene left no doubt as to the time of year.

Jilly rejoined him and gestured toward one of the chairs. "Sit."

Just like her mom, issuing commands. He obeyed while she paced across the room and turned, hands fisted at her hips. The natural look suited her better than the pile of makeup she used to wear. She was still slender, but a few extra pounds made her more womanly and even sexier.

Not that her defiant stance and narrow-eyed expression were all that sexy. "Why are you here? Are you stopping the support payments? Because if so, we can do just fine—"

"No." He cut off the flow of words, leaning forward, his hands gripping his jean-clad knees. This wasn't the time for lust—though it was hard to ignore the sheer physical desire he felt for her—but for seriousness and honesty. "I have no intention of stopping them. Ever. Well, at least until Cole's finished university, or whatever kind of training he wants to do."

Might the boy, with his fondness for Legos, decide to become an architect? Michael had believed that his parents' insistence that he study medicine or law was about status and income, but now he wondered. Had they felt the urge to see their child share their interests? "He's a great kid, isn't he? And he looks like me." It had stunned him, that first glimpse of mini-him.

"Yes, he's great and yeah, he does look like you." She didn't sound happy.

"Sorry. I guess that's not exactly fair. You put in nine months of pregnancy, had to deliver him, and you've raised him, where all I did was have a good time with you one night." Was there a man in her life now, sharing those sexy good times with her? Playing a fatherly role with Michael's son? For some selfish, primitive reason that didn't bear analysis, he hoped not.

"I have to admit, those thoughts crossed my mind." Still glaring from across the small room, she went on. "But, Michael, you still haven't said. Why *are* you here?"

"I didn't think this through as well as I should have," he admitted. "I wanted to see Cole. Do you realize I didn't even know if our child was a boy or a girl?"

"You never asked. Never wanted to know."

"No. But I started wondering. Especially since I turned thirty and realized I'm actually an adult."

"Married?"

He shook his head. "Not even close. Being a husband doesn't appeal. But it hit me that I'm a father. Or"—he held up a hand before she could protest— "okay, more like a sperm donor. But I wondered if . . . maybe I could, I don't know, be part of his life. Maybe."

"You *maybe* want to be part of his life, *maybe*? What does that mean?"

"It means I don't know, okay?" He scrubbed a hand across his jaw, realizing he'd been in such a hurry to drive here from the B and B, he hadn't taken time to shave. "I don't know what I want. And before you point it out, I know I don't have any right to *want* anything, and you don't have any obligation to go along with me. But I kept thinking that there was this kid I'd helped to create. And maybe I owed that kid more than money. Or perhaps it's more selfish than that, just my curiosity or ego or something." It really was cool that Cole resembled him and played with Legos. "That's what I'm saying. I don't even know what I want."

She gave a huffy snort, but relaxed enough to perch on the edge of the chair opposite his. "You used to be more articulate."

He still was, when it came to his work and to the

women he dated. "Now my words aren't fueled by drink. They're connected to my brain and my brain honestly doesn't know what it's thinking. I'm not trying to be mysterious or obscure or . . . or to totally annoy or frustrate you. I'm being honest here."

Her face softened, something that had been rare tonight. It made her even more appealing, and again he had to battle against arousal. "Okay," she said. "I kind of get it. But, Michael, if you don't know what you want, how can I react? I have to protect my son."

"I see that. You're a mom. It's weird." At her raised-eyebrow expression, he went on. "I mean, I only knew you as a party girl. Of course I realized, objectively, that you had a baby. But I never formed an image of you being all domestic and maternal. You were just, you know, hot."

"And now I'm maternal."

"But still hot."

She sucked in a breath and that thing, that same chemistry thing, arced between them. He wondered, if she wasn't in a relationship, was there a chance the two of them—? No. What was he thinking? He'd come here because of the child. "So I wanted to see Cole and see if . . . see how . . ."

"To see if Cole measured up?" She jerked her head in a motion that made her blond curls dance under the light of a floor lamp. "To see if you thought he was worthy of your attention?"

He shook his head. "No. More to see if I could imagine myself being, uh, paternal. Being a part of his life."

"Do *not* tell me you want to share custody and have Cole spend half his time in Toronto. That is totally not happening." Sky-blue eyes couldn't literally spit fire, but hers came close.

"Of course not." That thought had never, not once, crossed his mind. "But I thought maybe I could spend time with him. With you present, or however you want to do it. Get to know him. See if . . . we form a bond." They'd already started to, over broccoli and Legos. "And if we did, then I could fly out and see him sometimes." If that happened, would he break the news to his parents and his auntie that he had a son? They'd been after him to settle down, to start a family, and he could imagine their shock at finding out about the youthful indiscretion he'd kept a secret for years and years. They'd end up being happy, though, and they'd want to meet Cole—and how would Jilly react to that?

"At your convenience? Cole has a stable, happy life. He has a family. He doesn't need a stranger getting him confused. If you tell him you're his father, and then see him, like, twice a year, I don't see how that'd be good for him."

"I don't know, Jilly. As I said—"

"Don't call me that. My name's Jillian. Jilly was the Toronto me."

"Okay, fair enough. Anyhow, as I was saying, I don't have a clear picture of how this might go. Can I spend a little time with him and we can take it from there?"

She sighed, her shoulders rounding, and he realized what a burden he'd laid on her.

"I suppose," she said. "But we're not telling him you're his father. Being a father's about more than just genetics."

"I hear you."

Chapter Five

Jillian longed for nothing more than a hot bubble bath, an entire wineglass full of Baileys Irish Cream, and privacy to release the flood of tears dammed up behind her eyes. Not tears of sadness, but of confusion and frustration.

She could relate to Michael wanting to get to know Cole. Yet how dare he shake up their lives? She and Cole had a special bond and she didn't want anyone messing with it. And how dare Michael shake *her* up, making her feel the kind of attraction—of arousal— she hadn't felt in all those years?

One thing she'd learned as a mom: her own desires didn't come first. Cole's needs did.

If Michael proved to be a decent man and decided he genuinely wanted to build a relationship with Cole, not just with fancy architect-type *designs* but by laying a solid foundation and then putting in the hard labor and emotion, how could she deny her son that? At most, Cole's and Michael's would be a part-time, long-distance relationship. She shouldn't feel threatened.

Yes, if Michael proved to be serious, she'd have to

give him and Cole the opportunity to become father and son. But they weren't there yet. What next, though? "I need to get back to Cole and my parents. We're trimming the Christmas tree tonight."

"I should go. That's family time." There was a hint of wistfulness in his voice.

It made her wonder if his family celebrated Christmas. They'd never talked about religion, but given his Indian heritage, she wondered if he might be Sikh, Hindu, or Muslim. He'd eaten ham at dinner, and wasn't pork a taboo food for Muslims? "Did your parents put up a Christmas tree when you were a child?"

"Yeah. Well, Deepa did. It was—"

"Deepa?"

"My auntie. Technically she's my mom's cousin. She was widowed just before I was born. Childless, not much education, not well off. She came from India to live with us. She got a home and family, and Mom and Dad got a housekeeper, cook, and nanny. Anyhow, yes, we had a tree. One of those artificial ones, silver with blue lights. Mom and Deepa thought it was pretty. We'd exchange a few presents and have a turkey dinner, cooked by Deepa. Mom sometimes missed dinner because she had surgery. The holiday was low key. My parents were busy, and the traditions weren't part of their culture." He stood. "Thanks for letting me meet Cole. You should sleep on this. See what you think in the morning."

That made sense. She remained sitting, deliberating over whether to invite him to help with the tree. "Where are you staying?"

"A B and B in the village. The Once in a Blue Moon."

"It's very nice." And not cheap, but money had never been a problem for Michael. "You've got the whole village and harbor on your doorstep. Did you fly in?" Now, that would have been weird, if she'd been the pilot and he'd turned up as one of her passengers.

"No. I rented a car at Victoria International Airport and then caught the ferry. This place is pretty remote."

"Yes. That can be annoying sometimes, but mostly we islanders love it."

A firm knock sounded on the door separating her and Cole's small two-bedroom apartment from her parents' house. Her dad called, "Jillian, we've got the lights and decorations out. We're waiting for you."

"Be right there," she called back. Before she could angst it to death, she said, "Do you want to stay and help with the tree?"

Michael's dark, melted chocolate eyes, so like Cole's, lit up. "Really?"

She dropped her face into her hands and scrubbed her fingers over her tension-knotted forehead. Was this the right thing to do? She'd thought life was complicated back when she'd found out she was pregnant, but tonight took *complicated* to a whole new level. And in both cases, it was Michael's fault.

Warm fingers touched the back of her neck, feeling oh, too good. She jerked, the fingers fell away, and she gazed up to see Michael peering down at her, looking sympathetic.

"I'm sorry to do this to you," he said. "I was thinking of me. And of the child. I didn't really imagine how this would affect you."

"That's me," she said wryly. "Easy not to think about. Well, I didn't think of you all those years either. I didn't even realize how much Cole resembled you until I saw you tonight."

"And now here we are. Seeing you again . . . Well, it's hard to believe I'd more or less forgotten you. How pretty you are, how sexy."

She drew in a breath. He'd always been a charmer. No way should she be flattered, or stirred, by words that tripped so easily off his talented tongue. "I'm not the same woman. I'm a mother now. My idea of parties involves kids, parents, and cake."

"Cake's good." He smiled and reached out both hands. "And, by the way, you may be a mom but you're even prettier and sexier than you used to be."

Of their own volition, her hands fitted themselves into his and she let him tug her to her feet. Their bodies were only inches apart and she'd swear that an electric charge hummed back and forth between them. Now that he was touching her, it seemed impossible that she'd spared him so little thought over the years.

He let go of one of her hands and she should have thought *Good* and tugged her other hand free, but then he was reaching out to cup the back of her head and she was resting her hand on his shoulder, feeling the warm strength of the muscles under his Henley and aware of a faint, woodsy scent like sunshine on cedar boughs. And then she was rising on her toes as he tipped his head down, and *oh God!* their lips were touching and it was all there, all the passion she used to feel and maybe even more because she was sober now, and it had been so long, and he felt so amazingly, incredibly good, and *right* and—

"Jillian?" The loud call and double-knock on the door sent her thudding down, flat-footed and panting for breath, breaking contact with Michael.

"Coming, Dad," she called, struggling to control her voice.

Michael looked as dazed as she felt, which was a small consolation.

"That wasn't a good idea," she said, trying to sound assertive but failing miserably. What was wrong with her? Hadn't she learned her lesson years ago? That falling in lust with Michael could mess up her life?

"I suppose not. I guess it'd confuse things?"

"You think?" she said sarcastically. "Damn, Michael, I'm so confused I barely know my own name. But we have to get out there and help with the tree, and act, act . . ."

"Normal?"

"Hah! Nothing about this is normal." She shot him a narrow-eyed glare and stalked past him to the door.

Chapter Six

Shaken by the intensity of that barely there lip press, Michael followed Jilly's—no, make that Jillian's—shapely butt as she strode, long-legged, back to her parents' side of the house. When he'd come to see her, it had never occurred to him that the physical attraction, a force so powerful it had a mind of its own, would still be there. He had the distinct impression that, as in the past, it wasn't one-sided either.

Fortunately, as he stepped into the Summers's living room, the family atmosphere went a long way to restoring his sanity. Music was playing, good King Wenceslas looking out on the Feast of Stephen while Michael looked out at a six-foot fir tree in a bucket of water, plastic storage bins of decorations, a little boy in flannel pajamas patterned with airplanes, and a black-and-white spotted dog lying on a hearth mat in front of a real wood fire. Not to mention a middle-aged woman and man who both favored him with cool stares.

He addressed them. "Jilly—Jillian—invited me to

help with the tree. But I know this is a family night, so if you'd rather I didn't . . ."

Cole said, "You should stay. You're taller than Gramps. He always has to stand on a step stool to reach the top of the tree, and Granny always worries he'll fall off."

"I wouldn't fall off," John said, sounding offended. He exchanged a glance with his wife, and then said, "Stay if you want to, Michael. We can always use another pair of hands. Speaking of which, how about you grab that tree while I hold the tree stand, and the ladies and Cole can tell us when we've got it sitting straight."

As Michael stepped forward to clasp the tree, Jillian said, "Wait, you could get pitch on your shirt. Dad, have you got an old one he could borrow?"

"Don't worry about it," Michael said. He didn't want to wear her father's clothes and he guessed the feeling was mutual. Ruining a Henley was no big deal. He could always buy another.

When he grabbed the tree, it smelled so green and tangy, he was tempted to bury his face in its soft boughs. Instead, he heaved it up and followed everyone's instructions until it was locked into the stand.

And that was the story of the evening. He took direction and each time his sense of design made him open his mouth, he shut it again. This was their tree, and they knew what they wanted, so he draped strings of multicolored lights and then chains of cranberries that Cole said he'd strung after school. When Michael admired the clunky, obviously child-made ornaments, he learned they weren't just the product of Cole's efforts but that some dated back to Jillian's childhood. The boy's were the more artistic.

As Michael worked, he snuck glances at Cole and they exchanged a few comments. It blew him away that this was his biological son. A cute, smart kid who might, based on the pjs' airplanes, share his mom's interest in flying, but who also shared Michael's artistic talent and love of Legos.

The new Jillian also kind of blew him away. A red sweater and tight black leggings hugged a slim but sweetly curved body. Her blond hair was mussed from an encounter with a fir branch. She snapped photographs, joked with her parents, switched the music when "Santa Baby" began to play, and gave Cole affectionate touches without seeming to notice she was doing it. This woman was multifaceted and fascinating. Definitely Jillian, not Jilly. Was there a man in her life?

Why should he care?

The final touch for the tree was three or four dozen snowflake ornaments. "Because it isn't Christmas without snow," Cole said, yawning, "and it doesn't usually snow here."

Jillian's parents sank down on the couch with exaggerated sighs of exhaustion. "That's all the effort you're going to get out of us," Amanda said.

Cole, with another yawn, said, "The tree's perfect. Santa's going to put lots of presents under it on Christmas Eve." Then he shot Michael a glance. "I don't really believe in Santa Claus. We just like to pretend, 'cause it's more fun that way."

"You're right," Michael agreed. But since no white-bearded man in a reindeer-drawn sleigh was going to deliver gifts, Michael needed to make some quick purchases. He'd go online and research the best architecture and engineering toys for kids Cole's age.

Probably he should also get presents for Jillian and her parents.

"It's your bedtime, honey," Jillian told Cole. "You go over to our place and brush your teeth, and I'll be there in a few minutes."

The boy gave both his grandparents a hug and kiss and then went over to Michael, who still had a box of faux snowflakes in his hand.

"Good night, Cole. It was nice to meet you. Thanks for letting me help with the tree."

"Night-night, Michael." The boy gazed up at him and then threw his arms around him for a quick hug before rubbing his eyes and heading out of the room.

Touched and disconcerted, Michael looked over at Jillian, who was gazing after her son.

"We should turn in, too," Amanda said with a yawn of her own. "Tomorrow will be another busy day at the store."

Michael turned to the pair of them, an attractive couple about his parents' age, though they looked fitter and less stressed than his mom and dad. They were both fair haired like Jillian, her dad with the same bright blue eyes as his daughter. "You own a store? What kind?"

"We sell outdoor clothing, supplies, and equipment," the man said. "Summers' Seasons is the family business. Well"—he flicked his head in Jillian's direction—"except for our renegade here, our fly-girl."

"The store's great," she said. "But it's not my calling. And I should know, after slaving away part-time all through high school, and then summers and Christmas holidays while I was at university." Her tone was teasing.

So was her father's when he said, "Slaving for a decent salary, I'll point out."

"Which I needed, to go to university. As for decent, I made more when I was waitressing in Toronto." She gave a cheeky grin. "I did darned well with tips."

Michael didn't remember that she'd waitressed. He did know she'd never had a lot of free time. "Tell me more about the store," he said to her dad. "When you say family business . . ."

"My parents opened it back in the mid-sixties," he said. "My sister and I grew up working there, just like Jillian and her brother in their turn."

He hadn't known Jillian had a brother. Not wanting her parents to realize how little they knew each other, he kept quiet.

"John and I met at the store," her mom said. "I lived in Sidney, on Vancouver Island, and came over to Destiny Island with three girlfriends for a week of bicycle camping. We rode off the ferry and popped into the store to buy a few supplies. John waited on us and it was, like, pow!"

When she said that, Michael could see the young Amanda, her expression excited and glowing.

She went on. "I'd always thought people were crazy to talk about love at first sight, but I swear that's what I felt. Him too. Right, sweetheart?"

"Exactly right," he said fondly, and reached out to clasp her hand.

Michael felt a pang of envy, which was odd because he'd never felt the desire for a serious relationship.

"She came back almost every day during that camping trip," John said, "and by the end of the week—"

"I'd not only fallen for him but for the island." Amanda finished his sentence. "I found a job at one of the tourist shops. To shorten a long story, as soon as I graduated we got married."

Her husband took up the story. "My parents slowly phased out of running the store and Amanda and I took over. Now the same thing's happening with Jillian's brother, Samuel, and his wife, Lynette." He stretched and rose slowly. "But we'll need all hands on deck bright and early tomorrow, so it's time to turn in." He reached a hand down for his wife's. "Come on, Amanda."

She let him pull her up and then, still holding his hand, turned to Michael. "You and Jillian will want to talk."

"Yes," he said. "Thank you for your hospitality. It was nice meeting you."

They both gave a nod of acknowledgment but kept silent as they left the room.

"I'll walk you to the door," Jillian said to him.

Michael put on his coat, scarf, and city shoes and stood just inside the door with her.

"How long do you plan to stay in Blue Moon Harbor?" she asked.

"Work is slow over the holidays, so I shut down the office until January second. I've got a couple of projects to work on, but it's computer work. I can do it anywhere."

"You really plan to stay here for . . . how long is that?"

"Uh, twelve days, I guess. But it depends on whether you're okay with me seeing more of Cole."

"I want to sleep on it. I'll call you in the morning."

After they exchanged cell numbers, he shoved his hands into the pockets of his coat, forcing himself to resist the urge to tug her into his arms and kiss her again. "This is weird. It's us, but we're such different people." He wanted so badly to ask if she was seeing someone, but doubted that would earn him any Brownie points.

"We're pretty much strangers. You realize that, don't you? We hooked up what, not more than a dozen nights over the space of two or three months? Didn't talk about anything of significance, so we never really knew each other." She frowned. "And now you want to come into Cole's life, and mine."

He clenched his hand, not out of anger but to fight the need to stroke the worry lines from her forehead. "I may be a stranger, but I'm not a bad person. Give me a chance to prove that, Jillian. Please."

Chapter Seven

At noon the next day, a Friday, Jillian again answered the door. But this time it was the door of her and Cole's apartment, and this time she knew that when she opened it she'd see Michael. She was also at least semiprepared for the hot, tingly rush that pulsed through her veins, the physical craving to kiss him again. Bad enough she had to worry about his influence on Cole; it was totally unfair that he had this impact on her.

He stepped past her, the chilly air that came with him not doing much to cool her down. "Thanks for asking me over."

She'd texted him before her morning round-trip flight to Vancouver and asked him to come over for lunch. Though she was upset that he'd reentered her life, she believed in tackling problems rather than deferring them. "Obviously, we need to talk. My parents are at the store and Cole's spending the day with his best friend, Jordan, a couple of doors down."

Michael pulled off his scarf, unbuttoned his coat, and tossed both over the back of a chair. He wore jeans again, and a lightweight turtleneck the color of bittersweet chocolate. The same shade as his lovely eyes. Eyes that were a touch bloodshot, like her own.

"You didn't sleep well," she guessed.

He shook his head. "You?"

"No." She sat in a chair and gestured him toward the couch. "I spent the night thinking, and I talked to my parents this morning. Bottom line: we all want what's best for Cole. But what is that? If we go any-where together—you, Cole, and me—people will see us and guess. If he didn't look so much like you . . . But he does. You could spend time with him here, but it's the holidays and he wants to go out and have fun. I'm just not sure—"

"Jillian." He cut her off, leaning forward. "Would it help if I told you that I've cleared up that *maybe* thing I was talking about last night? I *do* want to be part of Cole's life. I don't know what form that'd take, but I want to be there as a regular presence, even if it's mostly by Skype. I want him to know that I'm his father."

Well . . . wow. "That was a quick decision." And not one she was inclined to trust in. "Are you sure?"

"Yeah. Seeing him . . . Now he's real to me. He's more than a birth control malfunction and a financial responsibility. He's a boy. Cole Summers. My son. I can't imagine returning to Toronto and having things go back to the way they were."

She bit her bottom lip. "Even if you mean that now, how can I count on it? I don't want us telling Cole you're his father, and you being attentive for a while but then getting bored—or marrying and having other kids and leaving him behind."

"Jillian, I'm committed. I'm responsible. I have

no"—he paused briefly, shook his head—"no plans to marry and have more kids."

"I'd like to believe in your commitment. But we're still virtual strangers."

"Did I ever miss a support payment? And if you look at my Web site, you'll—"

"I did. Last night." That had killed more than an hour of couldn't-sleep time. "It's impressive."

"Those projects require commitment and responsibility. They're complex, they involve a bunch of people, and I'm at the center of it. I'm the one who makes them happen and I'm good at it. When I commit, I follow through."

She liked the way he said it. Not boasting, just stating a fact. Sounding, yeah, responsible. "A project that takes a year, even two, is different from having a child. A child is forever."

He stared her straight in the eyes. "I'm prepared to commit forever."

She blew out air in a silent *whew.* Who'd have thought party boy Michael would ever speak those words? She should be glad but instead felt threatened. If Michael was in her son's life *forever,* what would that do to her relationship with Cole? And how would she handle having a permanent tie to Michael? Slowly, she said, "If that's true, you really have changed."

"I grew up. Is that so surprising? I was twenty-two." The grin he used to flash all the time made an appearance. "And a spoiled only child. Now I've passed thirty and own my own business. You're, uh, thirty as well?" At her nod, he went on. "You're a mom and a pilot. You're a grown-up, so why can't I be one, too?" He put on a little boy pouty voice that reminded her of Cole, and his dark eyes danced with mischief.

This side of Michael was pretty irresistible, yet she was in no mood to laugh. "Okay, that's fair. We're grown-ups, parents of a wonderful boy, and virtual strangers. What do you say we throw together some lunch and get to know each other a bit?"

"An excellent idea."

She led him into the kitchen, but a few minutes later regretted it. The room never seemed small when it was her and Cole, but Michael, at six feet or so, broad shouldered and narrow hipped, took up too much space as he moved around, taking sliced turkey and mozzarella from the fridge and washing carrots. Too much air as well—which must be why she had trouble breathing evenly as she spread mayonnaise on bread and then sliced a tomato.

Her nerve endings tingled and every time his clothing brushed hers, she almost jumped out of her skin. It was a relief when they sat across from each other at the four-seater dining room table—until his knee bumped hers. She scooted her chair back a couple of inches.

If Michael did become a permanent part of her and Cole's lives, it might be the biggest challenge she'd ever faced.

Chapter Eight

Though he'd hoped for a quick "yes," Michael respected that Jillian wanted to know him better before deciding whether she was okay with Cole hearing the truth.

So he'd try not to think about the fact that the "getting to know" he'd most like to do was exploring her curvy body, naked between the sheets. Too bad she looked so sexy in a snug navy sweater that made her blue eyes even brighter.

Munching his sandwich, he waited for her to ask her first question. She seemed distracted, though, as she nibbled a carrot stick, not even looking up at him. She had said "get to know each other," and that went both ways, so he would get the ball rolling. And he'd start with the question that hovered at the top of his mind. "So, is there a man in your life these days?"

That brought her head up. "No. I don't date much. I'm too busy with Cole and my job."

Which meant the closest thing Cole had to a father figure was his granddad. And Jillian's lush body wasn't getting the attention it deserved. And he shouldn't be thinking about her body. "How did you decide to be a pilot? I don't remember you mentioning it, back in school."

A smile flashed. "Like we talked about career paths? But no, I had no idea then." Holding a triangle of sandwich, she went on. "It was on my return to the island. Aaron Gabriel—who's my boss now—had a fledgling seaplane business, Blue Moon Air. I was on his flight and, well, I was pretty upset. About the baby, about having to tell my parents, about how my entire life was going to change."

Her brow crinkled and he felt sorry for the girl she'd been. All he'd had to do was cut back on expenses so as to put a portion of his healthy monthly allowance toward child support.

"After Aaron let the other two passengers off at Galiano Island," she went on, "he invited me to sit in the seat beside him. He asked if I was okay, and I kind of hiccupped out a 'no.' He said, 'Take the yoke.'"

"You mean the controls?"

"Yes, the steering wheel thingie. In his Cessna 180, there's one on each side. He took his hands off his and I gingerly put my hands on the other one." Her face brightened. "He told me about altitude and direction, and then he said, 'There you go, you're flying.' And I was. Slowly, it sank in." Her blue eyes were as bright as a summer sky now. "I was flying like a bird, the whole beautiful, amazing world spread out below. My problems faded from my mind. I felt lighter, hopeful. For the first time, I was happy I was having a baby."

So even though she'd decided against an abortion, she hadn't been happy about being pregnant. He hadn't really thought about that back then, just respected her decision and been relieved when she turned down his proposal. But of course she wouldn't have been happy, not when a birth control failure had screwed up her life. "Flying the plane made you feel happy you were pregnant?"

"It was like the glass half empty switched over to half full. Suddenly, I saw the positives." She flicked her head. "Oh, I knew there'd be problems, but life was good. I thought how nice it would be in the future, if things were getting me down, to be able to go up in a plane and fly, just fly into the wild blue yonder, and leave all those problems down on the ground."

She smiled at Michael. "I glanced over at Aaron and said, 'You get to do this for a living?' and he laughed. He said it was the best job ever. I saw the joy in his eyes, and that's when I knew. So I told him, 'I want to be a pilot.' And he helped. He got his instructor rating and taught me. I still had to go over to the Victoria Flying Club, to get my private pilot license and then my commercial license. It was expensive, but those monthly payments of yours helped a lot, and Cole and I stayed with Mom's parents, who live in Sidney not far from the airport."

"It must have taken a lot of hard work and discipline."

She chuckled. "Not things I was noted for back when you knew me."

"Well, I only saw the party side of you."

"I admit that the student side wasn't all that serious. For me, university was more about getting away from a small community where everyone's up in your business. I wanted freedom."

"And you ended up going home and being tied down by a kid."

Even as he said those words, words he'd have believed totally only a day ago, they felt hollow to him. Until he'd met Cole, he'd never really considered settling down and raising a family. But now . . . if there was a paternal instinct switch in the brain or heart, it seemed to have flipped on last night. When he'd started to tell Jillian he had no plans to marry and have other children, the words had stalled and he'd had to force them out. Maybe he no longer believed them? That notion was one he'd need to explore in the months to come.

"Yes, but no," she said. "Now I see the benefits of Destiny Island, and of my parents. And of my big brother and Dad's parents, who live here, too. As for Cole, yes, a child is a huge responsibility, but he's so much fun." She grinned, looking almost like a child herself. "Kids know how to have fun better than adults. Besides, if I want freedom, I just leap into the sky."

"Fun and freedom. I'm glad you have those things, Jillian."

"Me too. Now, how about you?" She picked up her sandwich again. "How did you decide on architecture?"

He shook his head ruefully, remembering how unfocused he'd been as a brand-new university graduate. "Can you believe I actually went to a career counselor?"

"Really?"

"When my parents found out I hadn't applied to med school or law school, following in one set of their footsteps, they were pissed off. But I'd seen what their lives were like. They do both enjoy their work, but they're type A people and their work rules them rather than vice versa. They nagged me to get serious about a career and I had no sense of direction, so we agreed I'd see a counselor. I took tests, which indicated I had the skills and attributes to be an architect."

"And you had that big 'aha' moment like I did with flying?"

"Not then. I went home and researched it online, and realized it was perfect."

She'd finished her sandwich and now rested her elbows on the table and propped her chin on her fists. "How so?"

This was strange, the two of them stone cold sober, sitting and talking over turkey-and-cheese sandwiches. But it was good. He still felt a buzz of lust, but he saw that Jillian was more than just a sexy woman and a responsible mom; she was an intriguing person in her own right. He liked that she seemed interested in him, too, though probably her main motivation was making sure he was a fit parent for Cole.

"On the tech side," he said, "as well as the Lego thing, I've always enjoyed math and science and been good at art, especially the drafting kind. I'm practical-creative."

"I'm not sure what you mean."

"Painting a picture doesn't grab me, but I get excited about designing a structure—house, shopping mall, whatever—that achieves multiple purposes and is attractive and eco-friendly. So anyhow, I've always had the skills and the interests that apply to architecture, so I'd taken a number of undergrad courses that proved to be relevant. I have the right personality traits, too."

"Such as?"

"Being confident, a good communicator, a problem

solver, a negotiator. Flexible. Able to lead but also to really listen to what people are saying."

"Don't forget charm," she said wryly. "I bet you can persuade clients and contractors to do almost anything you want."

Chapter Nine

Michael chuckled, flattered that she still found him charming. "Except it's not about what *I* want. It's about what the client wants—really wants, which isn't necessarily what they first say they want—and figuring out how to best bring that to life. That involves intuition, creativity, research. I like to learn, at least if it's a subject that intrigues me. I'm pretty organized when I'm motivated, and I have an assistant who keeps track of all the important stuff."

"Looking at your Web site, it seems it's just you and your assistant, right? Louise Jones?"

He smiled fondly, picturing the stylish, personable, and supremely efficient woman he'd been lucky enough to hire. "Yes, and she's as important to the firm as I am. I thrive on being my own boss and working flexible hours. Louise organizes things so I can do that and so the firm's still efficient. She's the office manager, my assistant, the bookkeeper, and she's even learned how to update the Web site, although she insists she's a tech dinosaur."

"I didn't know tech dinosaurs still existed, except for seniors."

"That's her excuse. She's sixty-six."

"You hired a senior? Here I'd assumed she'd be young, sleek, gorgeous."

Had she felt a twinge of jealousy? For some reason, he hoped so. "Shows how little you know me. And, by the way, don't ever call Louise old. She says sixty's the new forty."

Jillian chuckled. "She sounds great. Are your parents okay with your career choice?"

"*Okay* being the operative word. Not thrilled, but at least it's a respectable career. Once they reconciled themselves to it, they started referring friends and colleagues to me." He rolled his eyes. "After all, it wouldn't do to have a son who wasn't a success. I hate to admit this, but it's in large part due to them that I've been able to build the firm so quickly." Them, and the investment of some of the money he'd inherited when his grandmother died.

"I assume you wouldn't get ongoing referrals if you didn't do good work."

He smiled at her. "Thanks for that. And no, I wouldn't. I do very good work. It just rankles a bit that I didn't make it entirely on my own."

She shrugged. "Part of me wants to criticize you as being a spoiled rich kid. But then I've taken lots of help from my parents. Family should be there for each other."

If Jillian agreed to let Michael be part of Cole's life, he would tell his family about the boy. Deepa would be a wonderful great-auntie, but as for his parents . . . Would they be any more involved in their grandson's life than they had been in his?

"I guess that's true," he said. "In fact, right now I'm designing renos for their house, and of course I won't charge for the work."

"There you go." She sat back and stretched. "So you, too, have a job that offers fun and a fair bit of freedom."

"Exactly. And every project is so different, complicated in a unique way, I'll never get bored."

Her brow wrinkled. "Do you get bored easily? What happens if you get bored with Cole?"

He didn't want to give a flip answer, so he considered her question. Then, shaking his head, he said, "How could a child ever be boring? Especially when he's your own."

"That's so true." Her eyes crinkled at the corners. "There's still a fair bit of the boy in you, right?"

"I promise I'm responsible."

"Sorry, that's not how I meant it. It was more that you like to have fun and you approach your job with excitement. The same as I do."

He nodded. "In that sense, I hope I never entirely grow up."

An alarm beeped and she stood. "That's my reminder. I have a flight." She went to the island separating the dining area from the kitchen, and picked up her phone.

"What's your work schedule like?" He rose to join her.

"It varies by season. Winter's slower, though it's picked up now because of the holidays. We're doing at least one morning and one afternoon return trip to Vancouver, with stops in Victoria and wherever else people need to go. We also have individual charters and, with tourists here now, a few sightseeing flights.

We have two planes, a de Havilland Beaver that takes six passengers and a Cessna 180 that takes three. Aaron and I try to juggle the flights so we each get time off when we need it."

"And your parents help out with Cole?"

She nodded. "If I have an early flight, they take him to school when they go to the store. If I can't pick him up after school, either he goes home with his friend Jordan or Mom or Dad get him and take him to the store." She grinned. "When he finishes his homework, they have him help out. My parents start early with the kids in the family."

He smiled. "It seems everyone wants a child to follow in their footsteps." Then his smile faded and he asked the most important question. "So, what happens next for me and Cole?" One thing he'd realized last night was that, if he consulted a lawyer, he'd probably find that he had the legal right to be recognized as Cole's dad and to have visitation privileges. He only hoped he'd never have to go that route, though. He wanted a good relationship with Jillian, not a strained one with each of them resenting the other.

She gazed at him, her blue eyes serious. "Dinner here, the three of us. You can spend the evening playing Legos or we'll watch a video. But I'm not ready to tell him you're his father."

It was a step in the right direction. Relieved, he said, "Fair enough. Thanks. How about I pick up groceries and cook dinner?"

"You can cook?" she said incredulously. Then, probably remembering his similar question the previous night, she laughed. "Sorry. We still have some getting-to-know-you to do."

Chapter Ten

When she'd trusted Michael with her house key so he could arrive before her and get a start on dinner, Jillian hadn't expected to come home to an utterly delicious aroma. Cole, whom she'd picked up at Jordan's house, said, "Mmm. Is Granny cooking?"

She hadn't told her son Michael would be there because she hadn't been one hundred percent sure he'd show, but the spicy scent was definitely not from one of her mom's recipes. Besides, Mom always used her own larger kitchen.

Cole didn't wait for an answer. Nor did he take off his gum boots before running to the kitchen. "Granny, are you—oh! Michael, it's you. Hi."

Michael's deep voice greeted Cole as Jillian took off her boots and placed them on the mat by the door, beside Michael's city shoes. She peeled off her coat and toque and, glancing in the mirror by the door, fluffed her hat-flattened curls.

In the kitchen, she found Michael in the same clothes as earlier, washing dishes. He cooked and he cleaned up after himself? Impressive. And a good role model for their son.

"Cole, go take off your boots," she said. And then, to Michael, "What smells so good?"

"Butter chicken. It's always been one of my favorites. It isn't as spicy as a lot of Indian food, so it should be kid-friendly."

"A family recipe?"

"It's a quicker, easier variation of Deepa's. And it's almost done." Cole had returned, and Michael said, "Why don't you two wash up or whatever while I finish the dishes?"

From that excellent start, the evening went better than Jillian could have hoped. The butter chicken, served over rice and accompanied by store-bought naan bread, was delicious. Michael hadn't brought dessert, so they ate crisp slices of apple along with shortbread with red and green sprinkles, which Jillian and Cole had made.

She cleaned up the dinner dishes while Cole and Michael got a fire going. Then she relaxed in her recliner and pretended to read, but really just enjoyed watching the two "boys" down on the living room floor playing with Cole's Mystery Mansion Legos. Their mutual task and similar approaches led to a quick rapport and she knew she'd made the right decision, inviting Michael over tonight.

But darn it, something pinched inside her at seeing how much fun they were having. She'd never been construction oriented herself, and the only Lego kits she related to were the ones with planes and helicopters.

Michael will never replace me, she told herself. *I'm Cole's mom. Michael will stay for a few days and then go back to*

Toronto. Cole will be all mine again, except for a few minutes of Skyping each week.

And, once Michael had gone, the increasingly powerful attraction she felt for him would fade away, too. Of course it would.

Somewhat reassured by her conclusions, and bearing her son's best interests in mind, she stood and said, "Michael, can I see you in the kitchen for a moment?"

He said, "Sure," but his slow movements expressed his reluctance to tear himself away from Cole and the construction zone.

In the kitchen, she asked quietly, "Do you still want to commit to being a lifelong dad? Not just for play time, but really being there for Cole?"

"Even more strongly, if that's possible."

She studied him, trying to look past his sexy physique and stunning features, reading the sincerity in his eyes. She swallowed, took a breath, and then said, "Okay."

Those dark eyes widened. "Okay to what, exactly?"

Praying she was doing the right thing, she said, "If you're absolutely sure you want this, and you'll never ignore or run out on Cole, then I'm okay with us telling him you're his dad."

"Yes!" It exploded out of him, bringing a reluctant smile to her face. "When?" he asked.

Her approach to tough challenges was to face them and get them over with, rather than agonize over them. "Now."

Chapter Eleven

For the second time in his life, Michael's heart pounded so vigorously he could hardly draw breath. Back in the front room, Jillian sat on the couch and he seated himself beside her, not touching. Cole was still intent on the mystery mansion, oblivious to the tension in the air.

"Cole," Jillian said, "leave that alone for a minute. Michael and I want to talk to you."

"But I'm constructing," he protested.

"This is more important," she said.

Huffing, the boy looked up. "What?"

Michael forced breath into his cramped lungs and let it out again. He and Jillian, in a quick strategy talk, had agreed on how to handle this. The announcement would be his. He only wished his son wasn't glaring so sulkily at them.

"Cole, there's something we want you to know," he started. "I'm not just an old friend of your mom's." He took another breath and said the rest in a rush. "I'm actually your father." There was no going back now, and he was glad. But terrified. What if Cole rejected him?

The petulant expression turned into a puzzled frown. "My father? Huh?"

Now it was over to Jillian. "I told you how your father and I agreed that it didn't make sense for him to be with us, since we lived far apart and had such different lives. But how he sent money every month to make sure you had everything you needed."

"I don't have a smartphone," Cole complained.

Michael promptly added that to his mental Christmas shopping list. He'd already ordered a bunch of stuff online last night, paying for expedited delivery.

"Because you don't need one," Jillian said.

Cole tilted his head toward Michael. "So why are you here now?"

"Because I want to know you."

"You're moving to Destiny Island? Are you marrying Mom?"

"Uh . . ." Neither he nor Jillian had guessed the boy might leap to these conclusions. "No, Cole. But I'm here for Christmas and I'd like to spend time with you. Then, after I go home to Toronto, I'd like us to keep in touch. Do you know what Skype is? Or FaceTime?"

The boy nodded. "I use Skype with my great-grandparents in Sidney."

"We can use it, too, and e-mail." They could text and phone as well, once Cole had opened his Christmas gifts. "And I can come visit again." Previously, Michael's vacations—alone or with whatever girlfriend he'd been dating at the time—had been to places with intriguing architecture. His life was in for a big change, but this boy was worth it.

He couldn't honestly say that he loved Cole, not yet, but he felt something different from anything he'd ever experienced before. Protectiveness, the desire to build the connection between them. The wish for his son to have two parents who were really there for him and supported him, who didn't just dump a bunch of expectations on him and leave him to the care of an auntie. *No offense, Deepa—you're awesome.*

"Huh." Cole's eyes squinted like they did when he worked on modifying a Lego design.

"What do you think of all this?" Michael asked.

"It's okay, I guess." He cocked his head. "What do I call you?"

He and Jillian had anticipated that question. "Whatever you want to. You could call me Dad or Daddy, or Michael."

The boy considered. "The kids at school say 'dad' or 'daddy' unless they have two dads." He glanced at Jillian. "I don't have two of them, do I?"

"No, honey," she said, a touch of humor in her voice. "You definitely don't."

"Two dads?" Michael queried. How was that biologically possible?

"A father and a stepfather," she clarified, "or two gay dads."

"Oh, got it. That's not where my mind went first."

She gave a quick snort of laughter and then said, "You get used to the permutations and combinations of 'family' when you're a parent."

"Cole," he said, "you don't have to decide now. See what you're good with after we've spent more time together. Okay?"

"Okay." The boy nodded. He seemed more puzzled

than upset by tonight's revelation. "Are you coming to my school's holiday spectacular tomorrow night? I'm an elf!"

Michael again glanced at Jillian. Would it be awkward for her?

She picked up the ball. "Would you like him to, honey?"

He nodded firmly. "Parents come. I have two parents now."

Jillian gave a subtle nod of her own, and Michael said, "Then I'd be proud to be there."

"By the next morning," she said wryly, "the entire island will know Cole's dad is here."

"Are you okay with that?" Michael asked.

She sighed. "Nothing in life stands still."

Obviously, she was less than happy. Michael, on the other hand, was pretty thrilled. He was a dad, and he was going to see his son up on stage playing an elf. That was damned cool.

Chapter Twelve

On Christmas morning, in her parents' living room, Jillian raised her Nikon as Cole tore off the paper on the book she'd bought him. It was the third in a series he'd recently discovered, called Spirit Animals. He was down on the floor beside the Christmas tree with an excited Freckles, who pounced on each bit of wrapping paper as Cole discarded it.

A fire crackled in the fireplace, the white snowflake ornaments on the tree glimmered multicolored from the strings of lights, and her parents sat side by side on the couch. Jillian had her mom's reading chair and Michael sat upright in her dad's recliner. They'd all assembled at nine, which had allowed Jillian some alone time with her son. He'd been up by six, eager to tear into his stocking. The Scratch Art magic kit in it, along with the pancake breakfast she prepared, had kept him occupied until it was time for the official family Christmas.

A family that now included Michael. As most of the island knew as of two days ago.

The day before last—a Saturday of chilly winter

sun—while she'd been flying, Michael, Cole, Freckles, and Cole's best friend, Jordan, had gone for a hike in Spirit Bluff Park, followed by hot chocolate at Dreamspinner coffee shop. When Jillian had returned home for a quick, early supper, she'd found a picnic laid out. She, Cole, and Michael had snacked on barbecued chicken from the deli, a couple of deli salads, fresh bread from the bakery, and local cheeses.

After, they'd gone to the elementary school for the secular spectacular where each class gave a presentation: songs, plays, whatever they chose. Her parents had picked up her dad's parents, and Jillian's brother Samuel and his wife were there too since their daughter, who was in fourth grade, was also participating in the event.

Conversation at that initial meeting with Michael was stilted, though Jillian had filled her relatives in over the phone ahead of time. Samuel and Grandma Joan in particular surveyed Cole's father with narrowed eyes. But even they warmed to him when he cheered loudly as Elf Cole took his bow at the conclusion of the Santa's Workshop skit.

Yesterday, a very busy one for Blue Moon Air, Aaron had brought in the relief pilot he occasionally used, which had allowed both him and Jillian a half day off. She'd flown in the morning, and in the afternoon had gone with Michael and Cole to the Christmas Eve market in Blue Moon Harbor Park by the ocean. They'd bought more treats to supplement last night's leftovers, and then after dinner driven back to the village for carol singing around the giant decorated tree.

Her parents had gone, too, in their own car, and again her dad's parents as well as her brother and his family had joined them. She'd always loved how her family stood side by side, a cohesive, supportive unit within the larger community, as together the islanders and a few tourists sang the old, familiar songs. She wondered how it felt for Michael to be part of all this.

After the carol singing, her parents and grand-parents followed their own tradition and went off to church. As Michael drove her and Cole home along the west shore of the harbor, he said quietly to her, "I bet you could use an evening alone with your son." She'd appreciated his sensitivity and taken him up on the offer.

She had needed not only time with Cole, but also time away from Michael. Sometimes playing "family" with him felt too natural, as if they were a real couple. Conversation flowed easily; they laughed together, teased each other. Her hand kept reaching out to touch him, and she had to stop herself. She craved physical intimacy with him.

Eight years ago, he'd been sexy and fun. He was even sexier now, fun in a much better way, and far too interesting and nice and just an all-around good guy. A guy who lived in Toronto. Though he was becoming part of her and Cole's life in Blue Moon Harbor, she would have no place in his Toronto life. She had to constantly remind herself of that.

And now here they were again, all together. When Michael had arrived this morning, he'd had two huge bags full of beautifully wrapped presents. Some were from him, he'd said. Then, with a *you and I know we're just pretending* wink to Cole, he'd said the rest were from Santa, who'd asked him to play delivery boy with the items he couldn't fit down the Summers's chimney. Jillian had frowned at the number of gifts, hoping he didn't intend to spoil Cole rotten.

Cole reached for one of the boxes Michael had brought, and ripped off the paper. "Oh, cool!" Cheeks flushed with excitement, he held up a box labeled "Young Architect."

Jillian suppressed a grin. Could Michael be any more obvious about his desire to share his interests with his son? It didn't seem Cole needed much persuasion, though, because he was trying to pry the lid off the box.

"Cole, there are more gifts," his grandmother reminded him. "Maybe you could find one for me under there?"

"Okay, Granny." Diverted, he plowed back into the pile under the tree, and handed her a package. "This one's from Santa."

The fancy wrapping gave "Santa" away as being Michael. Jillian wondered whether he'd had a store do his wrapping or applied his own creative, detail-oriented brain.

Curious, she watched as her mother unwrapped the gift with neat, precise motions and pulled a gorgeous purple and green silk scarf from a flat box. "This is lovely." She gazed straight at Michael, looking surprised.

"Santa must have figured you like scarves," he said.

She did in fact wear them with almost every outfit—and this one would bring out the greenish highlights in her hazel eyes. "Find Santa's gift for Gramps," Jillian instructed Cole.

It proved to be a book called *The Wild in You*, again indicating Michael's perceptiveness. Her dad loved the outdoors, and the family store carried all the gear he might ever want, but this book with its gorgeous photos and evocative poems celebrated the spirit of the wilderness.

When her turn came, her gift was a chain with a gold seaplane pendant. She gasped. "Oh, Michael"— she caught herself before breaking the pretend-Santa rule—"look what Santa brought me! It's beautiful."

He gave a smile of acknowledgment, and Cole returned to doling out presents. Her parents had given Michael a pair of sturdy walking/hiking shoes and a rain jacket—both items from the store. Arriving in Blue Moon Harbor with only city clothes, he'd been borrowing her dad's outdoor gear until now. Jillian interpreted the gift as signifying acceptance of Michael's ongoing presence in their lives. Maybe he did, too, because he grinned widely and said, "These are great. They'll be getting a lot of use."

Jillian's gift to him had been scrambled together in every spare moment over the past days. It was an old-fashioned photo album with shots from each year of Cole's life and from each major event, including a few from the past couple of days. When Michael glanced up from taking his first look through it, she'd swear his eyes were damp.

"I'll give them all to you as a digital slide show as well," she told him. "But sometimes it's nice to have something more concrete."

He nodded and his Adam's apple moved as he swallowed.

The tender moment passed quickly as Cole continued to pull gifts from under the tree. As Jillian had feared, the majority were for him, from Michael. When Cole opened yet another box and found a smartphone, he was ecstatic and threw his arms around his dad.

He hadn't hugged her or her parents in thanks for their more modest gifts. Irritation built within Jillian, and she took a few slow, deliberate breaths. Fastening her new necklace around her neck, she reminded herself that Michael was, in addition to being too wealthy for his own good, a generous guy and a brand-new parent. She should have explained the family rules.

When the gifts had all been opened, Jillian's mom refilled the adults' coffee mugs. "Michael," she said, "are you calling your parents today?"

He dragged his attention away from Cole, who was busy checking apps on his phone. "Since it's three hours ahead in Toronto, I talked to Dad before I came over. He was at home catching up on work. Deepa, my auntie, and I had a good chat, too. I left a message on Mom's phone. She's at the hospital."

"Your mother works on Christmas Day?" Jillian's mom asked.

"Usually. It lets a doctor who's more into the holiday spend it with his or her family." He glanced around the room and then back to her mom. "They don't know what they're missing. Thank you for letting me share this with you."

Her mom sighed. "Of course. You're family now." Jillian knew that her parents, like her, worried about how this would go in the long run. Mom went on. "Have you told them about . . . ?" She cocked her head toward Cole, who was paying no attention to their conversation.

"Not yet. I figure it requires face to face."

"Yes," her dad said dryly, "that's not something I'd want to learn about in a voice mail."

A vigorous knock sounded on the door. Freckles

barked, Cole yelled, "That's Jordan!" and the boy and dog pelted toward the door. There followed an excited boy-babble along the lines of "What did you get?" and "Wait till you see what I got!" Jordan did at least remember his manners enough to greet the adults, but in mere seconds the boys were down on the floor, going through Cole's presents.

Jillian's mom rose and held out her hand to her husband. "Time to stuff the turkey."

"Woman's work," he muttered with a mischievous glint in his eye.

"If you want to carve it, you have to stuff it," she retorted.

When he went to the kitchen, Amanda held back and, with a head gesture, indicated that she wanted to speak to Jillian. Jillian went over and her mom quietly said, "Those gifts . . ."

"It's my fault for not telling Michael our rules. I'll talk to him."

She'd rather not have this conversation on Christmas Day, but her annoyance would fester if she didn't. Going over to Michael, she said, "We need to talk."

Chapter Thirteen

Looking puzzled, Michael followed her to the apartment. "Is something wrong?" he asked as she seated herself at the table and gestured him to the chair across from her.

"Those presents for Cole. They're excessive."

"I'm pretty well off, financially. My business is growing and I inherited some money. I want Cole to have nice stuff."

She scowled. "I give him nice stuff. So do his other relatives."

"Sorry. Of course you do. I just mean, well, more stuff. Stuff from me, as his dad."

"It's not a competition." Michael was used to getting what he wanted, and right now she figured he wanted Cole's affection. Words spilled out, fueled by an anger and fear she hadn't been aware of until now. "You can't buy him away from me!"

His eyes widened. "Jeez, is that what you think? Jillian, you're his mom and he's with you full time. I only want to build something special between him and me."

A little embarrassed by her outburst, she sat back, crossing her arms over her chest. "Okay, I get that. But fancy gifts aren't the way to do it. Spoiling a child isn't the same as loving him, and a kid who feels entitled isn't the same as a loving child."

His eyes narrowed slightly, and after a moment he said, "No. You're right."

"I don't mean to make this about you and your parents, but . . . well, it kind of is about how each of us was raised. I was taught the value of money. Taught to save for things I wanted, not expect my parents to give them to me. I had an allowance but I also worked in my parents' store. And like I said, at university I wait-ressed. The deal with my parents was, if I wanted to go to university somewhere other than Victoria where I could live with Mom's parents, I had to pay for my flights and some of my housing expenses. To me, that was entirely fair."

He nodded slowly. "Yeah, that's far different from how I was raised. My parents gave me pretty much everything I ever wanted, much less needed."

She put together a few things he'd said, and guessed quietly, "Except for their time?"

"Yeah."

Poor little rich boy. She'd had the better childhood. She'd been loved, listened to, supported, taught im-portant values. Those things counted far more than wealth. And she had to wonder what kind of grand-parents his parents would be.

"Well, anyhow," he was saying, "I didn't pay any-thing toward my university education. My parents even bought me that condo. The only condition was that I maintain an A average."

Sidetracked, she said, "You had an A average? I

never got the impression you took school all that seriously." She herself had struggled to maintain a B.

He shrugged. "I do well at subjects that interest me. Besides, I wasn't holding down a part-time job. Do you know, my very first 'employment' was as an unpaid intern at an architecture firm, to make sure I was choosing the right career path?"

"I don't want Cole's life to be like that." Michael opened his mouth but she held up a hand, stopping him. "I admit that you seem to have turned out pretty well, okay? But I've seen some of Cole's classmates and they're spoiled, entitled, pain-in-the-ass brats."

"Cole sure isn't." He smiled a little. "And you'll tell me that's because of your philosophy of child rearing."

"Yes, I will." She leaned forward, gazing into his eyes. Her annoyance and fear had faded and she felt a little sorry for him. Not to mention, still attracted. But this wasn't about her feelings; it was about Cole. "So will you agree with me? No spoiling, no competing, no letting him play one parent off against the other?"

"I guess. But how do we define *spoiling*?"

He really had no notion. "Check with me before making any major purchases or decisions. Like those fancy games and toys today, and the smartphone. You heard me say the other day that he doesn't need one."

"Maybe he didn't, but now I'm in his life. We need to be able to text and call."

She pressed her lips together. "Okay. I'd probably have said yes to that one."

They gazed across the table at each other and she gave a smile that quivered slightly. This was the right thing for Cole, but the idea of sharing her boy still hurt. "We can do this. Be his parents. Together." Life had been so much easier before. It would also be easier now if Michael hadn't grown up so damned handsome and sexy and nice.

"Together," he echoed. "Does that mean you'll consult me?"

"About what?"

"What you said. Major decisions and purchases."

Her mouth opened on a silent *What?* That notion had never occurred to her. "You want *me* to consult *you?* But I've been making decisions about Cole's life ever since . . . well, ever since I decided not to have an abortion."

"For which I'm very grateful. And sure, of course you made the decisions. But I'm in his life now. I'm committed to being his dad. You made a big deal about whether I was a responsible person, so doesn't that mean I should share some of the responsibility for how he grows up?"

No. The flat negative hovered in her mind.

"I can see that doesn't sit well with you."

She raised a hand to rub her temple. "He's been mine for so long. . . ." Her voice wavered, just as her smile had done a minute ago. These few days had, honest to God, been the most stressful ones of her entire life. Her hand rose to finger the seaplane pendant. Thank heaven she was flying this afternoon. Aaron, newly engaged but childless, had taken the morning flight and she'd have the afternoon one. Being in the sky would soothe her frazzled nerves.

Michael rose and came around the table, to crouch beside her chair. "I know this is hard. He's been yours and you don't want to share him. Especially with some guy you've never even thought of in eight years."

"That's about it," she confessed, feeling selfish and vulnerable.

"We'll figure it out. Get it in writing, all legal."

Her body clenched at that word. Michael did have legal rights, he was used to getting his way, and he had the money to hire an excellent lawyer. She might find herself in for a serious battle, maybe even resulting in shared custody. It was unimaginable. Or maybe not so unimaginable, because the very thought brought tears to her eyes.

"What's wrong?"

"You want to involve lawyers?" She hiccupped back a sob. "You're going to sue me for . . . for what?"

"Sue you?" His forehead creased. "Of course not. I just figured that when we agree how we want to do things, we'd put it in writing. Like with all my projects. We have contracts for everything so everyone's clear on the details."

"Cole isn't a p-project."

"That's not what I meant." He sighed and then, as a couple of tears rolled down her cheeks, his eyes softened like melted chocolate. "Aw, Jillian." He rose, reaching for her hands and pulling her up, too, and then putting his arms around her.

Unable to stop herself, she sank into the embrace of the man who threatened the core of her existence. Burying her face against the shoulder of his Henley, she let the soft cotton absorb a few more tears. "This is so complicated." Her words came out muffled.

"Let's try not to make it any more complicated than it has to be. We'll focus on what's best for Cole. We'll keep talking, we'll be flexible and keep adjusting. How does that sound?"

"Smart, actually," she said a little grudgingly. It didn't bother her—not much—that he'd been smarter than her at school, but he had no right to be smarter at parenting. Sniffing back the last tears, she said, "And I'll try not to feel threatened and defensive."

His arms tightened around her. "I never want you to feel threatened."

But she did. And right now it wasn't as much about her son as how good this embrace felt. She should step back, but instead her hands gripped Michael's powerful shoulders through the snug-fitting shirt. The scent of cedar made her inhale appreciatively. One day she'd have to find out if that was soap, shampoo, or cologne. For an outdoorsy woman like her, it was certainly an aphrodisiac.

The ever-present buzz of sexual awareness sparked like a lightning bolt, sizzling through her and making her forget her worries. All that existed was her too-long-celibate body and the man she lusted after. When her hips moved forward, his were there to meet them.

She'd only been intimate with two men in the post-Michael years, and the experiences had been unmemorable. This, right now, the simple press of their two clothed bodies, was sexier than actual intercourse with those other guys.

She stared up at him, dazed, lips opening to say something, though she wasn't sure what. He didn't give her the chance anyhow, but crushed his own mouth against hers, hard and fierce. She groaned and then his tongue was probing between her lips, tasting her as if she were a delicious feast spread before a starving man.

Years ago, there'd been passion between them, but never this intense. Her fingers flew over his back, clutching, gripping. She reached under the bottom of his Henley and caressed the bare skin of his lower back above the waist of his jeans and—

A knock sounded.

Chapter Fourteen

The rapping barely penetrated Michael's brain, but Jillian jerked away and then he heard it. His hands and hers tangled briefly in clothing before they managed to pull free of each other.

The knock sounded again, coming not from the door joining her apartment to her parents' house, but from the outside door of the apartment.

She tugged down her sweater, shot a panicky glance at Michael, and hurried down the short hall. He heard her exchanging Christmas greetings with Jordan's mom. He'd met Marjorie the other day, when the boy came along with him and Cole to Spirit Bluff Park.

Michael went to the kitchen sink where he shoved up his sleeves and splashed cold water on his face. Drying off on a hand towel, he heard Marjorie saying she'd come to pick up her son because they were going over to his grandparents'.

"They're in Mom and Dad's front room." Jillian's voice was higher pitched than usual. "Come on in."

Michael joined them, exchanging holiday greetings

with Marjorie, and went with them to Jillian's parents' gift and paper–strewn living room.

When Marjorie told the boys it was time for Jordan to go, they whined. She rolled her eyes and said, "There'll be more presents at your grandparents' place," which had her son scrambling up from the floor.

When the pair had departed, Cole said, "Michael, come play with me."

Michael glanced at Jillian. Obviously, this wasn't the time to continue their sexy encounter, and he knew she had a couple of afternoon flights. They'd arranged that he would look after Cole while she was at work and her parents prepared the meal and tidied the house. Later this afternoon, Jillian's brother and his family would pick up Cole's great-grandparents and they'd come over for more gift exchanging and to share the turkey dinner.

"You two can take Cole's new toys and games over to our place," she said, "and get out of Granny and Gramps's hair. But first, I need a minute more with Michael."

Oh yeah, he could use a minute more, though an hour would be even better. But when they returned to the apartment, she didn't step back into his embrace. Instead, she moved away from him, to stand with her back against the kitchen island. "That can't happen again."

"Not when Cole's around," he agreed, leaning a hip against the table.

She shook her head. "Not at all. It's not a good idea."

It had sure felt good, and he knew he hadn't been alone in that. "Why not?"

"It would confuse things. You're here for Cole. This isn't about us."

"Can't we do both?"

"That's not a good idea."

"You're repeating yourself." Clearly, she felt strongly about this, but he didn't understand why she thought it was a problem.

"Damn. I can't think straight." She rubbed her forehead. "Right, that's exactly it. When you kiss me, it scrambles my thoughts. I need to be clearheaded and logical, and so do you. We agree that what counts is Cole's best interests, so—"

"How's it going to hurt Cole if we kiss and"—he winked—"do what naturally follows?"

"Lust is selfish and it's distracting. Look what happened the last time we gave in to it." She waved a hand. "Not that I'd ever wish Cole away, you know that. But we could do something stupid again."

This felt a whole lot different from university days. "What if it's not just lust?"

"What?" Her gaze scanned his face, flicked down his body. "But I . . ."

"It feels to me like something more." Those words— *something more*—felt a little scary. For his sake, and Jillian's, he hurried to clarify. "I mean, we're older now. It takes more than just physical attraction to want to spend time with someone, right? You have to like them, be interested in them, feel some kind of connection."

"Ri-ight." She drew the word out, as if considering whether it sounded accurate. "Yes, you no longer leap into bed with someone right away. At least I don't." She cocked an eyebrow.

"That's what I'm saying. I don't either. It stopped being fun, waking up with some woman I didn't know."

"Okay." Her brow furrowed. "So we like each other. This is a good thing, because it'll make it easier to be good parents to Cole. But if you and I, uh, dated or whatever, that seems more complicated than dating someone else. Which, for me, is complicated enough. I always have to think how he and Cole would get along, where the relationship might go, how Cole would be affected if it does or doesn't work." She gave a dismissive shrug. "It's easier to not date. Besides, I don't have time for it."

She didn't date? That sounded lonely.

"And if you and I," she went on, "had some kind of intimate relationship, it could have a negative effect on Cole."

"In what way?"

She snorted. "Let me count the ways. He could feel shut out. Or, d'you remember what he said when we told him you're his dad? He jumped to the conclusion that you might move here and we'd get married. We don't want to reinforce that hope."

"No, that's true." Although, having spent time with his son and with Jillian, he'd felt a real sense of family. More than he did with his parents.

"And intimacy leads to expectations and all sorts of possible conflicts. If our personal relationship tanked—which it's bound to do—would that lead to disagreements about Cole-related decisions? Would it be harder for all of us if you came to visit?"

"Why are you so sure we'd tank?"

"You live and work in Toronto. I'm here. Long distance relationships are hard. You'd probably want to date when you're back home." She frowned. "I wouldn't like that. If I'm in a relationship, I want exclusivity. I can't imagine that working for you. Can you?"

He'd been in exclusive relationships, but with women he saw regularly. Not ones who lived so far away, whom he'd only be able to get together with at most a few times a year. "I guess not," he admitted.

She nodded. "Once emotions are involved, things get really complicated."

He was growing to hate that word. But he saw her point. "Cole is more important than our attraction to each other," he said slowly.

The tension in her face relaxed and she smiled. "Yes. So we'll be friends. Just friends." The smile faded when she added, "No more kissing."

"No more kissing," he echoed regretfully.

She was right, but something inside him ached all the same.

Chapter Fifteen

On Thursday morning, three days after Christmas, Jillian closed the door of the Blue Moon Air office and stood at the top of the ramp that led down to the network of wharves.

The village of Blue Moon Harbor spread along the end of the bay, a few blocks of shops and restaurants that served the fifteen hundred or so locals throughout the year and then geared up for the influx of thousands of summer tourists. The houses and condominiums scattered along the shore on either side of the harbor were owned either by those who'd been lucky enough to purchase them decades ago or by people rich enough to afford waterfront. Knowing just where to look on the west shore, she glimpsed the peaked roof and upstairs bedroom window of her family's home, which sat across the road from one of those more expensive properties.

On that same shore was a private marina, but here below the village the wharves were working ones. The ferry dock sat at one end, and the other wooden fingers housed commercial fish boats, the pleasure craft of visitors who paid for moorage, and the seaplane dock used by Blue Moon Air and a few off-island airlines that also serviced Destiny Island. Aaron's blue-and-white de Havilland Beaver and Cessna 180 gleamed in the early morning sunshine.

On this crisp, lovely day, frost rimmed the wood, sparkling like ground-up diamonds in the sun. Dazzling and slippery. Kam Nguyen, the airline's other employee, would caution the passengers to watch their step. She hoped Cole had warned Michael.

Right now the pair stood beside a fish boat, with Cole pointing and talking excitedly. A true Destiny Islander, her son knew a lot about boats, the ocean, and fishing. No doubt he enjoyed showing off that knowledge to his father. Michael might be a big city architect, but he looked surprisingly outdoorsy and at home here, wearing the jacket and boots her parents had given him. She pulled out her phone and snapped a couple of photos.

Much as Michael might fit in here, she had to remember this wasn't his home. They had promised to be friends and nothing more, and it was the right decision, for many reasons. Too bad that the more time she spent with him, the more drawn to him she was, even though they took pains to avoid even touching. Last night, eating popcorn and watching *Harry Potter and the Sorcerer's Stone* with Cole—a movie they'd all seen several times before—she had so wished that after she and Michael put their son to bed, they'd be going to her bedroom together. Their two kisses had told her that if they had sex, it would be even better than before. That thought was ever-present in her awareness of him.

Her parents had fallen in love at first sight. When

Jillian had first seen Michael years ago, it had been lust at first sight but never turned to love. Over the past week, though, her growing feelings for him were stronger than, different from, anything she'd ever experienced. Was she falling in love? That would be so stupid. Even if he might care for her, and obviously did have strong feelings for Cole, he was established in Toronto, loving his career and taking well-justified pride in it. She was just as established here, as was Cole. Not that she could imagine Michael asking them to leave the island and follow him to Toronto.

When she'd said good-bye to him at university, she'd barely felt a pang. Her focus had shifted from lust and the party life to being pregnant and figuring out her future. He'd been just a sexy hookup, easy to leave behind. Now, if they got involved, she could end up with a broken heart. Not to mention how she and Michael might mess things up for Cole. She clicked a final photo and sighed, feeling regret but also a reconfirmed resolve.

Quick but careful steps took her down the skid-stripped ramp and across the frosty wharf to the Beaver. She conducted her preflight inspection, then phoned Kam giving the okay to send passengers down. "Cole!" she called. "Michael! We're boarding."

There were three passengers booked on the flight over to Vancouver, and four on the return, plus a tiny baby. With two free seats on the plane, she had asked Aaron for permission to invite her son and his dad along. Michael had expressed an interest in experiencing her world, and Cole loved to go flying. She'd like to remind her boy of that fact before Michael, with those fancy Christmas gifts, convinced him he wanted to be an architect.

The first two passengers, a married couple from Vancouver who'd spent the holiday on the island, approached, holding hands and smiling. Kam had already brought down their luggage and stowed it in the plane. He came down the ramp behind the couple, carefully supporting Mrs. Perkins, an eighty-something-year-old bundled up in a wool coat and a bright red knitted hat. Over Kam's shoulder hung a flowered tote bag.

"Good morning, Mrs. Perkins," Jillian said. "Just a day trip today, I see." The woman, who was flying to Victoria, was booked to return that afternoon.

"I'm getting another pesky test at the hospital and I've an appointment with my ophthalmologist to discuss whether it's time to get my second cataract done." The woman tapped the frame of her thick-lensed glasses. "The joys of aging, my dear. It's not for the faint of heart. But my granddaughter's off for Christmas break so she'll drive me around and we'll have a lovely lunch somewhere."

While Cole and Michael waited on the wharf, Jillian and Kam got the elderly woman settled in the middle row and the married couple in the back row. "I'll let you two fight over who sits up front and who keeps Mrs. Perkins company," Jillian told her son and his father.

Cole, who always wanted to sit beside her, surprised her. "Dad can have the best seat."

It had taken him a few days to call Michael "Dad." Jillian felt a poignant tug at her heart every time he did it and every time she saw the resulting glow in Michael's dark eyes.

Mrs. Perkins's eyesight might be failing but her hearing proved sharp because, as Michael slid past her to take the seat beside Jillian's, she said, "You're Cole's father? I heard a rumor you were on Destiny Island."

Of course you did, Jillian thought.

"Yes, ma'am," he said. Once seated, he turned to look at the woman. "I'm Michael Dhillon. I came to visit Cole and Jillian for the holidays."

"He lives in Toronto," Cole chipped in, slipping into the seat beside Mrs. Perkins. "He's an architect! He designs all kinds of buildings but he doesn't actually build them himself."

"Is that right?" she said.

Jillian took the pilot's seat, started the engine, and made sure everyone was buckled in. She did the engine run-up and then, assured it was functioning properly, signaled Kam to untie the plane. Scanning the harbor, Jillian taxied away from the dock, giving her passengers the standard safety and flight information.

After completing her preflight checklist, she faced into the wind and increased speed, glad the ocean and the skies were calm. Michael would have a great first flight.

She retracted the water rudders, opened the throttle, and eased back on the steering yoke. The Beaver's nose rose, which always made her think that the plane was as eager as she to leap into the sky. She moved the stick forward and the seaplane climbed onto the step, the water pressure moving back along the floats. More speed; she felt the plane's response; and they were free of the ocean.

Behind her, Cole cheered and Mrs. Perkins, speaking loudly enough to be heard over the engine, said, "I never get tired of that moment."

"Me either," Jillian said, adjusting the angle of the plane's nose and setting her course for the Port of Victoria.

She glanced at Michael, very aware of his strong, blue-jeaned thighs and the faint scent of cedar. She really, really hoped he could relate to this magical world of hers. "What do you think?"

Chapter Sixteen

When Michael turned to look at her, his eyes were wide and a grin lit his face. "This is pretty damned—darned—cool."

"It is." But for once she didn't mean flying as much as having him beside her sharing the experience.

He gazed at her hands on the steering yoke, and then at the instrument panel, and he began to ask questions. She gave him the usual "Seaplane Flying 101" lesson she reserved for inquisitive passengers, and Cole eagerly added his perspective.

When she descended into Victoria's busy, scenic harbor, Cole pointed out the stately Empress Hotel and dignified legislative buildings. Sounding proud of his knowledge, he told Michael that both were the work of the famous architect Francis Rattenbury.

Once she'd docked, Jillian helped Mrs. Perkins deplane and meet up with her granddaughter, and then she took off again, Cole in the window seat the woman had occupied.

Michael asked more questions about the technical aspects of flying as well as about the islands and ocean traffic below them. She was pleased by his interest and happy that the conversation left her little time to muse over how appealing he was. And yet flying was so much about simply being "at one" with the experience—it was a rather Zen-like state, she and Aaron agreed—and she wanted Michael to feel that.

Reaching Vancouver, they flew over English Bay with its usual scattering of tankers and container ships waiting to enter the port. She pointed out the beaches, West End condominiums, and Stanley Park. "This is the First Narrows Bridge," she said as they approached the elegant structure, "more commonly called Lions Gate."

Cole pointed out more things of interest: tourists walking the Stanley Park seawall, the huge sulfur pile at a commercial dock, a seaplane taking off below them, a tug towing a ship stacked with multicolored containers looking no bigger than Lego bricks from up here.

Cleared for landing by the air control tower, Jillian took the Beaver down and taxied into the Vancouver Harbour Flight Centre seaplane terminal. Blue Moon Air was one of several companies using the terminal, their logo sign marking their spot on a finger of wharf.

There, she helped the married couple deplane and gave them their luggage. Michael and Cole climbed out to stretch their legs, and followed Jillian up to the terminal. She checked in with Tracy, who worked for Blue Moon Air and several other small, local seaplane businesses.

Jillian then escorted the next group of passengers down the ramp. The single mom and her two-month-old baby were Destiny Islanders returning from a holiday visit with the baby's grandparents. The other family, a fortyish couple with a boy a year or two older than Cole, said they were tourists spending their winter holiday in the Pacific Northwest. The kid, wide-eyed, said, "These seaplanes are the coolest thing I've ever seen! I can't believe I get to fly in one."

Cole said, "My mom's the pilot!"

"That is so super cool!"

Michael came close to murmur to Jillian, "Want to give the boy my seat?"

Did his breath really caress her ear like a warm, erotic touch, or was it imagination that made her shiver? "He'd love it. Thanks."

When she made the offer, the kid almost levitated with excitement.

Jillian stowed the luggage, then settled the single mom in the two-seat last row, her baby in her arms. The excited boy's parents went in the three-seat middle row with Cole.

"Michael," she said, before he climbed in to take the seat beside the single mom, "for this flight, try turning off your brain and being in the moment."

"What do you mean?"

"It's great that you're interested in flying, and I'd be happy to answer all your questions some other time. But try just experiencing it. Use all your senses. Mellow out and enjoy."

Humor twinkled in his eyes. "I won't need to ask questions this time anyhow."

What did that mean? Had he already learned everything he wanted to know? This wasn't the time to ask.

Everyone was bound for Destiny, so the flight could have been an as-the-crow-flies one, but instead, for the sake of the tourists as well as Michael, she made it more scenic, flying west to Nanaimo on Vancouver Island, then down through the scattered islands off the coast. She pointed out some sights and responded to questions from the boy and his parents, with Cole again offering comments.

She was proud of her son. He was smart, a quick learner, personable, and confident. So far, Michael's unexpected appearance in their lives didn't seem to have had any adverse effect, and she'd do everything in her power to make sure things stayed that way.

When they landed at Blue Moon Harbor, Kam was waiting on the wharf to tie up the Beaver. "A beautiful day for flying," he said when Jillian hopped out of the plane. Reading the envy in his brown eyes, she said, "Sorry you haven't had a chance to get up during the holidays. We'll make it happen next week, for sure."

The slim young man, who under Aaron's supervision handled the business end of Blue Moon Air, was an aspiring pilot. For Christmas, Aaron had given him a gift certificate for a dozen lessons, which meant Jillian handling more flights so Aaron would be free to take Kam up.

After everyone had deplaned, the tourist family, with Kam's and Cole's help, toted their luggage up to the office where they would phone for their rental car and collect brochures. Cole promised to tell them about his favorite places and things to do.

Alone on the wharf with Michael, Jillian gazed up at him. "How did you like it? Did you find out what I meant about mellowing out and experiencing it?"

"I did. Being in the back row helped."

"Really? But the view's better from the front."

"It sure as hell is." The twinkle was back in his eyes.

Unsure what he meant, she said, "So . . ."

The twinkle gave way to something hotter, more intense. "You are so sexy when you fly."

"Oh," she breathed as corresponding heat raced through her.

"I wanted so badly to touch you, so I tried to distract myself by asking questions." He swallowed. "Nothing helps. It's driving me crazy."

The wise thing would be to say the attraction was one sided and he needed to get over it. Instead, she admitted, "Me too." It took all her willpower to not step closer to him. "I'm afraid to touch you," she said. "Because I want to so much, and I shouldn't."

"Being with you is painful, but when I'm not with you all I want is to see you again."

As he spoke, she nodded in agreement. "Yes." She shot a glance up to the office at the top of the ramp, to make sure Cole was still inside.

"The attraction's way more intense than it used to be," he said.

"I know." For her, it was because she'd come to know him and to care deeply. Was there any chance he felt the same way?

"Do you think it's the appeal of the forbidden?" he asked.

Her eyes widened. "The what?"

"Like how, with Cole, if you tell him he can't download a particular app, he gets even more determined to do it. We've decided we can't have sex, so it's even more appealing. Until it's this all-consuming desire."

She squeezed her eyes shut, an automatic reaction to hide the pain they must reflect. No, he didn't have feelings for her. She was only a taboo lust object. Well, that certainly set things straight. No way should she fantasize about any kind of happy family ending for them. Fighting to keep her voice level, she said, "That's an interesting theory. I suppose it's possible. Which means the obsession will fade as soon as the next shiny new thing comes along."

In other words, when Michael returned to Toronto and dated one of his sleek city women, his desire would transfer to her.

Leaving Jillian here on Destiny Island trying to forget that she'd come close to falling in love with her son's father. The man who would be in their lives as a permanent fixture.

Chapter Seventeen

On the second to last day of December, Michael sat at the table in Jillian's dining room alcove, working on his laptop to refine the plans for his parents' reno. Cole sprawled on the floor using his Young Architect kit to design the kind of house he thought Harry Potter would like to live in.

The door to the apartment opened and Freckles, who'd been dozing near Cole, jumped up with a bark. Jillian's voice called, "Anyone home?"

"Hi, Mom! We're in here."

Michael looked up as she entered the room, her cheeks pink from the cold, pulling a long blue scarf from around her neck and looking too damned beautiful. Remaining "just friends" was sheer hell. "Did the flight go okay?" he asked. Fog had delayed the departure of her morning flight to Vancouver.

"Great. There were only wisps of fog, making the scenery moody and beautiful."

"We've eaten lunch," he said, "but we left some for you."

"Chicken and rice soup," Cole said enthusiastically, "with PB and RJ sandwiches."

"How did I know that?" Jillian joked.

Michael had been skeptical when Cole introduced him to his favorite lunch, but he'd become a fan. When you dipped a peanut butter and raspberry jam sandwich into chicken and rice soup, culinary magic happened. "And carrots and apples," Michael added, to let her know he was making sure their son got his veggies and fruit. He glanced at the computer screen, where he'd been right in the middle of something.

"Go back to work," she said.

"Thanks, I'm just . . ." As he clicked the mouse, he lost track of what he'd been saying.

Engrossed in the design, he was only vaguely aware of Jillian returning to the table to eat her soup and sandwich, then going back to the kitchen and then into the living room. He was also only marginally aware of Cole on the floor, as involved in his project as Michael was in his.

Jillian's voice broke his focus. "You're two peas in a pod and not the best company."

He gazed up at her, where she sat in a recliner with a book. "Sorry. When I'm caught up in something, I can lose track of the world around me." Although now she was in his field of vision, he wondered how he could ever find anything more fascinating than this woman with her curvy body, bright eyes, and expression of mild annoyance. "You have the afternoon off," he remembered. "We should all do something. Cole?"

When his son didn't look up, he raised his voice. "Hey, Cole!"

The boy raised his head. "Huh?"

"You can work on that later." Outside the window, it was cloudy but not raining. "Let's go out somewhere."

Cole tilted his head. "The beach? Freckles loves to chase sticks."

The dog, who'd seemed to be sleeping, leaped to his feet, tail wagging madly.

Michael grinned at the boy and dog. "Sounds good to me." He turned to Jillian. "Does that work for you?"

"If the two of you wash the dog when we come back."

"Sure," he said, having learned that Freckles didn't hold back when he explored his environment.

"Sunset Cove?" Cole asked.

"Okay," Jillian said. "It's near the northwest end of the island," she told Michael.

It didn't take them long to get organized, and soon they were in Jillian's old minivan with her in the driver's seat, Michael beside her, and Cole and the dog behind them.

Michael had learned that Destiny Island formed a rough hourglass, the top portion smaller and less populated. Blue Moon Harbor was at the south end. One main road ran roughly up the middle of the island and he'd been on it before, noting how undeveloped Destiny was. The main industry was tourism, followed by agriculture, fishing, and the arts, so they passed a lot of farmland and fields of sheep as well as signs for artisan studios.

Sunset Cove, located on the ocean, consisted of three or four shops, a pub, and roughly three dozen houses. He noted the disparate styles of architecture, always looking for ideas.

Jillian turned left onto a narrow, tree-lined road called Orca Song Drive. Here and there a driveway, most of them unpaved, meandered off into the trees toward what he guessed were waterfront homes. She took a narrow dirt-and-gravel track, and came out not at a house but at a dead end. There was room enough to park three or four cars, but theirs was the only vehicle.

When they'd climbed out, Freckles raced ahead to a trail through the trees. Cole followed, then Jillian and then Michael, single file. Carpeted with soggy leaves and pine needles, the trail came out ten feet above a long stretch of beach that curved gently between two rocky points. Logs were scattered along the shore and most of the beach was made up of rocks and pebbles, but there was also an arc of grayish brown sand. The cloudy sky gave everything a pewter tone Michael found artistically appealing.

"Good," Jillian said. "It's low tide."

"Nice beach. I didn't see a sign for it."

"It's the islanders' secret one. It's not on the tourist maps."

The place was deserted but for a man and a black dog. Freckles had already scampered down the last zigzag of trail to the beach and was racing to greet the other dog. The two barked, tails wagging, and began what looked like a game of tag. Jillian, who'd brought her Nikon, clicked off a couple of shots.

As she and Michael trailed Cole down to the beach, the man raised a hand in greeting and they waved back. But rather than come toward them, he strode away, calling something that got lost on the wind. His dog broke off playing, stared after him, and then trotted in his wake.

"Not very sociable," Michael commented as Freckles ran back to rejoin them.

"He's reclusive," Jillian said. "Some of the islanders

are like that. Destiny's a good place for eccentrics. Don't tell a soul, but that's Kellan Hawke, a successful thriller writer."

Flattered that she'd shared this secret, as well as the islanders' special beach, he said, "Huh. I saw his books on the local author table at the bookstore." He'd noted the author's name, to maybe buy one for his e-reader for the flight home. "They looked—"

"Come on, Dad," Cole, who'd picked up a sturdy stick, broke in impatiently.

Michael and Jillian followed the boy across the hard-packed sand to the water's edge, where Cole threw the stick as hard as he could into the ocean. The spotted dog flew after it, splashing into the water and swimming to fetch the stick. When Freckles swam back, Michael would swear he was grinning around his prize. The water must not be as cold as it looked.

It was, though. He found that out when the dog dropped the stick at Cole's feet and shook energetically, spraying the boy and Michael with icy droplets. Jillian, who'd stepped back a few feet and aimed her camera, laughed. "Don't know much about dogs, do you, Toronto boy?"

"It's true. I never had a pet."

In his jeans pocket, his cell phone pulsed. He pulled it out to check. "Sorry, I should take this. It's my mom. We've been playing phone tag since Christmas."

"Of course," Jillian said. He knew that his relationship with his parents seemed odd to her, and that she was concerned about how they'd react once he got back home and told them about Cole.

Stepping away from her and his son, he tapped the phone and held it to his ear. "Hi, Mom."

"Hello, Michael. Thanks for calling at Christmas. I'm sorry it's taken so long to connect."

"Not a problem." He'd walked down the beach and now turned to watch Cole heave the stick into the ocean again. Freckles raced after it, flinging himself into the cold water just as enthusiastically as he had the first time. Jillian was squatting down to photograph brown streamers of what he'd learned was kelp.

"I hope you're having a good holiday, though it doesn't sound like your usual spot," his mother continued.

Normally, he chose destinations based on architecture that intrigued him. "It isn't, but I'm having fun." Being with Cole, Jillian, and her family made him realize how much he and his parents had missed out on. He'd have to arrange his life to spend more holidays with Cole. It dawned on him that he didn't know his son's birthday. He'd be turning eight soon.

"Interesting architectural designs?"

Her question made him refocus. "Eclectic. Everything from cantilevered cedar and glass to tiny A-frames and yurts."

"Yurts?"

"Octagonal huts. They originated with nomads in Central Asia and those were portable. Now, many are more permanent and the idea's become trendy. By the way, I've almost finished the plans for your renos. Let's you, Dad, Deepa, and I get together when I'm back after New Year's." He'd tell them about Cole and show them the album Jillian had made. He'd deal with the recriminations and questions, and then they'd all figure out how to handle the new reality.

"Good. Speaking of getting together, you haven't forgotten about the black tie dinner dance next week?"

"Of course not." He had, but now he remembered telling her he'd attend a hospital event to raise funds to buy some fancy new piece of medical equipment.

"We hope it'll be good timing. People should still be filled with Christmas generosity as well as New Year's resolutions. Have you invited a date?"

"Uh, no." Dressing in a tux, picking up a stylish woman in an evening gown, making polite chat with a bunch of wealthy people while they all ate a fancy six-course dinner, dancing to a small orchestra playing "New York, New York" and "In the Mood" . . . It didn't sound anywhere near as much fun as this afternoon's entertainment. Watching Freckles drop the stick and dig up sand with his front feet, spraying it out behind him as a laughing Cole dodged it. Appreciating the curve of Jillian's fine butt as she hunkered down with her camera.

"Good, because I have someone in mind," his mother said.

"Are you matchmaking again?" She and his dad, both second generation Canadians, hadn't had an arranged marriage, but they had been introduced by their parents. Periodically, she tried to interest Michael in some eligible young woman. Her choices were often pretty good and he'd dated two or three of them, after making it clear he wasn't in the market for marriage.

"She's an intern. Very smart. And attractive."

He did a quick mental flip through his contact list, thinking of women he'd dated recently. Was there anyone he'd like to sit beside and dance with?

Now Jillian was shooing Freckles away from a pile
of seaweed that he was trying to roll in. She was scold-
ing, laughing, her cheeks pink, her curves partially
revealed and partially concealed by those slim-fitting
jeans and a down vest worn over a heavy sweater. She'd
look dynamite in an evening dress, though likely she
didn't own one.

She was the woman he wanted to be with. But since
that wasn't going to happen, he said, "Fine, Mom. Set
it up, if she's free." Maybe the woman would be interesting, and if not, at least he'd make his mother happy.

They talked a while longer and he thought how
strange it was that, while he loved his parents, it was a
rather distant love. It was sad for all of them that he'd
never had much in common with his parents, not
their interests nor their personalities. Watching Cole
romp with the dog, Michael wondered how he'd have
felt if, on meeting his son, he'd found they had nothing in common. But they did. He saw himself in this
boy. He saw Jillian, too. As well as things that were dis-
tinctly Cole.

All of it made him feel connected, protective, and
almost fierce in his desire that Cole have a good,
happy, healthy life.

He loved his son.

How about that? Watching the kid run down the
beach with the dog, Michael grinned widely. When he'd
come here, he hadn't known what outcome he was
looking for. But he'd found this special, amazing boy
and he'd learned what it was to love your child. Though
he and his son might live in different places, he vowed
that their love would *not* be emotionally distant.

Michael's mom, who'd been talking about a new
surgical procedure she'd recently tried, wound up. "I

must get back to work. It's been good talking to you, Michael. Have a happy new year."

"You too, Mom." An impulse made him add, "I love you. You and Dad and Deepa."

The momentary pause made him realize how rarely he said that. "We love you too," she said, her voice softer than before.

As he put the phone back in his pocket, he again wondered how his mom and dad would react to the news that they were grandparents—and had been for almost eight years. There'd be recriminations and questions. He'd probably end up playing the role of intermediary, trying to make sure his parents stayed involved in Cole's life without overdoing it. Deepa, he had no concerns about. She would be a loving great-auntie.

Freckles had pelted down the beach, chasing seagulls. It seemed to Michael that the birds were taunting the dog, strolling the shore nonchalantly until Freckles roared up to them, and then at the very last moment soaring into the air.

Cole was crouched over something on the beach, Jillian bending down too with her camera. Michael walked over to see that the subject of their interest was an orange-shelled crab.

The boy straightened. "You were talking to your mom?"

"Yes."

"Do she and your dad know about me?"

Michael was aware of Jillian standing up too, but he kept his gaze on his son's face. "Not yet. I'll tell them as soon as I get home."

"Will they want to meet me?" he asked hesitantly.

"I'd bet on it. We'll have to figure out how to make

that happen." His parents were so busy, it wasn't likely they'd take time off and come to Destiny Island. Maybe Cole could visit Toronto at spring break. Was he old enough to fly alone? Michael could come and get him. Or Jillian could accompany him, if she could get time off from Blue Moon Air. Would it be awkward, Jillian meeting his parents? And where would she stay? Cole could stay with Michael, but having Jillian in his apartment, sleeping down the hall . . . that was way too much temptation.

"Cole, what's wrong?" Jillian asked.

Michael stopped musing and focused on his son, who was staring down at the beach, kicking at some broken purple shells. "Cole?"

Not looking up, the boy muttered, "I guess you didn't want me."

It took a moment to figure out what he meant. "Back when your mom got pregnant?"

His head dipped in a nod.

"I told you about that," Jillian said. "How your dad and I had such different lives."

"It's true," Michael said. He would never tell his son that he'd assumed Jillian would have an abortion, but he didn't want to lie to him. "And the fact is that I didn't want a child. I was nowhere near ready. I was immature and, well, if you'd met me back then, you probably wouldn't have liked me much."

The boy's head tipped up and he studied Michael. "Mom liked you."

Jillian stepped in again. "You know how babies get made. The best way is when two people love each other very much and want to start a family. But that's not always how it goes. With your dad and me, we were just casual friends who had fun together. I did like him, but we didn't know each other well at all. Neither of us intended to create a baby. When we did, we had to figure out how we felt about it."

"You don't have to have a baby just because you're pregnant," Cole said, surprising Michael by how savvy he was for an almost-eight-year-old.

"That's right," she agreed. "But I realized I did want to have a baby. I wanted to have *you.*"

Cole gazed at her. "You were more mature than him."

She grinned. "You bet I was."

"She was," Michael agreed. "And now that I've met you, I'm really glad about that."

Cole turned to him. "I wondered about you. Mom didn't tell me much."

"I didn't know all that much about him," she said.

Michael took Cole's hand and guided him up the beach to a log, where they sat side by side. Jillian came, too, sitting on the other side of Cole. "I didn't want you," Michael said, "because I was stupid. And because I didn't know you. The best thing I've ever done in my life was coming to Blue Moon Harbor to meet you."

Cole cocked his head up. "The best thing?"

"Yes. The absolute best." He meant that, completely. "Until now, the best thing was getting my architecture firm going. But this is better. You're better than anything."

Jillian moved slightly, drawing his attention. She'd raised a hand to wipe a tear from her cheek. He gave her a wry smile and turned back to his son. "I'm sorry it took me so long to figure that out." He touched the boy's shoulder. "I love you, Cole."

His son's dark eyes appraised him for a long moment,

and then he said, "I love you, too, Dad," and he leaned forward to hug Michael.

Michael enfolded him, closing his own eyes to hold back the tears of joy.

He mustn't have been successful, because he felt dampness on his cheeks. No, wait, it was starting to rain. He and Cole broke apart, both pulling up the hoods on their rain jackets. Jillian, bare headed, called, "Freckles! Time to go!" Cole ran to meet the dog and the two of them sprinted for the trail.

Jillian broke the no-touching rule by slipping her hand into Michael's. "That was lovely."

He nodded. "I meant every word."

"I know." Too soon, she released his hand. "Let's go before we get soaked. Sorry about the weather. You need to come here in summer. Or spring or fall. Winter isn't our best season."

"In Toronto, the temperature will barely rise above freezing for months. A little rain feels fine to me."

"I actually like days like this. Let's stop at Dreamspinner for takeout hot chocolate, then go home and curl up by the fire."

The coffee shop was part of the bookstore. "If we're going to Dreamspinner, I might buy one of Hawke's books. And read the old-fashioned way for once. Seems like the right thing to do, in front of a wood-burning fire."

As Jillian smiled at him, he thought that the whole package—fire and book, woman and child, even the wet dog—felt like exactly the right thing.

Chapter Eighteen

"Don't go back," her son pleaded with Michael.

It was New Year's Eve. After dinner, Jillian's family had driven through fat, drifting snowflakes the few miles to Blue Moon Harbor Park. Fireworks were scheduled to start in ten minutes, at eight o'clock. Her parents had gone to find Samuel and his family, leaving Jillian alone with Cole and Michael. Tomorrow, Michael would fly back to Toronto.

"You don't have to go back," Cole continued. "I don't want you to!"

Despite sharing her son's feelings, Jillian said, "Honey, you know he has to. He has his job, his apartment, his family, his friends." And girlfriends, no doubt.

While father tried to reason with son, she mused that she couldn't imagine dating again. Not when Michael had gone and made her fall in love with him. Not, of course, that he'd intended to. But when you combined sexual chemistry, his unique blend of responsibility and a knack for having fun, the way he treated Cole, and oh, so many other things . . . well, she'd

been powerless to resist. The capper had happened
yesterday at the beach when he'd told Cole he loved
him. Her heart had broken a little: in happiness for
her son, in resignation to no longer being Cole's sole
parent, and in the pain of knowing that Michael
would never say those words to her. He might be attracted to her, but it was only, as he'd said, the lure of
the forbidden.

She tuned back in to the father-son conversation to
hear Cole say, "Fine!" His dark eyes, so like his dad's,
glittered fiercely. "Go back! It's not like I care anyhow!"
He stalked off in the gently falling snow.

"Cole," she called. "Where are you going?"

He didn't glance back. "To watch the fireworks with
Jordan's family!"

Michael stared after his son, the tense lines of his
face revealing his anguish.

"Sorry he's being a brat," she said. "He does care.
That's why he's so upset." They'd all been on edge
today. Even the snow, a rare event that usually engen-
dered excitement, hadn't lifted anyone's spirits.

Michael sighed. "I know." Turning to her, he took
a breath and squared his shoulders. "Here's a question for you. Do you care?"

"C-care?" Her tongue stumbled over the word. What
was he asking?

"Do you care if I go? I know my suddenly appearing
in your lives was tough on you. It's been hard for you
to share Cole with me."

She nodded, brushing damp flakes from her cheeks,
still uncertain what he was getting at.

"I guess that'll be easier if I go back to Toronto."

If. He'd said *if,* not *when.* Michael was usually precise with language, so did this mean he was thinking of

not leaving? No, she must be misunderstanding. He had so much waiting for him there. "From that perspective, I guess you're right," she admitted. Though it probably wasn't wise to continue, she couldn't stop. "But I'll miss you. I've gotten used to the idea of the three of us as, well, family. Together, I mean. Not separated by more than half a continent."

He nodded, but his eyes were narrowed and he didn't smile. "I guess I asked the wrong question. Do you care about me?"

Her heart stuttered. "I . . . yes, of course."

"Of course? Before, when we were hooking up, you weren't even sure you liked me."

"But now I know you. I like the man you've become."

"Like?"

She drew in a breath and let it out, her breathing quavery. So was her entire body, not to mention her emotions. "I don't know what you're asking."

"Here's the thing. When we knew each other before, it was all about having a good time. We didn't talk much. Over the past eleven days, it's been the opposite. I think you were smart saying we shouldn't have sex, though it's been sheer hell. But we've done so many other things. Hung out together with Cole. Talked about all sorts of things. I've seen you, Jillian. Seen who you are as a mom, a daughter, a pilot. A woman."

She nodded. "Yes, that's exactly what it's been like."

"On the beach, when Cole asked why I hadn't wanted him when I found out you were pregnant, it hit me that I don't just want him now. I love him."

"I know. I can see it. He loves you, too."

"I feel that. But there's something else I feel.

Tonight, you telling Cole why I needed to go back to Toronto, and then me trying to explain it to him . . . Well, it hit me. Yes, I have a life there and a business I love and am proud of. But none of that feels as meaningful now."

"You'd rather be with Cole?" She felt even more quavery. Did he want to move here and share custody? How could she bear not tucking Cole in every single night?

"Yes. And with you. Because it also hit me—" He broke off as a thunderous boom and a dazzling burst of fireworks indicated the start of the show. Laughing, he stared upward. "A lightbulb moment, multiplied by a million."

Much as she loved fireworks, she wasn't about to let anything interrupt this conversation. Raising her voice, she asked, "What hit you?"

"That I love you." He'd increased volume, too, but his statement happened to fall in the aftermath of a second explosion of pyrotechnics, so his words boomed loudly on the night air.

"Oh!" She was so shocked that her exclamation was no more than a soft puff of air.

"What did you say?" he almost yelled over the next burst of sound and dazzling colors.

Who cared that they were attracting annoyed and amused gazes from spectators around them? This was one of the most important conversations of her life—after the one where she'd told him she was pregnant, and the one where she'd said she wasn't getting an abortion and had turned down his proposal.

At high volume, she asked, "How do you love me? Do you mean as your son's mom? As a friend?"

"Yes, all of that, but more. Everything. As a woman.

An amazing woman. Do you think there's any chance you could come to feel the same way and—"

"Yes!" At the top of her lungs, she cut him off. "Oh yes. Every day for the past eleven days, I've been falling more and more in love with you."

"Really?"

Maybe he read the truth in her eyes, because rather than wait for her to respond, he threw his arms around her and kissed her.

As showers of gold and silver filled the sky behind his head, snowflakes brushed their faces, and laughter and applause sounded around them, Jillian gazed into his eyes and kissed him back with all her heart.

Chapter Nineteen

Michael glanced at his watch. "Five minutes to midnight," he told the woman he loved. "Bring those glasses into the front room."

"So this is how it's going to be. Now that you've got me, you're bossing me around," she teased, gathering the two flute glasses.

Carrying the chilled bottle of champagne, he followed her, enjoying the straightness of her slender back, the sweet curve of her hips and butt. His. Yes, she was his. And he was hers. At some point soon, they'd stand up in her parents' church with Cole beside them, and they'd make it official. Not that it got a whole lot more official than having a couple dozen residents of Blue Moon Harbor witness their bellowed declarations of love.

By now, likely the entire island knew. The notion made him smile. His new home would take some getting used to, after the impersonality of Toronto.

Another thought made him smile, too. "I'm glad Cole forgave me," he said. When Michael had explained that he wanted to move to Blue Moon Harbor, set up his architecture firm here, and have the three of them become a family, his son had said, "Took you long enough to figure it out." But then he'd thrown his arms around Michael and squeezed as hard as he could.

Much as Michael loved his son and looked forward to all the days and years ahead, right now he was very glad that Jillian's parents had invited the boy to spend the night—and that the door between this apartment and their house was firmly locked.

Here, there was a fire in the fireplace, chilled champagne, and the woman he loved. It was only a couple of minutes to midnight. On the couch, his thigh touching hers, he eased the cork out of the bottle, poured carefully into two glasses, and handed her one. "When I came to Blue Moon Harbor, I didn't know what I was looking for. How incredible it is that in this short time I've found a family and found love."

"Do you realize," she said wonderingly, "we've had our own version of the twelve days of Christmas?"

"You're right. Each day there's been a new gift, a new connection between us." A revelation struck him. "Years ago, you said we had no foundation for building a family. I just realized, that's what we've been doing since I came here. Building that foundation one moment, one day, one gift at a time."

"It's a strong foundation, and it'll grow even stronger."

He raised his glass. "Only ten seconds until midnight. Here's to a new year, a new love, a new life together."

She clicked her glass against his. "A new year, a new love, a new life together."

They gazed into each other's eyes and drank the toast. Then they put their glasses down and kissed deeply, intimately, a kiss full of promise.

Second Chance Christmas

JULES BENNETT

Chapter One

Ruby Blanton smoothed a hand down her emerald green sheath dress and wondered if she'd gotten too dressed up for this blind date. Considering the stranger waited on the other side of her cottage door, it was a little too late to worry.

"Why do I agree to these things?" she muttered as she flicked the lock. The blind date from hell was inevitable considering she'd never had a successful one. But, here she was again, about to put herself out there for some guy who probably lived in his mother's basement or thought Ruby would go home with him between dinner and dessert to continue on their time in private . . . sans clothes.

Was it too late to back out and fake a stomach bug? Because thinking of the endless possibilities of how this could all end in disaster was giving her indigestion.

Pulling in a deep breath, Ruby swung the door open. A gasp escaped her lips before she could suppress it. This blind date wasn't a stranger at all. She hadn't seen him in six years, but she'd recognize those bright blue eyes and that strong jawline anywhere.

"Ruby?"

She smiled, though nerves curled low in her belly. Knox Walker returned her smile and she was instantly thrust back to when she'd first met him . . . and the last time she'd seen him. Pain laced with anticipation and she had never felt more out of her comfort zone.

"This is unexpected," she replied.

That was a vast understatement. The last time she'd seen him had been under heartbreaking circumstances—circumstances that had changed her life.

Ruby had never forgotten him and had always wondered where he'd ended up. Never in her wildest imagination did she dream he'd be on her doorstep ready to take her for a night out.

She'd expected a disaster of a date, but she truly had no clue now how this could even work out. Awkward, party of two? Your table is ready.

"I . . ." Ruby shook her head, trying to find the right words. "I wasn't sure whom to expect. Are you comfortable with this?"

Knox stepped over the threshold and she mentally cringed at her poor manners of not inviting him in. If she hadn't been so shocked, she would've been a bit more hospitable.

Ruby moved out of the way as his large frame took up the entire space of her entryway. As he closed the door behind him, his eyes never left hers. Did he recognize her? Surely he did. Granted he'd been grieving and worried at the bedside of his wife when he first met Ruby, so maybe at that time he hadn't paid Ruby any attention whatsoever.

"I mean . . ." She hurried to backtrack and get her

words caught up with the spiraling thoughts in her mind. "Do you know who I am?"

Those perfectly shaped lips offered a wide smile that did much to ease her nerves, but ramped up her anxiety and attraction.

"Of course I remember," he informed her. His voice, smooth as whiskey, washed over her. "Are you uncomfortable? I don't want to make this difficult. I had no clue you were my date."

Considering she'd been the midnight nurse to his ailing wife only six years ago, this was a tad rough. But he seemed like a completely different man. Not just his looks—he had slight wrinkles around his eyes now, and broader shoulders—but there was an aura about him that seemed much more peaceful.

And there was a ruggedness about him she didn't remember. He'd gotten broader, the fine wrinkles around his eyes and mouth more prominent, yet it all made him seem extremely distinguished. His hair was shorter, littered with a sprinkle of silver around the temples.

No, she couldn't be attracted to the man of a patient she'd taken care of . . . could she?

"I guess I'm just shocked it was you on the other side of my door," she admitted. "But if you'd rather cancel, I understand."

Knox shifted, stepping farther inside her entryway. "Quite a bit has happened since my wife passed. And I'm actually just looking for a friend and a fun night out. No pressure. If you want to still go, I can fill you in on the past six years."

Knox and his wife Lydia had always left a special place in Ruby's life. Lydia was her first patient right after nursing school. Day in and day out, Ruby got to know the young couple. After Ruby had cared for her for five weeks, Lydia finally succumbed to her illness.

Ruby hadn't seen Knox since. She also hadn't returned to that unit and had promptly asked to be transferred to the emergency department. She'd rather deal with broken bones and wounds than terminal patients every day.

Now when she lost one, they had usually just been brought in and Ruby hadn't gotten to know the family, hadn't fallen in love with them. Ruby still mourned and grieved the loss of patients, but nothing like when Lydia had slipped away in the quiet hours of the morning.

She shook away the memory that threatened to steal this moment and thrust her down a path she never wanted to revisit. It was obvious Knox had moved on, though she was sure he still struggled with the pain and lived with it daily. He was here and he was asking for a friend for the night. She wasn't about to turn him away.

"Well, if you're okay with this, then I'm ready." She reached beside him to grab her wrap coat from the hook beside the door. "At least this is already starting off as a better blind date than my last. He showed up driving his mother's car and had her credit card to pay for our dinner."

"Who says I don't have my mother's credit card?" he joked.

Ruby couldn't help but laugh, and be thankful he'd lightened the mood with a bit of humor. Maybe this night would prove to be something magical and perfect. If they reconnected as friends, that would be so amazing.

Knox held her coat open and adjusted it up over her shoulders once her arms were in. When his fingertips feathered innocently against the base of her neck, Ruby trembled and tried to ignore the unexpected jolt.

"You had many bad blind dates?" he asked.

Ruby tied the straps around her waist and turned to face him. "I've had enough, but the last one was such a disaster, I vowed never to do it again."

Yet she'd gone out and bought a brand new pair of shoes for this occasion. Hey, if she was going to be paired with a loser, she at least deserved a killer pair of heels, right?

But she knew for a fact Knox wasn't a loser. Granted she hadn't seen him in years, but she didn't believe the man she'd gotten to know at the side of his ailing wife would be anything less than amazing. Looks aside—and he was devastatingly handsome—Knox had been a great guy.

He flashed that smile, showcasing his twin dimples. "What made you change your mind about giving another shot at a blind date?"

"I trust Jackson's judgment."

Jackson Morgan, pilot and part owner of the small airport in Haven, Georgia, was a good friend. He'd actually bought her old house when she decided to move closer to the hospital and park. He was a single father and her old house had been perfect for him and his adorable little girl. They'd struck up a friendship and he'd mentioned a new pilot who was in town for a short time. Ruby figured she needed the distraction because holidays simply weren't as jolly as they used to be for her.

"I'm renting a hangar from him for my plane," Knox stated. "For the time being, at least."

Ruby picked up her purse and tucked it beneath her arm. "He mentioned a new pilot that had been in town a couple of months, but he didn't give me a name or anything else. He was pretty vague, now that I think about it."

Not that Jackson knew their history. Maybe he hadn't known all the details of Knox's past life either.

"Then I'm doubly glad you agreed." Knox pulled the door open to let her pass through. "I joined the Navy after Lydia passed, became a Naval pilot, and decided to carry that over into civilian life. I've been out about two months now, but I still love the skies."

Wow, he hadn't been kidding when he said quite a bit had changed since he'd last seen Ruby. She'd had no idea what happened to him after Lydia. Considering she'd been the nurse, there was no reason for her to have further contact. But she'd always wondered. Certain patients just stuck with you and, considering Lydia had been Ruby's first terminal patient, her family had definitely held a special place.

That whole period spanning several months had been such a crushing time for him . . . and for her as a new nurse.

As Knox led her toward the drive where his truck was parked, he held on to her elbow to guide her through the snow. He was certainly a gentleman—that was a rarity considering her last few dates.

"Your house is the only one on the block without lights." He pulled the door to his truck open and glanced down to her. "You don't like lights or you're too busy to put them up? I'm not judging. I just put a wreath on my rental yesterday."

Since she was alone and her father had passed this time last year, she simply wasn't in the mood for cheery decor. She'd wrestled up the tiny tree from the basement and plunked it in her living room corner. That was as far as she'd gone before she had herself a solitary pity party and had eaten half a roll of cookie dough.

Putting that tree up was a ridiculous effort on her part. She'd ignored it for the past week. Ruby hadn't even gotten the ornaments, lights, or any other decor out of storage.

"I've been working some double shifts at the hospital and my time off is spent at the animal shelter walking dogs and cleaning kennels."

Wow. When she said that out loud her life seriously sounded boring. No wonder she was single. She was either assisting patients or playing with dogs. Not much room there for finding the man of her dreams, unless this faceless man appreciated a woman in scrubs or sweats. That was pretty much her wardrobe considering her job and her volunteer work. So this fun sheath and her new heels were quite the change of pace. Perhaps she should've greeted Knox as she usually looked so there would be no preconceived notions in the future.

Wait. Future? They hadn't even pulled from her drive and she was already thinking of more dates?

Knox walked her to his truck and she couldn't help but steal a glance at him. The lights from the decorated homes on her street illuminated his profile. This man exuded strength and sexiness and all the appeal she shouldn't find attractive considering their unique history. But she did, and there was no denying her instant attraction.

"I hope I'm not overdressed," she told him, those nerves still getting the best of her. "I wasn't really sure what to wear when you said dinner, but I tend to get excited when I can put on something other than scrubs or ratty T-shirts when I volunteer."

He assisted her up into the truck. "You look beautiful and perfect for where we're going, but I would've even taken you in scrubs and ratty tees."

When he closed the door, Ruby smiled at the compliment. It had been a long time since someone called her beautiful. And when he said he'd take her in her crappy clothes, she truly believed him. Knox was a gentleman in every sense of the word. She needed to remember that he'd said he was looking for a friend. One day she'd like to settle down and marry, have some children, and make the family she'd always wanted.

She rarely had an evening off, so for tonight, she'd just enjoy the company and not worry about anything else . . . especially the way she still had those nerves swirling through her. Knox was beyond handsome and that sliver of a touch earlier still had her tingling.

Knox had had no clue his blind date was going to be Ruby. This was his first date since coming back stateside. He'd meant it when he said he was only looking for a fun night out, but one look at Ruby in that green dress and all the air had vanished from his lungs. The black, strappy heels she wore accentuated her toned legs. He shouldn't be admiring her this much, shouldn't be relishing in that instant attraction, but he was a guy and she was one very beautiful woman.

When he'd helped her with her coat and her sweet floral scent had surrounded him, it was all he could do not to lean down and nuzzle the side of her neck.

Thankfully he had self-control, because that action most likely would've creeped her out . . . as it should've, because they were still virtual strangers.

The sweet nurse who had comforted him during the most trying time of his life was now in his truck and wreaking havoc on his emotions. She looked too damn good and he was struggling with the fact he wasn't looking for anything other than a friend while he was in town. All too soon he'd be moving on anyway.

Knox maneuvered through the streets and headed toward the restaurant in the next town over. He'd heard great things about Plantation House, a five-star restaurant that opened while he'd been overseas, and he was eager to try it. It may have been a bit much for the first date, but he didn't care. He wanted to do things right and have a good time. Just because he wasn't looking for something serious didn't mean he would take his date to some fast-food joint. And with the way Ruby looked, the way she smelled, he was glad he'd gone all out and made reservations.

"So you're still a nurse at the hospital?" he asked.

The dash lights lit up Ruby's face, showcasing those pink lips and long lashes. His gut tightened and he was having a difficult time focusing on anything else.

Eyes on the road.

She was even more stunning than he'd remembered. Granted that time in his life when he'd met her was a blur and not too many details remained. But he did recall her gentle bedside manner, her compassion, and her concern for her patients. Ruby was undoubtedly a phenomenal nurse.

In all honesty, he wasn't sorry she was his date. Their history put them already at an advantage, if you looked at it from that angle, which he did. He didn't have to pretend anything and he didn't expect her to, either. As crazy as it sounded, there was already a deeper bond between them than most first dates.

"I've moved to the ER," she told him. "I'm usually put in the trauma department there. Car wrecks, gunshot wounds—not that we have many, but they're usually accidental. I never know what I'm going to encounter with each shift."

"And you've doubled your hours?"

Ruby shifted in her seat and crossed her legs. "I've been taking some of the hours from coworkers who have little kids. It's just for the season. I know they have shopping to do, Santa pictures to get, cookies to bake."

Knox turned onto the two-lane highway that led out of Haven. "You don't bake cookies or get a picture with Santa?"

Ruby laughed. That sensual, low laughter filled the small space and clenched his chest. But she didn't have that flirty giggle that grated on his nerves. She was genuinely amused, and damn if that didn't make her even more attractive.

"I'm not the best in the kitchen, but I have been known to buy a roll of cookie dough and make those for the other volunteers at the animal shelter. As for

Santa, I'm pretty sure I'm too old to be asking for gifts or sitting on his lap."

"Never too old to ask for gifts," he replied. "I'd like a brand new Cessna Skyhawk. It's not going to happen, but I'm not above asking anyone who will listen."

"You really love flying," she murmured. "Have you done much since you've been back?"

"I'd be in the air every day if I could," he admitted. "I'm still trying to decide what I want to do, but I do have something lined up if I want it."

"So Haven is just a stepping stone?"

He'd been restless since Lydia's death, but over the past year or so, he'd come to terms with the fact he'd have to settle down at some point and start setting roots for his life. Buying a house alone just didn't have much appeal, though.

Once he found the town he wanted to stay in for good, he'd rent until the right house came along. He clearly didn't need anything too large since it was just him and he didn't plan on marrying again. A dog, though. He definitely needed a dog wherever he ended up.

Knox turned onto a side street and nodded. "Pretty much. I was given a job opportunity in Atlanta, though I'm not real sure I want to live in the city. But it's a solid opportunity and hard to pass up."

"What's the job?"

"Nothing as rewarding as nursing."

He pulled into the parking lot and Ruby let out a gasp. "I've been wanting to eat here, but never had a reason to come."

Knox found a parking spot and killed the engine before turning to face her. "Then I'm glad we have the chance to try this together. I've heard how amazing it is."

He hopped out of the truck and circled the hood to get her door. Of course she had already opened it and was in the process of getting out when he caught her by the elbow and helped her down. He didn't step back and her flush body against his had him reevaluating that whole speech about "friends only."

Ruby felt too good, too right. That was insane, wasn't it? They'd just reconnected after six years and he didn't know her. His body betrayed him as he heated up from her touch. Apparently his hormones didn't care how well he knew her.

"Apparently your past dates weren't gentlemen."

Ruby's eyes held his as a smile flashed across her face. "Not many of them."

"That's a shame." He looped her arm through his and led her toward the festive entrance. "Let me make this clear. I'll get all the doors and I plan on pulling your seat out. When we get back to your place, I'll walk you to your door."

Ruby reached up and placed her hand on his over her arm. "And I'm just Southern enough that I'm going to let you—and enjoy every minute of it."

Her megawatt smile was like a punch of lust to his gut—not the first he'd had since she opened her door. There was such a natural beauty about her that was refreshing. He wasn't looking for anything more than a date, but having a little bit of history with Ruby made this evening a little less stressful. She already knew his backstory, so he didn't have to go into the reasons for not looking for happily ever after. It just wasn't in the cards for him.

They headed into the two-story restaurant, which had been completely decked out for the holidays. Bright twinkling lights wrapped around fresh greenery draped over each doorway and along the banister leading upstairs. Two tall nutcrackers flanked the entrance to the main dining area, and the tables that he could see all had a variety of green and gold centerpieces.

"This is beautiful," Ruby murmured as she glanced around the area.

Knox couldn't help but instantly think she fit right in here. With her long black hair curled down her back, her green dress that matched her eyes, and the sweet elegance about her, she was truly breathtaking.

Dinner. That's all this was. There was no reason for him to get swept into any sort of fantasy. This was simply a relaxing evening out.

Only, he wasn't so relaxed. Not when his body was strung so tight and their date had only just begun.

Chapter Two

"There was no way I could've eaten dessert."

"Good thing, since the kitchen caught fire while we were there. Being evacuated does put a damper on finishing your dessert." Knox placed his hand on the small of Ruby's back as he led her to her front door. "Sorry, that wasn't a good joke."

"At least the fire department was able to put it out and keep it contained to just a small area in the kitchen." She pulled her keys from her purse and stepped up onto the porch. "I'm telling you, blind dates are disastrous for me."

"I don't think the fire was your doing," he laughed.

She turned, the lights from either side of the door illuminating her beautifully. "Do you want to come in for a bit?" she asked. "I feel like we still need dessert. We could make up a batch of those Christmas cookies you mentioned."

Knox wasn't ready to call it a night. They'd had a good time, even with being rushed from the restaurant. They didn't have one lull in the conversation and she looked him in the eye when he spoke. That act was so telling about a person. Most people listened just so they could chime in, but Ruby was listening because she was honestly interested.

He wasn't looking forward to heading home to his rental town house where he'd be alone and have to sit in the silence and think. There were too many decisions to make for his future and he didn't want to make them tonight. Ruby wouldn't have invited him in if she didn't want him to stay for a bit.

"I can't remember the last time I had homemade cookies," he told her.

Ruby's smile widened and there went that punch of attraction again. Did she even have a clue the impact she had? He wasn't looking to be impacted by another woman. He'd had his shot at love and he'd taken it. His life now was his own. He didn't believe he didn't deserve happiness, but he was also realistic in that love only happened once in a lifetime. . . . He just wished his would've lasted a bit longer.

People didn't get second chances, not with something as enchanted as love.

"Come on in," Ruby stated as she slid her key into the lock. "Do you like icing? Sprinkles? Sugar crystals?"

She led him into the foyer and he helped her with her coat. After hanging hers by the door, he removed his black leather jacket and hung it next to hers. There was something so intimate about their coats hanging side by side, like it was the most natural thing to do after an evening out.

"On the rare occasion I get homemade cookies, I tend to inhale about five as soon as they come out of the oven, burn the roof of my mouth, and swallow it all down with a large glass of milk. No time for all the decorating."

Ruby crossed her arms over her chest as her eyes raked over him. "You eat five cookies in one sitting and still look like that? If I ate five cookies, I'd bust my zipper."

An image of her sans dress assaulted him and he wasn't too eager to diminish the thought. He'd been attracted to women over the past few years, but he'd not had a pull like this. Maybe it was because there was already a history. Yes, that had to be why. Knox refused to believe there was this strong of a need for her for any other reason.

Ruby stepped into the living room and toed off her heels. Throwing a glance and a grin over her shoulder, she said, "Follow me."

Did she even realize she was taunting him? Those bare feet and the sway of her hips had him gladly obeying her command. Maybe cookies weren't the best idea. Outside on her porch the idea had all seemed so innocent. Now that they were behind closed doors, he was having a difficult time recalling that promise he'd made earlier of just wanting a friend.

The large island in the center of the kitchen had bar seating, but he wasn't going to be sitting this one out. He planned on helping where he could and making this date a continuation of fun.

Knox remained by the island as Ruby pulled an apron off the hook by the refrigerator and tied it around her waist and neck. This was all becoming so domestic and he had to mentally prepare himself to do this. He'd done domestic for a short time before his wife fell ill. He wasn't looking to do it again . . . at least not long term.

When Ruby turned her attention back to him, she cocked her head to the side. "Relax. It's just cookies. I promise I'm not making you do anything outside the friend zone."

"Did I have a look of panic on my face?"

Ruby smiled and flattened her palms on the island. "More like you were considering making a run for it."

Clearly he'd have to work on his game face because if she thought he was attracted, who knew what would happen. She was blunt and honest, usually values he appreciated in people. But he didn't want her calling him on anything he prided on keeping hidden.

"How good are you at baking?" she asked. "Because I was going to let you mix everything while I got busy with the icing."

He figured keeping this island between them was the smart move, but his mother didn't raise him to sit back and let someone wait on him. He'd been taught at an early age to help in the kitchen and he'd promised Ruby a nice evening . . . that included dessert.

"I'll help," he told her as he circled the island and started rolling up his sleeves. "Tell me what to do."

"Really?"

Her shocked tone caught him off guard. "Did you think I wouldn't help?"

With a shrug, she went to get him an apron. "I figured you'd rather sit and talk. But I'm grateful."

He eyed the red and white polka dot apron with ruffles around the hemline. "I will sit and talk if you make me wear that. There is a point where I draw the line."

"Suit yourself," she told him as she hung it back on the hook. "But don't get upset when you get cookie dough and food coloring all over that nice shirt."

"I'll take my chances and hold on to my man card."

Her bright, wide eyes sparkled as she continued to smile at him. There was something so comfortable about Ruby, something so . . . right. Was that the second time he'd used that word to describe her? Fine, she was right for someone, but not him. There was no way the first date he got set up on would somehow change his entire world. He wasn't a pessimist, but he was realistic, and that's just not how life worked.

Ruby would make a perfect friend for him while he was staying in Haven.

That's right. Friend. Nothing more. No more watching those swaying hips or admiring the way her toes were polished a festive shade of red. Nope. None of that.

She pulled out all of the ingredients and some mixing bowls. Once she had everything spread across the island, she pulled a recipe card from a drawer.

"This was my mother's recipe," she told him. "Why don't you follow this and I'll start working on the icing?"

He glanced down to the yellow-edged card with elegant penmanship. "I don't want to mess up your mother's recipe."

"You won't," she assured him. "Just read, measure, and mix. Nothing to be afraid of."

Knox started putting the ingredients in the bowl while Ruby worked beside him on the long island. She hummed a tune he didn't recognize as she stirred her icing mixture.

"Do you make these often?" he asked.

"I've actually only made this recipe once since she's been gone. They were a disaster and wouldn't even have served as a good hockey puck."

Well, he figured he couldn't do much worse. He'd piloted planes for the US government; how hard could this be? It was sugar, flour, eggs . . . nothing to be afraid of.

"Want to turn on some Christmas music?" he asked.

"I'm not much of a festive person," she replied, with a lift of one slender shoulder. "But I'm sure I can come up with some music."

Her open floor plan allowed him to watch her as she crossed to her television and pull up some music . . . not Christmas. She had one tiny tree in the corner, no lights, no ornaments, no presents beneath. There were no lights outside, either. If he didn't know the date, he'd never know it was Christmastime by the looks of the inside of her house.

All the telltale signs of grief. This wasn't just some Scrooge-persona he was witnessing. Ruby wouldn't be that type of person. He figured she'd be the one who shopped early, had presents for her friends beneath the tree, baked cookies for families on her street. She probably had some special ornaments and random knickknacks in storage that belonged to her grandmother or someone special in her life. Yet she had nothing at all out on display.

When some trendy rock song filled the room, she came back to the island and proceeded to pull out another mixing bowl and food coloring.

"You lost someone recently, didn't you?" he asked.

Those expressive green eyes shot to him. Knox offered a smile to soften the blow of his abrupt question.

He hadn't meant to come across as harsh. He was still adjusting to civilian life, but he had to do better to remember where he was.

"My father," she finally replied. "He passed last Christmas Eve, so this year is rough. I mean, I've had a year to deal with the loss, but I guess you can't fully prepare for something like this. Time moves on and drags you with it."

That last sentence summed up how he'd felt for so long. Over the past couple of years, though, he'd attempted to take that control back and not let life control him.

All that grief was no doubt another reason why Ruby was taking on so many hours at work. Still, that didn't mean she needed to shut down. He of all people knew when you lost someone, you couldn't just check out . . . no matter how much you wanted to. What better way to prove you were alive than to get back out among the living? Staying home alone, being shut in with your inner demons, was a combination that would eventually lead to self-destruction.

"You do actually own Christmas decorations, right?" He wiped his hands on the towel on the counter and turned to face her. "You just didn't want to get them all out?"

She squirted a few droplets of red into the white icing and stirred without looking up at him. "I didn't see any reason to. I don't have any family here, so nobody will be coming by. And at this point it's two weeks away, so why go to all the trouble now?"

"I'll do it."

Where had that come from? He always thought before he spoke . . . apparently not the case around

Ruby, who had somehow hypnotized him. Maybe it was that steel strength she tried to wrap her vulnerability in, or perhaps it was the dress—he didn't know. But he did know he wanted to make her Christmas a little brighter. Isn't that what any friend would do?

"Don't be silly," she replied with a gentle smile. "You don't have to do anything."

"I want to." And he realized just how much he wanted to now that the idea had taken root. "Tell me where the stuff is and I'll start while you finish here. My part is already done."

Ruby pursed her lips as if torn between arguing and giving in. Finally, she nodded her head. "Let me get the totes."

While she was gone, Knox went into the living room and figured out how to change the music channel. Finally, some classical Christmas music filled the room. There was about to be a Christmas overload here. He knew exactly how he'd felt that first Christmas after Lydia had passed. He'd already joined the Navy, but that still didn't fill the void. Holidays were rough, especially that initial one. He was about to show her that the holidays could still be joyful and that was the best way to honor your loved ones.

Ruby came up from the basement with a tote and set it in the middle of the kitchen floor. "There's one."

When she turned to go back for more, he crossed the space. "I'll go."

"It's no problem for me to get them. I'm the one who has done it every year and carts it all back down."

He placed a hand on her shoulder, instantly realizing that touching her only added to his already growing attraction. "It's also no problem for me to get them," he countered. "I'll do this; you get those cookies in the oven so I can eat my promised five."

Ruby rolled her eyes and shook her head. "You're only here for the cookies, aren't you?"

Unable to help himself, he smoothed her hair over her shoulder and kept his gaze on hers. "I'm here for the cookies *and* the company."

Her expressive eyes widened, then darted to his mouth. Knox may have thrown out the word *friend*, but he hadn't wanted to kiss any of his friends like this before. And he hadn't been sure, but now he was positive the attraction was definitely two sided.

This was dangerous territory. He wasn't looking for anything and he wasn't staying in Haven. *Friends* . . . the theme word of the evening was slowly getting pushed to the back of his mind and his hormones had taken over.

The timer on the oven beeped, indicating it was warm enough. He'd attest to that.

"I'll get everything," he told her as he took a step back and dropped his hand from her hair.

Ruby licked her lips. "Um . . . okay. There are four more totes and they're marked *Christmas*. I'll warn you, they are pretty big and one is heavy."

He shot her a wink. "I think I can handle it."

Knox bounded down the steps and attempted to get his head on straight. He wasn't here for anything other than company and helping her have one nice evening where she didn't dwell on her loss. Surely to goodness he could resist temptation . . . couldn't he?

Chapter Three

The moment he was out of sight, Ruby placed her palms flat on the island and exhaled. She was pretty sure she hadn't breathed at all from the second he'd touched her, then glanced to her lips, then stepped back as if he'd been just as turned on as she had been.

That man had the most potent stare, almost as if he could see into her soul. The last thing she needed was for this attraction to blossom into something. She'd seen exactly how much he'd loved his wife. Ruby had never seen anything like it before or since, other than her own parents. Those two instances had been true love.

Knox said nothing as he carried four oversized totes in only two trips.

"Show-off," she joked as she slid one pan of cookies in the oven. Though the display of his sheer strength wasn't helping to squelch her ever-growing desire.

Knox chuckled as he took everything into the living room and began surveying the contents of each tote. "I'm not showing off, just making fewer trips so we can get this place whipped into shape," he explained.

Ruby snorted her denial as she continued making dough cutouts of reindeer. She watched him across the way as he pulled out red iridescent beads, candlesticks, ceramic snowmen. This was all very foreign to her, having a man in her living room while she baked in the kitchen. The fact he had volunteered to do her decorating spoke volumes about his character.

For one, he probably missed this part during the holidays. No doubt he and his wife had shared things together, like picking out a tree and having a Christmas dinner or going to parties.

Second, he didn't hesitate to jump in and try to make her holiday brighter. He knew she'd lost her father and she figured Knox didn't want her to feel alone during this time of year. He was already a friend—that most important title he assured her was all they could be. She could honestly use more friends like him; she just wished she didn't fantasize about kissing him so much.

Surely this guy had a flaw. Could someone seriously be this attractive and this giving? It was such a shame he wasn't looking for more and their past wasn't so confusing and delicate. What was the protocol here? She was completely out of her element and she figured Knox was as well.

Ruby would love to see him again, and maybe see if anything could progress beyond a friendship. But even if he was looking to date seriously again, most likely he wouldn't want to get serious with the woman who had cared for his late wife.

Friends might be the best zone for them to stay in, especially considering he wasn't staying in Haven. Ruby had never gotten involved with a patient before, or the family member of one. Now was not the time to start.

"Sorry about the mess," Knox stated as he continued to unwrap items from the totes. Ornaments and tissue lay on nearly every stationary surface and littered the floor. "I'll pick everything up when I'm done."

Ruby gently placed the cutouts on another cookie sheet. "Don't worry about it. One of my dates had to clear all the empty beer cans off his couch when he invited me to dinner. He hadn't told me dinner was at his house and he was making me a frozen pizza."

With ornament in hand, Knox stilled. "You're kidding."

"Oh, I so wish I was. I've had some dandies and they all wonder why I don't go for date number two."

Knox stepped over the tissue to hang another ornament on the tree. Then he walked around to the side and bent down to plug the lights in. Instantly the room was illuminated, and between that, the aromas filling the house, and the music he'd obviously switched to, it was starting to feel like Christmas . . . just like before. She had missed her house feeling cozy and the promise of Christmas joyfulness. Having Knox here was almost too much, like life was showing her what she could have . . . but not right now and not with this man.

For the time being, she wasn't sad, she wasn't worrying about how she'd get through this first holiday with no family. She decided to stay in this moment because this was exactly what she needed.

"Just how many bad dates have you had?" he asked, reaching into the tote.

Ruby laughed and wiped her hands on her apron.

"You don't have that much time on your hands. Let's just say I'm going to be alone if all that's out there is guys who expect me to pay for their dinners, guys who wear their best NASCAR T-shirts on a first date, or guys that expect me to be the dessert when they can't even get my name right."

Knox propped his hands on his hips. "What kind of people do you agree to go out with? And who are the so-called friends setting you up?"

With a laugh, Ruby circled the island and opened another tote. "Oh, I've started screening heavily now. Which is why I hadn't been on a date in months before you. Trust me, Jax was threatened within an inch of his life if you turned out to be a troll."

Knox flashed that dimpled grin. "And is he safe? Have I proved I'm not a troll?"

Ruby cocked her head and grinned. "You're not too bad. If you hang that wreath on my door, I'll give you an extra cookie and see if Jax will deduct some on the rental of your monthly hangar fee."

"I'd put the wreath on the door anyway," he countered, then sent her a wink that had her toes curling into the plush rug. "But I'll take that cookie and you're more than welcome to try to haggle that fee down."

While he worked on the decorations, Ruby felt it best to keep her space and finish up the dessert. It was nearing eleven and she had no idea when he was leaving, but she wasn't ready for him to go. Even with the sexual tension and the giddiness in her belly, she wanted this night to go on forever. Even if nothing intimate came from this, she was having the best time.

It had been far too long since she'd had a rush of desire like this.

Come to think of it, she didn't know if she'd ever been hit this hard, this fast, with the power of another man. And it just so happened to be Knox. What were the chances of that?

Ruby was well aware Knox had thought about kissing her earlier. She'd seen that flare of interest in his eyes. But what had stopped him? Was it because she'd been Lydia's nurse? Was it because he truly wasn't looking for more? Maybe he only saw Ruby as a friend and had just gotten caught up in the moment.

Ruby wasn't one to play games or do that flirting that hinted she wanted something more. If Knox was interested in more, he'd let her know.

But that wouldn't stop her from wishing or wondering what his lips would feel like on hers. She was human, with needs and desires she tried to control, but sometimes she had no choice but to go along with her mind . . . her heart.

The front door closed and Knox came back into the kitchen. "It's getting colder out there."

"You're just in time to warm up with cookies, then."

She grabbed a pot holder and opened the wall oven just as the timer went off. After pulling out one pan, she slid another one in and reset the timer. Hopefully these turned out better than last time she attempted her mother's recipe, a few years ago.

"Do I have time to ice them or are they going straight to your mouth?"

Knox took a seat at the counter. "I'll make time for icing."

"They need to cool a little before I get them off

the pan. Plus, the icing would just run off if I put it on now."

His gaze met hers across the counter. That penetrating stare from those striking blue eyes had her feeling way too much, when there was obviously nowhere this could go. He'd made that clear.

Why, why, why did he have to have such power over her emotions? And how was he able to do such things when he'd not done a single thing?

"Dance with me while we wait."

His request caught her off guard. "Excuse me?"

Knox came to his feet and rounded the island, coming within a breath of her. "Dance with me. We're still on our date."

Ruby stared up at him, more than ready to have his hands on her, his arms around her. "To Christmas music?"

"It's a slow song and just instrumental. We've got the time, right?"

Who was she to say no to a hunky guy asking her to dance in her kitchen? This was by far the best blind date, or any date for that matter, that she'd ever had.

But, didn't dancing in the kitchen barefoot resemble something utterly intimate and . . . well, sexy? Because she was feeling like they were pushing the envelope of this friend zone and about to bust into the next level.

Pulling in a breath, Ruby reached out and wrapped her arm around his waist as he clasped her other hand in his. The second they were torso to torso, every single nerve ending in her sizzled. As corny and ridiculous as that sounded, there was no other way to describe the sensations spiraling through her.

Knox's large hand covered her back, making her feel feminine and protected. There was something so attractive about a man who possessed such power without throwing it around and shoving it in your face. Or maybe she found him so alluring because he was showing her with his giving actions just how good a man could be. He was proving to her that good guys still existed.

But he wasn't for her.

"We didn't get to dance at the restaurant, either," he murmured, his breath falling on her cheek. "I feel like I owe you another date."

Ruby was so glad he couldn't see her face because she was positive her smile was utterly ridiculous. After a moment, she eased her head back to look him in the eye as they continued to sway.

"Are you asking me out again?"

Knox tucked their joined hands against his chest. "Would you say yes if I was asking?"

"Is this as friends?"

Knox's lips thinned, the muscle in his jaw ticking. "That's all it can be."

Disappointment coursed through her, but she kept her emotions hidden. "Then I'm saying yes if you're asking."

A slow smile spread across his face as he continued to lead the dance. "I think this is going to be a Christmas to remember."

"I'm pretty sure we cannot do any more decorating." Ruby pulled her coat tighter around her and stared up at her house. "This is much more than I ever thought you'd do when you volunteered."

Knox shoved his hands in his pockets as he stood beside her, admiring their work. "Oh, there's always more decorating. Lydia used to string garland and lights on every doorway, around every spindle, across the mantel. Basically anywhere she could. We didn't need to use actual lights during the Christmas season."

"I used to be like that," Ruby murmured, recalling just two Christmases ago. "She sounds like she was an amazing lady."

"She was," Knox agreed. "It was nice to decorate again. I clearly didn't do much of that in the Navy and, honestly, I haven't done any since Lydia and I had our house. Our last Christmas together was in the hospital."

So maybe he wasn't saving her after all; perhaps they were healing each other. This was just another step in the process of moving forward.

"There are stores still open if you want to go get more lights or anything," he suggested as he glanced over. "We didn't do your back porch yet."

She turned and smacked his arm. "It's one in the morning."

That grin he flashed her way never failed to thrill her. "And here you just thought you were getting dinner."

Yet she'd gotten so much more. Dinner, home-made cookies, her house decorated, a toe-curling dance, and a man that she never expected in her life.

When she wrapped her arms around her waist, Knox pulled her against his side. The gesture was so simple, yet so intimate. They'd spent the entire evening together and now . . . well, probably they were drawing this memorable date to a close. What else could they do?

Okay, well, there was plenty they could do, but what else could they do and still keep this friend status in line?

Ruby turned her head slightly, inhaling that masculine scent, something woodsy from his cologne combined with the leather from his jacket.

"Are you smelling my armpit?" he asked.

Busted. Ruby cringed.

"Not your armpit." Not exactly. She couldn't help she was shorter than him and that's just where her face landed. "Whatever that cologne is, it's pretty amazing."

Knox chuckled, his body vibrating beneath her cheek. "I didn't realize you enjoyed it so much."

"I didn't either until I snuggled you," she laughed. "This is a little embarrassing, so let's pretend the last ten seconds didn't happen."

Knox eased back and turned to grip both her shoulders. The lights from her house illuminated his face and the bold blue of his eyes. Yeah, she never wanted him to leave, to bring their date to a close. Time seemed to stand still for them and she wanted to hold on just a little longer.

"I don't want to forget a second of this night," he told her as he stepped into her. "This has been the best time I've had since coming home."

Ruby couldn't help but laugh, probably more from nerves and arousal than actual humor. "Manual labor and having your date get a whiff of your armpit? You clearly need to get out more."

"I plan on it." His hands moved to frame her face. "I'm taking you out again."

"Maybe to a restaurant where the fire department doesn't have to be called," she joked.

His hand slid over her cheek. "Maybe I'll just cook for you at my place. Something a little more exciting than a frozen pizza."

When his eyes darted to her lips, the knot in her stomach tightened. "Are you getting ready to kiss me?"

"Thinking about it."

"I thought we were friends," she murmured as he continued to close the gap between them.

"Oh, I'm feeling friendly."

The next second his lips slid over hers. There was no rush, but the potency was no less powerful. Knox framed her face with his hands and completely took over every part of her with just one simple kiss.

Simple? No. How could standing on her sidewalk in the middle of the night kissing a man she hadn't seen in six years be simple? This night, this man couldn't be summed up with such a tame word. Everything about this situation was complex and confusing . . . yet oh so glorious, and she didn't care about the red flags waving around in her head. Knox was finally kissing her and she couldn't get close enough.

Knox shifted, his body molding against hers as he secured them even closer together. His lips continued to stroke hers as he lifted his head and changed his angle. Ruby gripped his shoulders and willingly opened for him. It had been such a long time since a man made her ache this way, made her want things she figured were never going to happen for her.

With his hands still on her face, Knox eased back

and rested his forehead against hers. Was he trying to catch his breath, too? Because she was pretty sure she didn't breathe through that entire kiss. Not to mention the fact she needed to continue leaning on him just a moment longer, until her legs were stronger.

"What about that friend rule?" she asked, hating that her thoughts slipped out of her mouth.

He let out a clipped laugh as he lifted his head to look in her eyes. "I'm still not looking for anything, especially because I'm probably not staying here. It wouldn't be fair to lead you on, but, I enjoyed our night and the kiss. I wouldn't mind kissing you again. Is there a label for that?"

"Confusion?" she asked, wrinkling her nose.

Knox dropped his hands to her shoulders, a much less intimate stance. "If this is too back and forth for you with the attraction and me telling you there can't be more, I would completely understand if you don't want to see me again."

Ruby shook her head, amazed he would even think such a thing. "Considering the insane dates I've had, I'll take your friendship and the kisses. I'll even take the kitchen fire."

Stepping back, Knox shoved his hands in his jacket pocket. "At least I rank above the guy who made a frozen pizza. My ego would be crushed if he beat me."

"Trust me, you rank above all the blind dates I've ever had."

"So you're not uncomfortable considering . . ."

Ruby crossed her arms over her chest. "I was when you first showed up, but it's interesting how our lives circled back around. I'm glad you're getting along so well."

"There was a time when I wasn't," he admitted, turning to look at her decorated house once again. "But, that's a story for another time, and I'd say we both need to get to bed."

"Wow, you jump from friendship to a kiss to the bed."

Knox threw her a side eye. "Separately," he amended. "I'm beat."

Ruby stifled a yawn and realized she'd been fine until just now. "So, when are you cooking for me?"

Knox shrugged. "Later today?" he suggested with a laugh.

"I'm off the next two days, so that works for me," she told him as they fell in step beside each other back to the house. "What should I bring?"

"Just yourself." He didn't hesitate in his response. "I'll take care of everything."

She started to reach for her front door when he stepped in front of her and opened it for her, gesturing her inside.

"I can't get used to this," she muttered as she went in. "Cooking me dinner, opening doors, decorating my house, and carrying heavy totes."

"You should get used to this because when I'm gone, you better expect your guy to be a gentleman or he's not worth your time."

When he was gone. Yes, that reminder needed to stay in the forefront of her mind to avoid heartache on down the road. Ruby was starting to see exactly what type of gentleman was worth her time, but he wasn't a long-term guy. Ruby settled into the notion that she was just going to have to enjoy Knox while he was here. Besides, it wasn't like she wasn't busy herself, right?

But this evening only solidified the fact that she did indeed want more. She wasn't filling the void from her family she'd lost. She had always wanted a family of her own.

Christmas was a time for miracles . . . so who knew what the next few weeks would hold.

Chapter Four

Knox jogged through the park and was just about to start cooling down when he spotted a familiar woman with an unfamiliar, feisty, oversized dog by the fountain.

His first instinct was to go to her aid, but then he started laughing. The dog jumped up, placing his bearlike paws on Ruby's shoulders, and proceeded to lick her face like she was his very best friend.

Crossing the paved path, Knox began laughing even harder before he reached her. Ruby's head snapped in his direction.

"He's new to the shelter," she explained, dodging the slobbery kisses. "And he's very loving."

Ruby's hands were full of chocolate fur and she seemed to love the mammoth as much as he loved her. Knox pulled in a deep breath of crisp air. He'd gotten in about ten miles and really needed to get home and shower, but suddenly he wasn't in such a hurry. His errands could wait. Since leaving her house last night—or early this morning—he'd thought of her more than he should.

"What's his name?" Knox reached up to pat the dog's head and was greeted when the dog turned to prop his paws on Knox's shoulders.

"Chance." She tried to pull him away, not having much luck. "Sorry, Knox."

Knox patted Chance. "He's fine. Just let him get some energy out."

"He really needs to learn not to maul people," she replied. "He was doing so well walking from the shelter to here, but that was only two blocks. I guess he couldn't take the excitement anymore. His owner was elderly and had to go live in a nursing home. No other family members wanted him. Poor guy."

Knox bent down onto one knee, easing Chance down with him. "You're a good boy, aren't you?"

He rubbed on the giddy dog for a bit before something struck him as odd. He glanced up to Ruby, who was shielding her face from the sun with her hand.

"Why don't you have a dog if you love them so much?"

"I work crazy hours," she replied. "I'd always wanted a dog, but my dad was allergic. Honestly, after he passed I considered it, but with living alone and never knowing if I'm going to have to pull a double shift . . . I've just never brought one home."

After a few minutes, the dog seemed to calm down. He'd stopped licking all over Knox's face and now all paws were on the ground. Slowly, Knox came to his feet, but made sure to keep one hand rubbing the dog's ear.

Ruby's smile was just as vibrant and breathtaking today. "You're good with animals."

"We always had dogs growing up," he explained.

"Once I settle down, one of the first things I plan on doing is seeking a shelter dog."

"They're the best pets."

She wrapped a portion of the leash around her wrist and kept a tight hold on her rambunctious friend.

"Do you have time to walk with us?" she asked, pulling him from his questioning thoughts.

He needed to shower, get to the store, and start making one hell of a dinner for her, but what would another few minutes be. He liked spending time with her and she looked just as sexy and beautiful today in her yoga pants and hoodie with her hair in a ponytail as she did last night in her dress and makeup.

Ruby was a vixen—there was no doubt about that. She could draw him in with the arc of a brow or the tilt of her head. And that smile . . . His heart kicked up a notch every time she flashed it his way. What man could deny her?

And that thought had jealousy sliding through him. The thought of her with another man didn't set well with Knox, at least not the image he'd conjured up. The fact that he was instantly jealous of a faceless man was rather telling, but he didn't want to access that area of emotions in his mind—not quite yet.

"Sure," he told her.

Knox fell into step beside her as she tried to maneuver Chance into some sort of pattern. But this St. Bernard mix didn't have a care in the world. He was just happy to be out in the fresh air.

"So do you always run in the mornings?" she asked as they rounded the fountain and took the path leading toward the tree-lined walkways.

"Always. It's a great stress reliever, plus it keeps me in shape."

"Maybe I should make time for a workout," she muttered, pulling back slightly on the leash.

Knox reached over and slid the leash from her hand and took it into his. "I think you're getting enough right now. Besides, you look fine . . . if that's why you were thinking you need to work out."

"I'm a woman. We always find something wrong with our bodies."

Knox glanced over at her. "There's not one thing wrong with your body, and I should know because you were plastered against mine last night."

Her mouth dropped open. "Excuse me? I believe you're the one who did the plastering."

He couldn't help but laugh as he shrugged. "Guilty."

And he planned on taking full advantage of this extremely odd friendship again. Kissing Ruby wasn't what he thought it would be. He figured a kiss was something he could handle. Nothing wrong with a little physical contact. But then he'd done it once, and all he could think of was how soon they could do it again. He hadn't slept well, not for planning and figuring out what to make for dinner. He wanted to impress her and he wanted to make sure she had just as good a time as last night.

Despite the emotional shock right at first, and the restaurant catching fire, that had been the best date he'd ever had. Ruby was a special woman; there was no denying that.

Fear held him back from ever seeking more from anyone. He'd vowed long ago never to put his heart on the line again because there was no way he could ever love another woman. He hadn't expected to care so much, though. Having Ruby reenter his life had seriously thrown him and his plans for a loop.

"So, if I bring wine for dinner, what do you prefer?" she asked. "Or are you more of a beer guy?"

"Honestly, I don't drink," he told her. "But you are more than welcome to bring wine."

"Oh, no. I didn't know. I'm sorry."

Knox held the leash in one hand and slid his other hand into hers. "Nothing to apologize for. I drank my fair share in the military. I just decided to become healthier now that I'm out, and that was one of the things I cut."

"But you still devour cookies?" she asked, quirking a brow.

Knox guided Chance back onto the path when he tried to head off onto the grass as a squirrel ran toward a tree. "Cookies are important and it's so rare that I have them."

"I can't just show up at your house empty handed."

He tried to think, but there wasn't anything that came to mind. "I'm cooking, I'm making dessert, and you are just going to show up and have a good time. No arguments."

She opened her mouth to say something else, but he squeezed her hand and guided her through the park. Ruby wised up and didn't say another word about dinner. They walked in silence and he wondered what she was thinking. Was she replaying that kiss? Was she wondering what tonight held?

Knox didn't recall wanting to impress anyone the way he wanted to impress Ruby. When he'd dated Lydia, they'd been so young, getting her attention and keeping her satisfied was pretty easy. What did he know now about this whole dating thing? Was it even fair to Ruby to drag this out? She was obviously a settling down type of woman and he'd already put a line in the proverbial sand, not allowing anyone to pull him over that long-term boundary again.

"What time should I be at your house?" she asked after several minutes.

Chance spotted a flock of birds and attempted to take off. Knox held tight to the leash and guided him back the way they came.

"Dinner will probably be ready closer to seven, but come over whenever."

Ruby reached for the leash, her hand gliding over his. "I'll come a little early. Thanks for helping me walk this big guy. I think he likes you."

Chance turned and reached one paw up, swatting at Knox's stomach as if to ask for more affection. There was no denying this dog was loving and absolutely adorable. If Knox were staying in Haven, he'd seriously consider adopting Chance.

"I better get him back," Ruby stated. "I have several more to walk before I clean some of the cages. See you this evening."

Knox didn't know how she juggled it all. And by "it all" he meant all of the lives, human and canine, that she sacrificed her life for. Did anyone truly appreciate her? Did anyone ever give back to her and make her take a break? Who pampered her?

Knox watched her walk across the street, picking up into a light jog to keep up with Chance. As she disappeared into the shelter, a wonderful idea crossed his mind.

He'd promised dinner, but there was no reason he couldn't throw in another little surprise.

* * *

Knox opened the door to his rental town house and greeted Ruby. As fine as the man looked in his long-sleeved black T-shirt and well-worn jeans, the aromas that hit her in the face were positively mouth-watering. He knew how to pack a punch between his looks and his cooking.

"Whatever you're making, I already want seconds," she told him as she stepped over the threshold with a bundle of bright red flowers in her hand. "These are for you."

Knox closed the door and took the bouquet. "Isn't the guy supposed to bring flowers?"

Ruby shrugged and turned to face him. "Nothing about our relationship seems traditional and you wouldn't let me bring food, so flowers it is."

He stared down at the bouquet, his eyes widening as if seeing them for the first time.

"You're not going to believe this." He clutched the flowers and shook his head with a slight laugh. "These were Lydia's favorite. I had them delivered to her grave every month while I was overseas."

Ruby's heart clenched. "Knox, I'm sorry. I didn't mean to bring up bad memories."

"Bad memories? I have amazing memories of her. It's nice to remember. You bringing these almost feels like a sign, you know?"

A sign of . . . what? That he should move on?

The man was beyond remarkable with the outlook he took on life and the recovery he'd made since losing his wife. "You must have done some serious counseling to have that attitude."

Knox held the flowers in one hand and wrapped his other arm around her shoulders as he led her into the living room. "I did do counseling, but I soon realized that Lydia wouldn't have wanted me to remember the bad times at the end. So I choose to focus on the best."

Ruby turned to face him, still in awe at how he'd circled back into her life and how he was seriously helping her heal a year after she'd lost her father. She firmly believed everything happened for a reason and she knew . . .

She pulled in a deep breath. He'd come into her life at this moment, but she couldn't say for sure why. Was it just to help her heal? Or was there to be more? Ruby needn't get her hopes up—he'd made things perfectly clear. But at the same time, she couldn't help it. She was human.

"Come on into the kitchen," he told her. "Dinner is just about ready."

"Whatever that aroma is, it's amazing."

As she passed through the living room, she noticed the leather couch, some weights in the corner by a treadmill, a few end tables, lamps, pictures on the walls. It was like he lived here, but not fully here. The pictures were floral prints and the lamps were fairly feminine, as were the throw pillows on the sofa and the rug.

"Did the place come furnished?" she asked.

He threw her a glance and a side grin. "The motif doesn't necessarily fit me, does it?"

Ruby merely shrugged as they rounded the corner to the small galley kitchen. There was a pass-through with a bar and stools.

"Do you need help?" she asked, standing in the doorway.

"If you want to grab a mason jar to put these flowers in, they're with the glasses by the fridge." He went to the oven and pulled out a glass dish. "Sorry, I don't keep vases on hand."

Something she should've thought of. But she figured flowers were at least a nice gesture to show him how much she appreciated him.

Ruby grabbed a mason jar from the cabinet and filled it with water. The stems were clearly too long for the jar, so she snapped them down to a shorter size and made a new arrangement.

"How long did you volunteer today?"

Picking up the jar of flowers, Ruby turned to figure out where to put it. "Until about three. We had two dogs get adopted out today. It's always so bittersweet. I'm happy they found their forever homes, but I miss them. Chance is still there even though I thought for sure one family was going to take him."

Knox readied their plates and took them to the small table in the dining area. Ruby followed and sat her bouquet right in the middle. Instant romantic dinner.

No. No romantic dinners. Just a dinner between friends. Friends who kissed. Friends who have seen each other two days in a row and have a good time and there just happens to be a sexual energy charging around them. Nothing to worry about.

"Is that chicken parmesan?" she asked as she stared down at the plates.

"It is." He rounded the table and pulled out the

white, wooden chair. "And there's bread I'll grab, too. Is sweet tea okay?"

She took a seat and glanced up at him. "Perfect."

He quizzed her about her day a little more and she found out he not only used his mother's recipe for dinner, but he'd made the noodles from scratch. Was this guy for real? Scratch? Who in the world had time for such things? She barely had time for *not* scratch dinners.

"You're lying."

He met her gaze across the table. "Do you think I need to lie to impress you at this point?"

Ruby swirled her fork for another bite of noodles. "No, but I cannot believe you're this talented in the kitchen."

"My mother insisted I be raised helping to cook and learning all she knew. She was Italian, by the way, so I do have a few tricks up my sleeve."

Swallowing her bite of chicken, noodles, and an amazing red sauce, Ruby replied, "God bless her. This is the best thing I've eaten in a long time."

Knox chuckled. "I haven't made it in years. Six, actually."

Not since Lydia. The words hung in the air just the same as if they'd been said aloud. So what did that mean that he'd opted to pull this recipe out now and fix this for her?

"It's not much fun cooking for one," she replied, wiping her mouth with her napkin. "It's cheaper to eat out or make a sandwich."

"It's cheaper for you when your dates pay for dinner, but you've been set up with jerks."

Ruby laughed as she picked up her tea glass. "That's a very good point."

There was so much she wanted to ask him about, but she wondered if she had the right to do so. They were friends, yes, but did that mean he wanted to open up to her?

"I don't want to pry, but can I ask why you haven't dated since you've been back? You said it had been two months."

Knox dropped his fork to his plate and eased forward on his forearms. "I haven't found anyone that I wanted to date. I haven't been looking, either. I know I'm not staying here and I'm not planning to settle down again, so dating didn't seem like a priority."

Not settling down. Not staying. The words went into her head, but her heart wasn't quite grasping. How could there be such an emotional pull when the end result would only be heartache on her end? Was life this cruel?

"Why did you agree when Jax offered?"

"Honestly, I'm not sure," he stated. "I guess I figured what would it hurt. I planned on being up front with whomever I went out with, but then it ended up being you and I was a little relieved."

"Relieved?" That hadn't been her first response upon seeing him when she opened her door.

With a grin, he eased back in his seat. The wide shoulders and broad chest hid the entire chair. "You already knew my past, so I didn't have to tell you all about it in the get to know you stage."

Well, there was that. "I still don't know you very well."

When his dark brow quirked and his eyes dropped to her lips, Ruby's entire body tingled just the same as if he'd reached across the table and touched her . . . or captured her mouth again.

"I bet you do," he countered. "Think of some things you know about me that you didn't know when we met six years ago."

Ruby slid her thumb over the condensation on her glass. Had it only been a little over twenty-four hours since she opened her door to him? Her mind traveled through the last day and all she'd experienced.

"You're an amazing cook," she started, her mind rolling through the list. "You can decorate for Christmas like a pro. You love animals and you're a pretty good kisser."

His eyes widened. "Pretty good? You call that pretty good?"

Fine, their kiss had been toe-curling and palm-dampening, but she didn't figure she should throw those terms around to her *friend*.

Ruby shrugged and came to her feet. "Pretty good," she confirmed as she picked up her plate to take it into the kitchen.

She put her dish in the sink and was immediately caged in. Knox's firm chest rested against her back, those thick, muscular arms settled on either side of her. Heart beating quicker than ever, she tipped her head back to attempt to meet his gaze.

"Pretty good," he muttered a second before his lips descended onto hers.

Ruby shifted and instantly found herself being turned by strong hands. Knox had plunged one hand through her hair and the other was on her back, pulling her in closer. This kiss was nothing like the sweet, sultry kiss of last night. No, this one held promise and passion and everything she knew he could deliver.

And there was nothing she could do but hold on for the ride and savor every blessed moment. There had been so many belly-tingling moments since yesterday, Ruby had lost count.

A low moan escaped her and she should have been embarrassed at the way she was clinging to him, but then she realized his hands had traveled and were gripping her waist. His fingers eased beneath the hem of her shirt and just that simple, harmless touch set her on fire. She'd been playing with the matches since she opened the door.

Knox lifted his head and Ruby was just about to say something—what, she didn't know—when he dove back in for more.

Yes. This was exactly what she thought. He wasn't immune to the attraction between them. He could give all the well-meaning speeches he wanted, but they were all for naught. His body told her more than any of his words ever could.

Knox's teeth nipped gently on her bottom lip before he eased back just enough to disconnect their mouths. His warm breath came out in pants just as wild as hers. The man made her feel reckless, needed, desired, and absolutely glorious.

Never before had she experienced such an onslaught of emotions.

"Don't tell me that was just pretty good," he murmured against her lips, his forehead pressed to hers. "I pulled a moan out of you."

Not to mention she was still clutching his biceps like he was her only lifeline and the only reason she was still remaining upright when her legs had turned to complete jelly.

"Did you only kiss me to prove a point?" she asked.

Knox lifted his head. Those dark, heavy-lidded eyes told her all she needed to know before he opened his mouth.

"That was one of the reasons," he admitted.

"And the other?"

"Because every time you're near me, I want to kiss you. So I did."

Well, at least he was honest. Ruby went up on her toes and nipped at his lips.

"What are you doing?" he whispered.

"I wanted to kiss you." She repeated his words back to him. "So I am."

Chapter Five

Five days had passed since Knox had cooked Ruby his mother's recipe in his kitchen. And for the past five days he'd seen her every day.

Knox knew full well he was teetering on a thin line. For a man who didn't want any type of a relationship, he was doing a poor job of following his own rules.

But he honestly didn't care. He hadn't felt this alive, this attracted to anyone since Lydia. He had no idea what was going to happen, no clue as to when he'd actually leave for Atlanta, but for now, he was going to enjoy Ruby because he deserved some happiness . . . and she made him happier than he'd been in years.

Her work schedule was grueling. He'd figured that out the first day she'd gone back. How that woman managed everything and still remained awake was beyond him. She was like a machine always on the go and only rested when she had to refuel to get back up and start all over. It was tiresome just trying to keep up.

Ruby had worked until midnight last night and said she'd be free about two in the afternoon once she got some sleep. Knox waited until two-thirty before knocking on her door. Today was a special surprise. The past few days when she'd gotten off work, he'd brought food over and they'd watched movies, laughed, talked.

But today he wanted to mix it up a bit and show her a little more of his life. Again, what was he doing? Pulling her deeper into his world was only adding another layer to this already deep bond. Honestly, though, he didn't care. Ruby was special and he was anxious to show her something.

When she opened her door, she looked just as refreshed as ever. If someone didn't know her, they'd never guess she'd spent all night saving lives.

His chest tightened. There was so much irony in this entire situation, but he couldn't dwell on that right now. He couldn't go back in time.

"Come on in," she told him as she turned to lead the way.

"Actually, why don't you grab your shoes?" he suggested.

Ruby glanced over her shoulder. "Where are we going? I'm not exactly dressed for an outing."

That's one of the reasons he found her so amazing. She was comfortable around him with her jeans and simple V-neck tee. With her hair in a ponytail, she looked ten years younger than what she was. So far he'd seen her in a variety of states and every single one appealed to him.

"I promise, you look perfect for what I have in mind." He did step into the house and close the door, but he remained in the foyer. "Just grab some shoes and a light jacket."

Knox waited in the doorway, eager to get their day

started. He knew she'd have to be back by this evening to get sleep before heading back into work. He intended to make the most of their situation.

When she came back, she still had her brows drawn in, her eyes locked onto his. "You're making me nervous. When are you going to tell me what we're doing?"

He reached for her hands, because he missed her touch and he wanted to feel her. "Are you afraid of heights?"

Ruby stared at him a second before her brows rose and her mouth dropped open. "Are you taking me flying?"

Knox merely smiled.

"Really?" she squealed. "I've never been in a plane before."

"Never? You live in Haven and you've never taken advantage of the airport? You're not afraid, are you?"

Lydia had been terrified of flying. He hated comparing the two women, but it was difficult not to when he'd only had this strong of a pull twice in his life. Lydia had been his everything. Their slow romance had evolved into a short marriage.

Suddenly, this fast-paced whirlwind he was in with Ruby was just as intense and exhilarating as his marriage. How the hell had this happened? Hadn't he warned himself not to get too involved? One day had led to another and here they were . . . and he wasn't about to call it quits.

At some point though, he'd have to make some major decisions regarding his future. Call it quits and walk away from her, or figure out what exactly they were doing with each other. Atlanta wouldn't wait on his answer forever. He'd been in contact with an old

Navy buddy and had lined up something working for a company that specialized in the engineering of new jets and the dynamics of state-of-the-art models. He was fortunate to have something so meaningful and perfect for him fall into his lap.

Yet he still hadn't agreed to the position.

"You okay?" she asked.

Knox pulled himself from the inevitable future decisions and kissed her hand. "Let's go. You're going to love this."

He purposely didn't answer her, but she grabbed her keys from the hook and followed him out the door. From her enthusiasm, he couldn't help but smile. This would be a memorable Christmas for her. He'd make sure she didn't have time to grieve, but to remain positive and happy.

And so what if he wanted to kiss her? What was the big deal in fantasizing about more? Ruby knew where he stood and she was well aware he wasn't staying. Because he wasn't. He'd be telling the firm he was taking the job . . . just as soon as he got around to calling them.

The more leaving crossed his mind, the less appeal it held.

Knox helped her into his truck and decided he didn't have to make any life-altering decisions right now. Nothing would happen until after Christmas anyway, so it would be best to just enjoy the day, the woman.

He couldn't wait to get her in the air and see her reaction to his favorite pastime.

* * *

"This is insane." Ruby adjusted the mic by her mouth as she stared down at the patchwork-like view. "Everything is so tiny. Isn't it strange how little this makes you feel in the grand scheme of things?"

Knox's soft chuckle came through the headset. "There are no problems up here. I leave everything down there."

Ruby shifted in her seat to face him. "Is that why you went into the military? To get away from your problems?"

He stared out over the horizon as silence filled the tiny cockpit. "That's exactly why I joined. I'd always wanted to, but then I met Lydia and fell in love, so we married. I knew she was sick when we married, but we didn't know if she'd get better, so we jumped right in. Obviously I couldn't leave her, so after she passed, I fulfilled a dream and escaped my pain. Or tried to anyway."

Ruby couldn't imagine the pain of finding the love of your life and then experiencing such a devastating loss. That whole ordeal of seeing Knox and Lydia had changed something in Ruby as a person and a nurse. She knew she wanted that kind of love in her life one day, but she also knew she needed to remove herself from that type of atmosphere where she'd be subjected to getting emotionally involved with the families. Being a nurse was emotional regardless, but she had to guard her heart where she could.

"And did that work?" she asked. "Running away."

"No. I ended up seeing a counselor and that's what helped. The pain is something I've learned to live with and I know that Lydia would want me to move on. We actually talked about that before she passed, because we knew the outcome."

Ruby swallowed the lump in her throat. "You loved her so much."

"I did," Knox replied. "We had a good life and I can't complain, but I always thought marriage would last longer, you know?"

Yeah, she did know. She wanted a marriage that lasted forever. She didn't fantasize about the dream wedding; she daydreamed about the happily ever after portion. So many people put too much focus on the wedding—the perfect dress, the right location, the flowers, the seating charts. Ruby didn't care if she got married in her living room so long as she was loved and the marriage lasted.

"So tell me about why you're not seeing anyone."

His voice cut through her thoughts and Ruby shifted again to look back down at the strip of blue that was the winding river a few towns over from Haven.

"I'm seeing you," she joked.

"True. But before I came onto the scene. I know you dated jerks, but I can't believe there's not an eligible doctor at the hospital who hasn't flirted with you."

Ruby rolled her eyes and threw him a look. "You're kidding, right? Yeah, they flirt, but they're also married, which is an absolute no from me. I feel sorry for their wives."

"Is that why you switched departments?" he asked.

The plane banked slightly as they turned. Ruby loved the thrill that shot through her with each movement. No wonder Knox adored this sport. She could become completely addicted to flying. And with the airport practically in her backyard, she should take advantage of this. There was probably quite a bit in her little town that she needed to take advantage of but never had time for.

The new women's-only resort and spa that had opened last Christmas was thriving and all the buzz was about the men who opened it in memory of their late sister. Perhaps she'd call and see about a massage on her next day off.

"Ruby." Knox's voice came through the headset. "Why did you switch departments? Was it an issue with a coworker?"

If the answer were that simple, she would've responded the first time he asked. She'd always prided herself on honesty and she didn't see the need to lie now.

"I switched departments when I lost a patient who touched me." She shifted her gaze from the picturesque view to Knox's profile. "She was a young wife and had her whole future ahead of her."

His audible swallow echoed in her ears.

"I'm sorry," she told him. "You asked."

His knuckles turned white as he gripped the control. "I didn't realize she had such an impact on you."

"She was my first terminal patient and I was fresh from nursing school. I got to know her, got to know you, though I know you probably don't remember much about me from that time."

"Not much," he admitted. "That's a chapter in my life that's a blur when I look back on it. I was so focused on making her final days perfect. But I remember you. You were the most compassionate nurse we had. You were so attentive to her needs and mine. You worked harder than anyone we had the entire time we were there. I actually sent a note to the CEO about the care you provided."

Ruby jerked in her seat. "You did? My word, Knox. You'd just lost your wife."

"I sent it after the funeral. You know, when I was alone with my thoughts in that house and going out of my mind. I needed to do something and you deserved the praise."

There was so much to take in about his statement—a statement and action he was so cavalier about. Through his pain he made a point to remember the care his wife had received. That would explain why Ruby had been given such high praise when she asked for the transfer to the ER. She'd had no idea.

And now she was getting swept up with a man who clearly loved his late wife more than anything. Why did Ruby even think for one minute that she could penetrate that strong a bond? Why did she let herself hope? Someone like Knox loved with his whole heart. Even though he seemed to be doing so well, that didn't mean he'd make room for anyone else in his life.

"We better get you back so you can get rested for work," he told her as he banked the plane and turned toward Haven.

Ruby fisted her hands in her lap as the harsh reality settled in. She had two options right now: she could call it quits and go back to her life the way she knew it, or she could enjoy the time she had with Knox while he was in town.

As much as her heart would hurt in the end, Ruby knew there was no way she would stop seeing him, even if it was on a friend level.

"Maybe we'll get in another flight before I leave," he told her. "I plan on keeping my plane here until I figure out what to do in Atlanta."

"Sounds good," she lied as the wheels hit the runway.

"Maybe I should take you to dinner in this," he added. "You can pick anywhere you want."

Okay, now fate was just rubbing it in.

He circled the runway, slowly bringing the plane to a stop. They put their headphones on the controls and Knox hopped out before coming around to assist her.

When her hand slid into his as she stepped down, she tried not to shiver. Every time he touched her the jolts were just as potent as the first time. Why, why, why did it have to be this man?

"Hey, guys."

Ruby turned to see Jackson Morgan walking with his daughter, Piper. They were crossing the grassy path that led to one of the hangars. Well, Jax was walking. Piper was skipping and holding on to her father's hand. Her little ponytails bounced against the side of her head and Ruby didn't think this little girl could get any more adorable.

"Hey, man." Knox reached out to Jax as he neared and the two shook hands. "You all going up?"

"We are," Jax confirmed, glancing to his daughter, who eagerly nodded her head. "We have a pretty free day and Piper planned it for us. Now we're just trying to beat the rain. I saw the forecast and it looks like it might just miss us, but we're going to hang around and see."

Ruby smiled down at Piper. "I just took my very first flight. I bet this isn't your first. You're probably a pro by now, aren't you?"

Piper's mouth dropped. "Your first? I've been up like a gazillion times."

Laughing, Ruby nodded. "I'd say that's not too far from the truth with your daddy owning the airport."

"Part owner," he replied.

Ruby forgot Jax was part owner with the late owner's daughter. Granted the woman had been MIA since they graduated high school, so Ruby didn't know how much of a partner she was.

"Well, we need to get going," Knox said. "Great to see you."

Jax's eyes went from Knox to Ruby, back to Knox. "Looks like things are working out."

"We're just friends," Ruby was quick to say, and quick to remind herself.

Jax's lips twitched and he nodded. "Okay, then. Good to see you both."

Piper waved bye as they headed into the hangar.

When Ruby turned to face Knox, he was staring at her, his mouth in a frown, his eyes . . . Honestly, she couldn't read what was in his eyes.

"What is it?"

He stared at her for a minute before he spoke. "Why don't you head on into the lounge. I'll get the plane put away and meet you there shortly."

"Something's wrong," she told him.

Knox shook his head and started back toward the plane. "I won't be long."

Ruby watched his back as he walked away from her. Something had happened, something he obviously didn't want to talk about. He'd shut down on her and that was the first time she'd witnessed that type of response from him.

As she made her way to the lounge area inside the main building, she wondered what had happened during their flight. Had he been thinking like she had? Had the dynamics of their relationship been more than he'd originally thought?

All of this uncertainty could honestly drive her out of her mind. But Ruby needed to guard her heart above all else or she could end up seriously hurt.

Chapter Six

What the hell am I so upset about? Knox asked himself. *I'm the one who put the restrictions on this relationship. I'm the one who insisted that anything more than a friendship is impossible.*

Yet the second Ruby had told Jax that they were just friends, Knox had the sudden urge to hit something . . . mainly his past self. She had been quick to answer, which told him she was either in denial about the amount of chemistry sizzling between them or she was perfectly content in the friend zone.

And from the way she kissed him the other day, he didn't think that was the case at all.

He stepped outside and closed the hangar door, taking a minute to collect his thoughts. There was no reason to lie to her when she'd asked what was wrong, so he completely dodged the question altogether. He hadn't been sure how to respond because he wasn't even sure of his own thoughts.

Knox wanted Ruby. That was pretty much the bottom line and the crux of the entire situation.

But what happened if she fell for him and he

couldn't commit? That may have sounded egotistical, but all of this wasn't about him. He cared for Ruby, more than he thought he would, and he worried she'd get hurt if he found out that he couldn't move on . . . not in that way. Hell, he had no clue if he could emotionally invest in a woman the way she deserved. He hadn't tried since losing Lydia and he certainly didn't want to make Ruby his experiment to see if his feelings still worked.

On a groan, Knox raked his hands through his hair. What was he going to do?

Before he could have that mental pep talk with himself, raindrops hit his face. So much for that nice day and that sunshine that had been out moments ago. Jax hadn't taken off yet; most likely he and Piper were still in the other hangar.

Running through the rain, Knox headed to the main office area. Ruby wasn't inside in the lounge, she was standing beneath the overhang watching him. A worried look on her face was all the proof he needed that he'd handled things badly. He never wanted her hurt, and he sure as hell never wanted to be the cause of the pain.

Knox stopped just beneath the sheltered covering and shook the water from his body. He raked a hand over his wet hair and met her gaze.

"I can pull the truck close to the front if you want to go through the building so you don't get soaked."

Ruby reached up, her palm flattening against his cheek. "What happened between the flight and now?"

Uncertainty formed like a ball in his throat and he attempted to find the words. Nothing came to him.

Well, several things came to mind, but none of them would help this immediate situation.

Knox did the only thing he could think of. He reached out, snaking one arm around her waist and plunging the other one into her hair. Then he captured her lips.

This. This is what felt right. Words were meaningless and just jumbled up an already complex situation. He wanted to feel her, taste her. Consume her.

Ruby wrapped her arms around his neck and threaded her fingers through his hair. She opened for him, arched against him. This was so much more than a friendship. He knew it, she knew it. But right now, he didn't want to dissect the situation, he wanted to feel.

The sound of a metal hangar door sliding pulled Knox from the moment. They were out in the open where Jax or Piper could easily see them. For someone who wanted to keep this light and simple, he was doing a poor job of proving that.

"Did you kiss me to shut me up?" she asked, wiping her thumb across her bottom lip.

Knox watched her movement, his body heating all over again. "I kissed you because I wanted to. We've been over this."

Ruby tipped her head and sighed. "We have, but you keep putting this wall between us and I honestly don't know what's going on."

Yeah, he wasn't too sure, either.

"Can you give me some time?" he asked her. Even that question surprised him. "I don't know what I'm doing and I can't have you hurt. I just . . . I can't."

Above all else, that was imperative. Ruby needed to come out on the other side with her heart fully intact.

She took a step back and gave a clipped nod. "I don't want you to feel pressured. My feelings are growing, I won't lie. But you can't let that hinder your life. You either feel something for me or you don't."

Rain beat down on the metal overhang. The sound of Piper squealing in the background and Jax laughing had Knox wondering if this was the best place for this all-important conversation.

"We need to go."

Ruby's shoulders fell, her lids lowered as she turned and started heading to the back door of the building. His silence had hurt her when he'd just preached to himself how much she needed to remain safe.

Just as she reached for the handle, Knox couldn't bear the tension anymore.

"I feel, Ruby. I feel more than I ever thought I would again."

She opened the door and went in without even glancing back, without a word to acknowledge him speaking, and he wondered if she even heard him over the pounding rain.

Ruby shoved her key in the door to her house and cursed herself for being a fool. She'd known going into this exactly how much Knox had loved his wife, and she'd known full well how determined he was to move on and keep any type of intimacy at a distance.

They hadn't spoken on the drive home. She wasn't sure what to say so she just let the awkward silence settle between them like an unwanted third party.

Just as she pushed the door open, a firm hand gripped her shoulder.

"Wait, Ruby."

She stepped inside, ignoring his plea. Of course he followed her. Ruby toed off her shoes and set her keys on the accent table inside the foyer. She swiped the rain from her face before turning to Knox.

He stood with his back at the closed door, raindrops covered his shirt, his face, his hair. Those muscular forearms glistened with moisture. Ruby scolded herself. Now was not the time to get swept away by his ridiculously good looks or how her stomach knotted at the idea of him leaving Haven and of her never seeing him again.

"Look, I know we never claimed this would be more than a friendship," she started, needing him to know that she understood. "I can't help how I feel and I didn't mean to let my emotions . . ."

She shook her head and turned toward the living room. The festive tree in the corner mocked her with all the twinkling lights and glittery ornaments. She had nobody to blame but herself in this situation.

Hands gripped both her shoulders and Ruby found herself being pulled back against Knox's firm chest. She closed her eyes and willed the pain away. Now he was only giving her pity comfort because he was trying to let her down easy. How mortifying.

"Ruby." Knox's breath tickled the side of her face as he leaned into her. "I've given you the impression that I don't care for you."

Ruby pulled in a shaky breath. "I'm well aware you care for me," she replied. "I can tell by the way you're treading so carefully now that you don't want to hurt me."

"Never." He shifted her so she faced him, then he

slid his hands over her jawline and held her in place. "I'd never purposely hurt you. Which is why I'm struggling here."

She could see that struggle. She could practically feel his frustration rolling off him in waves. Still, she couldn't coddle him because she'd been playing by his rules. He'd set up all the restrictions in the beginning and suddenly he seemed angry about it . . . but not angry enough to admit he cared for her as so much more than a friend.

"You don't have to—"

"I do," he retorted, giving her a slight shake. "I need you to understand that you drive me out of my mind."

Okay, not the approach I thought he'd take.

"I swore I wouldn't get emotionally attached to anyone again and then you opened the door," he went on. "You can't possibly know how much I wish I could have more with you."

He rested his forehead against hers and sighed. "But I'm terrified," he whispered.

Those three words painted a much clearer picture for her. He'd moved on, sure. He'd gone through the motions of day-to-day living, but he hadn't fully let himself feel in six years. That amount of time in and of itself proved just how broken he'd been.

Knox eased back slightly, his eyes searching hers. "I want so much, but if I take everything and this ends in heartache, I won't be able to handle it. You have to understand, Ruby."

She reached up and gripped his wrists. "I understand that we're never promised another day. I see that often enough at work and I've experienced it in my personal life—so have you. I know that when I want something, I don't let fear get in my way because I could be missing out on the greatest thing—"

His mouth crushed hers. There was no other way to describe it. It was almost as if he'd snapped and couldn't stand it another second.

Knox slid his hands through her damp hair. Ruby flattened her palms against his chest, then curled her fingertips against his T-shirt. He walked her backward until her legs hit the sofa. When she fell onto the cushions, Knox stared down at her, his eyes full of desire and passion. Ruby had never, ever had anyone look at her like this before. Her entire body shivered.

"Knox . . ."

He sank down on his knees before her and settled between her parted legs. Gripping her waist, he pulled her to the edge of the sofa. Heavy lids partially masked that flare of need, but he couldn't hide it completely.

"I'm done denying this," he murmured, his eyes dropping to her lips. "If you want me to go, I will."

Ruby reached up to grip his shoulders, then closed the gap to nip at his lips. "Stay," she murmured, arousal spiraling through her.

She didn't care she should be resting before her shift; she could nap tomorrow after work. Right now she wanted Knox and he was here. He was opening himself to her in a way she never thought would happen. She'd be a fool to turn him away.

Without warning, Knox lifted her in his arms and headed toward the steps. "Bedroom up here?" he asked.

"You can't carry me up these stairs," she protested, smacking his shoulder.

The smile that spread across his lips only added to her desire. Anticipation coiled low in her belly and she knew this wasn't something she wanted to spend her time arguing about. If he wanted to carry her to bed, à la Rhett Butler, who was she to stop him?

Ruby laced her fingers behind his neck and leaned her head against his shoulder. "Top of the stairs. First room on the right."

He wasted no time climbing the steps and entering her room. Her immediate thought was the disarray of her bed. Had she left her bras and underwear all over the place? Was the bed even made? Would he trip over the basket of laundry that still needed to be put away?

Seriously? She was thinking of the state of her room when she was finally in Knox's arms, finally going to bed with him?

When he set her on her feet at the foot of the bed, he wasted no time in capturing her lips, thrusting his hands in her hair, and arching her back. The man knew what he wanted and the fact he wanted her with such conviction had a whole new level of desire pumping through her.

Knox eased back just enough to grip the hem of her shirt and strip it up and over her head. She hadn't been with someone in so long, insecurities slithered between them. Ruby crossed her arms over her chest, but Knox immediately pulled them away, taking her hands behind her back and gripping her wrists with one hand.

"We're beyond hiding from each other."

He released her long enough to reach behind his neck and tug his shirt off. He flung the unwanted item to the side, never taking those mesmerizing eyes off her.

Part of her wanted to say something to take the tension away, but the other part didn't want words to interfere with this moment. She wanted just to feel with her heart, her hands. Words had no place here.

Knox closed the gap between them and yanked the snap on her jeans. Glancing down, she trembled at the sight of his large, tan hand against her pale abdomen. She sucked in a breath as his knuckles brushed against her heated skin.

And as much as that was all glorious, Ruby couldn't help but admire his perfectly toned chest, shoulders, and abs. He didn't get that way from sitting in a cockpit the entire time he'd been in the military.

When her eyes met his once again, something crackled between them. There was a charge she couldn't explain, but in the next minute they were in a frenzy of shedding clothes and stealing kisses. Knox pulled protection from his wallet and covered himself.

As soon as they were both bare, Knox lifted her and settled her back onto the bed. He followed her down and Ruby relished in his weight pressing into her.

He rested his forearms on either side of her head and stared down at her. "Ruby . . ."

Yeah. She knew. He couldn't make promises. She covered his lips with her fingertip and shifted so he was settled perfectly between her thighs.

When he joined their bodies, Ruby couldn't stop the groan from escaping her. Her body arched . . . her hands curled around his shoulders . . . their bodies moved so perfectly together.

Knox slid his lips over her exposed neck as he

murmured her name over and over. Ruby trailed her fingertips down his back, needing to feel all of him, wanting this moment to last forever.

Darkness settled into the room, blanketing them in a euphoric atmosphere. It was almost as if nothing else existed—actually in her world, nothing else did.

Ruby's body tightened. She closed her eyes and tipped her head back as waves of pleasure washed over her. Knox muttered something she couldn't make out just as his body stilled against hers. Ruby wrapped her arms around him as her body settled.

Knox dropped his head beside hers, his breathing just as ragged as her own. But he'd mentally withdrawn. The rigid back was a pretty telling sign that he wasn't relaxed as one normally is after intimacy.

He shifted off her and moved to sit on the edge of the bed. A chill instantly covered her, leaving her cold and alone—two things that definitely shouldn't accompany them to the bed.

"I'll get going so you can rest before work."

Was he kidding? Did he honestly believe she could rest now? Her body was revved up for one thing, and another, she wanted to know why he was having the obvious regret.

"Is this how you're going to be?" she asked, needing to call him on this behavior. She understood that he was conflicted, but she also needed him to be fully aware that she had feelings, too.

Even in the darkness, Ruby caught the way his silhouette showcased those tense shoulders. "I'm not trying to be anything," he replied. "You have to work later."

She reached across the bed and clicked on the

accent lamp. The harshness from the light had her blinking.

"So, what? Was this just you testing the waters?"

He pushed to his feet and started gathering his clothes. "I've been with people since Lydia. So you weren't an experiment."

Ruby yanked the yellow sheet up to her chest. "And how many of those women did you care about the way you say you care for me?"

Knox clutched his shirt in his hands and finally met her gaze. "None."

"Exactly. So why don't you stop pushing me away and just stay for a while."

He stared at her for so long, Ruby was convinced he was going to give in and toss his clothes to the side.

"I can't," he whispered. "This was more than . . ."

Shaking his head, he turned and started for the door, his clothes in hand. Ruby sat in her bed, watching as he clearly battled some internal demon that he refused to let her see.

He paused in the doorway. "You're too important to me, Ruby. Too important for me to screw this up, and if I stay, that's exactly what I'd do."

And then he walked out. The bedroom door closed. She heard him in there for about a minute or two, then he headed down the steps and out the front door.

Still she sat. Her body humming from their love-making, yet her heart breaking because he'd admitted just how much he cared for her, but he wasn't quite ready to fully open himself up to the chance that something beautiful could grow from this. He was running and didn't even realize it. He was using the excuse that he didn't want to hurt her, but not staying and facing the issue was hurting so much more.

Ruby fell back against the pillows, inhaling Knox's familiar masculine scent. He'd only been in her bed a short time and had already left his imprint.

Ironically he'd been in her life a short time as well, and had imbedded himself into her heart.

Chapter Seven

Even flying wasn't helping him clear his head.

Knox taxied to a stop after taking a long flight to try to make sense of his life. He'd left Ruby's bed four days ago and hadn't seen her since. Oh, he'd texted her because he wasn't a jerk. Well, he wasn't a total jerk. He was confused as hell and didn't want to approach her until he had his head on straight.

Sleeping with Ruby had completely muddled everything in his mind. The attraction had been there from the moment she opened her door to their blind date. Then the uncertainty had settled in and he'd questioned whether he should be having such strong feelings again. He wondered if seeing her had just made memories of Lydia rush to the forefront and jumble up his mind.

Knox glanced to the vacant seat beside him. He didn't even have to close his eyes to remember Ruby's excitement over her first flight. She'd been like a little kid, all smiles. He'd given her that and she'd shown him how easy it could be to care again. To, dare he say, love again.

He stared down the runway as another plane was set to take off. These past four days had been boring, full of doubts and fears and a whole host of emotions he wanted nothing to do with. No matter the emotion, though, his life came down to two things: the job in Atlanta or Ruby here in Haven.

How crazy was this? He'd only been seeing her for two weeks. Less than, actually. Christmas was tomorrow and here he sat all alone and wondering what to do with his life, his future.

But he'd known Ruby for so much longer than two weeks. She'd been there at the absolute lowest point in his life. She was caring with her patients, loving with the animals at the shelter, and determined to show him that life didn't always provide second chances, but when it did, perhaps you should perk up and take notice.

Knox raked a hand through his hair. What was he supposed to do? Could he actually give up the future he'd started to finally set in place in Atlanta? After six years of being a widower, he'd come to grips with the fact he should put down roots somewhere and start over. Was he really willing to give that sure thing up on a risk that might end in heartbreak? He'd barely survived the brokenness after Lydia and here he was considering putting everything on the line again.

Jax walked from the hangar to the side entrance where his office was located. The man was raising a little girl all on his own because his wife had literally just walked out one day. Knox wondered if Jax would give love another go. Would he take that terrifying leap?

The more Knox thought, the more he knew what

he should do. This was crazy. He had to be out of his ever-loving mind. Yet there was really only one decision. All along the answer had been there, but he'd needed time. He'd needed to clear his head and attempt to process all of this unexpectedness.

A wide smile spread across his face. There was only one way to go about this and he had just the solution. He only prayed his plan would flawlessly fall into place.

Her first Christmas Eve service in years had been absolutely beautiful. The candlelight, the music, the smiles on faces, and the eagerness in children's eyes . . . yet through all of that Ruby had felt utterly alone.

She'd been given the night off and she didn't want to sit at home. There were too many memories of Knox all throughout her cottage, from the kitchen where he baked her mother's cookies, to the tree and decor he'd insisted on putting up, to her bedroom.

For the past four nights she'd slept in the guest room because she simply couldn't bring herself to lie on her bed, not when it still smelled like him.

For nearly two weeks she'd tried to remind herself that he was not staying, that he was never going to fall for someone like he had his wife, and that she was not the one for him. Her heart completely ignored every single warning.

She pulled her car into the garage and grabbed her purse. Ruby had opted to wear the emerald sheath she'd worn for their date. She'd also strapped on the same new shoes. Part of her tried to tell herself that it was her favorite outfit because it wasn't scrubs or sweats, but she knew the truth. She'd worn this because she'd loved the way Knox had looked at her, the way he could make her feel beautiful and special without saying one word.

The twinkling lights on her house were an ever-present reminder of the man who helped her through her first Christmas without her father. But now all the festive decorations seemed to be mocking her. Would her neighbors think she was nuts if she opted to start taking things down?

Perhaps she could start inside tonight and work on the outside tomorrow. She needed to do something to work off her frustrations, and if she kept eating cookie dough, this dress would have to be donated.

Ruby let herself inside the back door and dropped her purse and keys on the small breakfast table. She reached back and started pulling the bobby pins from her hair, setting them on the table as well. She'd just started raking her fingers through her strands to let her hair down when her doorbell rang.

Please, please, don't let this be carolers. She was so not in the mood to hear "Jingle Bells" or any other cheery song.

The sun had set and it was nearing seven. She'd gone to the early service at the church, but still, who just dropped by on Christmas Eve?

When she glanced out her front window and spotted a familiar truck in her drive, her heart kicked up. What was he doing here? She hadn't seen him in days, though he'd sent a few messages just to say hi or ask how her day was. He'd kept the line of communication open, but not nearly like it had been.

She shook the rest of her hair out, realizing it probably looked like a knotted mess, and headed to the door. With a shaky hand, she smoothed down her dress and pulled in a deep breath.

Ruby flicked the dead bolt and opened the door. The fact that Knox stood at her door was shock enough, but the fact he had a gigantic dog at his side was laughable.

"Can we come in?" Knox asked.

Without a word, Ruby stepped to the side and gestured them in. After closing the door, she turned to face them and got a good look at the dog.

"Wait," she said, crossing the room. "Is this . . . ?"

Knox nodded. "Chance."

Her eyes darted from Chance back up to Knox. "You adopted him?"

When he nodded, tears pricked her eyes. Chance leaped up and mauled her shoulders with those massive paws just as he'd done in the park when they were out for a walk.

"We're going to look into obedience school." Knox laughed as he eased Chance off her.

"I can't believe you got him," she cried as she followed the dog down and buried her face in his fur.

When she glanced up at Knox, he was looking down at her with uncertainty in his eyes. She had no clue what this meant, but he'd come to her house for a reason.

"Did you come here just to show me Chance?" she asked as she stood straight up.

"He's part of the reason."

Hope started to slither through her, but she tried to ignore it. He could be here to say good-bye, so she'd better not start rejoicing just yet.

"Come on in," she told him.

Ruby led him into the living room and Chance

immediately jumped up onto her sofa and lay down like he'd been here for years. She couldn't help but laugh at the oversized dog on her delicate yellow couch.

"Do you want him down?" Knox asked.

"Leave him be," she demanded. "I'm glad he's not walking around peeing and marking his territory."

"Why don't you have a seat," he suggested, pointing to the only other chair in the living room.

"I'm fine." She crossed her arms over her chest. "I can stand."

Knox shrugged and remained too far away, but those eyes held hers from across the room. "You may want to be sitting when I tell you that I think I'm in love with you."

Ruby felt for the edge of the chair behind her and slowly sank into it. Immediately Chance hopped off the sofa and came to sit at her feet, putting one large paw on her lap. Still staring at Knox after that verbal bomb he'd just dropped, she rubbed on Chance's ear.

"You . . . you love me?"

Now he crossed the room and squatted down before her. "Someone once told me that you don't always get a second chance."

Ruby smiled. "Sounds like a smart woman."

"She's the best."

Knox rested his hand on her knee. Chance shifted and gave Knox a lick to the side of the face.

"Come on, man, cool it or we're both going to lose her."

The room seemed to be spinning as his words sank in. He loved her. He didn't want to lose her and he'd adopted Chance.

"Knox?"

He glanced back to her, a smile on his face. "Can we forget the past several days where I was a fool and too scared to realize how precious you are in my life?"

Oh, that did it. Tears spilled down her cheeks. Knox reached up and swiped the moisture away.

"Why now?" she asked. "What made you realize that you . . . that you . . ."

"That I love you?" he finished. "Because my cockpit was empty. Because I want a dog and Chance is perfect for both of us. Because when I decorated your house I instantly saw me here next year doing the same thing. And then when you told Jax we were friends I was furious with myself because we were clearly so much more. It just took my stubborn mind a while to catch up to my heart."

"I don't know what to say," she whispered.

Knox smoothed her hair away from her face and stroked his thumb across her cheek. "Say you're ready to take this leap with me. Say Chance and I are welcome here because we're a package deal now."

The man she'd so quickly fallen for was using a shelter dog to lay his heart on the line and he was literally on his knees.

"How did this happen?" she asked, leaning her face into his palm. "How did I get so lucky to have you come into my life and see that you deserve more than being alone?"

"I was content with being alone," he replied as he wrapped his other arm around Chance and patted his side. "But you proved to me that there's still so much living left to do, and nobody has made me want to do that more than you. When I saw you with Chance at the park, something stirred inside me. His name seemed to just smack me in the face. Then the flowers you brought and the fact we were set up on a blind date to begin with . . . it all just seemed like signs."

"Do you believe in signs?" she asked.

He shook his head. "Never did until recently, but these are kind of difficult to ignore. I wanted to fight my feelings for you because I didn't think I could put myself on the line again."

"And now?"

Knox eased forward and slid his lips over hers. "Now I want to take every risk imaginable if it means I can be with you."

Chance wedged his way between them and rested his head on her lap. "If I didn't know better, I'd say you trained him to do that," Ruby said.

"If I'd had the time, maybe I would have," he replied with a chuckle. "But I literally just got him this afternoon and ran to the store to get everything he'd need."

Ruby leaned over Chance and nipped at Knox's lips. "And I suppose you think you two are going to stay here?"

Knox shrugged. "You surely won't turn us away on Christmas Eve."

"I think I can make room for you both."

The corners of his mouth tipped up into a grin, flashing those dimples once again. "That's going to work out well since I brought a bag for me and all of his stuff is in the truck as well."

Ruby couldn't help the laugh that escaped her as relief and anticipation flooded her. "I didn't think you'd love anyone the way you did Lydia."

Those bright eyes held hers as he continued to

palm the side of her face. "Lydia was a special woman. So are you. I never thought I'd find anyone who made me feel this way again. I never thought someone could come into my life and the thought of them leaving made me feel empty inside."

He said all the right words. Every single one of them from his heart and directly into hers.

"I knew you were torn," she explained as she stroked Chance's head. "I didn't want to confuse you more, but I fell for you. I think I fell for you when you steamrolled my decorating and took over. You were so determined to show me there's nothing to be afraid of when the holidays approach and you're alone. I needed you more than I thought and . . . I fell in love with you."

"Finally," he declared on an exhale. "I was hoping I wasn't laying my heart on the line for nothing."

There was such a renewed hope curling through her, Ruby wasn't sure what to do with all of her emotions. She'd wanted someone to come into her life, had wondered if anyone existed who was actually for her. And he was here. Knox was the man she'd been waiting for, and after all this time, their lives had circled back around to join once again.

"What about Atlanta?" she asked.

Knox lifted a shoulder. "I'll call them after the holidays and tell them thanks but no thanks. I have a better offer here."

"Another job?"

"I don't need a job," he retorted, his brows raised. "I have you."

Ruby rolled her eyes. "Please tell me you're going to find a job here."

"I'm not sure. I was thinking we could eat frozen

pizzas, and then when we go out I could just borrow a credit card."

She swatted his chest. "Not funny."

Knox came to his feet and pulled her up with him. Chance thought that was his cue to hop up as well. The crazy dog literally planted a giant paw on each of their shoulders.

"I'll take care of you," Knox vowed. "I'll get a job in Haven and we'll make this work because I'm just crazy enough to believe it will."

Ruby smiled. "So, are we a family of three now?"

Knox glanced to Chance, then back to her. "For now. What do you say about children?"

Her heart couldn't swell any more. "I'd say this is the greatest Christmas present I've ever had."

Knox snaked an arm around her waist and tipped her back as he closed his lips over hers. Ruby wrapped an arm around his neck to hold on.

Chance's paws proved to be too much and he got overly excited and knocked them into the chair. Knox landed on Ruby and laughed.

"Obedience school is a must because he cannot interrupt my alone time," Knox declared.

"What are we going to do about tonight?" she asked, looking up at him.

Desire flooded his eyes as he stared down at her. "I promised to take care of you, didn't I?"

Oh, that question held so much promise. Ruby knew he was going to love her, care for her, and be with her forever. There wasn't a doubt in her mind.

Knox hadn't believed in second chances, but she'd known all along that they could be something special together. And to think she'd been worried about that blind date setup. But Knox had been right when he'd told her this would be a Christmas to remember.

Dear Reader,

Merry Christmas! There's something so magical about this time of year, which is why I'm thrilled to be able to bring you Second Chance Christmas. *This romance is loosely based on my parents' meet and happily ever after.*

*I so hope you've enjoyed your quick visit to Haven, Georgia. This quaint, fictitious town was first introduced in the Monroe Trilogy (*Wrapped in You, Caught Up in You, *and* Lost in You*), featuring three gruff yet loyal brothers who came together to honor their late sister.*

Haven will once again be the setting in my upcoming series featuring the small-town airport and the single-father pilot who now runs the place . . . until the late owner's daughter shows up to claim what's hers. Look for it in April 2018!

Thank you for visiting Haven with me. I wish you all a fabulous Christmas and the happiest of holidays!

Jules

Finding Colin

LEAH MARIE BROWN

Chapter One

HORRIBLE BOSSES

Movie > A Year Without Summer
By: AngelsFall86
A mysterious horse and rider appear one night and
transport a young woman to a world of dark desires.
Rated: Fiction M
Words: 925
Reviews: 23

> *He came to her on a winter's night, when the moon-
> light spilled like quicksilver upon the frozen gardens
> and the world beyond her father's walls rested snuggly
> beneath a new blanket of downy snow. She felt his
> presence, knew he would be waiting for her even before
> she wiped away the lacy sheet of ice covering her
> windowpane. He sat atop a magnificent white stallion,
> his thick black hair hanging rakishly over one eye,
> his strong hands clutching the magical beast's reins.*

She moved through the dark house as if in a dream, oblivious to the cold, heedless of the dangerous world that might be waiting for her just beyond. She stepped into the garden, her bare feet moving over the gravel path, until the distance and space between them could be filled only with a breath and an unspoken desire.

"Why have you come?" she whispered. "Are you a burglar? Do you mean to steal something?"

"Aye," he said, his Irish brogue thick, his brown eyes sparkling dangerously. "I mean to steal you."

"Me?"

He nodded. "I mean to steal your . . ."

"Grace!"

OMG! This is not happening! Please tell me this is not happening.

I look over my shoulder and realize it is, in fact, happening. Roberta is standing behind me, her flinty gaze focused on the blinking cursor on my computer screen. The only thing worse than getting caught writing fan fic is getting caught writing fan fic by your boss.

She narrows her gaze.

"Is that the *Dark Desires* copy?"

Wild heat spreads up my chest, neck, cheeks, to the tips of my ears. I put my computer in sleep mode and swivel my chair around, fixing a falsely bright smile on my face.

"Yeah." I reach for a stack of papers and pretend to organize them so I don't have to look into her eyes. "I wanted to read it over one more time before sending it to the Art Department for a galley proof. It's great. Désir is going to love it."

I work at one of the largest full-service advertising agencies in the world, and Désir, a Belgian chocolate company on the verge of breaking in to the North American market with a new line of artisan chocolates called Dark Desires, is one of our biggest accounts.

Our team has been working overtime since Labor Day to come up with a killer multipronged strategy targeting social media, broadcast outlets, and print media. Roberta has been pinging big-time, stressing over every little detail. Even under the best of circumstances—when all of the planets align, her espresso machine keeps pumping out the dark caffeinated liquid that is her lifeblood, the copy reads clean, new accounts roll in, and the minions that work in the mail room sacrifice lambs to assuage the Beast—Roberta is a horrible boss, a brutal, brutal beast of a boss.

She snatches the stack of papers from my hand.

"'Désir is going to love it,'" she mimics, batting her eyelashes and raising her voice several octaves. "I'm sorry, but did the Wharton School offer a class in fortune-telling for their MBA students? No? Then please spare me your peppy prognostications, Pollyanna."

"Of course." I swallow the bitter lump of indignation in my throat and remind myself that landing a job at Oglethorpe & Larkin right out of grad school is every would-be marketer's dream. "I am sorry, Roberta."

"Remember what I told you," she says, crossing her arms and tapping her stiletto-heeled foot on the polished concrete floor. "Winners are motivated by doubt; losers by confidence. Are you a loser?"

"No," I say, looking her in the eye.

"Are you sure?"

"Yes."

She stares at me through her narrowed, emotionless eyes for several agonizing seconds before emitting a doubtful "Hmm," and stalking back into her office.

Nike has *Just Do It*. McDonald's has *I'm Lovin' It*. L'Oréal has *Because You're Worth It*. If Roberta Pellett, executive creative director for Oglethorpe & Larkin Philadelphia, had a slogan, it would be *Hmm*. The one memorable sound that succinctly expresses the essence of Roberta. Doubt. Condescension. Suspicion. Ridicule. It's all there in that one little close-lipped expression.

The intercom buzzes. I snatch the handle off the cradle and hold it to my ear.

"I am out of coffee." Roberta's cool, clipped tone fills my ear. "Handle it."

"Of course. I will bring you another cup immediately."

"No," she sighs heavily. "I am out of coffee beans."

"But . . ." I am certain I filled Roberta's airtight, stainless steel coffee cask with beans three days ago.

"But . . . but," she stammers. "What comes after the 'but' is irrelevant. Handle it."

She disconnects with a deceptively soft click.

My name is Grace Elizabeth Murphy. I won a full-ride swimming scholarship to the University of California, Davis, graduated at the top of my class, attended the prestigious Wharton School of Business, landed a job at one of the largest advertising firms in the country before finishing grad school, and . . . I fetch coffee. This is my life. I am probably the only barista in the world who has $62,000 in school loans and an expense account.

I kick my heels off under my desk and shove my

feet into my fur-lined boots, grab my coat, wind my scarf around my neck three times, slide my iPhone and company credit card in my pocket, and brace myself to head out into the harsh, bitter world that is Philadelphia in December.

I am a Southern California girl by birth and at heart, which means I am genetically wired to hate precipitation, especially the frozen kind.

I take the elevator to the lobby, tromp past the receptionist, and leave the sleek, jewel-box building that houses Oglethorpe & Larkin's Philadelphia offices. I usually take the bus when I run errands for Roberta, but today I walk to the taxi stand on the corner and climb into the first yellow and black cab idling at the curb.

"Bean to Sumatra and Back," I say, slamming the door. "Twenty-Ninth and Oxford."

Roberta doesn't do peasant coffee. I found that out the hard way when I brought her a Starbucks on my first day of work. She turned her head, raised her hand, and shooed away my offering as if it were an offensive goblet of swill. *"Away, thou dost offend my refined sensibilities with such a rancid offering."* Her Majesty will only consume Kopi luwak coffee, an outrageously expensive Indonesian blend made using partially digested coffee cherries eaten and defecated by an Asian palm civet.

You heard me. Roberta Pellett, Queen of the Adverts and Tormentor of Underlings, drinks espresso made from the turds of a beady-eyed rodent. Thirty-five dollars per cup, which, coincidentally, is the same amount I spend for a crate of Ichiban Ramen noodles at Costco. Ah, the plight of the little people!

My phone vibrates in my pocket, letting me know I

have just received a new text. It's probably Roberta
asking me to fetch a tin of Harrods Sweet Biscuits to
go with her rat shit coffee. Maybe she wants me to fly
world-renowned pastry chef Jimmy Leclerc in to
make her a fluffy vanilla sponge with orange currant
buttercream frosting or a tray of his Ladurée Vanilla
Macaron.

I pull my phone out of my pocket, look at my
screen, and smile. The text is from my college roomie
and good pal, Vivia.

> Did you know cold weather can cause depression
> and kill your sex drive? That explains why they call
> sexless people frigid.
> #ThingsThatMakeYouGoHmm

I immediately respond:

> Preach. There's nothing hot about thermal
> underwear, chapped lips, and red, runny noses.
> Send me some California sunshine before my
> libido enters permanent hibernation.

Vivia texts me back:

> Ha! You mean Queen Roberta hasn't commanded
> you to rearrange the heavens so the sun shines
> only on Oglethorpe & Larkin?

I laugh out loud. The taxi driver looks at me through
the rearview mirror and I shrug.

"Funny text," I explain.

He nods his head. I go back to messaging Vivia.

Guess what I am doing right now?

Having sex with Colin Monaghan? Fight the cold, shag an Irishman.

I snort and text back:

I wish. 21 degrees with a wind chill of -6 and I am on an expedition to fetch Her Majesty's coffee beans.

She's Shackletoning you. Brutal.

Shackletoning? Is that some new slang?

Vivia explains:

Shackleton. Sir Ernest Shackleton, the dude who went on all of those polar expeditions. You're bravely venturing into hostile environs in search of the Kopi luwak. Hopefully, your mission will turn out better than Shackleton's.

Didn't he die on his last expedition?

That's what I am saying. GTG but wanted to tell you I read your latest Colin Monaghan fan fic. Good stuff. Keep writing.

Thanks!

I write fan fiction about Irish actor Colin James Monaghan (born May 1, 1982, in Dublin, Ireland, to Catriona and James Monaghan). I have been fangirling over him ever since my freshman year in high school, when I went on a date with Camden Jeffries to see *Kiosk*. While the other girls in my class were sighing over Ben Affleck's boyish charm and Josh Hartnett's apple-pie grin, I was daydreaming about Colin's unruly hair, expressive eyebrows, and bad-boy snarl.

Some people—mostly ex-boyfriends—have suggested my feelings for Colin have made a detour from fangirl to obsessive simply because I write fan fic about his movies and RPF (real person fiction) about him.

I disagree.

Writing fan fic provides an outlet for my untapped creativity. It's not like I am stretching my imagination fetching coffee and proofing copy written by other people. And yes, it also lets me indulge my passion for all things Colin.

I used to operate a Colin Monaghan fan site, but market research shows that microblogging platforms like Twitter, Tumblr, and Facebook are more popular. In other words, blogs and comprehensive Web sites require sustained attention. We've become information and stimulation junkies. We need a hit and we need it fast. Besides, managing a Web site and blog took too much of my time so I shut it down and opened a Tumblr account instead. *Fecking Love Colin* is the number one Colin Monaghan feed on Tumblr. My most popular post got 86,127 notes, which speaks more to the enduring appeal of the OOMA (object of my affection) than my mad Tumblr-posting skills.

"Twenty-Ninth and Oxford," the driver says, pulling to a stop in front of Bean to Sumatra and Back. "That's twenty-six dollars and fifteen cents."

I hand him my company card. He slides it through his credit card machine and hands it back to me. I slip the card back into my pocket and climb out of the cab. The cold air bitch slaps my cheeks and knocks the breath from my lungs. I will never get used to living in such an abusive climate.

The tinkling of bells and the warm earthy scent of coffee beans greets me when I push the door open and step into Sumatra.

"Hey, Grace! Back so soon?"

Yes. I am on a first name basis with the owner of a coffee store even though I don't drink coffee. It's just another one of the peculiarities of my life.

"Hey, Rafi," I say, climbing onto one of the stools and unwinding my scarf. "Roberta must have binged on the stash I hid for emergencies. She's going through serious Kopi luwak withdrawals. Any way you can hook us up with a few bags of beans?"

"Sorry," he says, dispensing hot chocolate from a machine he keeps for children into a mug and spraying whip cream on top. "I'm out."

"No way!"

"Way." He puts the mug on the counter in front of me and sprinkles chocolate jimmies on top of the whip cream. "I am expecting a delivery anytime, if you want to hang."

"Sure."

The doorbells tinkle. A cluster of red-cheeked, camera-toting tourists hurry through the door, stomping the snow from their boots. Rafi excuses himself and greets the customers. I wrap my hands around the mug of chocolate and inhale the sweet-scented curls of steam. I drink my chocolate and work on my latest fan fic piece, a romantic, slightly dark tale loosely based on Colin's movie, *A Year Without Summer.* It's the same piece I was working on when Roberta surprised me, but the beauty of Google docs is I can work on my stories on any device and they're never saved on Oglethorpe & Larkin's servers.

Forty minutes later and fully tanked up on creamy

hot chocolate, I am armed with three bags of Roberta's precious beans and huddled in the back of a taxi inching down Twenty-Ninth Street. An accident has brought traffic to a near standstill.

I pull out my iPhone, open Google docs, and continue working on my *Without Summer* fan fic.

> *. . . I kept my arms wrapped around his waist as his magnificent beast carried us over the slumbering city to an abandoned warehouse beside Grand Central station. He vaulted off the horse and reached up to help me down, his strong, unfamiliar hands lifting me from the back of the beast. Hand in hand, we moved through the darkened warehouse, climbing the stairs to the place he called home. And it was there, in his lookout above the city, that he made good on his promise to steal my . . .*

"We're here, miss," the cab driver says, startling me. "Oglethorpe and Larkin building, right?"

I look out the window at the steel and glass building towering into the clouds and nod my head, still lost in the dreamlike world of my creation, the world where a burglar (played by Colin Monaghan) seduces me. I pay the driver, grab the Bean to Sumatra and Back bag, and jump out of the cab.

Continuing to type, I walk into the lobby, step onto the elevator, and jab the button for the sixteenth floor.

> *. . . innocence. He removed my pelisse, dropped it on the floor, and lifted me in his arms, staring deep into my eyes as he carried me to his bed.*
>
> *"Do not worry, my beauty," he says, brushing my hair off my cheek. "Nothing will happen between us that is not meant to be."*

The elevator *dings* and the doors slide open. I step out, my fingers flying over the screen. I keep typing as I walk back to my cubby.

> . . . *he stands over the bed, staring at my naked body with his strange, ageless gaze. I hear the steady, urgent rumbling of a train approaching, feel the vibrations in my bones. Golden light from the train's headlamp fills the warehouse. The light illuminates him—his sleek black hair, the sharp angles of his handsome face, his broad* . . .

It takes me a moment to realize I am hearing the words as I am typing. Not in my head. Out loud. I look up from my phone and my heart plunges to my Caribou boots.

"Don't leave us in suspense," Roberta says, smiling tightly. "Does the Irish rogue steal her innocence?"

She is sitting at my computer with several of my coworkers clustered around her, including Kale, the guy I've sorta been seeing. He looks at me and his lip curls up like he's just gotten a whiff of rancid milk.

It's then I realize I left my Google doc open on my computer. That means everything I typed into my iPhone was instantaneously synched with the document on the screen. Roberta has been reading my story aloud, word for word, as I was typing it.

A wave of bile rises in my throat. I think I am going to be sick. I drop the bag of coffee beans and slap my hand over my mouth. Tears fill my eyes and blur my vision.

Roberta claps her hands.

"Let's go, minions," she says. "We've all had a good laugh, but now it's time to get back to work."

My fellow minions scramble back to their cubbies,

a few of them smiling sympathetically or mumbling a "sorry" as they pass. Kale brushes by me without a backward glance.

"Grace," Roberta says, turning on her heel and stalking back into her office. "A word."

My feet feel as if they are sunk in concrete. Each step is an effort. Somehow I make it into Roberta's office, shut the door, and sink down onto the chair opposite her desk.

"I am not your therapist, so I'm not going to analyze what that sad psychodrama means," she says, leaning back in her chair and forming a steeple with her fingers. "However, I am your superior, and your misuse of company time and equipment leave me no choice but to discipline you."

I blink, still lost in the haze of the nightmare.

"I don't understand."

"What don't you understand, Grace? You were attending to private business on company time and corporate policy as dictated by Human Resources requires I draft a formal letter of discipline and suspend you for an appropriate duration."

"Private business?" I say, blinking back fresh tears. "I was getting your coffee."

She narrows her gaze.

"Are you blaming this on me?"

"What?" I shake my head to clear the fog. "What do you mean? I don't even know what 'this' is."

"Look," she says. "Perhaps you were writing your little romance while running an errand for me, but that doesn't excuse the fact that one of our clients could have walked by your station and read the words popping up on your screen. Do you know how humiliating that would have been for me?"

This is a joke, right? Roberta is joking. *I* humiliated *her*? The rat shit coffee has finally gone to her brain. She's probably contracted some rare brain-eating disease from the partially digested coffee cherries. It's the only explanation.

"Do you want to be here, Grace?"

"Of course."

She narrows her gaze. "Are you certain?"

"Working at Oglethorpe and Larkin is the culmination of seven years of sacrifice, commitment, study, and debt."

"That still didn't answer my question." Roberta cracks a smile, but it's one of those creepy smiles that usually come just before the butcher knife is plunged into the unwitting victim. "It's not uncommon for postgrads to experience career disillusionment. You've finally achieved everything you worked so hard for, but is it what you had hoped?"

I am in crazy debt. I spend my days fetching coffee for a tyrant and my nights eating ramen noodles. I thought I would be writing CLIO Award–winning commercials and landing major accounts. Of course my life post college isn't what I had hoped. Not that Roberta of the thirty-five dollars per cup coffee habit could possibly understand my frustrations.

"Your silence speaks volumes," she says. "I am not going to draft a formal letter of reprimand, but I am placing you on three-week unpaid administrative leave. I would like you to take the time to think seriously about your future. I will see you after the holidays and you can tell me if you wish to remain part of the Oglethorpe and Larkin team."

"That's not—"

"You're dismissed."

I stand and walk to the door.

"And, Grace?" I turn back around and look at my boss. "Have a merry Christmas."

Chapter Two

ELEVEN LUNATICS

I am hypnotically staring at the blinking lights on my sad Charlie Brown Christmas tree and trying to swallow a mouthful of Schweddy Balls when my phone rings.

A few Christmases ago, Ben & Jerry's released a limited edition flavor called Schweddy Balls, vanilla ice cream, malted milk balls, and rum-flavored fudge. After Roberta's harsh treatment, I decided to make my own version of Schweddy Balls by mixing rum, hot fudge, vanilla ice cream, and malted milk balls in my blender. I might have added more rum than Ben and Jerry added to their holiday flavor.

My phone stops ringing.

I know how this looks. I am hosting a pity party for one, right? Well, if your father abandoned you when you were eight and your mother was too absorbed in her own bitterness to recognize her rising level of toxicity, and you worked such crazy long hours that you barely had time to nurture a relationship with your house plant, let alone a steady boyfriend, and your boss humiliated and suspended you three weeks before Christmas, you'd slurp down some Schweddy Balls and host a pity party for one, too.

My life is just like the final, romantic scene from *Bridget Jones's Diary* only without the diary and the friends and the weekend in Paris . . . and Mark Darcy. Basically, my life is the pathetic beginning of that scene.

My phone rings again. I flip it over.

"Hey, Viv."

"Hey, girlfriend." Vivia's voice sounds unnaturally subdued. "What are you doing?"

"Sitting in my jammies, drinking Schweddy Balls, and watching the needles fall off the branches of my Christmas tree."

Vivia whistles. "Schweddy Balls? It's only . . . three o'clock there. Things must be bad."

"Horrible."

"I take it you saw the post?"

"What post?"

"What post?" Vivia cries. "Wait. Why are you home in the middle of the day?"

I tell her about returning from the coffee run to find Roberta reading my Colin Monaghan fan fic aloud to my coworkers.

"*OhmyfreakingGod!* That *so* did not happen."

"It *so* did."

"Did she fire you?"

"Suspended without pay for three weeks."

"Oh, Grace," Vivia coos. "I am so sorry."

"Thanks."

"Roberta sits on her Oglethorpe and Larkin throne declaring, 'Let them drink coffee.' But powdered heads always roll when royalty ignores the needs of the little people. Roberta's day is coming . . . and we will have front row seats at the scaffold, girlfriend."

Vivia's loyalty acts like a jackhammer to the dam holding back my tears.

"Go on, girl," she whispers. "Have a good cry and then take a ginormous swig of your drink. Have I told you how absolutely genius I think it is that you combined Ben and Jerry's with booze? Flannel jammies, sappy chick flicks, Ben and Jerry's, and booze. Those are my go-tos whenever I am suffering from a broken heart. I just never thought to combine them all at once."

I am about to tell Vivia that I am not suffering from a broken heart when I remember her comment about a post and I get a sick feeling in the pit of my stomach—a sick feeling that's definitely not from the ice cream and rum.

"You said something about a post," I say, walking over to my desk and waking my computer from sleep mode. "What post? What are you talking about?"

"Nothing."

"Vivia!"

"Seriously, Gem," she says, calling me by the pet name she gave me when she found out my initials. "Now might not be a good time to get into it. Just promise me you will stay off social media for the night, 'kay?"

My computer monitor flickers on and I slide my

mouse over the pad until the pointer is on the Facebook tab. I click it and hold my breath.

"You're going on Facebook now, aren't you?" she asks.

"Yes."

"Don't do it," she warns. "Step away from the computer, Grace. Just turn off the monitor and step away from the computer. Have another drink instead. I know, read me some of your Colin fan fic."

If Vivia is asking me to read her fan fic, I know whatever she is trying to keep me from seeing must be wicked bad. Vivia has never said anything negative about my writing, but I know it's not her thing.

The Facebook home page comes up on my screen. I type my log-in information and password into the boxes and wait.

"Jesus, Mary, and Jojo singing 'Leave,'" Vivia says. "You're doing it, aren't you? You're signing on to Facebook."

I chuckle. Vivia has a penchant for dramatics. It's one of the things I love about her.

"Jojo? That's an old ref . . ."

I stop talking when I see it. It. The post Vivia doesn't want me to see because she is worried it will be the gust of wind that pushes me from the ledge of bummed into the deep, dark chasm of depression.

"Wait!" she cries. "I am going to FaceTime you."

The line goes dead. A second later, my phone rings again. I push the button and Vivia's face pops up on the screen.

"Okay, girlfriend," she says. "I don't want you to read that d-bag's post alone. I am riding shotgun. Let's do this thing."

I take a deep breath and let it out slowly. Then, I prop my iPhone up against my computer screen and begin reading aloud.

Kale Keller > Grace Murphy 3 hrs

10 Things I Hate About You:

1. I hate the way your hair always smells like chlorine.

2. I hate your flannel frog prince pajamas.

3. I hate your laugh.

4. I hate that you would rather spend Friday night watching stupid movies, like *10 Things I Hate about You*, instead of going out.

5. I hate that you share every feeling/thought/event on Facebook.

6. I hate your desperate need to be loved by everyone.

7. I hate that you never stand up to Roberta. It's pathetic. Grow a spine.

8. I hate your weird friends, especially **Vivia Perpetua Grant**.

9. I hate your fucking creepy obsession with Colin Monaghan.

10. I hate that you emasculated me in front of everyone at work by writing a shitty story about whoring with some has-been actor.

I read somewhere that first-responders often find airplane crash survivors in a state of frozen animation. The shock of their overwhelming, tragic situation renders them catatonic.

"Talk to me, goose," Vivia says. "Give me a reading. What are you feeling?"

I shift my focus from the computer screen to Vivia's miniaturized face on my iPhone. *What am I feeling? What am I feeling? What am I feeling?* I keep repeating the question in my head until I have an answer.

"Pain," I say. "I am feeling pain."

"Of course you are," Vivia says. "The guy you were seeing just broke up with you in a savage, savage way. Do you want to cry?"

I shake my head.

"Damn Skippy my girl doesn't want to cry," Vivia says. "A testicularly challenged guy like Kale Keller isn't worth even one of your tears. Kale Keller. What kind of name is Kale anyway?"

I consider defending my now ex-boyfriend, but my gaze falls on annoying habit number six and I bite back the words.

"My stories aren't shitty, are they?" I sniffle. "Be honest."

"They're not shitty."

"What's wrong with my flannel pajamas?"

"Nothing."

"And my laugh?"

"Infectious."

I look at number six again.

"I don't have a desperate need to be loved by everyone, do I?"

Vivia doesn't say anything. She just stares at the screen.

"Do I?"

"Well . . ."

"Well, what? Tell me the truth."

"You want the truth?"

"Yes."

"Well, then," she says, drawling out her words like a cowboy. "I'll be your huckleberry."

I frown at her.

"Huckleberry?" she says again.

I shake my head.

"In the movie *Tombstone*, Johnny Ringo shows up expecting to have a gunfight with Wyatt Earp, but finds Doc Holliday instead. Doc says, 'I'll be your huckleberry.' Meaning, he is the man for the job, because he shoots straight, and he shoots fast."

"Oookay," I say. "Shoot."

"You have a desperate need to be loved by everyone."

"I don't!"

"You do," Vivia says, smiling softly. "Remember when we were roommates and I would leave my empty Chinese take-out cartons on your desk?"

"So?"

"So, you never once complained."

"Is that what I should have done?"

"That's what most people would have done. Most people would have chucked a carton at my head."

I splash a little more rum in my glass and mix it with a stainless steel stirrer. "What else you got?"

"Remember that time you were paired with Voldemort for an assignment in your Consumer Strategies course?"

Voldemort's real name is Vanessa Mortenson. Vivia called her Voldemort, or She Who Must Not Be Named, after the villain in *Harry Potter*. Vanessa dressed in black and had a legion of followers.

"What about it?"

"What about it?" She moves closer to the camera so her face takes up the entire screen. "She was a heinous bitch, ditching you in the library, making fun of your clothes, but you still did all of the work for the project and submitted it with both of your names."

"She was busy."

"Busy? Doing what? Summoning the death eaters to suck the joy from every living creature in a fifty-mile radius?" Vivia snorts. "Forget Voldemort. I've got another example."

I sigh. "Okay."

"Sophomore year. Thanksgiving break. Most students were home with their families gorging on turkey or getting shit-faced off campus on Sam Adams Fat Jack Double Pumpkin at the Rat Skeller. Where were you?"

I shrug even though I know the answer to her question.

"You were holed up in our room making Christmas stockings for every person on our floor."

"I wanted to spread joy."

"Why?"

"Do I need a reason for trying to make people happy?"

"Come on, girlfriend. Dig deeper."

What does Vivia want me to say? As the emotionally orphaned only child of a single parent, I didn't have a family waiting for me to come home and help bake apple pies. She knows my history, which is why she has invited me to celebrate Christmas with her family every year since.

"Forget Christmas."

"I would like to," I say, staring at the burnt-out

bulb on the string of lights hanging on my anorexic Christmas tree. "But there's a Stouffer's roast turkey dinner in the freezer and *Miracle on 34th Street* saved on my DVR."

Some families burn a yule log, sing carols, or go sledding on Christmas Day. I eat dinner alone in front of the television while watching *Miracle on 34th Street.*

"That's so sad."

"Don't hate. It's my tradition."

I don't tell my friend that I always fall asleep wishing a jolly whiskered nursing home escapee would leave a normal mom and dad beneath my Christmas tree.

"You know you're always welcome to celebrate Christmas with us. My 'rents love you."

"Thanks, but I'm afraid I wouldn't be very good company this year."

"You said that last year."

"Well, it was true. Last year, Drew ran off with my cousin a week before Christmas. I was nursing a seriously broken heart. I thought he was the one."

"Are you seeing the trend here?"

"Wait a minute!" I slam my cup down on the desk and the brownish concoction splatters on my keyboard. "What are you saying? It's not my fault my last two boyfriends have been losers."

"Eleven."

"Excuse me?"

"Your last ten boyfriends. Kale makes eleven."

"Eleven what?"

"Lunatics."

"Shut up!" I laugh.

"I am serious!" Vivia says. "If a screenwriter wrote a

movie about your love life, he could totally call it *Eleven Lunatics.* Your last eleven boyfriends have been as crazy as the dog napper in your fave movie."

She's right about Colin Monaghan's *Eleven Lunatics* being my favorite movie, but not about my boyfriends. Vivia is prone to exaggeration.

"They haven't all been crazy."

"Let's see," she says, holding up one finger. "First, there was Sean, the 'roided out mixed martial arts fighter who made Donald Duck noises when he orgasmed. Then, there was Zane, the guitarist who ran off with your life savings. David, the photographer who took you on a weekend getaway . . . to a nudist colony. The aforementioned Drew, who ran off with your cousin. And Gunner, the marine fighter pilot who ran off with your lingerie . . ."

I zone out as she brutally describes a few more of my failed relationships.

"Okay, okay!" I sigh. "So a few of them have been crazy, but not *Eleven Lunatics* crazy."

"Should I keep going?" She props her feet up on her desk and holds up another finger. "Lunatic number nine was J.P., the motorcycle cop who made you call him Sarge, refused to take off his underwear during sex, and called you thirty-eight times in one day because he thought you were cheating on him. He was a special brand of psycho. Lunatic number ten was 'Blade'"—she makes air quotes with her fingers— "the pathological liar who said he had a 'high level security job with the United States government' but couldn't talk about it because he was being monitored. Which brings us to . . ."

"Kale."

"Psychopath number eleven!"

"Kale is not a lunatic."

"Uh, yes he is. He eats coleslaw for breakfast every morning."

"That doesn't make him a psychopath."

"He pronounces it 'cold slaw.'"

"So! Mispronouncing a word doesn't make you crazy."

"He liked to lick your armpits."

"That was gross, but not totally crazy." I shrug. "What can I say? I smell good."

"He looked like Bea Arthur."

I see Kale's face in my head, strong black eyebrows, salt and pepper hair, thin lips. . . .

"Oh my God!"

"Right?" Vivia says, grinning. "I can't believe you never noticed it before."

The conversation lulls and I know Vivia is thinking about my coleslaw-eating, armpit-licking freak of an ex and wondering why I keep picking freaks.

"You know I love you, Grace, but I've gotta ask: why do you keep picking bad boys?"

"I don't think they're bad boys when I pick them."

"Okay, but at some point you figure out they're bad boys . . . bad for you, at least . . . yet you stay. Why?"

"I don't know."

"Yes, you do. Think about it."

I think about it for a nanosecond before answering her question with a question. "Are you saying I have Daddy issues?"

"I dunno." Vivia lets her feet fall from her desk and leans forward, her face inches from the screen. "Do you?"

I think about my last several boyfriends and realize

they were all bad apples. Some of them were obviously dented and bruised, but others hid their flaws beneath a seemingly perfect, shiny exterior. They were rotten to the core. Just like my dad.

"It doesn't make sense," I say, dropping my forehead to the desk. "My father leaving was the most damaging thing to ever happen to me, so why would I purposely seek out men who would poke at that wound, over and over again? That would be . . . masochistic."

"You're not masochistic, Grace. You're a creature of comfort. You grew up with abuse, abandonment, and neglect, so you unwittingly replicate that pattern in your relationships with men." Vivia's voice, usually animated and exuberant, is calm and gentle. "It's time to break that pattern."

"How?" I look up. "How do I break a pattern that was set twenty years ago?"

"First, you acknowledge that the pattern exists."

"Okay," I say, sighing. "I, Grace Elizabeth Murphy, am attracted to bad boys and seek them out knowing they will probably treat me like crap."

"Good," Vivia says. "Now you have to break the pattern by asking yourself difficult questions, like: Do I let men treat me like crap because I don't think I deserve better? Why don't I think I deserve better? Do I want to end up like my mom? Look inside to fix the outside."

"Damn, Vivia," I say, exhaling. "Have you been taking psychology classes?"

"Nah," she says, shaking her head. "I've always had crazy good bullshit-spotting goggles. They've just never worked when I look at myself. I've got more if you want to hear it."

"Okay."

"Have you ever thought that maybe you are so obsessed with Colin Monaghan because—"

"I am not obsessed."

"I love you, Gem, but you are a little obsessed."

"When you say 'obsessed' I think about those creepy stalkers who send hundreds of letters and bizarre gifts. I am not a creepy stalker."

"Of course you're not," she says. "Have you ever thought you are fixated with the ultimate bad boy because he's unobtainable? There's no risk of you ever getting dumped or abandoned. And writing fan fiction about him allows you to craft the ending you probably wouldn't ever get with him in real life."

"Colin has changed!" I argue. "He's not a bad boy anymore. Having a child born with a physical handicap has matured and grounded him."

"There you go!"

"There I go what?"

"You are obsess—"

"Fixated."

"Right. Sorry," she says. "You are *fixated* on Colin Monaghan because he represents an extremely rare creature: the reformed bad boy. He gives you hope that you will find your own bad boy, reform him, and somehow heal the wound your father inflicted on you."

"You're putting an awful lot on Colin, aren't you?" I say, chuckling.

"We aren't talking about Colin Monaghan."

"I would rather talk about him."

"Be serious. What do you think it would take to get you over Colin Monaghan?"

"I don't know. Maybe I have built him up in my mind. Maybe he has become this mythical creature by which I measure all other men. Maybe if I met him, I would change my mind."

"Okay."

"Okay, what?"

"Okay, go meet him."

"What?"

"With your holiday time off and suspension, you don't have to be back at work until after the new year. That's a month from now. You could come to California and celebrate Christmas at my house or you could fly to Ireland, a place you have always wanted to go, and track down the man of your dreams. He's there filming a movie, you know."

"You're crazy."

"Am I? Really?" She lowers her voice. "What's crazy? Spending your whole life being in love with a man you've never met or taking a chance and going to meet the man you love? Think about it."

"Okay, let's say the planets align and Irish fairies sprinkle me with pixie dust and I meet him. What then?"

"You fall in love. Duh."

I snort.

"Why couldn't Colin fall in love with you? You're not totally hideous."

"Gee, thanks."

"I'm kidding," she says, sticking out her tongue. "You know you're gorgeous, Grace. Long legs, long hair, freckles all over your perfectly angled face, and eyes as green as the *marshmallow clovers in me bowl of Lucky Charms.*"

She said the last bit in a ridiculously bad Irish accent.

"That's it? You think I am just going to hock my MacBook, buy a ticket to Dublin, track down one of the hottest actors on the planet, and a leprechaun will sprinkle us both with green clovers and we'll fall in love?"

"I don't think a leprechaun is going to sprinkle you with green clovers."

"Good."

"Because everyone knows leprechauns are agents of mischief. I think you mean Daoine Sidhe, fairy people, fallen angels who bridge the gap between divinity and humanity."

"Would you be serious, Vivia?"

"I am serious."

"Colin Monaghan is not going to fall in love with me, even if a band of leprechauns and fairies douse the shit out of me with pixie dust and clovers."

"Why not?"

"Because that would be the ultimate happy ending and happy endings just don't happen in real life. Not in my life."

"That's the problem, girlfriend. You don't believe you are worthy of a happy ending—and I'm not talking about the sexual kind, either."

"Ew."

"Grace, you deserve to be loved and you deserve happiness more than anyone I have ever known, but you have to stop wasting your love on people who aren't worthy of you. And the only way you are going to find someone worthy of you is to fix that broken picker you got, the one that inevitably points you to psychopaths. Go to Ireland. Track Colin Monaghan down . . . or don't. Whatever you do, take the time to get to know the Grace I already know: the one who is funny, smart, kind, and completely worthy of all that is good."

Tears fill my eyes.

"You're making me weepy."

"It's the Schweddy Balls. Schweddy Balls always make you weepy."

"Even if I admitted there was some logic in what you just said, how could I possibly go to Ireland? I have student loans and . . ."

"Bah!" Vivia raises her hands over her head. "If you were to die tomorrow, do you think your last words would be, 'Gee, I wish I would have paid more on my student loan'? I don't think so! You would say, 'I wish I would have listened to my wise old friend Vivia when she told me to go to Ireland and find Colin Monaghan.'"

I laugh, but Vivia's seed of an idea has planted itself in my brain and a million *what-ifs* are popping up.

"A last minute ticket to Ireland would be crazy expensive."

"Use your credit cards, dip into your savings. You have to risk big to win big, my friend."

I take a deep breath.

"Okay."

"Okay, you're doing it?"

"Yes. "

"Do it now."

"What do you mean, do it now?"

"I mean, turn your phone around so I can see your

computer screen and then get your fingers moving over to kayak.com. Buy the ticket right now, with me watching. Tell you what, I will skip sending you a Christmas gift and chip in half the airfare."

"You don't need to do that."

"I want to do it. Now get clicking."

Chapter Three

ONDINE

Ireland is the geographic equivalent to Prozac. If psychiatrists prescribed a week in the Emerald Isle, the world would be a mentally healthier place.

My heavy mood lifted moments after landing in Dublin. First, the An Garda Síochána working in the Passport Control booth complimented my hair. Then, a super sexy Chris Evans lookalike police officer flirted with me while I waited at the baggage carousel.

Even the double-decker bus ride from the airport to my hotel was filled with pleasant surprises, like free Wi-Fi and a sign that read, NOTICE TO NITELINK PASSENGERS: LADIES, THE POLES ARE FITTED FOR YOUR SAFETY. NO DANCING.

I cashed in my Hilton Honors points for two nights at the Morrison, a sleek boutique hotel favored by musicians and actors. The girl at the front desk apologized because my room wasn't ready by offering

me a glass of champagne and an upgrade to a suite.
When she said the concierge could assist in making
restaurant reservations, arranging for spa services,
recommending night life hot spots, and procuring
theater tickets, I asked her if he could get me a date
with Colin Monaghan.

"Ah, so ya fancy our Colin, do ya?" she said, then
leaned over the counter and lowered her voice. "He
was here last week. Had dinner in our own Morrison
Grill."

"Shut up! You're not serious?"

"Ah, sure." She smiled. "He's over County Kerry
way, shooting an action film."

"I know," I said, returning her smile. "I am headed
there next. In fact, finding Colin is the whole reason
I came to Ireland."

She frowned and glanced over at the burly valet
standing at the door

"Not in a creepy, stalker kinda way, though."

Now, I am making my way through the narrow
alleys of the Temple Bar district, reading the bright
neon signs promising PIZZA & BOOZE; SOUP OF THE
DAY: WHISKEY; and BOOZE: BECAUSE NO GREAT STORY
EVER STARTED WITH SALAD.

My phone vibrates, alerting me to a new text. I pull
it out of my pocket and open the message, which is
from Vivia.

I made a few phone calls, pulled a few strings,
promised my firstborn, and I have hooked a sister
up! Check your e-mail ASAP!!

I walk down the street, over a bridge spanning the
River Liffey, and to a colorful, bustling Christmas

market with stalls selling mugs of steaming whiskey-infused hot chocolate and bowls of seafood chowder, woolen sweaters, handmade scarves, artisan jewelry, jars of Shines Wild Irish Tuna, and Butlers chocolate reindeers. I step beneath a large candy cane with a FREE WI-FI sign hanging from it and wait for my e-mail to download.

To: Grace Murphy
From: Vivia Perpetua Grant
Subj: Get your groove on
Fáilte go hÉirinn! (That means "Welcome to Ireland!") If you are reading this, it means you have landed in the Isle O'Monaghan. I hope you have packed your dancing shoes because I scored you two VIP tickets to Lillie's Bordello, an uber-posh club that is *the* Dublin hang-place for celebs, including your boy, Colin. Grab a hot Irishman as your plus one. Do everything I would do and snap selfies to prove it (See attachment for the address to Lillie's Bordello, the POC, and your tickets).
I've also been burning up Google and calling all of my contacts in Hollywood. I found out exactly where Colin is filming in County Kerry. The shoot is near a little place called Sneem. They are looking for extras for the film. I have included the name and phone number of the casting director. Give her a call.
Love, V

I squeal. Literally squeal like a tween at a 5 Seconds of Summer concert.

"Are ya pissed from drinking too much whiskey nog at the Jameson booth or did Michael Fassbender just send you a sexty?"

I turn in the direction of the voice and find a pretty redhead leaning against a booth selling silver jewelry.

"Excuse me?"

"Ya just squealed."

"I did, didn't I?"

She nods her head and a long lock of her coppery hair falls over her eye. "If ya just got a sexty from Michael, be a pal and let me take a look," she says, blowing the hair away from her eye. "It is Christmas, after all."

I laugh.

"Sorry, no sexties from Michael Fassbender."

"Damn."

I walk over to her booth.

"My girlfriend just sent me two VIP tickets to some posh club called Lillie's Bordello."

"Feck me." She whistles. "That *is* a reason to squeal."

"Right?"

She nods her head. "Lillie's Bordello is jammers with celebs. Bono, Rihanna, Mick Jagger, Colin Monaghan, *and* even Michael Fassbender. They all party there."

"I am Grace, by the way."

"Pleased to meet ya, Grace," she says, grinning. "I'm Ondine."

"Nice to meet you, Ondine," I say. "Your jewelry is very pretty. Do you make it?"

"Guilty."

I pick up a delicate silver necklace with a round polished silver pendant engraved with strange words.

"Is this Gaelic?"

"Yes. It says, 'What lies behind us and what lies

ahead of us are tiny matters compared to what lies within us.'"

"Are you kidding me?"

"No," she says, frowning. "Why?"

"It's like"—I shake my head—"serendipity brought me to you. You can't begin to know how much the saying on your necklace resonates with me. I'll take it."

"Sounds like ya got a story to tell."

"A long story."

"Ooo, those are the best kinds." She pats the stool beside her. "I've got the time."

"Seriously?"

"Come on, then," she says, smiling. "Tell me your story while I wrap up your necklace."

I step into the booth, take a seat on her stool, warm my feet by her space heater, and unload my whole heavy story on her. I even tell her the bit about coming to Ireland to find Colin Monaghan . . . but not in a creepy way.

"You are brave to travel to a strange country, alone, for the holidays."

"So you don't think I am crazy?"

She laughs. "Oh, I think you are mad as a box of frogs! But, no worries, I like mad."

Ondine tells me her story. She's half Irish, half American. Her father is Irish and her mother is American. They couldn't bridge the cultural divide and divorced when she was ten years old. She has been bouncing back and forth between Ireland and the States ever since, studying international law at Columbia and spending summers and holidays working at her father's pub and restaurant in County Kerry, near her father's home. She tells me about her large family scattered from Dublin to Denver.

"It must be nice to have such a large family."

"Exhausting," she says, rolling her eyes. "What about you? Do you have a large family?"

I shake my head. "I don't have a family."

"Everyone has a family."

"Not me."

"Go on with ya."

I give her a pathetic half smile, half frown and shrug my shoulders.

"So you will be spending Christmas alone?"

"Yes . . . unless Colin invites me back to his place for a little whiskey nog."

"Listen," she says, handing me the wrapped box containing my necklace. "I know we just met, but you are welcome to spend Christmas with me, at my father's house."

My stomach clenches. It happens every time someone looks at me like I am a homeless, crippled war vet. Poor, pitiful Grace.

"Thank you, but . . ."

"Think on it," she says. "You said you were headed to Sneem. I live in Sneem. If that's not serendipity at work, I don't know what is."

I am about to stand up and say good-bye when I decide to step out of character. Instead of letting my pride get in the way of accepting a kindly offered handout, I decide to grab it with both hands.

"I would be happy to spend Christmas with you, but only if you agree to be my plus one at Lillie's Bordello tonight."

"Are ya fecking serious?"

I nod my head.

"I can't believe it. Lillie's Bordello! We are going to catch some good craic!"

"Crack?" I stand up. "I'm sorry, Ondine, but I don't do drugs."

"No, no," she says, laughing. "Craic doesn't mean what you think it means. Craic is Irish for 'fun, having a good time.'"

"Oh," I laugh. "Then we are going to have loads of craic."

Later, as I am stepping into a cab to go to Lillie's Bordello, I realize this trip is just like that old Nissan Sentra commercial—the one where a guy named Bob is speeding down a highway in a Nissan Sentra. A policeman pulls him over, but doesn't give him a ticket because . . . it's Bob. He passes a sign that says, NO PARKING, EXCEPT FOR BOB. Everything is golden for Bob.

I am Bob. And I am loving it.

Lillie's Bordello turns out to be a super swanky nightclub with a Victorian brothel vibe. Crushed red velvet wallpaper, leather sofas, wood paneling, and cozy nooks in dark corners perfect for getting down and dirty in a hurry. We order martinis and stand near the dance floor. A cute DJ with a buzz cut and mirrored sunglasses is spinning a pulsating electro beat while a bouncer aims a huffing fog machine at the people on the dance floor.

A gorgeous man in an Armani suit sans tie asks me to dance and before I know it we are grinding to a Calvin Harris and Rihanna remix. When the dance floor becomes too crowded, he takes my hand and leads me up the stairs to a members-only room called the library. He tells me he works as a second-unit director.

"For movies?"

"Movies and television shows," he says, draping his arm over my shoulders and leaning in close enough for me to smell the spicy cologne on his heated skin. "I just finished filming in County Wicklow. A show called *The Marauders*."

I am dying to ask him if he has ever worked with Colin Monaghan, but he is absently toying with the slender straps of my LBD and making it hard for me to concentrate. He leans in to kiss me and I let him. He tastes of whiskey and brash self-confidence. He tastes like a bad boy. If I am not careful, assistant director Seán's Armani suit is going to be balled up on my hotel room floor and I am going to be adding another notch to my lunatic belt.

By the time Ondine links her arm through mine and we stagger out of the club, past the golden velvet rope separating the in-crowd from the crowd outside, we are pissed on martinis and totally feeling the craic. We have also become fast friends.

Before parting ways, she asks me if I would like to drive with her to Sneem and crash on her pullout sofa at her cottage.

"You're serious? I wouldn't be an imposition?"

"Ah, away with ye then," she says, laughing. "I'd love to have ya. Besides, if ya manage to track down Colin, ya have to promise to come back and help me track down Michael Fassbender—but not in a creepy way."

Chapter Four

SAVING MR. BANKS

The four-hour drive from Dublin to Sneem takes us through rolling farmland, over gorse-covered hills dotted with fat, woolly sheep, and through forests of towering pines as ancient as the Celtic tribes that once lived here. At Ondine's suggestion, we make a quick detour to visit the Rock of Cashel, a castle and cathedral perched high on a hill with sweeping views of the countryside.

I worried spending four hours in a car with a virtual stranger would be uncomfortable, but we talk and laugh like we have known each other all our lives. No awkward pauses. No forced convos. The discussion flows as freely as an Irish spring.

We stop for dinner in Kenmare, a postcard-perfect town. The main road, Henry Street, is lined with Victorian-era row houses that remind me of an exuberant grade school student's art project. Each

building is painted a different color—mellow lavender,
sky blue, brick red, pea green, sunny yellow—and
strung with twinkling white fairy lights.

We have fish and chips at O'Donnabháin's, a
charming pub and restaurant with cozy wooden
booths and a potbellied stove. The air is tinged with
the scent of burning wood and foamy ale.

When I made my reservations for this trip, I booked
a single room at a B and B fifteen miles inland from
Sneem because that was all I could afford, but serendipity has decided to cram my stocking full of unexpected goodies this Christmas.

Ondine's cottage is within walking distance to the
Parknasilla Resort and Spa, which, according to the
waitress at O'Donnabháin's, is where Colin and cast
are staying while they film the movie.

By the time I take the last sip of my Bulmers Irish
Cider and swallow the last bite of my crispy-coated,
flaky fish, I am practically vibrating with anticipation.
In less than an hour, I am going to be within walking
distance of Colin *OhMyGod* Monaghan.

"Let's go," Ondine says, smiling.

"You're sure? You haven't finished your Guinness."

"I'm good." She stands and shoves her arms in the
sleeves of her coat. "I saw the look on your face when
the waitress said Colin is staying at Parknasilla."

Everything about Ondine's home is straight out of
an Irish fairy tale. The whitewashed cottage, with its
thatched roof and blue-painted flower boxes, sits at
the end of Oysterbed Road on a wooded hill overlooking the sea. The cottage and surrounding eighty
acres have belonged to her family for generations.
Her father lives in town, over his pub. He gave her
the cottage as an incentive to stay in Ireland full-time.

By the time we unload the car and unpack our suitcases, the sun looks like it is swimming in the sea, its slender golden rays dipping in and out of the water.

"If you follow the path through the forest, keeping the water on your right, you will eventually reach Parknasilla," Ondine says, handing me a flashlight. "Good luck, my friend."

I take the flashlight and hurry down the path. Twenty-two minutes later I arrive at the resort. The main building is an eighteenth-century stone manor, with towering chimneys and a slate roof. Other than a couple walking hand in hand along the water and a waiter bearing a silver tray with empty champagne glasses, the place is dead. I consider going inside the resort and inquiring at the front desk, but don't want to seem like a gauche American tourist. I keep walking until I arrive at a gravel parking lot. Three gigantic cranes affixed with lights are parked in the lot. They're the kind of lights you would expect to see on an outdoor movie set. You know that dry mouth, fluttery tummy feeling you get right before you are about to go on a first date with a new guy? That's what I am feeling right now. Any second, the man of my dreams could walk up to me, smile, and walk away with my heart.

I hold my iPhone low, snap a selfie with the movie lights in the background, and text it to Vivia with the message: Guess where I am?

It takes seconds for her response to hit my phone.

Colin Monaghan's arms? Get it, girl!

I laugh and switch my phone to airplane mode before continuing my not-so-subtle recon mission

around the resort. I walk through the gardens, peek
into windows, stop by the bar and order a Coke. I even
pop into the spa and schedule a massage for later in
the week. The girl working the desk at the spa tells me
all treatments include a complimentary day pass
to the facilities. If I still haven't found Colin by the
day of my appointment, I will use my saved B and B
money and get that massage.

Maybe I set an unrealistically high expectation in
hoping to find Colin on my very first day in County
Kerry, but I return to Ondine's cottage with a little air
missing from my buoy, the one that bobs around
inside me and contains all of my hopes.

The next day, while Ondine is working in her
father's pub, I am back at Parknasilla, skulking in the
bushes, peeking in more windows, pretending to be a
guest catching rays on the sun loungers. Other than a
few trailers parked behind the main lodge and some
people carrying clipboards and walkie-talkies, I see no
evidence that Parknasilla is the temporary home to a
major motion picture crew. And I certainly see no
evidence that Colin "Fell-From-Heaven" Monaghan
is in residence. No golden rings of light, no heavenly
choir singing, no bolts of lightning shooting from the
sky. By the time I return to Ondine's cottage, a little
more air has escaped from my hope buoy.

On my third morning in Sneem, I put on my
spandex running tights and jog the path through
the forest. I am not going to lie. My buoy is nearly
deflated. I spoke to a maid at Parknasilla yesterday

who hinted the crew had moved to another location. She said the director insisted everyone at the hotel sign strict confidentiality agreements and that she could get sacked just for saying the words *movie crew*.

Instead of following the path to the resort, I veer right and run through the forest. I keep running, breathing in the crisp, pine-scented air, until I come to an incline. I dig deep for that last bit of endurance and run up the hill. By the time I reach the top and break out of the forest, my breath is coming in sharp jags and my glutes are on fire. The view is spectacular, though. Totally worth the pain. I am standing on a rocky outcropping overlooking the water. I collapse on the rocks and stare up at the wispy clouds skittering across the cobalt sky. For the first time in . . . maybe ever, I am at peace. Lying on this rock, listening to the waves lapping below, I suddenly realize the frenetic energy that coursed through my veins back in Philadelphia, the urgent need to keep moving, keep working, has dissipated.

I close my eyes and let the warmth of the morning sun sink down deep to my bones. I am wrapped in a cocoon of well-being and utter contentment, about to drift off, when I hear the steady *thump-thump-thump* of helicopter blades. I sit up, shield my eyes with my hand, and stare out over the placid sea. The helicopter is flying parallel to the shore about a hundred feet over the water. The tail has a large green shamrock painted on it and I realize it is one of those see Ireland by air tours. I am about to lie back down when the helicopter banks left, the passenger door swings up, and a man tumbles out. My stomach drops to my tennis shoes as I watch him struggle to hold on to the landing skids, his feet flailing wildly.

If he survives the fall, the shock of hitting cold water will give him a burst of adrenaline that will quickly dissipate and render him incapable of completing the relatively short surface swim. He will drown.

I look over the side of the rocks and judge the ocean to be about twenty feet below. That's significantly less than the average high dive. I kick off my shoes, pull my fleece jacket over my head, and step to the edge of the cliff, my toes instinctively curling against the cold surface.

I am only able to take one deep breath, filling my lungs with air, holding it, and slowly releasing it, when he loses his grip on the landing skid and falls feet first toward the sea. I raise my hands over my head and dive off the rocks, mentally bracing myself for what is to come. I plunge into the sea, feel the breath knocked from my chest, and start swimming before I have even surfaced. Most people drown in cold water because they panic and forget to breathe. The trick is to stay calm, take steady breaths, and keep moving.

I did a New Year's Eve polar bear plunge off the coast of Virginia once. Yeah, this is nothing like that. The sea is calm, but much, much colder than I remember the waters off Virginia Beach. I keep my head down and concentrate on taking long, efficient strokes, even breaths, and before I know it, I reach him. He is calmly dog-paddling. He looks surprised to see me.

I position myself behind him and grab him in a lifeguard hold, the one I was trained to perform when I

worked the California beaches on my summer breaks
from college, but he resists.

"It's okay." I keep my arms around him in a backward hug, hands on his shoulders, and start swimming
him toward the shore. "I was a lifeguard."

"Are ya a fecking eegit?" His chest rumbling, his
voice thick with an Irish brogue. "Do ya want to die?"

He breaks free from my grasp, puts me in an ag-
gressive victim hold, and begins swimming us to shore
before I've even had time to think of a response.
When we reach the shallows, he scoops me up and
carries me the rest of the way to shore.

He drops me on the sand and stands over me, his
broad shoulders blocking out the sun.

"Who are you?" he demands.

I shield my eyes with my hand and look up at him
and . . . OH MY FECKING GOD! It's Colin "Divinely
Gorgeous" Monaghan.

"C . . . Colin?"

Chapter Five

TRIAGE

"How do you know my name?"

"Are you kidding me? I would know you anywhere. You're Colin Monaghan!"

He shoves his hand through his jet black hair and I am able to see a small, hairline scar near his right temple. Oh my God! He is not Colin Monaghan! He has the same dark hair, thick, expressive eyebrows, and melt-your-soul brown eyes as Colin, but he is taller, broader across the shoulders, and more muscular. I narrow my gaze. He's also missing a mole! Colin has two moles on his left cheek, not one!

"I'm Colin Banks, not Colin Monaghan"—he squats down and fixes me with a disconcertingly direct gaze—"and you are the woman who just ruined a three-million-dollar scene."

Someone shouts and I suddenly realize we are not alone. The beach is crawling with people wearing black Windbreakers and baseball caps. Some of them are holding equipment. Movie-making equipment.

"I'm s-s-sorry. I th-thought you w-w-were drowning."

I see his lips move, but my teeth are chattering together so loudly I can't hear what he is saying. I try to stand. A wave of dizziness washes over me and I fall back onto the ground in a shivering, seaweed-covered heap.

"What is your name?"

"Grayth Murthee."

Is it me or am I slurring my words?

"Right then," he says, grabbing a silver thermal blanket from a woman who suddenly appeared behind him and carefully wrapping it around me. "Grace, you are showing signs of hypothermia. We have an ambulance on standby at the top of the hill. I am going to pick you up and carry you to the paramedics."

He reaches for me and I clumsily slap his hands away.

"Don't be ridikileth . . . ridacaless," I say, trying to stand again. "I wath a lifeguard. I'm fine."

I fall back onto the ground and close my eyes. Hypothermia! I don't have hypothermia. I'm just tired. I need a nap and then I will be fit as a . . .

The Other Colin slides one hand under my legs and the other behind my neck and lifts me into his arms.

"Ow!" I lift my head and half open my eyes. "You're hurthing me."

"I'm sorry, *a a stór*," he says, his warm breath fanning over my cheeks. "Just a little longer and you will be somewhere warm."

"Okay," I say, resting my head against his shoulder. "But my name is Grayth, not Aster."

He laughs.

I don't know what I said that was so funny and I am too damned tired to try to figure it out. My eyelids are heavier than bricks, my teeth won't stop chattering, and my skin hurts. I close my eyes and slip into that half-awake, half-asleep stage. I am vaguely aware of movement, the rumble of an engine, and many people speaking in gibberish all at once. I can only make out a few words.

"... *went arseways.*"

"... *mad as a box of frogs* ..."

"... *call sheet* ... *four banger* ..."

"... *it's biscuits to a bear* ..."

When I wake up, I am on a gurney in a partitioned emergency room, an IV needle jammed into my arm, a heavy blue pool float lying on my chest and legs. A nurse is checking my vitals.

"How ya feeling, luv?"

"Tired." I blink several times. "How long have I been asleep?"

"Not long."

"What is this?" I say, trying to lift the pool raft off my chest.

"It's a hyper-hypothermia blanket, so it is." She lifts a tube hanging off the corner of the blanket. "Warm water is pumped through this tube and circulated around the blanket ta help restore your core temperature."

"I'm not hypothermic."

She chuckles softly. "Doctor O'Neil disagrees. He diagnosed you with moderate hypothermia and anemia, he did."

"Anemia?"

"Your hemoglobin levels were a wee bit below normal, they were." She pats my arm. "Nothing ta worry about. A vitamin B injection and iron tabs and ye'll be just grand."

Her heavily accented voice rises and falls as if she is singing her words instead of speaking them. She also drops the *h* from words with *th*, so *nothing* sounds like "nuh-ting" and *this* sounds like "tiss."

She takes my temperature, records it on a whiteboard affixed to the wall, and removes my IV.

"Now, would you fancy a wee cup of tea and digestives while your discharge paperwork is made ready?"

"If you wouldn't mind."

"Ah, 'tis nothing."

She disappears through a set of curtains and returns seconds later carrying a tray with a Styrofoam cup of tea and a small package of biscuits.

"Ring the buzzer if you need anything."

She steps through the curtains and closes them behind her. I gulp the tea down in a couple of swallows and am polishing off the last graham cracker–tasting biscuit when the Other Colin strides through the curtains.

For a nanosecond, I again think it is Colin "Heavenly Body" Monaghan and I catch my breath. My skin feels tingly all over, but I don't think it is from hypothermia.

"What are *you* doing here?"

Nice, Grace. How not to win friends and influence Irishmen.

"Is that a stereotypical American greeting? Because in Ireland we usually say 'hiya.'"

"I'm sorry," I say, blushing. "I didn't expect to see you again."

He crosses his muscular arms over his chest and frowns so deeply that his Colin Monaghan-like brows practically knit together. "Are ya kidding me? 'Tis not every day a man is rescued from a murky, watery grave by a beautiful woman. Maybe you're not a woman at all. Maybe you're a selkie who shed her sealskin to bewitch me."

I snort. "I am a woman."

He grins and his eyes sparkle with a mischievous light. His gaze moves from my face to my breasts, nearly visible beneath the threadbare hospital gown. "Yes, you are."

My cheeks flush with a familiar heat. It is an unfortunate side effect of being exposed to a bad boy. My late-developing Cadar (Cad Radar) is pinging like mad. *Whoop. Whoop. Cad. Cad.* The Other Colin has all of the outward attributes of a bad boy—the chiseled physique, roguish grin, breathtaking good looks, curious little scar with a story to tell, leather jacket. Why wouldn't I be attracted to him?

"I am sorry I ruined your three-million-dollar shot."

What in the hell? Are you crazy? Never apologize to a bad boy. It's like inviting him into the puppeteer's booth and handing him the strings. What would Vivia say? "Seize your power, girlfriend."

"Go on with ya, then." He shrugs out of his leather jacket and tosses it on a nearby chair, then sits on the edge of my bed and fixes me with his million-watt gaze. "Ya don't need to say you're sorry, Grace. I should be apologizing to ya."

Wait a minute. Hold up. Bad boys don't apologize. Ever. Either he is very, very good at working the strings or I have misjudged his flirty behavior and tribal tattoo. Yes, that is a Celtic tribal tattoo peeking out from under the sleeve of his tight-fitting tee.

"You? Apologize to me? What, for making sure I didn't die of hypothermia?"

"I am sorry I called ya a fecking eegit and I am sorry I yelled at ya, Grace. I hope ya will forgive me."

He smiles and dimples appear on either side of his mouth. Did I mention that Colin Monaghan doesn't have dimples? Colin Banks might not be Colin Monaghan, but he's crazy hot and his smile is making my palms sweat.

"Forgiven."

"'Tanks a million," he says, grinning again. "Now then, would ya like to go to dinner with me, Grace Murphy? So I can thank ya proper."

"You don't need to thank me. I mean, you didn't need saving."

"Ah, but ya didn't know that when ya jumped off a cliff into the ocean, now did ya?"

I shake my head.

"That was very brave."

"You don't need to take me to dinner."

"Dinner and a pint."

I smile. "It's not necessary."

"It's an Irish tradition."

I frown. "Is that so?"

"Ah sure," he says, his face suddenly serious. "If someone saves your life, you must buy them a pint. You can't ignore customs."

"Hmm," I say, smiling. "That seems to be the custom for a prodigious number of situations."

He chuckles. "Is that a yes?"

"Yes, I will have dinner with you."

"Grand."

I am expecting him to leave now, but he doesn't. He just sits on the edge of the gurney, his warm, strong leg pressing against my side, and stares into my eyes. My body flushes again and, to my complete mortification, my nipples harden beneath my thin hospital gown.

"So, you're an actor?"

"No."

"Then why were you in the water?"

"I am Colin Monaghan's stunt double."

Eff me! No wonder he looks so much like Colin Monaghan. Wait until I tell Vivia I rescued Colin Monaghan's stuntman. Colin Monaghan's crazy hot stuntman.

The curtains part and Ondine walks in.

The Other Colin stands and grabs his leather jacket. He greets Ondine with a smile and a "hiya," before turning back to me.

"Tomorrow at seven?"

I nod my head.

"Where ya staying?"

His brown eyes, fringed with thick dark lashes, are so beautiful, so transfixing, all I can do is stare at him blankly.

"One Oysterbed Road," Ondine says. "It is the first left after Parknasilla."

He squeezes my hand and leaves.

"Feck me," Ondine gasps. "I think I'm having a heart attack. Get one of those paddle things and give me a jolt, will ya?"

I laugh. "How did you know I was here?"

Ondine tilts her head and wrinkles her nose. "Are ya fecking kidding me? I work in a village pub in Ireland. Pubs are like the one-one-two operators of gossip."

"One-one-two?"

"Sorry. Nine-one-one." She smiles. "When I heard an American girl went mad as a box of frogs and jumped into the ocean to save Colin Monaghan's stunt double, I asked myself, 'Hmm, could they be talking about Grace?' So, did ya see himself, then? Did ya see our Colin Monaghan?"

I shake my head.

"No worries," she says. "I hear they're filming a sky-diving scene out Dingle way next week. Did ya pack a parachute in that suitcase?"

Chapter Six

A WINTER STORY

SEEING STARS IN SNEEM

Colin Monaghan's arrival in Sneem has the quiet coastal town seeing stars. The actor, in town filming an untitled action-adventure film with Academy Award–winning director Konstantin Niakaros, has been spotted buying apples in the SuperValu, reading a newspaper in the Blue Bull, and eating chicken curry with his crew at O'Donnabháin's, in nearby Kenmaretown. . . .

"Feck me!" I say in my best Irish accent, and toss the *Irish Times* onto Ondine's kitchen table. "Everyone in Sneem has seen Colin Monaghan except me!"

I am waiting for the Other Colin to pick me up for our date, after spending the day driving the Ring of Kerry in search of Colin Monaghan. A gardener at the Parknasilla told me they would be filming at Ballinskelligs Abbey, a priory founded in the twelfth century by Augustinian monks, located thirty miles west of Sneem. I stopped at a gas station in Ballinskelligs. The attendant told me the crew had moved to Portmagee, a coastal town reached via the "old Skellig Ring," a ridiculously narrow road hugging the rocky coast.

In Portmagee, the waitress who served me fish and chips said she heard the crew was filming on Valentia Island.

I drove over the bridge spanning the inlet that separates Portmagee from Valentia Island and spent two hours bumping over every dirt track—from Bruff to Knight's Town. At the northernmost point of the island, I paid a few euros to hike Geokaun Mountain and Fogher Cliffs. I looked out at the vast, churning sea from a promontory called Shepherd's View and snapped a selfie in front of a whitewashed lighthouse.

What I didn't do was find Colin fecking Monaghan.

"Bah," Ondine says, waving her hand. "Anyone can say they visited the restaurant where Colin Monaghan ate chicken curry, but only one person can say they risked their life to save the man's stunt double."

"I would rather watch Colin Monaghan eat chicken curry."

"So why don't ya just ask your man to introduce ya to himself?"

"First, he's not my man." I pull a tube of tinted lip balm from my pocket and dab it on my lips. "Second, I don't want him to think I am a crazed fan who traveled across the Atlantic just to meet Colin Monaghan."

"But ya are a crazed fan who traveled across the Atlantic just so ya could meet Colin Monaghan."

I put the lid back on my lip balm and slide the tube

into my jacket pocket. "Yes, but I don't want him to know that."

"Because ya want to snog him?"

I remember the dark stubble shadowing the Other Colin's jaw and upper lip and wonder what it would feel like to have it graze my face as he kissed me, and my breath catches in my throat.

My cheeks flush.

Outside, the sound of an engine and tires moving over gravel saves me from having to answer Ondine's teasing question. I stand up and look at my reflection in the toaster, wiping a flake of mascara from my cheek and licking my lips.

"Do I look okay?"

I am wearing a pair of dark rinse skinny jeans, a slouchy turtleneck I bought from a woolen mill on our drive from Dublin to Sneem, black knee-high boots, and a black leather moto jacket Ondine let me borrow.

"Gorge," she says. "Just gorge. Tall, slender, with cheekbones a cover model would envy. Ya look like ya should be on the arm of a handsome Hollywood type."

"Thanks."

The doorbell rings and I jump. I didn't realize it before this second, but my stomach is twisted up tighter than a Christmas bow.

"Relax, Cinderella," Ondine says, squeezing my arm on her way to answer the door. "You're gonna have a grand time at the ball. I promise. Just don't stay out past midnight or take off anything more than your glass slippers."

I snort.

When I walk into the living room, Ondine and

Colin are making polite conversation. He's wearing black jeans, low black boots, and the same leather jacket he wore when he visited me in the ER. His hair is hidden beneath a beanie and the air around him smells of fresh, cold air and woodsy cologne.

He stops talking when he sees me and whistles.

"Feck me," he says, pressing his hand to his chest. "You're awful gorgeous when you're not covered in seaweed. I mean, ya were gorgeous then, but . . ."

My cheeks flush with heat, even though I know complimenting appearance is a standard bad boy pickup line. *You look gorgeous when you're not wearing that flight attendant uniform/barista apron/business suit/fill in the blank.*

"Thanks," I say. "You look awful gorgeous yourself."

Feck me! Did I really just tell this confident bad boy that I find him attractive? I might as well just give him access to my bank accounts and lingerie drawer now. It will save him a lot of time and me a lot of heartache.

Ondine hides her mouth with her hand.

He reaches into his jacket and pulls out a bundle wrapped in tissue and tied with string.

"Here," he says, handing me the package. "I brought a gift for ya."

"What?" I take the bundle. "You didn't need to buy me a gift."

"Ah, it's nothing. Just a wee souvenir to remember your time in Ireland."

His voice is deeper and sexier than I remembered and his accent is thicker than his Colin Monaghan–like brows. When he says Ireland it sounds like "Our-Lend."

I untie the string, remove the tissue paper, and discover a neatly folded square of red cloth. I unfold it and laugh. It's a T-shirt with a white cross in the center and the words "Sneem Lifeguard" printed around it.

"Do ya like it, then?"

"Are you kidding," I say, holding it up to my chest and smiling. "I love it! Where did you find it?"

"One of my mates owns a T-shirt company based out of Galway. I asked him to make it custom."

"Thank you." I give him a quick hug and step back before it can get weird. "That's me. Bravely rescuing the able bodied since 2017!"

He laughs.

I put the T-shirt in my suitcase, grab a pair of cashmere gloves, and follow Colin out the door. When I imagined what kind of vehicle Colin would drive, I imagined a rugged SUV with black tinted windows or a mud-splattered Jeep, not a sleek, matte, gray BMW motorcycle that looks straight out of a Bond movie.

"I hope you don't mind," he says, handing me a matte gray helmet that matches the bike. "My hire car had a flat, so I borrowed one of the bikes from the set."

"What?" I practically squeal. "This motorcycle is going to be in a Colin Monaghan movie? Are you serious?"

He frowns. "Yes, why?"

Why? *Because I am a crazed fan who traveled all the way across the Atlantic hoping to see Colin Monaghan and now you tell me I am going to take a ride on the back of the motorcycle from his next film?*

"No reason," I say, casually drawing an arc in the gravel with the toe of my boot. "I didn't expect you to pick me up on a motorcycle. I've never been on one before."

"You're serious?"

I nod my head.

"This will be your first time, then?" I look up into his brown eyes, see the teasing light glimmering in them, and my heart does a strange loop-de-loop in my chest. "Do ya trust me?"

Do I trust him? The only thing I know about Colin Banks is that he willingly jumps out of helicopters into a freezing ocean. Can I trust a devastatingly hot adrenaline junkie who smells like sex in leather? My mouth goes dry. My mind goes blank. I can't think of a witty response, so I pull the helmet on my head and fumble with the straps.

"Let me help," he says, his long fingers brushing my cheeks. He pulls the strap and adjusts the buckle under my chin. "Is that too tight?"

"No."

"Grand," he says, smiling. "I have been riding since before I was legally allowed to operate a motorcycle, so just try to relax. There are a few things ya need to know, though. I will get on first and then help ya on. Put your feet here"—he flips down the footrests located on either side of the bike—"but keep them away from this long tube. It's the exhaust and it gets very hot."

He swings one of his long legs over the bike, puts his helmet on his head, and gestures for me to hop on. I climb on and sit up straight.

He looks over his shoulder.

"Put your arms around my waist, your chest against my back, and look over my inside shoulder. When we come to a curve or turn, just relax against me and let me do the leaning, okay?"

I do as he says, wrapping my arms around his waist and pressing my chest against his back. The engine roars to life and we take off down the gravel drive and onto Oysterbed Road.

I wasn't entirely honest when I told Colin I had never been on the back of a motorcycle before. Sean of the Donald Duck orgasm rode a motorcycle. He picked me up for lunch one day wearing a Cage Warriors Fighting Championship wife beater and enough Drakkar Noir to knock out an elephant. He jammed the brakes several times, which I later learned is a cheap move pulled by d-bags trying to cop a feel because it slams the passenger's breasts against the driver. It's called the "boob jam." We rode to a nearby park and made out beside a row of Dumpsters. It was a very brief ride and a very unsatisfying make-out session. Therefore, it doesn't really count.

This ride is totally different—and not just because Colin has mad riding skills, taking the curves with the precision of a Grand Prix racer—but because I feel different with him. He treats me with more respect than Sean ever did. He seems genuinely concerned about me. Each time he stops, he puts his hand on my knee and asks if I am okay. He has the body of a cad and the manners of a dad . . . and I kinda like it.

He takes the N71 toward Killarney, a ribbon of a road that unfurls over rolling hills and through pine-scented forests.

I'm not gonna lie: the vibration of the engine under our seat, the feel of my arms and legs wrapped around Colin's solid body, the thrill of being on the back of a powerful motorcycle with a stranger in a strange country, is doing something to me. With each mile that passes I am becoming more and more attracted to the Other Colin. I rest my head against his shoulder, inhale the scent of his leather jacket comingled with his cologne, and wonder what it would be like to slip my hands under his coat, run my fingers over the ridges of his abs.

When he finally pulls into the restaurant parking lot and kills the engine, he has revved me up way more than the motorcycle. He removes his helmet, climbs off the bike, and holds out his hand to help me off.

I put my gloved hand in his and climb off the bike.

"You're trembling," he says, rubbing his hands up and down my arms. "Was it too cold?"

Cold? Is he kidding? It was bone-marrow-melting hot.

I take my helmet off and hand it to him, grinning.

"Are you kidding me? I don't want to sound like a stereotypical American, but that was awesome."

He laughs and stops rubbing my arms.

"I am glad ya liked it."

While Colin attaches our helmets to the bike, I look around. It's the gloaming, that magical time just before dark when the world looks as if it has been suspended in amber. The cozy stone restaurant is situated in the Killarney National Forest, on the banks of Looscaunagh Lough, a mirror-smooth lake aglow with a translucent orangey-yellow light. A wreath is hanging on the restaurant's red-painted door and tall red candles burn in each window. A painted wooden sign hangs from an iron lamppost that reads: Seanmháthair Lodge, established in 1860. It looks like a Thomas Kincade painting.

"What does *sean-ma-there* mean?"

"*Seanmháthair* means 'old mother,'" Colin says, taking my hand and leading me toward the front door. "It's pronounced 'shan-a-WAW-her.'"

Colin opens the door and we step inside. The rustic restaurant has stone walls, rough timber beams spanning the ceiling, and logs crackling and hissing inside a massive fireplace. The air smells of roasting meat and cinnamon.

An older woman wearing a crisp white apron greets us and shows us to a table beside the fire. She hands us each a menu, hand printed on heavy cream card stock.

"The special tonight is Seanmháthair Yule Pork," she says, crossing her hands and resting them on her waist. "Pork fillet wrapped in crispy belly, stuffed with apple and black pudding, and served with spiced apple and rosemary-flavored roasting juices. We serve it with a potato and cauliflower puree and garden peas."

"Mmm, that sounds delicious," I say, handing my menu back. "I will have that."

Colin orders beef fillet served in a whiskey peppercorn sauce and champ, creamy mashed potatoes with scallions and loads of butter. Meat and potatoes sound so much classier in Ireland.

"Can I bring yous something to drink?"

If I spend the rest of my life living in a cozy cottage in County Kerry, I won't ever become used to hearing the word *you* pluralized.

"I would love a Bulmers," I say. "Unless you can recommend a local cider."

"Ah, sure," she says, grinning. "Moll McCarthy's is made not too far from here in Moll's Gap. Mind how much ya drink, though, or ya will be two sheets to the wind before ya know it."

"I'll take one, thank you."

Colin orders a Guinness.

Our server returns with our drinks and a basket of warm soda bread with a crock of whipped butter.

"So, Grace Murphy," Colin says, resting his elbows on his chair and lacing his fingers. "Tell me something about yourself. Something grand."

I take a long sip of my cider and try to think of something grand. Something grand. Something grand. An image of my cramped apartment with the leaky kitchen faucet and sad, needle-shedding Charlie Brown Christmas tree pops into my mind. There isn't a lot of grand in my life.

"I am spending Christmas in Ireland. That's pretty grand."

"Ah, sure. But what about your family?"

"What about them?"

I take another sip of the crisp, pale golden cider, savoring the smooth taste that makes the cider I drink back home taste like cheap apple-flavored Kool-Aid by comparison.

"Aren't they going to miss ya?"

"I don't have a family."

His brows knit together, his lips turn down at the corners. "Everyone has a family, Grace."

I don't want to tell this tall, dark, gorgeous Irishman my sad, sordid, soap-opera-worthy story because I don't want him to pity me—pity is the worst, like razor blades on the heart—but he is staring at me with his soul-piercing eyes, beneath those thick, expressive Colin Monaghan-ish eyebrows.

"My grandparents died before I was born. My father left when I was a little girl. I don't have any siblings, aunts, or uncles."

"What about your mam?"

I shrug. "She told me once she never wanted a kid.

She thought a baby would be the superglue to hold my father, but he found a solvent—another woman. He got my mother pregnant and left her. Apparently, I have several half siblings scattered from Bakersfield to Boston."

"Jaysus!" He runs his hand through his hair. "I am sorry, Grace. I don't know what I would do without me mam and me gran."

"Ain't nothing but a thang," I say, smiling even though my heart is aching.

"What?"

"Sorry, it's something my friend Vivia says when she's brushing something off. It's American slang for 'no big deal.'"

"It is a big deal and I am sorry"—he reaches across the table and puts his hand over mine—"truly."

"Thank you, but you know what they say—what doesn't kill you makes you stronger." I swallow back the lump forming in my throat. "I've learned to be independent. I graduated from high school valedictorian, won a swimming scholarship to UC Davis, put myself through college and grad school, and landed a killer job."

Colin stares at me, a sympathetic smile on his lips and a knowing glint in his eye. He sees right through my bravado.

"You have had to be strong and independent." He squeezes my hand, before pulling his hand away. "You've had nobody else to rely on. *Go raibh do theach i gcónaí ró-bheag a shealbhú go léir do chairde.*"

Either Irish cider is a lot more potent than the cider we have in the States or Colin is having a stroke.

"Excuse me?"

"It's an Irish Gaelic blessing." He says, cutting

himself a piece of soda bread and slathering it with butter. "I said, 'May your home always be too small to hold all your friends.' Until you have a family of your own, I pray God gives you many friends."

Tears fill my eyes at his unexpected kindness.

"Thank you," I say, my voice cracking.

"*Tá fáilte romhat.*" He finishes buttering the bread, puts it on my bread plate, and cuts himself a slice. "That means 'you're welcome.'"

"What about you?" I change the subject before I crawl into his lap and start blubbering like a toddler lost in the mall. "Do you have a big family?"

"Sure," he smiles. "Five brothers, eight aunts, seven uncles, thirty-one cousins. Holidays are barely managed chaos, they are. We gather at my gran's house, not too far from where ya are staying in Sneem. Where are you from, Grace?"

Every time he pronounces my name, with a slight tip of the *r* and the Irish lilt, my heart skips a beat. I could listen to him say Grace Murphy again and again. Would it be weird if I asked him to say it into my iPhone recorder? How cool would it be to have that as my text tone?

"I was born in California, but I live in Philadelphia."

"What do ya do in Philadelphia?"

"I am in advertising. In fact, I work for the largest advertising firm in North America."

"Like *Mad Men*?"

I smile. I actually get that a lot.

"Sorta like *Mad Men*, only without all of the cocktails and sordid office sex."

He looks up from buttering his soda bread, one

black eyebrow arched. "What's the point, then? Really, without the cocktails and sex, it's just an unrelenting grind toward heart attacks and lung cancer."

I laugh.

"Tell me a campaign you have worked on. Have I seen any of your ads?"

"For the last year, I have been working on the Désir campaign."

"The Belgium chocolates?"

"Yes."

He sits back, crosses his arms, and whistles. "I am impressed, Peggy."

"Peggy?"

"You're a Peggy Olson. Striking out alone to make a name for yourself in the cutthroat world of advertising."

"Something like that," I say, laughing again.

I don't tell him that, like Peggy, I focus on my career too much and pick deadbeat losers as boyfriends.

"Still, I am impressed. Lifeguard and advertising executive. Very impressive."

"What about you, do you like being a stunt double?"

"I get paid to do things I would do for fun."

"Like fall out of a helicopter?"

He shrugs. "Fall out of a helicopter. Dangle from a cliff. Drive a motorcycle off a bridge."

"You drive motorcycles off bridges just for fun? Please tell me you don't have any fun planned on our ride home."

He laughs.

"That depends on what you consider fun." He winks, his broad toothy grin stretching across his handsome face. "What sort of fun did you have in mind?"

My cheeks flush with heat. I know precisely what the charming Irish rogue is implying. I should pump the brakes on his fast flirting, but a bad boy addict rarely knows her limitations.

"Anything that doesn't involve pain," I say, flipping my hair over my shoulder and giving him a little wink. "Surprise me."

Chapter Seven

CRAZY HEART

Colin Monaghan once said, "My biggest problem is that I don't know how to abstain from love. I fall in love with nearly every girl I meet." By the end of dinner, I am feeling Colin's pain. I am not saying I am in love with Colin Banks, but I am well on my way to having a problem.

Of course, Colin Monaghan also said, "There's something massively empowering about running naked into a frozen lough with a bunch of lads."

So maybe I shouldn't read too much into Colin Monaghan quotes . . . or the way Colin Banks's leg kept brushing mine under the table, or the way he made me laugh a thousand times before dessert, or the way he fed me a bite of his sticky toffee pudding.

We are just about to put our helmets on and climb back onto the motorcycle when he grabs my hand, puts it to his lips, and kisses the tender spot on my palm.

"Do ya have to get home?"

"No. Why?"

"I know a place. . . ."

Don't all players know a place? Is Colin making a play? I can't tell. Sure, his banter has been a wee bit flirty, but other than that he has acted as if he were having a pint with a pal.

". . . and on a clear night you can see clear across to the Beara Peninsula and Dursey Island."

"Ah, sure," I say, mimicking his accent. "It sounds grand, it does. 'Tanks for inviting me. 'Tanks a million!"

He laughs and pushes the helmet over my head. I adjust the straps, wait for Colin to swing his long leg over the motorcycle, and climb on behind him.

We follow the same ribbon road back to Sneem, but this time I hold Colin a little tighter and rest my chin against his left shoulder, watching the countryside zip by as if in a movie. I wish there were a cameraman filming us because I don't ever want to forget the way the hills look bathed in the quicksilver light of a full moon or the way Colin reaches back and squeezes my knee each time we stop at a crossroad.

We drive to the outskirts of Sneem, to a dirt turnoff. Colin parks the bike and we hop off. He takes my hand, leading me down a narrow path, through a thicket of flowering whin bushes, and to a wide swath of sandy beach.

We stand side by side, staring out over the water, glimmering silver in the moonlight, to a distant silhouette rising out of the water.

"That's the Beara Peninsula." He points across the water. "It's where me gran lives."

We walk along the water. The cold air blowing off the sea whips my hair around. Colin pulls his beanie off his head and puts it on my head, tucking my hair behind my ears. He stares at me so long I am certain he can read every hope written on my soul, hear the thundering beat of my heart.

"Do ya know how fecking beautiful ya are, Grace Murphy?"

No. I don't know how beautiful I am, Colin Banks, but please, please tell me in excruciating detail with that drop-dead sexy Irish accent.

I am about to make a flippant, self-depreciating comment when he leans down and presses his lips to mine. If Santa Claus filled my stocking with all of the sugarplums in the world, they wouldn't be half as sweet as Colin's kiss. He tastes of toffee and Guinness, two flavors I will forever associate with this moment and Colin Banks.

I am about to slip my arms around his waist when he stops kissing me. A cold breeze blows a lock of my hair across my face and it becomes fixed to my damp lips. Colin reaches down, brushes the hair from my face, and then slowly, teasingly, traces the swollen curve of my bottom lip from corner to corner. I can taste the sea salt, feel the rough warmth of his finger.

He grabs my hand and I open my eyes, blinking away the fog of fantasy. He leads me to a seawall and we sit on top of it. Colin wraps his arm around my waist as if it is the most natural thing in the world for us to be together on this dark, deserted beach. The waves lap against the shore, a lone seagull circling overhead cries mournfully.

Who could have imagined when I was alone in my apartment drinking Schweddy Balls and feeling sorry for myself that I would end up here, in County Kerry, Ireland? I look up at the seagull and feel a pang of empathy for the lonely creature. Before coming to Ireland, I felt like a seagull, circling around and around in the dark, hoping to find my way.

Vivia once told me that she is her best self when she travels. I didn't get it before, but I get it now. In Philadelphia, I was a shadow of my best self, stretched thin with work and worry over student loans, but here in Ireland I feel relaxed, confident, centered.

"I have to work tomorrow, but I am free the day after," he says, his voice as warm and comforting as a woolen blanket. "I would like to spend the day with ya, Grace. Would ya like to spend the day with me?"

The day, week, month . . .

"Sure," I say, keeping my tone casual. "What did you have in mind?"

"I want it to be a surprise. I'll text ya tomorrow with the details."

He laces his fingers through mine and we walk across the beach, up the hill, down the path leading to the turnoff. He climbs onto the motorcycle and I climb on behind him, snuggling close for the short ride back to Ondine's cottage. When he turns onto Oysterbed Road, I close my eyes and savor our last few seconds together, enjoying the warmth of his solid body, the scent of his spicy cologne, and the way my blood is racing through my veins, making me feel younger and alive.

He pulls to a stop and kills the engine. I am about to unwrap my arms from his waist when he puts his hands on mine and holds them in place against his rock-hard abdomen. We sit like that for a few minutes, listening to the wind whispering through the trees, inhaling the scent of pine needles and coming snow, prolonging a moment that will soon be a memory. It's simple and sweet and makes my heart ache for something I didn't even know I wanted.

I climb off, remove my helmet, hand it to Colin, and wait while he secures it to the back of the bike. He lifts his visor and grins at me.

"I am awful glad ya saved my life, Grace Murphy."

He turns the key in the ignition and the engine growls to life. He winks, lowers his visor, and drives away, his taillight fading in the darkness.

So am I, Colin Banks. So am I.

Chapter Eight

DAREDEVIL

The next morning I notice I got a text from Vivia:

Am I to take from your radio silence, Mata Hari, that you have finally managed to infiltrate the set and are using your feminine wiles to seduce Mister Colin Monaghan? Does the object of your obsession ... er, affection ... know that you traveled over 3,000 miles to be near him?

"We are going to jump out of an airplane."

I am sitting in the front passenger seat of Colin's sleek black SUV, dressed in black leggings, ripped boyfriend jeans, a UC Davis tee, and a flannel shirt. Colin texted late last night to say that he arranged a big surprise for our day together and that I should dress casually, in layers. I figured we were going on a hike.

"Are you crazy?" I retort.

"I'm Irish," he says, winking. "We're all as fecking mad as a box of frogs."

"Where?"

"Excuse me?"

"Where is this insane event supposed to take place?"

"We are making our jump over Bere Island."

"Bear Island? Excellent. So, after we plummet to our deaths, bears will feast on whatever flesh is left on our shattered bones."

He laughs.

"No worries, *a stór*," he says, patting my knee. "There aren't bears on Bere Island. Our broken bodies will be undisturbed."

"Ha ha."

All joking aside, panic is rising inside me like a tide, ominous, unrelenting. I twist the corner of my flannel shirt around my finger, making a knot, and wonder what big, bad, brave Colin Banks would do if I clutched the sides of the door and refused to leave the SUV. I did that once. First day of third grade. New school. You move a lot when you're poor—move to a cheaper place, move to avoid paying back rent, move to public housing. I don't know why, but I became convinced my mom was going to leave me at the new school, that she would drop me off in the morning, drive away, and never come back. I clutched the door handle of her Ford hatchback and refused to get out. It took Mom and my new teacher to pull me out of the car and into the school. I blink away the memory, and the tears collecting in my eyes, and unknot my shirt.

Colin flips his turn signal on and pulls off the side of the road.

"Grace," he says, turning to face me. "Look at me, please."

I look at him and feel ridiculous, stupid even, for acting like a weak, weepy baby. The man jumps out of helicopters and drives off bridges for a living; I don't want him to think I am a big fat coward.

"I would never make ya do something ya didn't want to do, a *stór.*" His low, husky voice rumbles in his chest. He reaches out and puts his hand on my cheek, stroking the tender skin just behind my ear with his thumb. "If ya don't want to skydive, just tell me. If ya decide ya do want to jump, ya need to know that we will be tethered together. I won't let anything bad happen to ya . . . ever."

I look into his brown eyes and the panic recedes. I don't know what it is about Colin Banks, but he makes me feel safe—my heart, my body, my thoughts—even as he is making me feel terrified and thrilled.

"Do ya trust me, Grace Murphy?"

"Ah, sure," I say, smiling. "I trust you."

Thirty minutes later we pull into a parking lot beside a narrow strip of a runway and a Quonset hut with chipping yellow paint.

We hop out of the SUV and walk across the gravel lot into the Quonset hut. Over the next three hours, Colin briefs me on how to sit securely in the airplane during takeoff and ascent, how to safely exit the aircraft together, the proper body position during free fall, and how we will perform our landing.

We gear up and go out to the plane. Before I have time to reconsider the lunacy of this date—or sign on to the Geico app to see if my life insurance policy covers death by skydiving—the plane is in the air and climbing to fourteen thousand feet.

We've only been cruising a little while when Colin stands and makes a fist, his thumb and pinky raised. It's the skydiver's hand signal for relax. It looks like the shaka sign the surfers used to make on Huntington Beach, and I am waiting for him to say, "Hang loose, duuude."

Instead, we hook up, shuffle over to the door, and wait for the red light to flash green. I close my eyes, take a deep breath, and then we are falling, falling, falling through clear blue sky. During my briefing, Colin told me the free-fall part only lasts about sixty-five seconds. It feels like six seconds. We are weightless, floating, flying together, our arms outstretched, legs bent and touching. It's exhilarating and sexy.

The view is breathtaking . . . literally. The ocean stretches endlessly, a rolling blanket of deep blue.

Colin pulls a cord, the chute deploys, and we are jerked up through wispy clouds. Then, we are spiraling, spiraling, spiraling toward the sea. Colin maneuvers us toward an island covered in a patchwork quilt of green. The island gets closer and closer. I pull my knees as Colin instructed and keep them up until he lands feet first on spongy ground.

He has barely untethered us when I turn around and jump on him, wrapping my wobbly legs around his waist and my arms around his neck.

"That was amazing!"

He laughs.

"Ya liked it then?"

"Are you kidding? I fecking loved it!"

My wind-chapped cheeks flush with heat as I suddenly realize that Colin is supporting me by cupping my bottom in his hands. I unwrap my legs and drop onto my feet.

He crosses his arms over his chest and grins. "Are ya impressed?"

"Crazy impressed." I look into his twinkling eyes and it feels as if my heart has decided to skydive, free-falling inside my chest. "This is the best date ever."

"It's not over yet," he says, winking.

By the time we finish gathering the parachute, a mud-splattered Jeep with the "Aerodrome Ireland" logo emblazoned on its hood is bouncing over the ground toward us. We hop inside and drive over dirt roads to the small town of Rerrin, where we catch a ferry back to the mainland.

It isn't long before we are back in Colin's SUV, racing along the circular road that is the Ring of Beara. Colin pulls off the paved road and follows a rutted dirt track until it ends. He hops out, gets something from the trunk, and comes around to open my door.

"I thought we could have a picnic lunch."

He is carrying a big black backpack, the kind soldiers wear when they are on special ops missions. Colin leads the way over mushy, marshy ground, up a slight rocky incline, until we come to what looks like the ruined tower of a castle perched on the edge of a cliff.

He leads me into the tower, pulls a blanket out of his backpack, spreads it on the ground, and invites me to sit. Then he busies himself gathering rocks and using them to form a circle in the center of the tower. He pulls a camping log and a small bundle of twigs out of his backpack and positions them in the circle, removes a lighter from his pocket, and soon we have a cozy campfire.

He joins me on the blanket and we eat roasted chicken sandwiches, sliced apples, and drink bottles of apple cider while staring out the gaping hole in the tower's wall at the ocean beyond.

"To all our days here and after," he says, holding his cider bottle in the air. "May they be filled with fond memories, happiness, and laughter."

"*Sláinte,*" I say, clinking my bottle against his.

"*Sláinte!*"

Colin waits until I have taken a sip of cider before grabbing the bottle from my hand and setting it aside. He pulls me into his arms and we fall back on the blanket, lips on lips, legs tangled together. We explore each other's bodies with our hands and mouths until we are fevered and gasping for breath. I know I should pump the brakes on this holiday romance, but a dangerous little voice in my head is telling me to grip it and hit it. I slide my hand down his chest, tugging on his jeans button.

He groans against my lips and shoves his hands under my tee, cupping my breasts.

I feel as if I am free-falling through a night-blackened sky, tumbling blindly toward danger, powerless to stop what is happening. Words spin around and around in my brain. Lunatic. Break the pattern. Holiday romance. Broken heart. Colin. Colin.

"Colin," I moan. "I want . . ."

"What, *a stór*? What do ya want?"

I want you to stop before we have sex and I fall hopelessly, helplessly in love with you and ruin this amazing, special thing we have . . . like I have ruined every other relationship I have ever had. I want you to stop so I can tell you the truth—that I came to find one Colin and fell in love with another.

"I want . . ." My skin flushes with my arousal. "I want . . . I want you."

Colin growls low in his throat.

We lay together under another blanket he pulled out of his miraculous, Mary Poppins, never-ending backpack, and stare out the window as snowflakes tumble out of the sky, making the same spiraling descent we made a few hours before.

It's one of those perfect moments, like when you plug the Christmas tree lights in for the first time and they all light up, or like when you stand on the beach and a wave curls onto shore and washes over your bare feet. The Vienna Boys Choir came to Philadelphia two years ago and I scored a free ticket. I sat in the pew, listening to those angelic voices, and my heart felt whole and content.

That's how I feel right now, lying beside Colin. Whole and content.

I am sitting in his SUV, holding my hands in front of the heater vents, when I remember Kale and his "10 Things" list on my Facebook wall.

"Colin?"

The snow is pouring out of the sky and he is concentrating on the road.

"Yes, *a stór?*"

"Do you think my hair smells like chlorine?"

"No."

"If I told you I liked to wear flannel pajamas with frog princes on them, what would you say?"

"Are they easy to remove?"

"Be serious."

"I am serious," he says, laughing. "I don't care what ya wear to bed as long as it's easy to take off."

"Okay," I say, tucking my hands under my armpits. "Let's say it was a Friday night and you wanted to go out, but I wanted to stay home and watch *10 Things I Hate about You*."

"With Heath Ledger?"

"Yes."

"I fecking love that movie."

A warning bell goes off in my head. Something is wrong here. Colin is too perfect. He likes the way my hair smells, doesn't care if I wear flannel pajamas, and plans rom-com-worthy dates.

"What if I told you I have quirky friends, write fan fiction, and—"

He glances over at me, frowning.

"What is this about, Grace?"

I take a deep breath and then I tell him about getting suspended from work (omitting the Colin Monaghan bit) and how Kale dumped me on Facebook.

"Your ex-boyfriend is a fecking rawny Muppet."

"A what?"

"A spineless fool."

"What would you have done?"

"I would have taken the piss out of ya."

"Eww."

"It means I would have teased ya. I would have given ya a hard time, Grace."

"That's it?"

"That's it." He squeezes my knee. "I am confident enough in my masculinity not to be threatened because ya write a bit of romantic fiction. It's a wee man who feels he can't compete with a fantasy." He takes his hand off my knee and puts it back on the steering wheel. "Any other questions?"

"No. Yes." I turn to look at him. "Why do you keep calling me '*a stór*'? What does it mean?"

He turns off the road and follows a driveway up a hill, parking in front of a thatch-roofed cottage with windows glowing golden in the darkness.

"It's an Irish term of endearment."

I smile a big, beaming, toothy smile like the kid from *A Christmas Story* when he finally got his Red Ryder BB gun.

"What's it mean?"

"It doesn't matter."

I poke him in the sides, tickling him.

"Tell me."

"No."

"I'll keep tickling you."

He squirms to get away, laughing.

"Fine," he says. "I have broken six bones, suffered hypothermia, a stab wound, and second-degree burns, but I can't stand to be tickled."

I stop tickling him.

"It means 'my treasure.'"

And just like that, my battered and abandoned heart grows three sizes. It's amazing how a little love and tenderness can heal a person.

"Thank you," I whisper. "That's a lovely thing to say."

Then, I lean over and kiss his cheek. He turns his head and kisses me on the lips.

"I hope ya don't mind, but I promised my gran I would drop by and introduce ya to her."

I look out the window at the whitewashed cottage and the new-fallen snowflakes sparkling like glitter on the thatched roof and my eyes fill with tears, my throat constricts.

"You brought me to meet your grandmother?"

"Sure. Why not?"

He jumps out of the car and comes around, opening my door and holding his hand out to help me down. I have never had a date introduce me to his family—not after two dates, not after twenty-two dates.

If Santa had asked me to make a list (and check it twice) of the traits found in an ideal grandmother, I would probably just write: see Catriona Banks. Colin's gran is as short as an elf, with twinkling green eyes, silver hair, and a kind smile. She speaks with a thick Irish accent and her words rise and fall in a most charming, lyrical way.

Although Colin tells her we can only stay for a few minutes, she waves him away with a "go on, will ya," links her arm through mine, and leads me to a set of overstuffed chairs facing the fireplace.

She is a brilliant conversationalist, as skilled at asking questions as she is at listening. She cuts through all of the gristle and gets right down to the bones of my life. I don't know why, but I tell her things I've only told my closest friends. When a timer in the kitchen begins ringing, she apologizes and hurries to turn it off.

Colin walks over and whispers in my ear, "She likes ya, which means she is going to insist ya stay for dinner."

We have shepherd's pie, mushy peas, and buttery rolls. After we have cleared the table and helped wash the dishes, she prepares a tray with homemade cinnamon oatmeal cookies and a pot of tea, and we settle beside the fire. She tells me funny stories about Colin when he was a boy, and by the time we are pulling our coats back on and saying our good-byes, I am hopelessly, helplessly in love with Catriona Banks.

"'Tanks a million," she says, giving me a hug. "It was grand to meet ya. Just grand."

"Would you adopt me?"

She pats my cheek.

We are almost to the SUV when she calls to Colin. He helps me inside, tells me he will be right back, and shuts the door.

I watch as he lowers his head so his grandma doesn't have to raise her voice, and a lump forms in my throat. Colin is one of the good ones, a decent guy who treats me with respect and loves his grandmother. I look up at the wintry sky, find the brightest twinkling star, and make a wish.

"I don't know if this thing I have going with Colin is more than a Christmas holiday romance, but whatever happens, please let me get a good one. Let me get a good one with a gran who smells like lavender and bakes oatmeal cookies."

Colin runs back to the SUV and climbs inside.

"Gran would like ya to join us for Christmas Eve dinner," he says, turning the key in the ignition and backing down the driveway. "That is, if there isn't somewhere else ya would rather be."

My heart feels like a big, shiny Mylar balloon pumped full of helium. It's the same feeling I used to get in elementary school gym class when I would be chosen first for a kickball team . . . only better. Much, much better.

"There's nowhere else I would rather be."

Chapter Nine

ORDINARY DECENT CRIMINAL

The next week passes like a chick flick montage. I help Ondine sell her silver necklaces at Christmas markets in Galway, Cork, and Limerick, hike the ancient forests around Killarney, snap selfies beside the Cliffs of Moher. I spend an evening sitting beside the fire with Colin's gran while she patiently tries to teach me how to knit, and another drinking thick, foam-topped ale and listening to upbeat traditional Irish music in a pub with Colin.

Colin spends his days filming intense, high-action scenes, staggering back to his hotel half frozen and completely exhausted. One night I got a text from him:

I would love to take you out tonight, *a stór*, but I am in tatters. Fancy a quiet night with a passably good-looking, battered Irishman?

I replied instantly:

Go way outta that, ya fecking gorgeous Irishman.
How about I pick up some fish and chips from the
Blue Bull and we watch whatever's on the
television?

(When Ondine's father offered to arrange a tour
of a local whiskey distillery and I told him I didn't
want him troubling himself, he said, "Go way outta
that!" Ondine told me it meant "Don't be silly.")
Colin texted me back:

Ah, what a ride you are, Grace Murphy! Keep it up
and I will fall in love with you.

You mean you're not already?

Not answering that question. I need to keep some
things secret for Christmas.

I arrive at his room armed with steaming, crispy
fish and chips wrapped in paper and a bottle of pep-
permint-scented massage oil topped with a red bow.
Colin is staying in one of the courtyard lodges, one-
bedroom apartments nestled in the forest behind the
main lodge.

He opens the door wearing a towel around his
lean waist, his hair damp from the shower, an angry
purple bruise on his massive right bicep. My breath
catches in my throat. For a nanosecond, I think I
have knocked on Colin Monaghan's door, but then
he pulls me into the room, bends me backward over
his arm, and kisses me the way only Colin Banks can
kiss me.

"I missed ya today, Grace Murphy," he says, looking
into my eyes.

"I missed you, too."

"I'm glad."

He goes into the bedroom to get dressed while I turn on the gas fireplace and unpack the fish and chips, arranging them on plates I find in the kitchen cupboard.

Colin returns wearing charcoal cashmere lounge pants and a matching hoodie that hugs his chest and biceps. We eat our fish and chips and talk about everything and nothing, like two old friends or familiar lovers. I have never felt such a comforting, easy familiarity with a man before.

It's after eleven when Colin leans back in his chair, raises his fists in the air, and yawns.

"I should go," I say, standing and carrying the dishes to the sink. "It is getting late and you have an early call tomorrow morning."

He grabs me around the waist and pulls me onto his lap, nuzzling my neck with his nose, kissing my collarbone.

"Not so fast," he says, growling in my ear. "I believe you said something about a shoulder massage . . . unless you want me to massage you?"

Considering he spent twelve hours hanging from a helicopter's landing skids, I am more than a little impressed and flattered that he would even make such an offer.

I follow him to the bedroom. He pulls off his hoodie and tosses it on the floor, collapsing on the bed facedown. I stare at his broad shoulders, rippled back tapering to a narrow waist, and lust flickers inside me, like the flames in the gas fireplace, growing fiercer by the second.

I remove the lid from the bottle, pour a generous

amount of oil onto my hand, and rub my hands together until my palms are warm. I start at the sexy valley at the base of his spine and slowly move up, up, up, until I reach his shoulders, pushing my palms against his deltoids, and kneading the knots away.

I haven't been massaging him for long before I am aware of the soft, even rise and fall of his back. I sit on the edge of his bed, staring at his handsome face, illuminated by a shaft of moonlight streaming through a gap in the curtains, and I wish I could freeze this moment, capture it in a snow globe to gaze upon again and again.

I cover him with a blanket and creep to the door when he mumbles something. I walk back to the bed and his hand shoots out, grabbing me by the wrist and pulling me into bed beside him.

"Stay, *a stór*," he says, his voice thick with sleep, his eyes sealed shut. "Please."

Of course I stay. What would you do if a sexy Irishman called you "his treasure" and begged you to spend the night with him? I kick off my boots and snuggle against him.

The first full night I spend with Colin "Could Be the Man of My Dreams" Banks, outrageously gorgeous, stud of a stuntman, we sleep fully clothed, spooning like two old married people. It's the best night's sleep I have ever had.

The next morning, I am hurrying down the path that leads away from Colin's room and back to the main lodge when I see Colin "Gorgeous but Shorter and Older than I Thought" Monaghan dressed in plaid flannel pajama bottoms and a heavy, navy blue pea coat.

I am so stunned, I stop dead on the sidewalk, staring with my mouth hanging open. In ten seconds, I am going to be face to face with the man I have dreamt about since high school and I look like the homeless woman that sleeps on the bench in Love Park, back in Philadelphia. My clothes are rumpled. I have a wicked case of bed head. And the sexy, smoky eyes I was working last night have smudged so much I look like a linebacker with two wide black swipes of liner on my upper cheeks.

And then it happens. . . .

Colin stops walking and looks at me, fixing his sweet Belgian-chocolate brown gaze on me. He is close enough for me to see the moles on his left cheek and the stray hairs fanning out from the top of his expressive, thick brows.

He smiles a little nervously and waits for me to move, but my feet are frozen to the path. I am literally transfixed by the lank of black hair, shot through with gray, hanging down the side of his face. Colin's hair is as thick and beautiful as his expressive brows, but grayer than I imagined.

"Oh. My. God!" My excited voice echoes around the quiet courtyard, bouncing off the stone path. "You're Colin Monaghan. I am Grace. Grace Elizabeth Murphy, from America."

He grabs my elbow and opens his mouth to speak.

"I write fan fiction about you!" My verbal locomotive has left the station and is full-steam ahead. It won't stop for anyone, not even Colin "I Finally Found Him" Monaghan. "I was thinking about writing a story about an American girl who is *totally* obsessed with you and travels to Ireland to track you down . . . but not in a creepy way."

I laugh . . . in a creepy way. Colin lets go of my arm.

"Everything all right here?"

I look over Colin's shoulder. A hulking man in a black sweatshirt with the word "Security" printed across the chest is hurrying toward us, followed by a maid and a woman carrying a clipboard and two smartphones. She's wearing the same black jacket and snapback members of the crew wore the day I botched their helicopter scene.

"You're the nutter from the beach, aren't you?" she says, squinting. "What are you doing here?"

Just then, Colin strolls up. The Other Colin. The only Colin. My Colin.

"Grace?"

Colin Monaghan backs away and the security guard steps in front of him, like security guards do when they are protecting megastars from deranged fans. It reminds me of a clip I saw on TMZ, when paparazzi swarmed around Britney Spears as she left a restaurant. Poor Brit-Brit had this terrified expression, like a little kitten backed into a corner by a pack of snarling dogs.

And then, suddenly, it hits me. I am the deranged fan. I am the one everyone is staring at. I am the one the megastar is trying to get away from.

"You have been observed lurking around the grounds many times over the last few weeks," the security guard says. "I know you are not a guest. So, what are you doing here?"

"She told me she was in love with Colin Monaghan. She said she came all the way from America just to meet him. She even said she would pay me two hundred euros and name her firstborn after me if I would sneak her into his room," the maid says.

"I was only kidding," I say, forcing a laugh. "Seriously? You didn't think I was for reals, did you?"

Colin, my Colin, looks at me through wide, disbelieving eyes with an expression that makes me feel ashamed and desperate and sad all at once.

"Is this true, Grace? Did you come to Ireland just to meet Colin Monaghan?"

I consider my options. I could pretend to faint. It always works in Jane Austen flicks. I could snort and roll my eyes in a totally "as if" way. Or, I could own it.

Yes. Yes, I did travel over three thousand miles, cash in my Hilton Honors points, and take a serious chunk out of my savings in the hopes of meeting the man who made me laugh out loud in In Forgetting My Mind, *made me cry with longing in* A Year Without Summer, *and scratch my head in utter confusion in* The Prophecy of Nobody. *You gotta problem with that?*

In the end, Colin "Thinks I Am a Stalker" Monaghan turns and walks away without so much as a "Top o' the morning to ya!" The security guard sticks close to the megastar. The maid clucks her tongue at me before hurrying back to her cart. Clipboard Girl shoots Colin, *my* Colin, a pointed, "ditch the groupie loser and get your shit together" look.

And Colin, my Colin, looks at me the same way he did the day we met on the beach. I am waiting for him to say, "Are ya a fecking eegit?" but he doesn't. Instead, he shakes his head, runs his hand through his hair, and says, "I have to go to work now. We'll talk later."

But we don't.

Chapter Ten

A HOME
AT THE END OF THE WORLD

After I text Vivia and tell her what happened, she texts back:

So what if you had a slightly disturbing obsession with the man who could be his older, grayer, less muscular doppelganger. That is hardly a reason for Colin Banks to end your relationship, is it? I don't think so. We all have our oddities. Even Colin— Probably Lets the Yellow Mellow—Banks. Go to him.

I reply:

I don't know what that means—lets the yellow mellow.

It means he probably doesn't flush the toilet every time he goes. But that's not really the point. The point is this: we are all flawed, fragile, cast-off china, collecting dust in the antique store that is life. The trick is finding someone who sees our worth despite the tiny, hairline cracks. You're a treasure, Grace.

Every Halloween I watch M. Night Shyamalan's *Signs,* a sci-fi thriller about hostile aliens invading earth. My favorite scene—besides the one where the long-legged alien pokes his gray head out from behind a tree—is the "which type of person are you" scene, when the main character says that people can be divided into two groups: the kind that see signs and the kind that explain things away as coincidences.

I see signs. I believe there are complex cosmic connections. I believe nothing happens randomly.

Vivia describing me as a treasure is a sign. It has to be. I didn't tell her Colin called me *a stór.* I don't believe she randomly chose that word to describe me.

I don't want to believe it.

I want to believe that a higher power compelled her to use that word to reignite my hope, to spur me into action.

It's the day before Christmas Eve. It's been thirty-five hours and forty-six minutes since I watched Colin walk down the path at Parknasilla. He promised we would talk, but he hasn't called, e-mailed, or texted. I've checked—eighty-four times. I click out of my texts and open my e-mail, just in case Colin decided to send me a note. No new e-mail messages.

Eighty-five times.

I have been stressing about Christmas Eve, debating whether I should show up at his gran's cottage in my Sunday best or stop trying to resuscitate a relationship too weak to survive beyond its infancy. I had just convinced myself to wait for Colin to reach out to me and then I got the sign.

I slip my feet into my boots and grab my coat.

"I am going to find Colin."

"It's about fecking time!" Ondine has been wrapping Christmas gifts for her family for the last few hours while I watched the snow fall and checked my phone for messages. She drops a shiny red bow and stands up. "Let's do this thing!"

"You've been a godsend, Ondine. Truly. My very own Clarence."

"Clarence?"

"Clarence Odbody," I say, smiling. "The angel who saves George Bailey in *It's a Wonderful Life.*"

"I get it." Ondine sits back down. "You need to do this alone, am I right?"

I nod. "Please don't be mad."

"Go way outta that," she says, waving her hand at me. "Go in with ya. Go get your man, Grace, but take a scarf because the snow is pouring like Guinness on Saint Patrick's Festival."

I give her a quick hug and hurry out the door, ignoring her suggestion to grab a scarf. Who needs a threadbare scarf? I have passion, purpose, and pure adrenaline to keep me warm. I am motivated by an ageless longing, driven by the purest of emotions. Surely, the fates are in my favor. Fate favors the bold.

I hop into my rental car and put the key in the ignition, turning the wipers on to clear the thick, fluffy snow from my windshield, and take off down Oysterbed Road. I wish I had wings so I could fly to Colin, because I want to be by his side now, for the rest of my life.

I've never felt this urgency, this overwhelming, all-powerful need to be with a man. Sure, I have fallen in and out of lust, but I've never been in love. Not really. Not like this. Maybe Vivia was right. Maybe I fell "in love" with Colin Monaghan to keep from falling in love with a mere mortal, to keep from feeling what I am feeling right now: vulnerable.

Oh my God!

I am a classic case, aren't I? Poor little fatherless girl who grows up so terrified of abandonment she finds the one unobtainable bad boy to idolize and a series of real, accessible bad boys to perpetuate the familiar.

I don't know if Colin Banks is the right guy, but I know he is a good guy. A real, flesh-and-blood man who makes my idol look like an illumination, a shadow, a mere projection of the reality.

"*Go to Ireland,*" Vivia said. "*Track Colin Monaghan down . . . or don't. Whatever you do, take the time to get to know the Grace I already know: the one who is funny, smart, kind, and completely worthy of all that is good.*"

I came to Ireland to find Colin Monaghan, but I have found something far more precious: a belief that I *am* worthy of what is good.

I navigate a series of switchbacks and make the turn onto the steep road leading to Colin's gran's cottage, but the snow is too thick and my little Volkswagen Polo gets stuck. I shift into reverse and give it gas. The wheels make a high-pitched whining sound, but the car doesn't move. I alternate between reverse and drive, hoping to rock the car out of the drift, but it only moves a few inches. I shift into park, open my door, and step out of the car, my boots sinking deep in the snow.

The VW is well and truly stuck—the tires have made channels in the dirt road. I am going to have to call the rental car company's roadside assistance for a tow truck. I get back into the car, crank the heat, and grab my iPhone out of my purse.

No signal. Of course.

It's getting dark and the snow is really coming down. Even if I could get a signal, there's a chance roadside assistance wouldn't be able to dispatch a tow truck before morning.

I will die if I wait until morning. Maybe not of hypothermia, but definitely of adrenaline overdose. I have to talk to Colin tonight. I have to make it better.

I turn the car off, strap my purse crosswise around my chest, and leave the warmth of my little rental car, stepping into the blowing, swirling snow.

The cottage is at the top of the hill, maybe a mile away. If I can jump off a cliff into a freezing sea, I can walk a mile, uphill, in a blizzard. I flip my collar up, shove my hands in my pockets, and trudge through the snow, sticking close to the side of the road.

By the time I finally reach the drive leading to the cottage, the snow has stopped falling and the sky is filled with a million silvery stars. Tall red candles burn in each of the cottage's glowing windows.

The door opens before I have a chance to use the knocker. Colin's gran is standing in the doorway.

"Ah, my poor, poor luv," she says, wrapping a thick heather-blue scarf around my shoulders. "You're frozen through. It's a good thing I made this scarf for ya."

I look at her through a haze of tears.

"For me?"

"Aye."

I nuzzle my nose against the scarf, catch the scent of lavender, and the tears spill down my frozen cheeks.

"Come in, luv," she says, stepping back. "Come in."

I shake my head. She pulls her cardigan tighter around and steps closer, pulling the door closed behind her.

"I am sorry," I sniffle. "It's just, growing up, I used to hear my friends talk about their grandparents and I always felt so envious. I wished I had a grandma to bake me cookies and knit me scarves and a grandpa to ruffle my hair and say silly things like 'Rubber baby buggy bumpers.'"

She pats my cheek with her weathered hand. The door opens and Colin appears. My heart skips a silly, sappy beat and fresh tears fill my eyes. Colin's gran pats my cheek again before going back inside and shutting the door.

"What are ya doing here, Grace?"

My tongue is frozen to the roof of my mouth. What *am* I doing here? I rehearsed what I wanted to say on the drive here, but the words seem to have been blown away by the blizzard. It doesn't help that Colin is scowling.

"I had to see you . . . to explain."

He looks over my shoulder, down the drive.

"Where is your car?"

"Stuck at the bottom of the hill."

"Are ya saying ya walked?"

I nod my head and my teeth chatter together.

"It's not the first time I have risked h-hypothermia to be near you."

His scowl softens and he reaches for me.

"Come inside before ya freeze, ya fecking eegit!"

"No," I say, shaking his arm off. "I need to say something and if I don't say it now, I might lose the nerve."

"Grace Murphy?" He chuckles softly. "Lose nerve? Impossible."

An SUV pulls into the driveway and I worry Colin is about to leave.

The words come to me, pour out of me. I tell him about my dysfunctional childhood and how I escaped into the make-believe world of television, watching movies about fathers who stayed, mothers who loved. I tell him I went to college and learned how to make a career out of selling illusions, packaging and marketing something to be better than the reality. I tell him that I came to Ireland to find my dream man because I wanted to see if the reality was as wonderful as the illusion.

He clenches his jaw.

"And I did . . ."

"Aye, you found Colin Monaghan, all right."

"No. I am talking about you, Colin Banks. You are the Colin of my dreams—only I didn't know that until I met you. I am sorry I didn't tell you about my Colin Monaghan thing. . . . I didn't want you to think I was a weird stalker or that I was using you to get a chance to meet Colin . . . the other Colin."

"So, are ya over Colin Monaghan?"

"Yes."

"Completely?"

"Totally."

"Does that mean ya don't want to meet him?"

I think about his question before answering and realize I don't want to meet Colin Monaghan. I have been cured of the madness.

"I really don't care about meeting Colin Fecking Monaghan. I would rather be with Colin Banks."

"That's too bad."

My heart drops to my boots. I blew it. He isn't going to give me another chance.

The door behind Colin opens and . . . Colin "Still Cute Even If He Does Have a Wee Bit of a Dad Bod" Monaghan walks out. He smiles at me, slaps Colin on the back, and climbs into the idling SUV.

I turn back to my Colin. He has his arms crossed over his broad chest and is staring at me with a mischievous grin on his face.

"Merry Christmas, Grace Murphy," he says, pulling me into his arms and giving me a big kiss.

"Merry Christmas, Colin . . . my Colin."

Dear Readers:

When I wrote Faking It, *the first book in my four-book It Girls series, I wanted to create a cast of young, quirky, pop-culture-savvy characters who face challenges that force them to look for the deeper meaning in their lives. Grace Murphy was a throw-away character—my heroine's college roommate who had a comical obsession with actor Colin Farrell.*

The more I thought about Grace and her obsession with Colin, the more I wanted to write a book about her. I told myself that the only way I could write a book about a girl who travels to Ireland to find Colin Farrell was to actually travel to Ireland and attempt to find Colin Farrell.

So, I talked my best friend into tagging along on a trip to Ireland. We bought our tickets and booked a hotel in Dublin and a cottage along the coast in County Kerry.

Then, I did a little Googling. You can imagine my shock when I discovered Colin lives in Los Angeles and only spends a small part of each year in Dublin. I spent hours on the Internet, searching fan sites, news sites, gossip sites—any site with information about Colin's Dublin. It paid off. I learned where Colin likes to jog, which restaurants he prefers, and which clubs and pubs he has frequented. If I couldn't

*meet Colin in person, I would have to content myself
with visiting his fave haunts.*

*A few weeks before we were supposed to depart for
Dublin, I learned that Colin was in Ireland filming*
The Lobster. *I did more digging and
hyperventilated when I discovered that Colin was
filming a few miles from the cottage we had rented in
County Kerry.*

Serendipity was working her magic.

*Thanks to the lovely and charming Peter O'Brien,
manager of Lillie's Bordello, I was able to score two
invites to the posh VIP club that celebs visit when they
are in Dublin. We spent two days in Dublin, visiting
Colin's favorite places before heading to County Kerry.*

*Everywhere we went in Ireland, we met someone
who had a Colin story. They all spoke fondly of the
actor and called him "our Colin." I rehearsed in my
head how my meeting with "my Colin" would go. I
would be cool and witty. He would be so attracted to
my magnetic personality that he would invite me to
grab a pint with him and his mates at a nearby pub.*

Some might call it delusions of grandeur.

*The reality? I was sitting in the lobby of the
Parknasilla Resort, waiting to have a spa treatment,
when my best friend whispered, "There he is." I looked
up just as he was walking out of the dining room (cue
choir of angels and rays of heavenly light). I jumped
up, ran over to him, and acted like the worst kind of
fangirl, gushing about his movies and telling him
how I was working on a novel about a girl who was
obsessed with him and tracks him down . . . but not
in a creepy way. I must have blacked out after that
because all I remember is him looking into my eyes,*

5

touching my arm, and calling me "lovely" (twice), and then he was gone in a cloud of woodsy aftershave.

I saw him in the corridor later that day. He smiled and nodded his head. Sigh. Over the next few days, we were able to watch Colin and his fellow actors filming. We made friends with one of the assistant directors and some of the extras (one gave me a call sheet from the movie as a souvenir). It was a closed set, which meant we weren't supposed to take pictures with the actors, but we were able to get a few memorable snappies. And then our magical, serendipitous trip to the Land O'Farrell was over.

I went home vowing I would never wash the place where Colin touched my arm. I bored my friends with the telling (and retelling) of how Colin touched my arm and called me "lovely" . . . twice.

And, I wrote this story.

I hope you enjoyed reading Grace's story as much as I enjoyed (researching) and writing it. I also hope you will read about the many adventures of Vivia Perpetua Grant and her friends in my It Girls series.

All the best and happy holidays,
Leah Marie Brown

Grace Murphy's Ireland Must-See List:

LILLIE'S BORDELLO, IN DUBLIN
1-2, Adam Court, Grafton Street

Glam up and bat your eyes at the doorman and you might find yourself admitted to this swank VIP club.

PEACOCK GREEN, DUBLIN
Lord Edward Street

A fab tea shop and bakery with the most darling painted, wood facade. I highly recommend the caramel-chocolate shortbread.

CAFÉ TOPOLIS, PARLIAMENT STREET, DUBLIN
37 Parliament St, Dublin Southside

Everything about this café is inviting, from the wide-plank wood floors and old brick walls to the garlic and bubbling cheese–scented air. It's the perfect place to tank up on pasta before a night of pubbing.

O'DONNABHÁIN'S RESTAURANT AND PUB, KENMARE
10 Henry Street

The owner, Jer Foley, is friendly and extremely knowledgeable about the area. His wife is a fantastic chef. Her shepherd's pie is heaven in your mouth.

CROWLEY'S BAR, HENRY STREET, KENMARE
26 Henry Street

If you blink, you might miss this small pub located on Kenmare's busiest commercial street. My advice: Don't blink! Crowley's is dark and a little dank and utterly fecking charming. If you are looking for the real Irish pub experience and some amazing trad (traditional Irish music), Crowley's is where you want to head.

BRAY HEAD LOOP HIKE, VALENTIA ISLAND
Off Route 565

This moderate hike takes approximately three hours and is well worth the effort, offering sweeping views of the sea and Valentia Island and culminating at a ruined guard tower perched on a rocky cliff.

PARKNASILLA SPA AND RESORT, SNEEM
Derryquin

The spa at Parknasilla has some of the finest views of Kenmare Bay. Schedule a massage or facial and then head to the deck to soak in the hot tub overlooking the forest and sea.

QUINLAN'S SEAFOOD BAR, HIGH STREET, KILLARNEY
77 High Street

Crazy good chipper, with golden crusted, flaky fish and perfectly crispy, salty chips. So fresh you half expect the fish to flop off the table and back into the ocean.